Praise for *One Puzzling Afternoon*

"*One Puzzling Afternoon* introduces
tagonist, at the dawn and dusk o
reader the satisfying task of slip
untangle the events of younger Edie's life that have begun to slip from older Edie's memory."

—Eva Jurczyk, bestselling author of *The Department of Rare Books and Special Collections*

"*One Puzzling Afternoon* is a quiet, compelling mystery of a woman untangling the secrets locked inside herself. This truly unique story blends past and present in a way that feels real. Great atmosphere and even better characters."

—Lucy Gilmore, author of *The Lonely Hearts Book Club*

"A captivating and poignant book, I was completely hooked. You can't help but fall for Edie as she desperately tries to find the lost friend from her past while she begins to lose herself to dementia in the present."

—Marianne Cronin, author of *The One Hundred Years of Lenni and Margot*

"An uplifting, bittersweet story with a page-turning mystery at its heart. Emily Critchley writes about aging and memory with huge warmth and compassion. A beautifully atmospheric and endearing book.'"

—Freya Sampson, author of *The Last Chance Library*

“A splendid read. *One Puzzling Afternoon* is like finding your way through a maze blindfolded while sipping your favorite drink. Both scintillating and sincere, the prose pays homage to the nuance of memory and the confluence of age and understanding. I plan to spend many a coming afternoon with a Critchley novel in my hand, watching the past meet the present through her captivating lens.”

—Lo Patrick, author of *The Floating Girls*

One Puzzling Afternoon

One Puzzling Afternoon

Emily Critchley

sourcebooks landmark

Cover design by Faceout Studio, Tim Green
Cover images © Javier Zayas Photography/Getty Images, brickrena/Shutterstock, venimo/Shutterstock, Rashad Ashur/Shutterstock, fotograzia/Getty Images, artuco/Shutterstock, musbila/Shutterstock
Internal design by Laura Boren/Sourcebooks

Published by Sourcebooks Landmark, an imprint of Sourcebooks
P.O. Box 4410, Naperville, Illinois 60567-4410
(630) 961-3900
sourcebooks.com

Cataloging-in-Publication Data is on file with the Library of Congress.

Printed and bound in Canada.
MBP 10 9 8 7 6 5 4 3 2

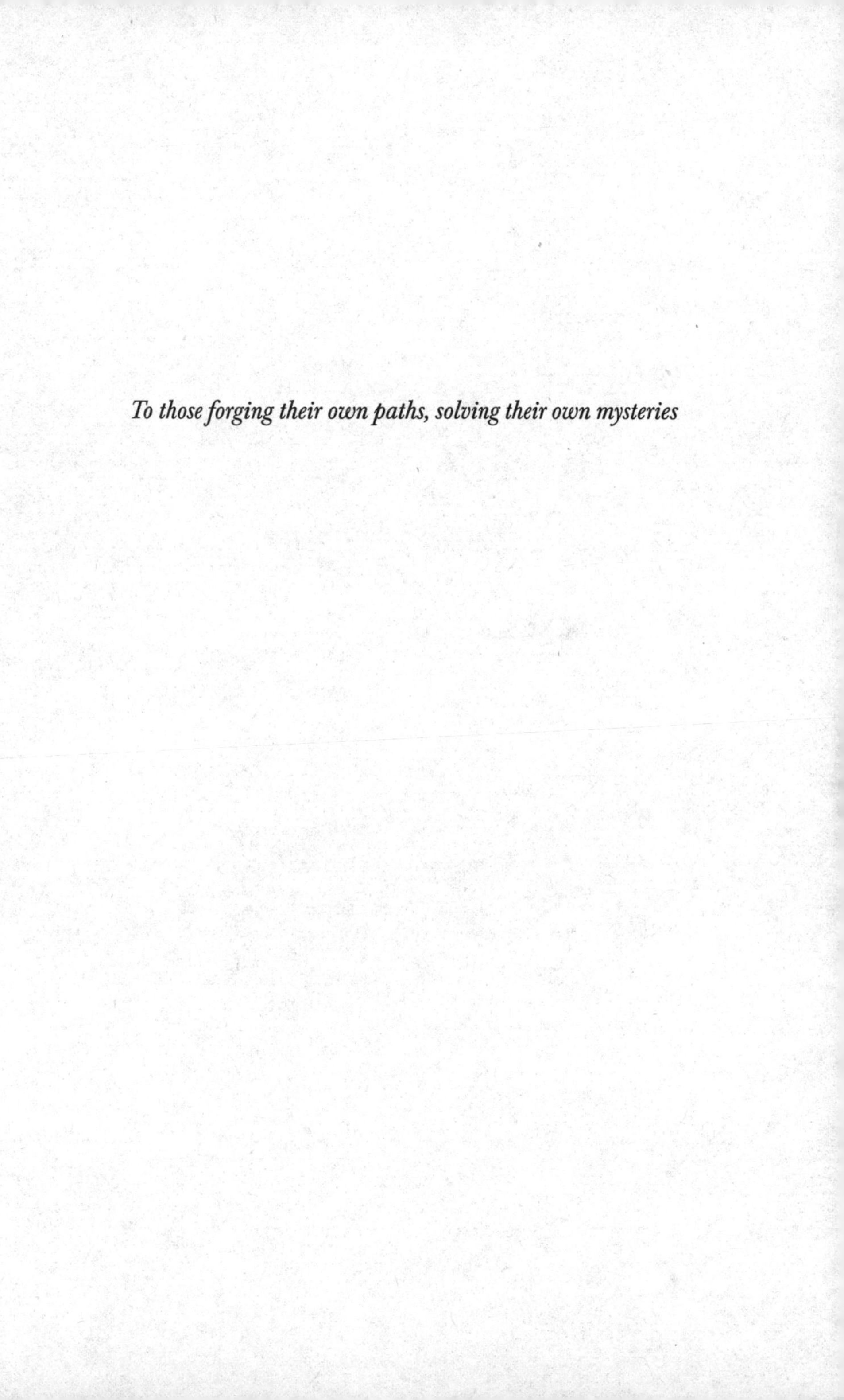

To those forging their own paths, solving their own mysteries

"Memory is the diary we all carry about with us."

—OSCAR WILDE

Prologue

I stand on the empty platform under the heat of the midmorning sun. The station is on the edge of a small town, and the surrounding fields are full of golden wheat waiting to be harvested. The huge sky stretches wide and cloudless, a clear, hard blue above the patchwork of green and yellow fields. From the station bridge, a few cows can be seen grazing, flicking away flies with their tails. A hand-printed sign advertises PICK YOUR OWN STRAWBERRIES. High above me, a starling spins his chatty song.

Very soon these familiar fields and lanes will be combed by police and volunteers. Bodies beating back the wheat, peering under the hedgerows, crawling across the land with their maps and torches, hoping to be the ones who can shed light on the local girl's disappearance, yet dreading what they may discover. Hundreds of statements will be taken, residents' questionnaires studied and analyzed, and of course the missing girl will be seen everywhere: riding a bus in Manchester, buying a packet of cigarettes in Norwich, working in a shoe shop in Hampshire. Local people will dream of her and wonder if their dreams have meaning. Committees will be formed, money raised, fingers pointed, hopes dashed again and again.

Of course it isn't me they'll be looking for. It's Lucy.

Right now, there is little breeze, and I can feel beads of perspiration forming on my forehead. My knee throbs under the blood-soaked handkerchief. I adjust the brim of my straw hat and glance up at the station clock. The anxiety curls itself into a tight ball in my chest, almost causing me to forget my grazed hands, my bloody knee, and scraped shin. "I'll be back before you know it," she'd said. I take a deep breath, trying to calm myself. She'll be here. She has to be.

The station is empty. The stationmaster is probably further along the track in the signal box.

He is not only stationmaster but porter, clerk, ticket inspector, and signalman. The station is used far less frequently than it was when my father was a young man and only the wealthy could own a motorcar. These days, there is no need for station staff; only a handful of trains pass through in a day and, unbeknownst to me now, in twelve years' time the station will close completely. The station house will be converted into a private residence, the signal box left derelict, the track either lifted or forgotten, the long grass and tangled weeds making it difficult to see where it was once laid. But this is all far off in the future, a future I am unable to envisage, a future I don't know will be forever changed by this day.

I shift my weight from one foot to the other, willing Lucy to hurry. The platform shimmers in the heat. Using my hand as a visor, I squint into the sun, looking at the long, narrow road that leads to the station. I expect to see her there, pedaling furiously, her hair tied back with her scarf, her skirt flapping around her knees. But there is nothing, just the empty road.

Come on.

My tweed skirt makes my bare legs itch and my feet feel hot inside my brown lace-ups, but I needed to bring them; they are the best things I own, and better to wear them than to carry them. My small brown suitcase is at my feet. I packed as much as I could, but I know it won't be enough. Never mind, we'll manage. As long as we're together. As long as we're far away from here.

The hands of the clock are edging toward five to eleven, and I can feel a sickness rising in my throat. She has to be here. She has to come back.

An awful thought dawns on me: what if she's changed her mind? Decided she wants to stay? But she was here, I remind myself. She was here and now she isn't, and it's all my fault.

She said it wouldn't take long. She promised she'd be back.

I reach into my pocket, checking for our tickets, the smooth paper slipping through my fingers. Then I see it: a black speck on the horizon growing steadily larger. A cloud of white steam.

I can hear it now too, the train's panting approach, the gentle *chug chug* as the familiar scent of the sweet oily smoke fills my nostrils. I watch as the small hand of the station clock shifts over to eleven and the train whistles its arrival. My chest hitches and I make no attempt to wipe my eyes, pricking with tears.

Where is she?

1

2018

I first see Lucy Theddle standing outside the post office on Tuesday afternoon. Looking exactly the same as she did in 1951.

I am on my way in when a young man accosts me, carrying a tray and wearing a paper hat.

"Free sweets," he says, pushing the tray under my nose.

"Free sweets?"

"It's our open day," he explains, gesturing to the small shop squashed between the post office and Sandy's Shoes. The shop used to be a key-cutting place. Before that, it sold sports equipment and school uniforms. The sign over the door now reads RETRO SWEETS. ALL YOUR CHILDHOOD FAVORITES.

"No, thank you."

"Oh, go on. One won't hurt." He nudges the tray toward me.

I peer down and there they are: Parma Violets. I reach for them. I can't help myself. "These used to be my favorites," I murmur, but the man isn't listening. He has spotted another customer and has dashed off. "*Free sweets!*"

I unwrap the tube and pop one of the tiny disks in my mouth. The taste is sweet and soapy. They remind me of spring flowers and warm days, of cycling down to the sea with the sun on my face, of secret whispers and kept promises.

That's when I see Lucy. She's standing next to the postbox, wearing white ankle socks and the school uniform we used to wear: a green pleated tunic over a blouse. Her hair is in two neat plaits; she's carrying her satchel and her violin case.

"Oh, hello, Lucy," I say.

A woman in a blue coat is coming out of Sandy's Shoes. She gives me a sympathetic smile. It's a look I am familiar with, one I don't like. When I glance back at the postbox, Lucy has vanished. I blink then crunch the sweet down, swallowing hard. A chill runs through me and I shake my head, trying to push the image of her from my mind; she's nothing to do with me anymore.

I quickly shove the rest of the Parma Violets into the pocket of my mackintosh raincoat and enter the post office, shuffling forward past the stationery and up to the counter.

"Ah, good morning, Edie."

"Hello, Sanjeev." I am pleased to have remembered Sanjeev's name, pleased it had been there for me instead of that awful void that exists, more often now, where a familiar word should sit.

"And what can we do for you?" Sanjeev smiles as his good-sized wife busily pastes labels onto packages behind him.

What is it I came in for?

"I'll have twelve stamps, please."

Perhaps I came for stamps. Everyone can always use a few extra stamps.

"Keeping well, are we, Edie?"

Sanjeev speaks loudly, probably because of the glass partition. I can tell by the way he leans forward that he wants his voice to carry.

"Very well indeed," I reply, trying to match his loudness.

"Autumn now," he says.

"Leaves everywhere," I offer.

He slides the stamps to me under the glass and I pay for them. I notice the collection box and the tray of red paper poppies with their green plastic stems. It must be that time of year again, the time for remembering. I slide a pound into the collection box, then fix a poppy to my buttonhole.

"Take care now, Edie," Sanjeev says cheerfully.

When I exit the post office, the boy with the sweet tray is offering a drumstick lolly to a man on a mobility scooter. I look around cautiously but can see no further sign of Lucy. Above me, the clouds are gathering; there is a gust of wind and I shiver, pulling at my coat.

As I pass the newsagents and the rack of papers outside, a headline catches my eye: "Local School to Close." The words mean something to me, only I can't think what. I lean in, peering at the photograph of a gray, imposing building. Then I remember—it's Daniel's school. The secondary school where he works as the deputy headmaster. Daniel says the school isn't closing but *merging*. Another school is getting a big development and all the children from Daniel's school are joining that one. Daniel could work there, but he doesn't want to. I frown, unable to remember why.

At home, I pick a bill up from the doormat, edge my coat off, and place my shoes on the rack Josie recently insisted I buy. When you reach my age, everything becomes a trip hazard.

I go straight through to the kitchen to put the kettle on. Ordinarily I'd wait for Josie, but the events of the morning, seeing Lucy, require a cup of tea before Josie's arrival. Whatever happened to her? I feel I should remember but I can't. I roll her name around in my mind. *Lucy Theddle, Lucy Theddle.* It feels strange, forbidden, and I bite my lip trying to quell the unease that squirms in my stomach.

Josie finds me, fifteen minutes later, sitting in my chair in the living room, sipping from the mug Daniel bought me last Christmas. It has a sketch of a cityscape and the word "Stockholm" written in a delicate script. A gift from his latest city break.

"Hello, Edie," Josie bellows at me from the hallway. "Have you been out?" She pokes her head round the living room door and peers in at me.

"The post office," I say.

"What for?"

"Stamps."

Josie frowns while shaking her coat off. She's holding a tiny collapsed umbrella and it gets caught in her sleeve. "I could have done that when I go to the shops tomorrow."

I attempt a shrug but find my shoulders don't obey. My joints, nowadays, often ignore my instructions.

"Not got the telly on?" she asks, looking at me suspiciously. Josie cannot understand how anybody would want to sit in a living room and not have the television on.

"No," I say. "I was thinking."

"Thinking?" Josie repeats the word with some wonderment. "Well, that would be nice, wouldn't it?"

Not waiting for my reply, she scoots off to the kitchen, then returns wearing my apron. "I'll just do this bit of washing up, Edie, take the rubbish out for you. Then I'll make us a cuppa. Oh. I see you've already made one."

"I'll have another."

She nods, disappears. I can hear her rattling around, turning on the tap, the sound of the cupboard door opening and closing. She's probably looking for the marigolds.

Josie comes for two hours, four days a week. Expensive. But worth it. It was Daniel's idea, and I was most against it at first, but I've got used to her now. I enjoy the way she bustles around, making sure she earns her nine pounds an hour—a perfectly reasonable rate, Daniel tells me. She isn't my carer, just to clarify. She helps out with the household chores. Daniel insisted on hiring her and I went along with it. Of course, I'd never let Josie go now I have her. She's a single mother, you see. She needs the extra income.

Josie was reluctant, at first, to sit down and have a cup of tea with me, during *working hours* as she calls them. She soon changed her mind when I persisted, although she often stands, leaning against the doorframe, or else she perches on the sofa arm, as if she isn't really stopping, only pausing. People don't like to take breaks anymore, I've noticed. They have to keep busy, as if something terrible will happen to them if they stop.

I push myself up from the chair and move unsteadily into the hallway. My kitchen, these days, is very beige and very clean (Josie is fond of bleach).

She's at the sink with her back to me, her shoulders slightly rounded, her dark hair tied with a thin red band.

"I saw Lucy Theddle today."

Josie jumps and turns around. "Oh, Edie. I thought you were in the living room." She recovers herself and continues rinsing a fork under the tap. "Who's Lucy Theddle then?"

"She disappeared in 1951." As I say the words aloud I feel surprised that this is something I know, and by my certainty.

"Mm." Josie puts a plate on the drying rack. "Perhaps she moved away? Did you eat an egg last night?" She holds up my blue and white striped eggcup.

Did I eat an egg last night? Perhaps I did. My mother always used to overdo them, cook them until they were dry and rubbery.

I can see my mother now, sitting at the kitchen table, her rollers in, cigarette in hand, the toast still warm in the rack, looking at the front page of the *Ludthorpe Leader*. She's got the wireless radio on and Eddie Fisher sings "Anytime You're Feeling Lonely." It must be a Saturday because the BBC Light Programme doesn't usually start until I'm at school. I've got a boiled egg on my plate—a real one, which means the weather is warm. We mostly have powdered egg in winter, although my mother swaps tinned egg for nylons, not strictly legal, but many people swap rations. *You wouldn't think we actually won the war*, my mother is fond of saying. The egg is probably supposed to be a treat, although it's overdone and I don't want it. My mother doesn't eat much as she worries about her figure. She blows her cigarette smoke out of the side of her mouth so it avoids me, glances down at the front page of the paper, at Lucy's picture: *I do hope they're doing all they can to find her.*

Of course, my mother knows all about Lucy. Lucy is in my year at school. Not only that, she's the mayor's daughter. Our town has talked of nothing else all week.

I'm looking at the paper, at the grainy photograph of Lucy standing in her back garden, rose bushes behind her. Her younger brother has been cut from the picture, but I can see his small fingers curled around hers. They'd been dressed in their Sunday best, told to stand still for the photograph. Lucy is wearing a white dress with a lace collar.

"Edie, are you okay?"

Josie is staring at me. Eddie Fisher's voice fades.

"Yes. I'm fine."

She peels off the marigolds and drapes them over the sink. "Well, go and sit down. I'll bring some biscuits through, shall I?"

"We don't have any. I've run out."

"Nonsense." Josie opens the cupboard. She waves a packet of custard creams at me. "I told you I bought these last Tuesday and put them in here for you."

"Oh, *those* biscuits," I say, pretending I hadn't forgotten about them. "Yes, let's have *those* biscuits then."

I pause next to my calendar. It's *National Geographic.* I'm in October—the Taj Mahal—although I'll be able to change it to November next week. Daniel is coming over on Friday; I've written *Daniel 5pm. Fish and Chips.*

I take a pen and write in today's square *Saw Lucy Theddle outside Post Office.*

In the living room, I pick up the crossword, intending to give it another go. I'm not very adept at them but I like to try. Daniel tells me they are good for my brain, like oily fish and walnuts, neither of which I am fond of. I usually end up getting stuck on the crossword and asking someone else if they have any ideas. Sometimes I just can't think quickly enough. It was much easier with Arthur. Arthur was always good at the crossword.

Josie finally appears with the mugs, the custard creams tucked under her arm. The tea is too hot but she takes quick, tiny sips. No doubt there is somewhere else she needs to be before she collects her small scabby-kneed son from school. I always forget his name. It's something silly like "Tree" or "Sky."

"So who's Lucy Theddle?"

Josie is talking to me but looking at the screen of her phone, perhaps thinking about something she needs to do. She's trying to be in two places at once. I know how she feels, although I never *try* to be in two places at once, it just happens. The problem is, when you've got so much past behind you, it creeps into the present.

I realize Josie is no longer looking at her phone. She's watching me, waiting for an answer. I put the crossword down on the coffee table.

"Lucy was in my year at school."

"Well, you're bound to bump into people, Edie. You've lived here your whole life." She takes a final gulp of tea, slips her coat on. "Gosh, it's almost three. I've got to get off. I need to nip to the shop before I collect Ocean. I don't know where the afternoons go. I'll see you tomorrow, Edie, get you a few bits from the Co-op."

"I'll make a list," I say.

Josie looks doubtful. "Well, all right then."

After she's gone, I stand by the window, lift the net curtain, and look out over the street. The sun is slowly moving around to the front of the house. Soon it will be spilling its light across the carpet where I stand now. The kitchen gets the sun in the morning. My mother's kitchen got it in the morning, too. She'd stand at the sink, washing the dishes in a shaft of sunlight, dust particles drifting in the air. She scrubbed the dishes until they sparkled. She scrubbed them as if they could never be clean enough.

I drop the curtain. I can hear the clock ticking on my mantelpiece, the rustling of the browning leaves belonging to the horse chestnut across the road. You wouldn't know it had rained earlier; the sky is as blue as a button, the clouds as fluffy as freshly whipped egg whites. I decide to take a walk.

I need to speak to Lucy.

2

2018

I pull my coat down from the peg rail, the waxy fabric slipping through my fingers, then fasten the large shiny tortoiseshell buttons. Keys. I find them in my pocket. I'm supposed to put them in the little wooden bowl on the hall table—one of Arthur's creations—but I must have forgotten.

I set off along the road. It's only a five-minute walk to the High Street. I take Willow Avenue then Beech Close, avoiding Sycamore Street. I always avoid Sycamore Street.

Ludthorpe is an average-size town. There's the post office, the newsagents, The Tea Tree, a hairdresser's, and a hardware shop, where you can buy all sorts. What else? The bakery, of course, and the British Red Cross charity shop. Oh, and there's Exquisite Fashion, which used to be the greengrocer's where my mother once worked. Everything used to be something else. Except for the post office, which has always been the post office.

The town center is busiest on Thursdays—market day, but

today isn't a Thursday. At least I don't think it is. I used to love market day when I was a girl. All the veg piled up. The smell of fresh fish reminding me of the seaside; the meat man in his blue and white apron calling out his offers. The jams and the marmalades, the cheeses and chutneys. The knitted baby clothes and silky handbags. I find it all a bit confusing now. Everything looks different on market day. I can no longer see the postbox, the war memorial, all the familiar landmarks that let me know where I am.

I've reached the end of the High Street. It's further than I usually go but I'm enjoying the warm autumn sunshine, the cool air on my cheeks, the sensation of moving forward with purpose. I pass the library and find myself on Alderbury Road.

The sign in front of me, fixed to the brick wall, reads THE GABLES. I peer through the black iron gates. The house hasn't changed much. New windows, and the front door is white instead of red, but otherwise it's the same. It's the sort of house you'd see on a Christmas card, or inside a snow globe; twin chimneys, redbrick, three rows of elegantly proportioned windows. *As pretty as a picture*, my mother would have said, and perhaps once did. The circular driveway has gone, though. There used to be a large round patch of bright green grass. And there's a different car parked outside now. One of those large silver things, not the black shiny Austin Somerset that Richard Theddle once drove.

I push against the black iron gates and they open more easily than I'd imagined. A large red leaf lies on the driveway. I slowly bend down to pick it up, tracing my finger along its veins like lines on a map, then put it safely in my pocket.

My finger poised above the bell, I pause. Wasn't I here before?

And aren't I supposed to be terribly worried about something? It's there at the back of my mind, a persistent, anxious flutter, like a moth trapped under glass: there is something I should know, something I need to remember.

I press the bell but there's no answer, so I go for the knocker, banging it as hard as I can, more desperate now. After a few minutes, a man opens the door. He's wearing a sweatshirt, tracksuit trousers, glasses, and those funny rubbery shoes—the ones with the holes in and no backs. Daniel has a pair he keeps by the door in his kitchen.

"Is Lucy in?" I ask.

The man frowns. "Sorry. You must have the wrong house. There's no Lucy here."

I shake my head and notice my hand has scrunched itself into a fist. I may not have been right about the biscuits, but I *know* Lucy lives here.

"I haven't got the wrong house," I say, a slight tremor in my voice.

The man looks around as if searching for help. His face softens.

"I'm sorry," he repeats kindly. "There's no one called Lucy at this address. Are you on your own?"

This is a question I know how to answer. I've heard it so many times over the years. *Edie's on her own now.* "Yes," I say. "My husband is dead."

The man looks taken aback. "I'm sorry," he says, staring at me.

"That's all right." Now I feel confused. This wasn't about Arthur. It was about Lucy.

The man continues to stare at me. He rubs his chin.

"Look," he says, stepping forward, "are you able to get home? Do you want me to call someone?"

"No," I say quickly, thinking about how cross Daniel will be if he has to leave school. "I can get home."

"Well, okay then." He's shutting the door.

"Wait!" I say, not wanting him to go. "Will you tell me if you see her? Lucy, I mean. She disappeared and everyone's looking for her."

The man studies me for a moment. "Yes," he says. "Yes, I'll do that." He smiles sadly. "You take care now." He shuts the door slowly but firmly.

I make my way down the drive. I should be pleased, but I feel I've got it all wrong. A huge current of worry is swirling inside me, making me sway a little from side to side. I lean against the gate. A memory slips into my mind. It's a warm spring evening and we're outside the village hall, the sun blinking behind the trees on the green. Laughter. The sound of the band. The sweet, plummy taste of fruit punch. Lucy is wearing a yellow dress, heeled shoes, her mother's earrings. She lights a cigarette, and I can see her face, anxious and flushed. Her hand on my arm. *It's my secret. You mustn't tell anyone, Edie.*

I kept your secret, Lucy, I tell her silently, as if she might be able to hear me. I've kept it for more than sixty years.

I just wish I knew what it was.

3

1951

It's a chilly afternoon early in March. A few hopeful daffodils proudly display their trumpets in neat front gardens; tiny white blackthorn buds are beginning to appear in the hedgerows. I am walking home from school, cutting up Cucumber Lane, running through my French verbs in my mind ahead of next week's test, almost halfway home, when I stop by the church, suddenly remembering the tin.

It's an old Lipton tea tin belonging to my mother. This morning in domestic science, we'd made scones and I'd put the scones in the tin and left them in the classroom, intending to collect them after school. Of course, I've forgotten all about them. It's not the scones I'm concerned about; they're terrible, and I know my mother will declare them completely inedible as soon as she sees them (*As hard as rocks, Edie! I should never have given you the sugar!*). No, it's the tea tin I'm worried about. My mother had been reluctant to let me borrow it in the first place, and now I've gone and left it up in Mrs. Beecham's classroom. I can just imagine the scene when I return home: *I knew you'd forget to bring that tin home. Honestly, Edie, you'd forget your head. I expect I've lost it forever now. And it was such a useful one.*

Being forgetful is one of many entries on my mother's long list of Edie's Regrettable Personality Traits. They include shyness, a tendency to avoid eye contact in most kinds of social situations, and what my mother calls "a lack of womanly intuition." Forgetfulness is probably up there somewhere alongside my inability to walk without slumping my shoulders, or to manage to get through a single day without staining my pinafore.

And so I turn around, head back toward school. There doesn't seem to be any rush now, not that I am ever in a particular rush to go anywhere, dawdling being another of my deficiencies. I enjoy the light breeze, the promise of the spring blossom, the soft, satisfying slapping noise my brown shoes make on the pavement.

The school gates are open but the playground is deserted. I skirt the edge of the art block. Inside one of the classrooms, a white-haired lady wearing a blue apron is mopping the floor, her movements slow and rhythmic. I picture my tin where I left it before break, sitting on the side by the window, and hurry on past the gymnasium and the two hastily erected prefabricated huts, used as extra classrooms, which is when I see them.

Mr. Wheaton, our history teacher, is inside his classroom, only he isn't alone. Lucy Theddle is there with him. They are standing very close, *too* close, and as I stop, trying to take in what I am seeing, Mr. Wheaton reaches forward and strokes Lucy's hair. I realize they are kissing, that I am watching Lucy Theddle and Mr. Wheaton *kissing*. Mr. Wheaton, with his bristly beard and stripy socks, Mr. Wheaton who paces backward and forward in front of the board when he speaks and who keeps pieces of chalk behind his ears; Mr. Wheaton *kissing Lucy Theddle.*

I stand staring at them through the grubby prefab window. Mr. Wheaton has his arms around Lucy, and his hands don't seem to be able to keep still; they sweep and grope as if he's misplaced something and is desperately trying to find it. They press against each other, merging, running into one another like the colors in a watercolor painting left out in the rain so that it is hard to tell where one ends and the other begins.

My hands are clammy, my face hot, as if I am the one who has been caught doing something I shouldn't.

Mr. Wheaton and Lucy Theddle.

Lucy Theddle and Mr. Wheaton.

I turn around and walk quickly away, forgetting about my tin, moving as fast as I can without drawing attention to myself, almost running out of the school gates. If I walk quickly enough, I might just be able to erase what I have seen, because surely such things don't happen in real life, not at Ludthorpe Grammar School for Girls, not to girls like Lucy Theddle.

Lucy is one of the tallest girls in our year and one of the oldest. She is what my mother would call well endowed. She doesn't need to stuff handkerchiefs in her bra like some of the girls do. Lucy is in a few of my classes but I cannot say I am friends with her, exactly. And why would we be? We come from different worlds. She's the mayor's daughter, and she's got a tennis court in her garden. The Theddles are well known in the community, renowned for throwing lavish parties and charity fundraising events. Lucy is one of those girls everyone wants to be friends with. She's clever, pretty, and popular. She possesses the easy confidence that accompanies wealth and status. She's never had to hide in the loos at break time, eat her lunch alone, or know what it feels like to be picked last for the netball team. Why would Lucy Theddle want to get involved with Mr. Wheaton? Lucy Theddle could go steady with any boy she wanted. Mr. Wheaton is our teacher, he's old, and he's *married*.

If it were Judy Simpson I'd seen, I might not have been so surprised; Judy is an outrageous flirt. The boys at St. Martin's are terrified of her: she's the kind of girl their mothers warn them not to get trapped by. I can just imagine Judy being the sort to stay behind after class, after orchestrating some misdemeanor or other, biting her lip, twirling her pigtail, drawing her shoulders back, and thrusting her chest forward (not that she has much to thrust), getting herself into a scrape like this. But Lucy Theddle?

And Mr. Wheaton, of course. What is *he* doing? Surely he must realize he could get into an awful lot of trouble. I can see it now: the officers arriving, handcuffing Mr. Wheaton in front of his class, dragging him out of the gates, a hand on his head as they shove him into the back of the Wolseley; his feeble protests, the one phone call to his wife. It would certainly be the talk of the town. There isn't much to fill the papers with around here, especially judging by last week's headline: "Chip Shop Uses Too Much Vinegar, Local Residents Complain."

But would Mr. Wheaton be in that much trouble? Lucy is a few months older than me, already sixteen. Still, he's our teacher. Surely there would be repercussions.

My mind continues to whirl all the way home. How did this happen? I wonder. And what should I do about it? Despite my visions of Mr. Wheaton's comeuppance, I don't think I could ever be a telltale. I'd be drawing too much attention to myself, and it would cause a scandal, which would be dreadful for poor Lucy. How do I know I'd be doing the right thing anyway? What do I know about relationships, about kissing? I know nothing, and clearly a girl like Lucy Theddle *does* know. Lucy knows what I have only read about in books or seen at the pictures, and I can't help being impressed by her and her involvement with Mr. Wheaton. Who am I to meddle? I shouldn't have even been there. If I'd remembered my tin, if I wasn't so forgetful, I'd never have seen anything at all.

I rush past the post office and the fish shop, wanting to be at home, wanting to be alone with my thoughts. I can't help experiencing a tingle of excitement when I think of what I know; it's nice to have a secret, even if it isn't my own. I'll be able to carry it around with me, like a warm biscuit in my pocket, a special piece of knowledge, a trump card. *I know something you don't*, I'll think when I see Lucy, or Mr. Wheaton, or any of the girls at school. The thought comforts me, and I smile to myself as I reach the front gate.

Who would suspect shy, boring, awkward, little ol' me of knowing a secret?

4

1951

It's seven thirty in the evening and I'm under my bedclothes, reading, shining my father's old torch over *First Term at Malory Towers.* Downstairs, the doorbell is ringing. I can hear my mother greeting her clients, the sound of the dining room door opening. *Rose, Margaret, do come in. Mr. and Mrs. James…so lovely of you to participate tonight.* She'll be hanging their coats on the peg rail in the hallway.

I know better than to go back to my book. Once, I forgot my task and Mother was cross. *People pay to see a show, Edie.*

Tonight, it's difficult to keep my mind focused; I can't stop thinking about Lucy and Mr. Wheaton. It has been one of those rare eventful days, a day when something has actually occurred beyond the boredom of school and homework and my mother's complaints about what we can't get at the butcher's. As soon as I arrived home from school, in the safety of my bedroom, I took out my diary and drew a little sun under the date to indicate it had been an interesting day.

I realize the doorbell has stopped ringing and the house has grown quiet, which means I had better concentrate. I'll give my mother five minutes, then I need to listen for my cue.

I wonder what my father would have thought of Mother's evening occupation. My classmate Cordelia Keal doesn't have a father; he was killed in Burma and she doesn't remember much about him. I remember everything about my father: how he used to put our slippers next to the copper boiler to warm them, how he'd wave at me as he opened the front gate, pushing his blue bicycle up the path when he returned from work in the evening. I can see him now, sitting in the garden in his deck chair on a Sunday afternoon, reading out bits of the paper while I sit at his feet and play with my rag doll. I can just about remember him putting the Anderson shelter together, giving up a part of his vegetable plot, edging the heavy piece of corrugated iron down the side passage. My mother thought it was silly. *For goodness' sake, Donald, they're not going to bomb Ludthorpe, are they? There's nothing here to bomb. I'm not sleeping in that hole with bugs crawling all over us.*

My father didn't fight in the war; he worked for the railway and was considered to be in essential services, something I know he felt ashamed of. "Someone's got to keep England moving," I can remember a friend of my father's telling him. Still, it was hard for my father, watching his friends go off to fight.

Cordelia's father died in a foreign land, fighting for his country. He died a hero. My father died after the war, just down the road at Sandy Bay. My mother won't speak of it. Neither does she speak much of my father in general except when she mentions that he left us nothing. I want to say that he was hardly planning on going anywhere. My father's death is an embarrassment to my mother. I think he embarrassed her when he was alive, too. She warned him not to swim after I'd joked with him: "*Bet you can't swim out to that buoy.*"

"*Bet you I can,*" he'd replied, grinning at me.

"*It's too windy, Donald, the current is strong,*" my mother had called out from behind the windbreak, her eyes never leaving *Woman's Own*. My father ignored my mother, a small act of defiance, and was swept away.

My mother often reminds me how it was me who suggested he swim, and I often wonder if he'd still be here if I hadn't. It's something I have to live with: my father's death was my fault.

I scramble to the edge of the bed, leaving the diary behind, then push my feet into my slippers and creep across the room in my pajamas. From the landing, I can just about hear Mother's voice. She calls out loudly and I catch the end of her sentence: "... make yourself known."

I dart back into my bedroom, pick up the broom and bang the handle on the floor three times, wait a few seconds, then bang it again three times.

Last month when I used the broom handle too vigorously, a blue china plate fell off the dresser. *I suppose it all adds to the excitement*, my mother had said, sweeping the pieces up after her guests had left. *Although perhaps don't bang quite so hard next time. I can't afford to keep replacing china.*

Once I'm finished with the broom, I grab my torch, keeping the beam low. The rest of the house is pitch black. There's an eerie moaning coming from the dining room, like wind trapped in a chimney. The moaning belongs to my mother and is all part of her act, but that doesn't make it any easier to hear and I can't help but shiver.

I stick to the edges of the stairs, avoiding the creaky steps, turning the torch off, feeling my way. My legs are shaky and there's a sour taste in my mouth, but I have to see. *Curiosity killed the cat*, Mother always says, but I often sneak out of my room to take a peek; it makes it less terrifying somehow, if I can see what's going on. Upstairs, alone in my room, I worry I will offend the spirits by imitating them, by interfering without fully being a part of things. I fear they will come for me.

Downstairs, the door to the dining room is open just a crack. Candlelight seeps onto the hallway floor. I can hear my mother's moans, louder now. She stops but continues to breathe heavily. "Don't break the circle," she says, her voice husky.

I edge closer and peep around the door. There are five people sitting at the dining room table with their eyes closed, holding hands: three women, a man, and my mother. The curtains are drawn, and Mother has the best lace tablecloth out. Six red candles have been lit. No doubt she swept and dusted the room before the arrival of her paying guests. *First impressions are everything, Edie.*

I stand, staring at them, my knees locked together. I recognize the man and one of the women: I've seen them in church. The woman is soft and rounded, small-eyed. Her husband, tall and broad, delivers our coal. Even when he's scrubbed up and in his Sunday best, you can still see the coal dust ground into the palms of his hands. Now his eyes are shut, his brow furrowed in concentration. I don't know the other two women, but one of them is wearing an expensive-looking black dress with a fur trim. Her face, in the dim light, is thin and pale. The other woman, slightly younger, is wearing a red hat, matching lipstick, and a dark green dress suit. The two women have the same nose. Perhaps they're sisters.

Shadows dance across the five pale faces as the candles on the table flicker and the wind whistles down the chimney. As usual, the window has been left open behind the curtains so the room is cold; the woman in the black dress shivers.

I stay as still as I can, hardly daring to breathe, my chest tight. I pray my stomach doesn't rumble, giving me away. My mother will be livid if she spots me.

I keep my eyes on her. She's wearing large dangly earrings with a green stone and a black and gold paisley scarf in her hair. She rolls her neck, loosens her shoulders, takes a deep breath. "I call upon the good spirit who responded to our prayers. Do you wish to communicate with us tonight?"

The woman in the red hat bows her head. Everyone waits with bated breath.

This is my mother's second job. She's busy at the greengrocer's during the day, weighing cooking apples, marrows, and turnips then putting them into brown paper bags, molding butter into rounds. She doesn't earn enough at the greengrocer's to keep us, which is what she always says. *Well, I wouldn't have to do two jobs, would I, Edie? If your father hadn't left us with nothing but his debts. I can't possibly make enough just at the greengrocer's. Not if we want to keep this house.* I never say anything about her new dresses, the hall table she had delivered in a van from Eve and Wenley, the wall lights with the peach-colored glass she simply couldn't do without, the new stockings she buys because she doesn't like to wear darned ones.

"I can hear whispers from the other side," she says. "Ooh, yes...I'm getting a sense of someone. A man." She tilts her head as though listening.

The woman in the black dress and fur gasps. "Oh, is it Gerry? Please let it be Gerry."

My mother frowns in concentration. "I know you are there, Gerry," she announces. "I can feel your presence. You've joined us from the spirit world. We welcome you. We thank you for your sacrifice. For you did make a sacrifice, didn't you, Gerry?" My mother opens one eye and glances in the direction of the woman in the fur, her gaze lingering on the women's left hand where a diamond sparkles.

"He did," the woman whispers. "He died in France."

My mother closes her eyes and takes a deep breath. "Gerry tells me he is at peace. He wants you to know it is time for you to move on, that he doesn't mind."

"I've been so worried," the woman says, her voice trembling.

As I watch, the candles on the table flicker more urgently.

I keep my body tight against the back of the door, expecting at any moment to feel an icy hand at my throat, a tap on my shoulder. I am always terrified of what she may summon.

The woman gives a small sob, and I notice her sister in the red hat tighten her grip on her hand. "Tell him I still miss him," the woman in black whispers. "Tell him we won the war. Tell him we can afford peaches again."

My mother has gone pale. She's sweating–I can see the beads of perspiration on her forehead. She should have been an actress. She wanted to be, but her own mother forbade it, said the stage was "common" and that she wouldn't have her daughter associating with "those theater people," so my mother gave up her dream.

As I watch, she moans, a deep, dark, piercing sound, and I want to creep back upstairs and carry on with *Malory Towers* where it's safe under my bedclothes. But I find I can't move. My eyes remain fixed on my mother as she rocks and sways.

"I can see his final moments," she gasps. "He's on the beach. The boats are leaving. He can see them but he can't reach them." She moans again, dropping her head forward. Her breathing is noisy and shallow and I put my hands over my ears. There is a sudden blast of cold air and I shiver. The cold gnaws at my insides, snaking its way up through my limbs. I expect to see a man wearing a khaki-green uniform. He'll be covered in sand and muck and blood. There'll be a large gaping hole in his side; a horrible, fetid smell, the smell of rotting flesh. He'll stare at me, his eyes full of fear, and I'll scream, giving myself away, breaking the circle in the dining room. My mother's eyes will fly open, her evening's work over, and it will be all my fault.

I drop my hands, take a deep, steadying breath, then turn slowly around. Of course, there is nothing there: no man, no rotting flesh, just the dark hallway, and the stairs that will take me back to bed.

5

2018

It's Friday evening, and I'm standing in the kitchen waiting for the kettle to boil. I notice I've written on my calendar in Tuesday's square *Saw Lucy Theddle outside Post Office* and drawn a little sun underneath the date to indicate that it had been an interesting day. That's good; there aren't too many suns on my calendar these days. Suns mean a good day, and gray clouds are a bad day. I draw little storm clouds when I feel something unfortunate is brewing.

When I was a girl, I used to write a diary, but I stopped for some reason. Diaries were then used for appointments only. Lately, diaries seem to be always getting misplaced and so Daniel insisted on fixing a calendar to the wall for me. *So you always know where you are, Mum.* As if I am in the habit of finding myself in mysterious places.

But how could I have seen Lucy? I wonder. Lucy vanished in 1951; I haven't thought of her for years. And if she's come back, she'll be a tiny old lady with upper lip hair and creaky knees, just like me. Although I have my facial hair under control, and Lucy was always so fair, perhaps it would never have been a problem for her. She'd still look beautiful, even in old age. I'd know her anywhere.

I shake my head. I couldn't have seen Lucy. I must have imagined it. Unless, after all this time, I'm finally inheriting my mother's gift—the gift of second sight, of being able to communicate with "those passed," as she liked to say. She believed I must possess the gift, that it was handed down through the female line. *It's like a muscle, Edie, you have to exercise it. And it's no good trying to suppress it. It will catch up with you eventually.*

Perhaps she was right, and the gift has finally caught up with me. But that would mean Lucy is dead. I shudder. My mother used to say the dead always want something. *They're forever pestering. We can't help them all, Edie.*

An image appears in my mind. I'm standing in an unfamiliar house outside a closed door. The carpet beneath my feet, plum-colored squares with orange and blue flowers, makes my head hurt. From somewhere in the house I can hear the wireless playing: "Don't Sit Under the Apple Tree." It's being played over and over again, and I want to put my hands over my ears and weep. From within the room comes the sound of a scream—Lucy's scream.

"Mum? Are you there?"

I blink. Daniel is calling me from the living room and I remember that I am here in my kitchen, that I was making tea. I shake my head, realizing the kettle has boiled and that I've already set the mugs out. Daniel always offers to make the tea, but I like to do it.

The remnants of our dinner are on the kitchen table: leftover chips and a tub of mushy peas. Greasy gray paper. I remember when fish and chips came wrapped in newspaper and you used to get little pieces of newsprint stuck to your batter.

"Mum?"

"Just coming," I call back, reaching for the milk. I don't know why Daniel worries so much. I'm perfectly capable of making a cup of tea.

In the living room, I set the tea down. Daniel has his laptop on his knees and I notice he's plugged a long white wire into my socket. I hope he remembers to plug my lamp back in. I shall have trouble later, if he forgets, trying to get to it behind the sofa.

"Mum, look at this."

Daniel is pointing the screen at me. It's very bright. I can see a cream house. There's a low stone wall and two apple trees.

"Who lives there?" I ask.

"Well, me. Possibly. I'm thinking of putting in an offer. It's an old dairy. What do you think?"

I fumble with the cuff of my blouse; the button has come undone.

"I've been offered a job in Devon, remember? We feel ready for a move, what with the school merging. And we all know Suzanne has never been that fond of Ludthorpe. With any luck I'll be able to retire in five or six years. We've always liked that part of the world."

I try to keep my hands still in my lap. "Devon?"

"Yes, Devon," he says patiently, smiling at me.

"But that's miles away. What about Amy?" My throat has gone dry and my voice sounds high pitched. I can't imagine being so far from Amy; I've always been close to my granddaughter.

"We've discussed it," Daniel says gently. "She feels sad about leaving her friends, but she'll be going off to university next year anyway. There are lots of good schools nearby, and we'll make sure she can keep her subject choices." He turns back to the screen. "Here, I'll show you a few pictures."

There is a photograph of something green and blurry, a duck pond perhaps, but I can't make sense of it. Is he really going all the way to Devon? My stomach clenches. "What about *me*?" I ask. He can't be serious. "What will I do if you move to Devon?"

"We'll take you with us, of course," Daniel says cheerfully, as if I'm a cat or a piece of furniture. "We'd never leave you behind, Mum. I did tell you," he adds.

"Well, I don't remember," I huff. "I think I'd remember something like this."

Daniel sighs. He's been doing a lot of that lately. He reaches for his tea. "Anyway, we'll find a nice place for you to live. Somewhere more manageable. Or, if we buy this place, you'll be able to live with us. It's got a granny annex, see?"

Daniel is pointing to the screen, to a sort of extension bit on the side of the house. I put my hand to my neck and touch my necklace, a thin silver chain with a tiny rose pendant I found in my jewelry box last week; it had slipped underneath the lining. "But I'd be under your feet all day. Suzanne wouldn't like it."

"No, you wouldn't. You'd have your own little kitchen, and a wet room."

"A *wet room*."

"A shower, Mum. Instead of a bath."

"I like a bath."

Daniel gulps down a mouthful of tea and replaces his mug

on the coaster. Someone's got him well trained. My mother was obsessed with protecting furniture. She made her own crocheted doilies. They were all over the house, little circles of lace supporting teapots, vases, clocks, and jewelry dishes.

"You haven't had a bath for years," Daniel is saying. "You've got the shower seat. And Suzanne doesn't mind. We'd be able to buy somewhere bigger, see, like the old dairy." He points at the screen again. "Once we've sold your house and ours."

"Sell my house? I don't know about that." I thread a cushion tassel through my fingers. It feels silky and familiar.

"If you lived with us, Mum, we'd be able to see you more, look out for you. Be there for you when you get in a muddle."

I open my mouth to protest but the words aren't there. Am I in a muddle? Life has become a little fuzzier around the edges in recent months and I am, perhaps, a little less sharp than I once was, but that must be perfectly normal at my age.

"We'd like to be there for you for when you forget things," Daniel says kindly.

"I manage just fine," I say, my voice louder than I'd intended. "I may well forget *some* things, but everyone forgets things, don't they? You forgot my birthday once."

Daniel grins. "And I've never heard the end of it."

"I always remember in the end," I say firmly. "And besides, I've lived in Ludthorpe all my life."

"Not *all* your life," Daniel corrects me. "You went to college, remember? In London. Then you came back."

I mull this over, remembering red buses, noise, traffic, the metallic taste of the smog, dorm rooms for young women, toasted crumpets, shared dresses, dances. The pictures aren't clear in my head, just a series of blurred snapshots like someone flicking through a slideshow. It all feels like a lifetime ago, a life that belonged to someone else, or perhaps should have belonged to someone else.

"Well, I've lived in Ludthorpe *most* of my life then," I say.

"Exactly," Daniel replies cheerfully. "It's never too late for a change, is it? And it's getting a bit tricky, isn't it? This house. It's a lot for you to cope with on your own."

What's he talking about? I've always been independent. Before I have a chance to say anything, he stands, picking up our mugs.

"I'll wash these up for you, Mum."

"No, I'll do it," I say, pushing myself up out of my chair slowly and taking the mugs from him.

Daniel smiles. "You've got to let us help out more."

"I don't need help," I tell him firmly.

In the kitchen, I put the mugs in the sink. I don't like to think of myself as being in a muddle, although I suppose I must be; otherwise, how could I have forgotten for all those years about Lucy going missing? Wasn't I her friend? It doesn't make any sense. I've also got a feeling I knew something about Lucy, something important. What was it?

When I think of Lucy it's like I'm pressing down on a stuck typewriter key; I press and press but there's nothing there. Just a big fat blank.

Perhaps it's not too late. Perhaps if I get the key unstuck, if I can find Lucy, I won't be in a muddle anymore. If I can remember what happened nearly seventy years ago, what I knew about Lucy, no one will be able to tell me I need help, will they? I won't be accused of being forgetful then. They'll soon realize I'm capable of managing in my own house and put an end to all this moving business. If I find Lucy, the dark thoughts, the twisting in my gut, the unsettling snippets of long-forgotten memories are bound to disappear. Why didn't I think of it before? I realize, now, exactly what I have to do.

Taking my pen from the pot, I write on my calendar in today's square: *Find Lucy.*

6

1951

"Freak."

The word is muttered under Judy Simpson's breath but is loud enough for me to hear, as was intended. Linda and Ann both giggle.

I'm crossing the playground at lunchtime, hugging my books and my brown lunch bag to my chest, trying to keep my head down, trying to go unnoticed. It doesn't always work.

I can hear them laughing. "There goes ghosty girl," is Linda's feeble attempt at an insult.

Linda is rounded and spotty with shiny skin and flat, straw-colored hair she describes as strawberry blond. Ann has bouncy ginger curls and a fringe (a mistake) that sticks up at the edges. The fringe has a mind of its own, unlike Ann herself, who copies everything Judy says and does. Judy is freckly and spot-free; she is sharp like her figure, which is all elbows, knees, and angles. Judy doesn't live far from me and, like me, is lucky to be at the

Grammar. She is friends with Lucy because Judy's mother, Martha Simpson, is employed by the Theddles as a cook and housekeeper and has been for years, which Judy believes gives her some kind of superior status, their families being closely linked, despite the fact that her mother *works* for them.

I pretend I haven't heard, that I can't see the three girls. Linda glances at me over her shoulder, whispers something in Judy's ear, and then they are gone, disappearing around the corner, a flurry of pleated tunics, legs, and giggles.

I haven't got many friends at school. People think we're strange. It's because of what my mother does in the evenings. It's difficult to keep something like that quiet in a small town. It's why I often eat my lunch alone on the bin bench, at the back of the hall on a patch of weedy gravel by the bicycle shed. The bin bench is called the bin bench because it's next to the bins. They are full of scraped-away school dinners and so it smells truly awful. At this time of year, the bins also attract flies. No one ever sits there, which is why I do.

I am passing the hall windows when I hear a strange snuffling, hiccuping sound. I stop, then take several steps cautiously around the side of the building, coming to an abrupt halt.

The bin bench is occupied by Lucy Theddle. She is making funny sniffing noises. Her cheeks are damp and I realize she's crying.

I take a step back, startled to see her; Lucy Theddle is not the type to be found crying on the bin bench at lunchtime.

I am about to sneak away when she looks up.

"Edie." She quickly wipes her eyes on her sleeve.

"Sorry. I didn't mean to–I was just, um..."

"It's fine," she says, giving me a weak smile. "You were looking for somewhere quiet to eat your lunch. I was too. Look, there's plenty of room."

She slides across the bench, holding her tunic over her knees, and I feel I have no option but to join her or she might think me rude. There's a fluttery feeling in my stomach: *I saw you. I know something about you.*

Lucy sniffs a little as I sit down, and I wonder if she's going to cry again.

"Are you unwell?" I have a feeling this isn't the reason she is crying, that it is more likely to have something to do with Mr. Wheaton, but I ask anyway.

She shakes her head, takes a handkerchief from her satchel, and dabs at her eyes. I notice the handkerchief has a lace edge and is embroidered with her initials.

"It isn't that." Her voice falters and a small sob escapes her throat.

"It'll be all right," I say, awkwardly. "Whatever it is, it will work itself out."

This is what my father used to tell me when I was upset. He'd pat my head and say, *It'll work itself out, chick.*

I must have said the wrong thing because Lucy dissolves into tears again. She leans into me, her cheek almost on my shoulder. I consider patting her head, then decide against it. I feel useless. I'm not used to comforting people. *Don't be a crybaby*, my mother always says. My mother rarely cries and I only saw my father cry once—one of my earliest memories. Neville Chamberlain announced on the wireless that we were at war with Germany, and my father put his head in his hands. *It hasn't been five minutes since the last*, he'd sobbed.

"It's really nothing," Lucy chokes.

"Well, it can't be nothing, can it? If it's upset you like this."

I have the sudden inspiration that she might confide in me. Perhaps because I am outside her immediate circle of friends, because I am somewhat remote from the gossip and the fallings-out and goings-on at school and, choosing to associate with very few people, I am so far down the social pecking order she might see me as a safe bet, the one person she might actually be able to trust. The thought brings a hopeful warmth to my chest.

She wipes her eyes. "It's all a bit silly. I'm feeling much better now, really, I am." Her smile is watery, unconvincing.

"It must be something," I press. "If it's made you so sad."

She shakes her head, an indication the conversation is closed. "How were your scones on Monday?" she asks, changing the subject.

I feel a stab of hurt; she doesn't want to confide in me after all.

"Dreadful," I mumble.

Lucy thinks I am making a joke and laughs. "Mine weren't much better. I'm terribly impractical. Not that I can tell my mother that. She thinks domestic science should be my specialist subject."

"Specialist subject?"

Lucy sniffs. "It's a compromise, you see. I want to go to a training college in London, to study to become a teacher. My father is most against it. He thinks I'll do perfectly well here in some dreary office for a few years. My mother too, although she's *finally* managed to convince my father to let me go as long as I specialize in domestic science." She sighs bitterly, then scrunches her handkerchief up in her fist. "I want to study history or English, but my father won't hear of it. He thinks, if I absolutely *must* go, that domestic science will be more appropriate. He believes at least it will be useful for when I marry, although I think my father would keep me at home forever if he could."

I wonder what Lucy's father would think of her being kissed by Wheaton in a prefab classroom after school. I want to tell Lucy I know, that I saw her, but then I won't have a secret anymore, and I worry she'll hate me for knowing.

I am also a little taken aback by Lucy's ambition to become a teacher. Most of the girls talk of getting jobs in shops, or secretarial work. Although not for long, of course; only until they have rings on their fingers. I'm not sure I can see Lucy as a teacher—most of our teachers are loud voiced and practical, former Girl Guides, air-raid wardens in the war, that sort of thing. Lucy isn't like that at all. But perhaps she's the other type of teacher, the type who wears long flowing skirts and twists flowers into their hair and gets enthusiastic about things. Yes, that would be Lucy.

"Do you really want to go to London?" I ask. "What if you get lost or something happens to you?" For most people in Ludthorpe, London is dangerous, a place seldom visited, full of thieves, rapists, and giant buses you might get squashed under.

"Oh, don't be silly, Edie," she says cheerfully. "London is perfectly safe now that the war is over. And that's exactly the point. I *want* something to happen to me." She looks at me earnestly. "Don't you want to move away, Edie? Don't you want to get out of Ludthorpe?"

"I haven't much thought about it," I say truthfully.

Lucy reaches for her satchel. "We really should eat our lunch. Before the bell rings. We'll be starving all afternoon otherwise."

I smile, wondering what the other girls would think if they saw me eating lunch with Lucy Theddle. And I can just imagine how pleased my mother would be; she's obsessed with the Theddles. *Did you see that coat she had on? Mink, I'm sure of it*, she said to me last time we saw Barbara Theddle in town. *And do you know they've just bought a new car?*

Lucy nibbles quietly at her sandwich and I begin to unwrap mine: meat paste as usual. I notice Lucy's eyelashes are still damp and experience an unexpected feeling of tenderness. It isn't right that Mr. Wheaton should be upsetting Lucy, that he reduces her to crying alone on bin benches. I feel even surer now, for some reason, that Mr. Wheaton is the cause of Lucy's tears.

"I heard what the girls said just then. They shouldn't say things like that," Lucy says.

"It doesn't matter." My voice comes out high and squeaky.

"Yes, it does. It's mean. They shouldn't call you names. It isn't nice. I suppose it's because of what your mother does."

"I suppose so," I say carefully. I've always felt uncomfortable discussing my mother's work, and I try to forget about the small part I play in it. People approach us in the market, the park, even after church. They shuffle out from behind a tree, the bandstand, or some corner or other. They all have that same look–slightly guilty and unsure. Hungry, too. They have a hunger for something else, something beyond their ordinary lives. Then there are the desperate ones. They are a different kettle of fish altogether. *We must try to do what we can*, Mother always tells me.

"Well, she's quite famous in Ludthorpe," Lucy says.

I smile because Mother would be pleased to hear this. I won't tell her though. I don't want to encourage her. It's embarrassing enough as it is, having people look at us the way they do, thinking we're either freaks or frauds.

"She's not really famous."

Lucy starts on her second sandwich. "But wasn't she in the *Ludthorpe Leader* last year? I read about her. She went to that old inn near Spilksby. The owners said it was haunted. They heard bumping noises on the stairs. Didn't she banish a monk?"

"He'd strangled a maid," I say reluctantly, remembering my mother's story.

"That's it," Lucy says, excitedly. "She said the monk had dragged the maid's body down the stairs, which accounted for the bumping sound." She shivers. "It must be exciting, having a mother who can communicate with the dead, banish spirits. I've always been interested in that sort of thing, ghosts and witches and magic. I suppose it's a bit childish, but I mean, there's got to be more, hasn't there? And all these people who say they've seen things. They can't all be lying, can they?"

"No," I say, not telling Lucy how it isn't interesting or exciting to me; how I hide in the shadows, watching my mother's séances because I am too frightened to be upstairs alone. I don't tell her about the nightmares I have: angry, malevolent spirits floating up the stairs or crawling out from under my bed, grasping at my ankles. I don't tell her that I feel this fear despite knowing my mother is putting on a performance, and what I do with the broom. I could never give away my mother's secrets.

"It's just so extraordinary," Lucy muses. "Nothing unusual ever happens in our house. Although I suppose it would be a burden. Being able to see the dead." She takes a bite of her apple.

"My mother says they always want something," I tell her. "She says it's best not to get involved, that you can't help them all."

Lucy nods gravely. "That's why they hang around, isn't it? Something awful happened and they can't come to terms with it. Like they were murdered, or something." Her eyes shine. "People are frightened of ghosts, but they're only trying to show the living how they died. You can't blame them really, can you? I'd be bitter too. I'd come back and haunt the hell out of whoever bumped me off."

She gives a little laugh, then finishes with her lunch, tucking what's left into the paper bag and slipping it inside her satchel.

"Well, I had better go, Edie. See you around." She stands, brushing the crumbs from her skirt.

I blink up at her, half a meat-paste sandwich still in my hand. I realize that once Lucy has gone, she won't give me a second thought. I came upon her quite by chance and she felt obliged to eat lunch with me out of politeness. Now she'll go back to her friends, to Linda, Ann, and Judy. I'll certainly "see her around," but I know for sure that she won't see me.

"I know," I say quickly. The words tumble out of my mouth before I can stop them. "I know why you were crying just now. It's over Mr. Wheaton, isn't it? I know about you and Mr. Wheaton."

Lucy stares at me, the color slowly draining from her face. She looks so terrified I almost wish I could take it back. Well, it's too late now.

"I was going to collect my scones—I'd forgotten the tin and it belongs to my mother. I saw you in one of the prefab classrooms."

Lucy sits slowly back down on the bench and presses her knees tightly together. "Have you told anyone about this, Edie?"

I shake my head and watch her features settle into an expression of relief.

"Because you absolutely mustn't. It would be dreadful for Max, given his position, and for me... Well, you can just imagine it, can't you?" She gives a little shudder.

"Of course I won't say anything."

Lucy studies me carefully. "It would be so silly," she says at last. "There's really no need to say anything at all."

"How did it happen? How did you...?"

She smiles. "I don't know, really. It just *did*. I was going to see him—after school, at lunch sometimes. We'd sit in his classroom and chat. First about my essay ideas, then about other things, about me going to a teaching college. He said he didn't know I could talk so much, that I had such plans. He said he'd help me with my application, that I was that rare thing, a student who wants to learn, someone who needs to make something of their life, someone who knows that there can be more. Then one afternoon he kissed me and now I can't think of anything but him. Whenever we're together—well, it's just incredible. We're like two powerful magnets, or two colliding stars. It's just the most wonderful thing, Edie."

I give her a dazed look. "So that wasn't the first time? When I saw you. It's been going on for a while?" I feel a flush of adrenaline. It's mind-boggling not only to know Lucy has been kissed by Mr. Wheaton but that it wasn't the first time. I wonder what it would feel like—to have a man desperate to kiss you like that, to have that kind of power.

"Only a little while," she says casually.

"How long?" I ask, slightly breathless and in awe of Lucy.

"Oh, I don't know." She frowns, then turns to look at me. "But that's just it. It's over now. You were right, I *was* crying over Mr. Wheaton." She sniffs and takes a deep breath. "He says it's over, that it has to stop."

"I suppose he's right," I say, disappointed but opting for the moral high ground. "He's our teacher, and he's married."

"I know all that," Lucy says grumpily. "But it's been so much fun. More than that. It's come to mean something to me, and now I've had it, I don't know if I can live without it. I don't think I can go back to the way things were before."

"But it's really over now?"

She stares glumly at a tiny yellow buttercup in front of us that has managed to shoot up from in between the cracked paving slabs. "He told me he couldn't see me anymore. That it's too risky."

"It's probably for the best," I say.

She looks at me, and I feel like she is once again assessing how bad it is for her that I know, and if she can trust me.

"We should walk to school together sometime," she says suddenly. "I've seen you. You always walk by yourself. You live on Sycamore Street, don't you?"

I am somewhat taken aback by this unexpected proposal, thrilled at the suggestion I walk with Lucy but also mortified that she knows where I live. Sycamore Street is what most people would consider "the wrong end of town." After you've left the greengrocer's, the butcher's, Goy's Fish Shop, the park, and the library far behind, once you're past Woolworths and Pool's Bicycles and the drapery shop, if you turn left at the T-junction and carry on for a bit, you'll see a scruffy parade of shops and will have found yourself in the land of pubs with beer-stained carpets and curtains that haven't been washed since before the war, of betting slips exchanged in backstreets, of egg and chips for supper and gossip over the garden fence. The houses on Sycamore Street are small terraced cottages, all the same: a little front room, a dining room, a kitchen at the back, a narrow staircase, two upstairs bedrooms, and an outside privy. The privy at number three is said to be haunted after a man came back from the first war and hanged himself there.

I know where Lucy lives; I pass The Gables often. It's out on Alderbury Road, very different from Sycamore Street. The Theddles employ a gardener and a housekeeper. I expect they've got a television, a radiogram, use Boots library cards and cubed sugar, and that they know what to do with cocktail sticks—unlike my mother who, after feeling aspirational one day, bought a packet and put them in the kitchen cupboard where they've remained ever since.

"I'm afraid I can't walk with you after school this afternoon," Lucy is saying. "I've got debating club. But I could meet you on the corner outside the post office tomorrow morning. It must be about halfway?"

"Yes." I hardly dare breathe in case she changes her mind.

"Well, great. I guess I'll see you tomorrow morning. Eight thirty?"

"I'll be there," I say, my voice coming out more enthusiastic than I'd planned.

Lucy stands then reaches into her pocket. "Would you like a Parma Violet?"

There are two small lilac disks in the palm of her hand.

"Oh, no. Your ration..."

"It's fine, Edie. Really. I've got a stash. Go on."

I take one and she pops the other in her mouth, straightening her pinafore and collecting her violin case. "See you tomorrow then. By the postbox. Oh, and Edie. Please, you really mustn't say anything about–"

"I won't tell a soul. Cross my heart." I put my hand on my chest for extra effect and Lucy nods, although she looks uncertain.

"Oh," she says, brightening, "and you should come to the youth dance at the end of the month. Have you been before?"

I shake my head. I've heard of the dance, of course. Most of the girls talk of nothing else the following Monday: who danced with whom, who left together, who bought the chips on the way home. I'm sure I'd feel shy and out of place, but perhaps I'd be able to bear it if I were with Lucy. I might even enjoy it.

"It's not for a few weeks, and it's only in the town hall, not a proper floor or anything. But they've got a band on, so it should be a good one. It's usually just Reverend Thurby and his tea ladies with the gramophone. He loves those dreary old waltzes."

"I can't imagine Reverend Thurby playing records."

Lucy laughs. "He says the dance keeps us out of trouble, whatever trouble is."

I stand, clutching the strap of my satchel. "I'd like to come. I'm just not sure–"

"You don't need to worry, Edie. A lot of the boys are completely useless. Billy Jones almost broke Ann's toe last month. You only need to know a couple of dances. You can dance, can't you?"

In fact, I can. Thanks to my mother, who used to make me

practice with her. We'd waltz up and down the living room in front of the fireplace, taking turns to lead. Mother loves to go dancing. She comes home flushed and excitable, still spinning around the kitchen in one of her dresses, pouring a brandy from the supply my father hoarded before the war. *Just a little drink to unwind... Oh, it was fabulous, Edie. There's nothing like dancing.*

"I can dance a little."

"Perfect! And Rupert will be there, of course." Lucy twirls a strand of hair around her finger. "In fact, that's why I'm going. He asked me." She blushes.

I give her a questioning look. I know who Rupert Mayhew is. His father owns the undergarment factory on the other side of town. It's one of Ludthorpe's biggest employers. Rupert's older brother left the boys' grammar a few years ago and is already working for his father. I expect Rupert will do the same. I see him sometimes, walking home with a group of his friends. He's got a boyish grin and dark, sweepy hair; my mother would say he is in need of a haircut.

"You're going with Rupert Mayhew?" I say, thinking that only a moment ago she was crying over Mr. Wheaton.

Lucy smiles. "He asked me to the dance, yes, but we're not *going* together, not like that. We're friends, that's all. Our parents are close and I've known him forever. He comes over and teaches George and me tennis. It would put Rupert in a bad mood if I said no. It's a younger brother thing, I think. His father has always favored Henry and now Rupert can't stand not getting his way or being rejected."

She looks at my face and laughs.

"Oh, Rupert's lovely, he really is, but he can be a bit intense.

If you come, you'll be doing me a huge favor. I'll have someone to talk to between dances. Otherwise Rupert will want them all."

I imagine sitting with Lucy watching the dancers on the floor. We'll be whispering and giggling together just like the other girls do. I'll be helping Lucy out and she'll have someone to confide in. She won't be stuck with intense, moody Rupert all evening.

"Rupert will bring a friend along," Lucy is saying. "I'll make sure you get a dance or two." She clutches my arm. "Oh, do say you'll come."

"Of course I'll come," I tell her.

7

2018

Libraries. That's where people go to find information, isn't it? It's Monday. Josie has been and gone, and the afternoon looms ahead of me, long and empty. It's time to find out about Lucy. Why are my memories of her disappearance so foggy? Why is no one looking for her? I refuse to be in a muddle about something so important. Ever since I saw Lucy, I've been plagued by disturbing images and feelings, incomplete and incoherent flashes of memory. I wish I could stop them, put the lid back on, bury them in whatever deep, dark hole they've surfaced from. If I can find out what happened to Lucy, I'm sure they'll go away.

I use the downstairs loo before I leave the house. It will be hopeless otherwise. I'll get halfway along the road then have to turn back. Daniel says I should have everything I need, what with Josie coming in and going to the shops for me twice a week, and his Friday evening and Sunday visits. *You shouldn't need to go out, Mum*, he says. But this feels important. This is about Lucy.

I set off down the road; the leaves rustle along the pavement and gather around the war memorial. The man on the radio earlier said there was a storm blowing in. Strong winds. I keep my head down, my coat tightly fastened.

The walk to the other end of town feels long, and I'm tired by the time I reach the library. I enter through the modern sliding doors and have a little sit-down in a red leather chair that looks more like something from a fairground ride, half a spinning teacup. The arms are too high for me to rest my elbows on comfortably, so I keep them in my lap. I watch people come and go: a man in a gray suit, a girl in a pair of low heels that go *clickety-click* across the polished entrance floor, a woman with silver hair holding the hand of a small child.

After a few minutes, I feel suitably rested and decide it's time to push myself up from the chair. The library hasn't changed much since I was a girl, although the librarians don't use stamps and cards anymore. It's all done by computers. There are barcodes to be scanned, and alarms that go off; it's more like Tesco. As I make my way along the aisles of books, light spills in through the high Victorian windows and onto the worn carpet. People sit at tables, working on their laptops. I can hear singing coming from somewhere. *The wheels on the bus go round and round.* I hum along as I walk slowly among the shelves: cookery, travel, foreign languages. *The horn on the bus goes beep beep beep...*

I find myself in front of books with dark spines and loud fonts and look up at the section sign: CRIME FICTION.

I take a book, easing it out carefully. It's got one of those plastic covers on it and it's called *Killing Floor*.

"It's good, that one."

I turn to find a young man standing next to me, not much more than a boy. He's got bright brown eyes and scuffed trainers. The boy is looking at the book in my hands. I push it quickly back onto the shelf. "I don't think this is what I'm looking for."

He takes a step closer. "I can recommend something, if you like? I've read lots of these. What sort of thing are you after? Hard-boiled? Courtroom? Spies? Nordic noir? They're my favorite right now. All that snow and frozen fjords. It's enough to chill you before you even open the first page." He shivers.

I frown. "I don't like hard-boiled," I say, thinking of the overdone eggs my mother used to give me.

"I can reach the top shelf for you. All the Christie is up there."

The boy is looking at me earnestly, wanting, for some reason, to help. Some people are like that. They think all old people need help.

"And there's a section of large-print books too. I've seen them."

"I don't need large print. I'm not blind."

The boy blinks. "Oh, sorry. I just thought..." He trails off and looks down at his trainers.

"I'm after information," I say. "About a crime." Was Lucy's disappearance a crime? I'm not sure.

The boy looks at me with interest. "What, a real crime?"

"Well, a disappearance. Lucy Theddle. She disappeared in 1951."

The boy's eyes grow big. He whistles. "That's a long time ago." He seems impressed.

"Yes. I was fifteen."

The boy stares at me, perhaps trying to see beyond the

wrinkles and the white hair to picture me at fifteen. I gave up dyeing my hair years ago but I like to keep it tidy. I don't want to look like one of those old bats sitting on the porch of the Windy Ridge care home, hair sticking up all over the place, matchstick legs poking out of gray socks, their expressions vacant. I brush my hair each morning, and Suzanne takes me to the hairdresser's every three months—an act of charity on her part.

When I was a girl, my hair was brown and mousy. My mother made me wear it above my shoulders as she said it was more respectable for a girl my age. Lucy's hair was long and fair, thick and wavy. I think a lot of girls were envious of it, that she was allowed it so long, even though that wasn't the fashion then. She often had it in two plaits. I remember the green ribbons she wore. Green to match our uniform. I realize the boy is still staring at me.

"Old people were young once, you know."

The boy laughs. "Yeah, I guess so." He adjusts his rucksack on his shoulder. "So what happened to her then?"

"I don't know. I'm trying to remember."

The boy considers this. "Have you tried googling her?"

This, I know, is something to do with computers. "No," I say. "I haven't done that yet."

"We could give it a go." He shrugs. "If you want to." He gestures toward a cluster of large computers at a group of tables in the corner. "There could be something about her online. I'd look on my phone, but the bigger screen might be better."

"I suppose it wouldn't hurt," I say, cautiously. "Although I'm afraid I'm not much good with..." I wave my hand in the direction of the computers, and the boy grins.

"Don't worry, I'll show you. I'm Halim, by the way."

"Edie."

Before I can say anything more, he's beetling off to the computers, and by the time I reach him, he's already done something to make one of them light up, pressing buttons and moving a black object around on the table. He pulls out a chair for me, and I have to say I'm grateful. I can't remember when I last had a little sit-down. It can't have been recently.

I watch his fingers as he moves them quickly over the keys. His hands are smooth, unblemished. I look down at my own hands, wrinkled and liver-spotted. The thin skin at my wrists sags. I used to have nice hands, once. My mother was obsessed with her hands, moisturizing them constantly. She always wore gloves to do the dishes, for any housework. She said dry hands, worn hands, were an indication of a lowly status. *Are you putting cream on your hands, Edie?* she used to ask me, making me hold them out so she could see them. *You don't want your hands to give you away now, do you?* For a long time, I could never work out what she meant. I saw my hands as the mirror of my soul, telling people something about me I didn't want them to know. I kept my hands behind my back, or sat on them, terrified they would leach out my secrets.

"Ah, here we are."

A blank page appears on the computer screen.

"Shouldn't you be in school?" I ask.

The boy laughs. "Nah, I'm in the sixth form. I've got a free afternoon. I like to come here to work. It's quiet, you know. Fewer distractions. And it gets me out of the house. Actually, right now I'm killing time. I've got a driving lesson in half an hour."

I nod, knowing all about wanting to get out of the house, about killing time.

"My granddaughter's taking driving lessons," I say, pleased to have remembered.

Halim moves the black object and a tiny blinking line appears on the screen. "What did you say the missing girl's name was?"

"Lucy Theddle." I spell the name for him and watch the letters appear on the computer inside a rectangle. He presses a button and a lot of writing comes up. I squint at the screen as Halim's eyes scan the writing.

"Hm. There's not much. A Wikipedia page, at least. Let's have a look at that."

I make a murmur of agreement, as if I know what he means. There was talk, a few years ago, of getting me "online," as Daniel called it. Daniel thought it might be useful for me, and Amy said she'd help. Suzanne was against it though. I overheard her telling Daniel it would be a waste of time and money–just like the mobile telephone. They decided it wasn't worth it in the end, and I was glad. It's difficult to learn new, complicated things at my age and they were probably right: I never use the mobile phone Daniel insisted on buying. Carrying a telephone around with you all day is just silly. Amy looks at hers constantly. When I asked her about it, she said she "checks it" to see if anyone's got in touch. How ridiculous. We don't go to our front doors several times an hour just to check if someone is there, do we? I told Daniel, if he needs me, he can call me at home on the usual telephone. If I don't answer I'm most likely out, or dead, in which case I won't be worrying about answering the telephone, mobile or otherwise.

"This is the wiki page: 'Disappearance of Lucy Theddle.'"

I look at where Halim is pointing, but the words are difficult to read, being so far away and against the bright light of the screen.

"Don't worry, I'll read it." He pulls up a chair next to me. "'Lucy Theddle, born on the eighth of September, 1935, was an English schoolgirl who disappeared on the twelfth of July, 1951, aged sixteen. Lucy was last seen cycling along the country roads'—"

"She had a lovely new bicycle," I interrupt.

Halim nods then carries on reading. "'Lucy is thought to have been wearing a navy skirt and a cream embroidered blouse. A white bicycle, belonging to Lucy, was found the following day in a field close to the side of the road. A small suitcase containing clothes, a toothbrush, an apple, and ten pounds was found next to her bicycle.'" Halim uses the object on the desk to move the writing on the screen. "'Despite an extensive search and police investigation, no trace of Lucy Theddle was found and the reason for her disappearance was never known.'" He leans back in his chair. "That's really frickin' sad. All that time, and nothing..."

"It put Ludthorpe on the map. That's what Reg said."

"And you knew her?"

"Oh, yes," I say. "And now I'm trying to find out what happened to her."

"Why?" Halim asks, gazing at me. "I mean, I think it's great, don't get me wrong. I'm just wondering, why now?"

"Because I knew her well," I say. "And because if I can find out what happened to her, no one will be able to tell me I'm in a muddle or that I can no longer live on my own. They'll all see—I'm as sharp as a pin, that's what Arthur always says."

"You could just try sudoku," Halim suggests. "It's what my grandmother does."

I shake my head. "I do the crossword. But now I'm going to find out what happened to Lucy."

I don't tell Halim about eating the Parma Violet, about seeing Lucy outside the post office last Tuesday afternoon, how I'd forgotten her completely for all this time. I don't mention the dark thoughts and the incomplete images, and the feeling I know something terrible.

"Well, it will certainly be cool if you do find out what happened." Halim looks doubtful. "Kind of a tough one, though. An unsolved mystery. Decades old. No clues. The police must have looked for her for years..."

"There are clues," I say. "But they're buried, that's the problem."

Halim looks up, his eyes gleaming. "Buried where?"

I blink and gaze across toward the windows. I can see the tall church steeple beyond the houses. The sky has filled with clouds again.

"Me," I say, turning back to Halim. "I think the clues are buried in me."

8

1951

When I arrive home from school, my mother is in the front room with a strange man. He's got himself comfy on the brown settee, his legs stretched out in front of him, his feet tucked under the footstool my father made in our shed. My mother embroidered the cushion with a kingfisher design. The beak isn't quite right, but you can tell it's a kingfisher from the colors, the turquoise and the orange. I remember her buying the thread.

My mother is perched on the armchair, leaning forward slightly, her hands in her lap. She's wearing her peach blouse with the Peter Pan collar and contrasting trim, and a skirt she made herself. The man is in a shabby brown suit with a flashy gold watch that doesn't quite go with the rest of him. His shirt collar is too tight, the knot of his tie too large; his thinning hair is parted in the middle with a wave on one side; he has a stubbly chin and dark eyes and he seems to take up a lot of space in the room. I can smell his aftershave, something spicy and unfamiliar, and I can see they've had tea. The teapot in its knitted cozy is sitting on the side table along with two cups and saucers. I wonder if she offered him sugar with his tea. It's almost the end of the month and we haven't got much left.

"Ah, and this must be Edna." The man gives me a fake smile, a smile grown-ups give to other people's children they are pretending to be interested in.

"Edie," I say dryly.

"Well, isn't this nice." The man grins and turns to my mother, who nods and smiles.

"Edie, this is Reginald Drakes."

"Oh, Reg'll do just fine."

He stays where he is so I don't move to shake his hand, something I am glad about. The man isn't tall, but he has big hands and a rounded stomach. His elbow rests casually on the arm of the settee.

"We've been discussing your mother's business," Reg tells me.

I frown. I am not sure when the séances became "my mother's business," or what they have to do with this man.

Reg taps his large fingers on the arm of the settee. "There's certainly potential there. Your mother's a real talent, isn't she, Edie?"

My mother giggles. "Oh, Reg..."

He grins at her again then turns his attention back to me. "Advertising. That's what we need. I can help, see. Get the word out."

I dig my nails into my hand. I can just imagine my mother's

face stuck on the church noticeboard or in the fish and chip shop: *Local medium and clairvoyant. Contact your loved ones. Flexible prices.* I can already hear Judy and Linda giggling.

My mother, though, is beaming. She loves it when a man offers to help.

"Most people know what she does," I say quietly.

My mother's smile fades and she rolls her eyes. "I embarrass Edie."

Not as much as I embarrass you, I think.

"What Edie doesn't understand," my mother says, shooting me a look, "is that it isn't easy, being left alone with a child. It isn't easy when you've got to look after someone *and* pay all the bills. *Especially* for someone like me, with my background and what I'm used to." She sniffs.

Reg pats my mother's hand and I frown. The gesture is too familiar, and I wonder how long they've known each other.

"I'd say you've done a blindin' job, Nancy."

My mother sighs as Reg glances at me out of the corner of his eye. "Here, look, Edie. I've brought you and your mother some beefsteaks." He gestures to the sideboard, and I can see two parcels wrapped in thick greaseproof paper sitting next to my mother's framed photograph of Laurence Olivier and Vivien Leigh.

"Steaks?"

"Reg is in the meat trade," my mother says proudly.

Reg puffs out his chest. "I deliver for the abattoir. You probably saw the van out front."

I shake my head. Not many people own cars around here, and I can tell my mother is impressed that Reg has a van. I know where the abattoir is. It's a few miles east of Ludthorpe, out toward the coast. I pass it sometimes on my bicycle. You can smell it before you see it.

"Oh, Edie wouldn't have noticed. She walks around with her eyes closed."

"I distribute around the county," Reg continues. "To all the local butchers. And I'm chief mechanic. It's my job to keep the vans running. We've got garages on-site." He nods at the meat packages on the sideboard. "There's got to be some perks to the job, eh, Edie?"

"We're most grateful, Reg," my mother says, touching her hair, checking if a pin is in place. "We could all do with a little extra iron after so many years of going without." She holds her hands up in front of her face, inspecting her nails. "My nails are terribly pitted."

Reg leans over. "They look perfect to me, Nancy. As does the rest of you. Perfectly healthy."

I grimace and my mother notices. "Edie, don't loiter. Run along and change out of your uniform."

My mother always insists I change out of my uniform after school. She worries I'll mess it up somehow, that she'll have to wash it or mend it. She thinks I'm irresponsible.

I know there are many ways in which I am a disappointment to my mother. When I got into the grammar school, she was pleased, as she was sure it would mean I would go on to marry a well-bred young man who would elevate me socially, pulling her up with me as I went, putting us both back in our rightful place. She knew by the time I was thirteen that it was unlikely to be the case. I turned out wrong; plain and frumpy, shy, uneasy in company. My limbs lack elegance; my hair, bounce. When my mother enters a room, people notice. The same cannot be said for me. In fact, the opposite occurs. I disappear into wallpaper, blend into sideboards, get lost on the ends of settees.

I mumble goodbye to Reg, tell him politely that it was nice to meet him. My mother is a stickler for manners (*manners cost nothing, Edie*). I try to keep my back straight, my shoulders down. (*For goodness' sake, Edie, don't slouch like that.*)

I slip out the door and up the stairs to my room where I flop straight onto my bed, lying with my hands on my stomach, thinking of how, tomorrow morning, I will be walking to school with Lucy. She could have chosen to walk to school with anyone, and yet she chose me. And she asked me to accompany her to the dance. I'll have a lot to write about in my diary tonight. This day most definitely constitutes a sunny day.

My mother absolutely mustn't find out I'm spending time with Lucy Theddle, though. She'll make a fuss, want to be involved, insist I invite Lucy over for tea. I can't think of anything worse than my mother putting on her best drawing room accent while serving up a limp salad starter followed by a Fray Bentos pie. She'll ask Lucy awkward questions, try to get herself invited to The Gables. She'll see this as the perfect opportunity to improve her social life.

No, she mustn't hear of it. I want to keep Lucy for myself and I can't have my mother meddling in my life like she always does.

From downstairs, I hear the clattering of teacups and I imagine my mother standing, smoothing down her skirt. She tells me a woman shouldn't bring attention to her clothes or hair in company, but she often forgets her own rules. She smooths nonexistent creases, touches her hair absentmindedly, checks her curls are still in place. She used to twirl her wedding ring on her finger, perhaps calming her nerves. She no longer wears the ring but she still has the nerves.

"Well, this was very nice indeed," Reg says, from the hallway.

"Lovely," my mother says.

"I'll see you Saturday?"

My mother confirms that she will and I wonder again how long they've known one another. The front door shuts and then there is the sound of my mother's high-heeled footsteps along the hallway. She's moving around in the kitchen, switching the wireless on. From my window, I can see Reg across the street, getting into a small white van, MEAT DISTRIBUTION printed on the side. He hooks a pair of glasses over his ears then takes a brown trilby from the passenger seat and puts it on, adjusting it in the rear-view mirror until he's satisfied. He sits in the van for a moment, lighting a cigarette, and I watch as he flicks the match onto the road, then starts the engine. I can see he's smiling.

9

1951

It isn't that my mother wouldn't like the idea or would forbid me from going to the dance. Quite the opposite. She'd want to know everything: who was there, if I'd danced with anyone and if so, who he was, and what sort of family he was from. I'd never hear the end of it. It's why I left the house in my ordinary clothes, telling her I was going to Ann's to work on a school project. I'm not even friends with Ann. And of course I don't mention Lucy.

I park my bicycle outside the town hall and wait anxiously. Already, girls are beginning to arrive in twos and threes, giggling and clutching each other's arms. A handful of boys lurk on the other side of the road in their peaked caps, smoking cigarettes, pretending not to be interested yet giving themselves away with constant glances and readjustments of their jackets.

She's stepping out of her father's Austin Somerset. A yellow dress, nipped in at the waist, with a fashionable square neckline. Shoes with a small heel. She's wearing her hair in a stylish updo.

"Edie." She calls to me and waves.

I wave back, hardly believing it's my name she's calling, and then she is rushing across the road toward me. Up close I can see she's wearing makeup, a thin chain with a rose pendant, and tiny silver clip-on pearl and sapphire earrings. Perhaps she borrowed the earrings from her mother. I imagine Barbara Theddle to have an extensive jewelry collection: she's rarely seen out without a string of pearls around her neck.

"Your hair is lovely," I tell her. "You look like an air hostess."

Lucy laughs. "They're so glamorous, aren't they? And all those places you'd see. But there's no money in it. Not that that's what the girls are interested in..."

I give her a questioning glance and she links her arm through mine.

"The pilots, silly. They're all hoping to bag one."

I blush. "You still look lovely. I like your earrings."

"Oh, they're my mother's. A present from a sweetheart many years ago, although I doubt my father knows that." She laughs.

We head straight to the ladies' room, Lucy waiting outside while I change into my Sunday dress with the sweet-pea print. It's my second-best dress after the blue voile, but my mother would be livid if I damaged that one: she spent ages making it and the material was expensive.

"Here," Lucy says, glancing down at my brown lace-ups. She reaches into her bag. "I brought you some shoes. I wasn't sure you'd have any."

I take the shoes from Lucy—navy blue with small heels and an ankle strap.

"Are you sure...?"

"Of course."

We enter the hall to find the dance in full swing. Colorful dresses, shined shoes, slicked-back hair, shy smiles and cheerful chatter. Paper streamers have been hung from the ceiling. The band is playing a swing tune, and Reverend Thurby is bustling around, throwing away empty paper cups. A few couples are spinning and bopping on the dance floor.

In Lucy's shoes, I feel tall and glamorous. Pushing my shoulders back, I experience a new sense of confidence. I think of what I'd usually be doing on a Saturday night: lying on my bed, reading *Malory Towers* or *Jane Eyre* for the millionth time, or in the kitchen with my mother helping with the dishes, listening to a dreary old play on the wireless. That Edie Green doesn't seem anything to do with me anymore. Being with Lucy feels as though someone has opened a window and I am experiencing a rush of cold air on my face.

There are plenty of girls I recognize from school, and some I don't. I expect they've come from the neighboring towns and villages. Word must have gotten around that the band was coming. Most of the girls who aren't dancing stand around in groups stealing glances at the boys; others are sitting down on the provided benches. Judy, Ann, and Linda are at the refreshment table: FRUIT PUNCH AND ICES. Linda is wearing a salmon-colored dress that washes out her pale complexion, and Ann has far too much eyeliner on. Judy notices us; she waves at Lucy, stares at me, then looks away.

I've been walking to and from school with Lucy for three weeks now. The envious glances of the other girls when Lucy meets me at the gate at four o'clock have not gone unnoticed. I don't care. I always thought Lucy and I could be friends; it feels perfectly natural, as if it should have been this way all along, and walking to and from school has become my favorite time of day. My diary is filled with suns.

Yesterday after school, Lucy had youth orchestra practice in the town hall, and I went with her and waited, even though it is the wrong way for me. I didn't mind. I enjoyed sitting outside on the step, plucking at the daisies, listening to the youth of Ludthorpe play sketchy renditions of Bach or Vivaldi. Not that I'm one to talk–I don't know much about classical music. My mother prefers to listen to popular stuff, swing and jazz.

On Wednesday at lunchtime, I was crossing the courtyard and Lucy was sitting with Judy Simpson at one of the picnic tables.

"Would you like to join us, Edie?" Lucy asked me. "We've plenty of space here. You needn't use that awful bench, you know."

Judy's face was a picture. She glowered all the way through lunch while messily eating a sausage roll, glancing up at me and trying to get Lucy's attention by going on about how beastly Miss Benson had been to us during maths.

"She's very fair, though," I said when Judy had finished her little speech. "I never understood long division before Miss Benson."

"Yes." Lucy immediately agreed with me. "I don't think she's all *that* horrid."

Judy looked as though she'd been slapped, and I had to stifle a smile behind my sandwich. I know Judy is jealous of my new friendship with Lucy, that she can't believe Lucy would rather spend time with me than with her. If Judy only knew that *I* share Lucy's biggest secret.

I've tried to encourage Lucy to talk about Mr. Wheaton, but

she is reluctant to discuss the subject other than to admit it was "all a mistake," or "all over now, so there's really nothing to talk about," and to confirm, several times, that I haven't told anyone. But then yesterday, I was walking along the lower corridor with Lucy between lessons when Mr. Wheaton came along, carrying a pile of books. He stopped when he saw us and asked, casually, if Lucy could come to his office after school to talk about her French Revolution essay. Our essays were handed in a week ago, marked, and given back to us. If he'd wanted to see Lucy, he would have said that last week when we got our marks. What could he possibly want to see her about now?

Lucy confirmed she would, and Mr. Wheaton had hurried off, a smile playing at the corners of his lips.

"Sorry, Edie. I guess I won't be able to walk with you tonight," Lucy had said apologetically.

"Are you sure it's wise? Going to see him on your own."

She'd glanced around nervously as if someone might have been listening to us. "Shh, of course. It's fine. He's still our teacher, isn't he?"

I'd opened my mouth but was silenced by a cackle of girls exiting the library. We were absorbed into the general throng of the corridor and I didn't think it a good idea to mention Mr. Wheaton again, as much as I had wanted to.

I haven't had a chance to ask Lucy what he wanted, but ever since he spoke to her in the corridor I've had a creeping, ominous feeling. After what happened between them, surely Mr. Wheaton should be doing everything he can to keep away from Lucy, not approaching her in the corridor in front of her friends, brazenly asking to see her, and giving no good reason?

A voice behind us. "Hello, Lucy. Have you been here long?"

It's Rupert Mayhew with another boy. Rupert is dressed in a smart striped blazer, and his hair is slick with Brylcreem. The second boy is wearing a green corduroy jacket and a red tie. They are both much better dressed than most of the other boys in the room. Rupert doesn't look like he's worked a day in his life. It's hard to imagine him at the undergarment factory with his father, sitting in the office all day, overseeing the factory floor.

"Oh, hello, Rupert," Lucy says casually, leaning in and giving him a friendly kiss on the cheek.

I can tell the kiss has pleased Rupert even though he smiles nonchalantly. There is an air of confidence and dignity about him, but something else, too—the stress and anxiety of a young man whom others expect things of. A younger brother never quite matching up to the elder, perhaps.

I can see from the way he keeps glancing at Lucy that he's smitten with her. Well, that doesn't matter. He's just a friend to Lucy. Still, my stomach quivers. I want Lucy to myself. I don't want to lose her to Rupert. I picture him waiting outside the school gates, ready to walk her home while I am left behind.

"This is Ivor." Lucy gestures, for my benefit, to the boy in the red tie. "You've both met Edie, haven't you?"

Rupert holds his hand out and I shake it. "I don't believe we have," he says, smiling at me.

Rupert's hand is cool, but Ivor's is warm and a little damp, and I fight the urge to wipe my hand on my dress.

"Well, for goodness' sake, let's dance!" Lucy exclaims as the band starts up with a new song. "That's what we're here for, isn't it?"

Rupert obligingly offers Lucy his hand, leading her to the

dance floor where they begin to move in time with the music, another fast swing. Lucy dances beautifully, twirling and spinning assuredly yet elegantly, in full possession of herself. Most of the girls sitting on the benches are watching Lucy and Rupert, and I have to admit they make quite a pair. They've known each other a long time, I remind myself; that's why they're so comfortable together.

"Do you dance, Edie?"

Ivor has leaned over and is talking close to my ear. His breath smells of mint humbugs, but it isn't unpleasant.

"Oh. Not really. I mean, only a little. I'm not very good."

"Well, I'm not much good either, but we could give it a go if you like."

Taking Ivor's arm, stepping onto the floor, I can feel the rhythm of the music pulsing through my body and somehow the steps come to me. I dance cautiously at first, then with more conviction. *Just feel the music*, my mother used to tell me as we waltzed or bopped across the hearthrug. Ivor isn't a bad dancer at all, a little clumsy at first but then he relaxes and leads well. He seems to enjoy letting me twirl away and come back to him. I go faster and faster, feeling exhilarated, the images and colors blurring in front of my eyes: the hem of a dress, an open collar, a flash of lipstick.

When the dance ends, I thank him politely. The band starts up again, a waltz this time. The dance floor is already thronged with entwined couples. Ivor looks at me with a slight shrug as if to say, *shall we do this one too?* But then Lucy appears. "Time to swap partners," she tells us. A flicker of disappointment crosses Rupert's face but then he's smiling, leading me to a clear spot on the floor.

I try to remember the steps but I don't feel quite so at ease with Rupert. Perhaps because I know he'd prefer to be dancing with Lucy. I concentrate on my feet, not wanting to make a fool of myself and remembering those waltzes with my mother. *Quick, quick, slow, Edie. Keep your arms up. That's it.*

"How long have you known Lucy?" Rupert asks as we dance, his hand firmly placed on the small of my back.

"Oh, just a little while," I shout into his ear. "We go to school together."

"I'm going to marry her."

I almost stop in surprise but Rupert doesn't seem to notice; he continues to move us effortlessly around the floor. We're further away from the band now, which makes it easier to hear him.

"You're going to marry Lucy? Have you asked her then?"

Rupert laughs. "No, of course not. Not yet. We'll have to wait a year or two. Well, until she's eighteen, I expect."

"What makes you think she'll say yes?"

Rupert's eyes sparkle. "Of course she'll say yes. We're great together. Everyone has always known we'll get married one day. She's hardly going to say no, is she?"

"But I thought you were just friends?"

"Is that what she told you?"

I say nothing, not wanting to betray Lucy.

"Well, she would say that. I mean, nothing's *official* yet."

A lump rises in my throat. Why did Lucy lie to me? And what else isn't she telling me?

The song ends and Rupert takes up with Judy, who practically throws her arms around him, smiling gleefully.

I look around, scanning the room, but can't see Lucy anywhere.

Eventually I find her outside, leaning against the wall, smoking a cigarette and holding a cup of fruit punch. The evening is warm for the first week of May. A light breeze rustles the newly unfurled leaves, and the air is tinged with smoke; someone must be having a bonfire.

"Oh, hello, Edie. Do you want one?" She offers me a cigarette.

I shake my head. "No, thanks."

"Here, have some of this, then."

I take a sip of the punch, the taste sweet and plummy, then hand it back to her.

"Rupert's quite a good dancer, really, isn't he?"

I frown. "He says he's going to marry you. Are you going steady, then?"

Lucy flinches and takes a drag on her cigarette. "We're all far too young to get married, Edie," she says quietly.

"Still, it doesn't seem right. That Rupert thinks you're going steady but you say you're not. You should tell him now so he's clear about it."

Lifting her chin, she exhales a plume of smoke, then sighs heavily. "I know. But I suppose I don't want to hurt him. And I've got a lot going on right now."

My throat tightens. "It's Mr. Wheaton, isn't it? When he asked to see you yesterday..."

Lucy's cheeks color. She has finished her cigarette and stamps on it with the heel of her shoe, rubbing it into the gravel.

"He didn't want to see you about your essay, did he?"

"No," she says, glancing at me coyly, then leaning back against the wall.

"Well, what's going on?"

"It's difficult to say, exactly."

I press my lips together. "Is he—harassing you? Because if he is—"

"He isn't *harassing* me, Edie. We're involved. I mean, we're having an affair."

I gape idiotically at her. "An affair?"

Lucy glances around nervously. "Shh. Keep your voice down, will you?"

But there is no one around, only two boys across the road on the green, too far away to hear us. One punches the other playfully on the arm and they laugh loudly, causing several pigeons to take off from the tree.

"Has this been going on all this time? Since I saw you..."

"Yes," she says.

I am cross with myself for believing her when she said it was over. "Lucy, this is very serious. He's our teacher. He's married."

For some reason she begins to giggle loudly, then finishes with a snort. "Sorry," she says, covering her mouth with her hand. "I know all of that, really I do." She swallows and takes a breath. "It's just that I've been waiting for something like this, something exciting, to happen to me my whole life. Now it finally has and I just can't give it up." She looks earnestly at me, wanting me to understand. "And Max simply adores me."

"Max?" I rub my forehead. *Mr. Wheaton. Our history teacher. A married man. It has been going on all this time and she never told me.*

"I've been seeing him outside of school," she continues. "We park up by the woods and talk and kiss..." She grips my arm, her eyes ablaze. "I know we shouldn't be doing it but I can't tell you how wonderful it is. I get this delicious pain in my stomach just thinking about him."

I stare at her.

"Oh, Edie, don't look at me like that. We're not doing any harm. How can something that feels so divine possibly be doing any harm?"

I blink, not knowing what to say. The boys are crossing the road now, making their way back into the hall; I can hear the band playing "Take the 'A' Train."

"What about Mr. Wheaton's wife? Don't you feel awful?"

Lucy shrugs. "No, not really. I know I should, but I don't. Max is so unhappy with her and people should be happy, Edie." She puts her hand on my arm. "It's my secret. No one knows. You obviously mustn't tell anyone." She shudders. "My parents would probably disown me and never talk to me again, like they did with Uncle Roland when he got divorced. My mother said she couldn't cope with the scandal. Her own brother. *Divorce!*"

I lower my head, my stomach hardening. She said it was all over.

"Why did you lie? You told me—"

"Yes, well, it wasn't a lie then. We did decide it mustn't go on, but then when we saw each other again... Of course it was just *impossible.* Like we'd tried to throw a cup of water on a house fire or something."

I straighten my back. However shocked I feel, whatever I think, Lucy has trusted me with her secret. I'm her best friend, I must be. Otherwise she wouldn't have told me. "Of course I won't say anything," I tell her.

She turns and flings her arms around me and I stumble backward, surprised at the sudden embrace.

"Gosh, it does feel good to tell someone," she says, releasing me. "It's been eating me alive. I do feel dreadfully guilty about Rupert. I am awfully fond of him but it just isn't the same. And I told you—my father doesn't want me to go to college; he wants me to marry as soon as I finish school, live just up the road where he can keep an eye on me. He'd be delighted if I married Rupert, but I just can't bear the thought of it all, of knowing exactly how it will be, staying here in Ludthorpe, being Mrs. Mayhew... Max, well, it's different. He's a *man*. He's had experience of things. We're so perfect together, and I make him happy, I know I do. I'm happy, too, happier than I've ever been, in fact." She smiles dreamily. "Max says he loves me."

I blink at her in astonishment. How can Mr. Wheaton possibly love her? I want to tell her not to be so stupid, but the thought nags at me that perhaps she's right, and what do I know? Who am I to stand in the way of love, to give my inexperienced opinions? But the uneasy feeling in the pit of my stomach lingers.

Lucy is dropping the cigarette packet into her handbag. "We'd better get back in, Edie. We've got time for a few more dances, I should think. Rupert's going to drive me home; he's borrowed the car. I hope you don't mind. My father only agreed to let me go if Rupert was going to be there to chaperone me. You'd think it's 1922, or something."

She gulps down the last of the punch and before I can say anything else, she's grabbing my hand and leading me back toward the hall, her little white shoes tap-tapping up the steps.

10

2018

It's three o'clock in the afternoon and I'm sitting in my chair mulling it all over: what Halim told me in the library about Lucy's disappearance, the disturbing images that keep popping into my mind, the panicky feeling I get when I think of Lucy. Halim gave me something so I won't forget. What was it? It doesn't matter, I've memorized it all, like lines in a play: *an English schoolgirl who disappeared. A white bicycle in a field. A small suitcase containing clothes, a toothbrush, a bottle of perfume, sandwiches, and ten pounds.* I sit up. *Perfume.* I can see Lucy offering me the bottle. "*Try some, Edie, isn't it dreamy?*" She sprays her own wrists and inhales deeply. I can smell it too: the heady scent of desire, of broken promises and stolen kisses. Someone gave Lucy that perfume. Someone who shouldn't have. A shiver down my spine. My fingers tingle. I remember now: Lucy's secret.

January was an odd time for a teacher to retire, but Miss Dray had a fall, cracked her head. I can recall it because it unsettled me. Teachers were formidable, invincible beings of authority. They did not fall over on their own doorsteps. She'd been sweeping the snow off her front path and had slipped on a patch of ice, we were told. I can see her, falling in slow motion, her feet in the air, her head catching the front step, blood on the snow. Of course I saw no such thing. What I did see, however, late one afternoon, during double domestic science, was her walking out of the school gates holding the vase she'd been given as a retirement gift. She walked slowly, uncertainly, a canvas bag over her shoulder, presumably containing the contents of her desk. She put the vase and her bag in her bicycle basket, then cycled, wobbling somewhat, away. That was the last I saw of her. She'd been at the school thirty years.

So then came Mr. Wheaton. It was a blue February afternoon, our first lesson after lunch. The trees outside the window were bare limbed, the winter sunlight streaming through the high windows onto the dark, oiled, wooden floorboards of our classroom—the smell of ink and pencil shavings. I can picture him, quite clearly now, as though it were only yesterday, standing in front of us for the first time, introducing himself. There was something rebellious about him; perhaps it was his loosened tie, the rolled-up shirtsleeves. We eyed him with interest as we slipped quietly into our seats.

He was tall. Dark hair, a full, thick beard, brown but with flecks of gingery red, the color of the Canadian maple syrup my mother had bought before the war. The hair on his forearms was dark, and he wore an unusually large watch with a thick brown strap.

He waited until we were all seated before perching casually

on his desk. I could see an inch of striped sock between his shoe and trouser leg.

"My name is Mr. Wheaton, and I will be taking you for history for the rest of the academic year."

There was a deep richness to his voice, a physical ease in the way he carried himself. His accent wasn't the same as ours. He sounded like he was off the telly, like he should be reading us the evening news or discussing the chance of easterly winds. We waited for him to go to the board, to write out the dates we would undoubtedly have to copy down in our yellow lined exercise books.

Instead, he smiled at us. "Can anyone tell me what history is?"

We glanced at each other uneasily. Was this a trick question, we wondered? Or did this man not know we were at the secondary grammar, that we had been studying history, or various parts of it at least, for years now, that we were, in fact, almost done with history and school completely, ready to be unleashed on the world? Not that we, as women, would be able to leave much of a mark on it, of course. *Your natural ambition, girls, is to attach yourself to a man who will provide for you*, Mrs. Beecham, our domestic science teacher, was fond of telling us. Learning *too* much was bad. We must, after all, strike the right balance at dinner parties, not appearing completely ignorant but certainly not knowing more than our husbands.

Ann put up her hand.

Mr. Wheaton nodded at her.

"History is the past," she said.

Our eyes returned to Mr. Wheaton, who tilted his head to one side, considering. "Anything more?"

Ann's eyebrows furrowed as Judy's hand shot up. "Facts about the past?"

Mr. Wheaton slid off the desk and stood in front of us. "Facts about the past," he repeated slowly, stroking his chin. "And are these facts to be trusted? Are these facts *truthful*?"

"Well, yes, if they're facts," Judy replied smugly.

We suspected her to be wrong but we said nothing.

"And what are these facts based on?" Mr. Wheaton asked, now pacing slowly up and down in front of the board. His gaze swept over us. His eyes reached Lucy and seemed to linger a moment too long.

"Evidence," Cordelia Keal replied, not bothering to put her hand up.

"Ah, *evidence*," Mr. Wheaton said, Sherlock Holmes–style, as if we had discovered something significant.

We said nothing more, and so he stopped pacing and perched on the desk again. There was something mesmerizing about him. We couldn't tear our eyes away. He was different from any of our other teachers, more present somehow; he appeared to *see* us. And younger, definitely younger. Old, of course, because all teachers were, but not old like Miss Dray with her gray, cracked head.

"Facts, yes, can be truthful, but they don't always give us the truth, do they? Not the whole truth, at least. And evidence." He rubbed his chin again. "Evidence is only ever partial evidence. When do we ever really know the full story?"

"We don't," Judy chirped.

The rest of us rolled our eyes.

"History," he continued, ignoring Judy and opening his arms as if to fit history inside them. "History is always interpreted. It is the method of organizing what has been left behind, the truths *and* the speculation. It is what has happened, along with what has been *said* about what has happened. Some facts may, of course, be undeniable. The Second World War, for example."

We blinked up at him. We had never considered the war, not our war, to be history.

"The Holocaust." He held our gaze. "These are undeniable facts. What do *they* tell us?" His expression clouded. He was looking somewhere over our heads. "That history is nothing more than death and mess and wasted lives?"

We said nothing.

He recovered himself, smiled encouragingly. "They *happened.* But evidence," he continued, "does not create the past. *We* create the past. We give the people who lived in the past a narrative—yet it can never *truly* be their story. Their voices are lost to us. And in their voices lies the truth. Except," here he held up his hand, "except that memory is unreliable. What we remember is not always what we saw."

We must have all looked blank.

He sighed, knowing he'd lost us. "To clarify, history is not just 'the past.' History is evidence *of* the past, but it is evidence that has gone through the wash, been spat out, regurgitated. It is the past pressed through cheesecloth, the *essence* of the past. Never, quite, the full story."

He stood and turned to the board. "Take the Norman invasion, for example..."

Here we breathed a sigh of relief. We were back in familiar territory. We opened our yellow exercise books, pencils poised. Some of us were already scribbling away, making our headings, a familiar date: 1066.

This is how I remember that blue February afternoon; the

sunlight on the floorboards, Mr. Wheaton's rolled-up shirtsleeves, the smooth sound of his voice. I had forgotten it all entirely until I saw Lucy outside the post office, until I thought of the bin bench, Lucy's revelation at the dance, and then Mr. Wheaton was there for me too, the past brought back to life through the unreliable cheesecloth of my memory.

A knock at the door interrupts my thoughts, bringing me sharply back into the present.

"Hello, Nan."

It's Amy, my granddaughter. She's standing on the doorstep, holding two paper cups of tea and a cardboard box I know will contain lemon drizzle cake. She does this often—pops round to see me for an hour or so after school, bringing cake from The Tea Tree. Lemon drizzle is my favorite. I don't know why she bothers to get the takeaway tea though—I've got a perfectly good kettle here, but she likes to do it. They all do. Suzanne can't go anywhere without buying a takeaway coffee. She's always got one on the go, glued to her hand. I'm sure it isn't good for her nerves, all that coffee. It's why she's so highly strung, why she can't ever unwind, I told Daniel once.

For goodness' sake, Mum, don't say that to her, Daniel replied. *Anyway, coffee has proven health benefits. It reduces the risk of all sorts of things.*

Like what? I said. Sleep?

Daniel rolled his eyes, but I could see he was suppressing a smile.

At least the takeaway tea saves on the washing up, but I don't like to think of Amy spending her money on me. I suppose it's Daniel's money really, although Amy does have a job now. She works Saturdays at Exquisite Fashion. She bought me a scarf for my birthday—a bit too mauve for me, but I didn't say anything.

In the living room, Amy is prying the lids off the paper cups. "So, what is it you wanted to talk to me about, Nan? You said it was urgent."

I frown, settling down into my chair. What was it I wanted to talk to Amy about? I feel like it was just there and now it's gone.

"Well, don't worry," Amy says, cheerfully. "I'm sure whatever it was will come back to you. Or are you stuck on your crossword again?"

I glance over at the newspaper folded on my chair arm. "I don't think it was the crossword."

"Well...perhaps you'll remember. I'll get us plates, shall I?" She darts off to the kitchen.

"Yes, plates," I murmur, still cross with myself for forgetting what I wanted to tell her. It's there, on the edges of my mind... There was *something*. Something about...

Amy returns from the kitchen with the plates and forks. She's waving a piece of paper at me. "What's this, Nan? It was pinned to your calendar."

I take the piece of paper from her, smooth it out on my lap, then smile to myself. "Lucy," I tell Amy. "That's what I wanted to talk to you about. Lucy."

Amy gives me a puzzled look, then takes the paper from me. She begins to read. "Lucy Theddle—born on the eighth of September, 1935—was an English schoolgirl who disappeared on the twelfth of July, 1951, aged sixteen, on the outskirts of the town of Ludthorpe—" She stops reading. "Where did you get this, Nan?"

"A boy printed it for me at the library," I say proudly. "He helped me to use the computer. It's about Lucy. She disappeared, and I'm trying to find her."

Amy studies the crumpled piece of paper. "Sorry... Did you know her, Nan, this girl?"

"We were at school together, but then I saw her last week outside the post office looking exactly the same as she did in 1951."

"You *saw* her?"

I nod as Amy sits down next to me, rubbing at her eyebrows. The steam rises from our paper cups.

"I ate a Parma Violet," I explain. "I hadn't had a Parma Violet in years. And we used to meet outside the post office to walk to school together, you see." I bring my hands together in my lap, then dig my nails into the soft tissue of my palm, something I'm sure I used to do as a child.

Amy studies the Wikipedia page. "I've never heard of this girl. It's so awful. To just vanish into thin air like that... Do you remember anything about her disappearance?"

I look thoughtfully toward my windows. Weak sunlight is breaking through the clouds, and two birds are sitting on the telegraph wire. I lifted the net curtains earlier to let a bit more light in. When Daniel came back from his Stockholm city break he told me about how much he liked the Scandinavian decor. *So clean and minimal,* he said. *And when you walk past the houses at night, you can see right inside. You should get rid of these nets, Mum. They're old fashioned.*

I am old fashioned, I told him. Anyway, who wants the neighbors peering in at you in the evenings? How awful.

Amy is sliding our cake slices onto the plates, and I notice she's wearing little silver earrings in the shape of butterflies, and rings on her fingers. I'm not sure I want to tell her about Mr. Wheaton just yet, not until I've figured it all out.

"That's why I wanted you to come over," I say. "I wanted to tell you about Lucy so I don't forget. And I thought perhaps you could help me find her."

"Help you find a girl who disappeared in 1951?"

"Yes."

Amy frowns. "Um, I'd love to help, Nan. It's just difficult to know where to start. It was such a long time ago. I mean, if the police weren't able to find her..." She nudges my tea toward me then takes a sip from her own.

"But she's still missing," I insist.

"I know, Nan," Amy says, gently. "But there isn't much we can do after all this time. And I'd hate for you to be disappointed. Sorry," she adds, touching my arm.

I knit my eyebrows together and stare into my tea. My mother wouldn't have approved of paper teacups. She used the Wedgwood when Constable Diprose came over to ask me about Lucy. He arrived on his bicycle and sat in our front room, holding his notepad and a sharp yellow pencil. He couldn't have been very old; he wore a fuzzy mustache like a hairy caterpillar, and he clearly hadn't dealt with a case like this before. Things like that—teenage girls from good homes disappearing—just didn't happen in Ludthorpe.

He asked me if I could think of any reason why Lucy might have wanted to run away, and I said I couldn't, despite the twisting in my gut.

Where is Constable Diprose now? I think of Halim in the library. *I could look it up for you on my phone.*

"Amy," I ask tentatively, "can you look things up on your telephone?"

She nods. "Would you like me to look something up for you, Nan?"

"Not some*thing*. Some*one*."

Amy puts her tea down "Who?"

"His name was Peter Diprose. He was a young police officer, maybe five or six years older than me. He came to interview me about Lucy. Perhaps he's still alive. He might remember the original investigation into Lucy's disappearance."

Amy sighs. "Like I said, Nan. It was all a very long time ago—"

"But we found Lucy. On the computer, I mean. At the library. So maybe we can find out about other people too." I smile hopefully.

Amy reluctantly reaches for her bag. "We can do a quick search, but I have to warn you it's very unlikely we'll find anything." She tucks a strand of loose hair behind her ear while looking at her telephone. "If he was five or six years older than you then, that would put him at almost ninety now." She taps slowly. "And obviously he could be anywhere—" She stops talking and stares at her tiny screen.

"What is it?" I ask, leaning forward, straining my neck.

"Well, you might just be in luck, Nan." Amy turns the screen toward me, but it's so small I have to squint to make out the words. *Retired Chief Inspector, Peter Diprose, aged eighty-seven, completes charity fun run, raising five hundred pounds for the Ludthorpe youth center.* I'm looking at a picture of an old man in a blue vest and shorts with a number stuck to his chest like he's a human raffle ticket. He's holding a check and grinning proudly. There is something familiar about his features, despite the wrinkles and lack of hair. "Constable Diprose?"

"Apparently so," Amy says, taking her telephone back. "The article was written three years ago but it means he stayed in Ludthorpe. He's local."

I nod, hoping he isn't *too* local, now in the cemetery along the road. Three years is a long time when you're in your late eighties—just like when you're a child. It's all the middle that rushes by too quickly.

Amy sighs then puts her telephone down on my coffee table. "I suppose we can try and find him if you really want to, but Nan..."

"Yes?"

"Are you sure this is what you want? Do you really want to know about all this? Won't it be upsetting for you? If she was your friend?"

I think of Lucy. I need to find out what happened to her. Doing nothing is no longer an option, not at my age, and not when I've got this strange untethered feeling, the feeling I could take off at any moment. I need to stay grounded, stay focused. It's the only way to keep the fogginess and the disturbing, incomplete memories at bay, to keep from being in a muddle. It's the only way to show them all I'm capable. Lucy was my friend and I need to fill the gaping hole that arises whenever I think of her.

"Yes," I say firmly. "I want to know."

Amy hesitates, then nods. "Okay, if this is important to you, and you're sure you won't be disappointed if it comes to nothing, then we'll see what we can find out."

There is a lightness in my chest: I knew Amy would help. "It *is* important."

11

1951

It's a little after ten o'clock. I've hung up my sweet-pea dress, scrubbed my face and am lying in bed, replaying the events of the evening in my mind. Over the last few weeks, my friendship with Lucy has grown and blossomed, and yet all that time she never told me the whole story. I wrote all of this down in my diary, then drew a little cloud and raindrops to indicate it has been a stormy day, before replacing the diary under the loose floorboard in my room.

My thoughts are interrupted by a pinging noise at my window. I ignore it but it comes again, and then again, and so I get out of bed, pull the curtain back, lean over the sill, and squint into the darkness.

Lucy is standing outside the house under the light of the streetlamp, looking up at me, her eyes wide. She looks disheveled: her stylish updo has come undone and tendrils of hair have escaped; one of her dress straps has fallen down over her shoulder. She's holding her shoes.

"Shh," I hiss, putting my finger to my lips, terrified she'll wake my mother. She makes an indecipherable gesture with her free hand, a sort of wave, and I grab my father's old brown cardigan and slip it on over my nightdress, push my feet into my slippers, then tiptoe past my mother's bedroom.

I quietly open the front door. "Edie," Lucy whispers as she limps toward me. "I'm so sorry, I needed to stop walking."

Her breath smells of alcohol, her makeup has smudged, and the skin around her eyes is red. She shivers and I usher her into the front room, closing the door as softly as I can, glancing up at the stairs. She hobbles in and sits straight down onto the settee, barely noticing her surroundings. I turn my mother's sewing lamp on.

"Had to take my shoes off—the straps were digging in. Only now I've got a splinter, I'm sure of it." She picks her foot up and inspects the sole. I can see her heels are red and raw. A blister is beginning to form.

"Lucy, what are you *doing* here?"

She drops her foot. "Sorry, Edie. My feet were really hurting."

"Do you need a plaster?" I glance down at her bare and grubby feet. "Why aren't you at home? I thought Rupert was dropping you back?"

"Well, he was. Only he told me he didn't have to get me back straightaway, that we had a little time and might as well continue enjoying the evening. We drove out to the edge of town then parked in that little lane, you know, the one that goes up to the Colliers' farm."

I nod.

"Well, we were just talking and laughing and Rupert insisted I drink some of this awful stuff he had in a flask in the glove compartment. Something he'd taken from his father's drinks cabinet. He kept telling me what a splendid evening it was and how everyone was looking at us, but after a while I said we had better get back." She pauses, wipes her nose on the back of her hand. "Rupert, well, he tried to kiss me. I panicked and got out of the car. Of course he kept calling out to me: 'Lucy, I'm sorry. Come on, get back in. Let me take you home.' He sounded so mournful, but I just couldn't."

"You walked all the way here?"

She nods. "I was planning to go home but my feet... I just needed to stop. Now I feel awful. Poor Rupert. What must he think?"

"I wouldn't worry about him," I say testily.

"I overreacted. I know I did. He'll feel terrible."

"He shouldn't have got carried away."

"Oh, Edie, don't be like that. It was probably my fault for agreeing to the drive. I should have known he might have expected something."

"No, you shouldn't have."

"Please, Edie, don't go on about it."

"Fine." I leave her alone while I fetch a plaster from my father's old first aid kit in the kitchen. When I return, she takes it gratefully.

"Much better, thank you, Edie," she says, smoothing down the edges. "I should be able to make it home now." She stands, pressing her feet into the rug, examining her plaster, then glances at the clock on the mantelpiece. "I shouldn't leave it too long, my father will be waiting up."

"Maybe you should tell him about Rupert."

Lucy rubs her temple. "I couldn't do that. You don't

understand. You don't know my father. He has all these rules. He only allows me to go dancing if I go with Rupert as he thinks Rupert is respectable because he knows who Rupert's parents are. I'll never be allowed out if I tell him Rupert tried to kiss me when we're not even engaged."

"Is he really *that* strict?"

She nods. "We're supposed to be this perfect happy family but we're not at all. George is miserable because he can't ever be clever enough for my father, and my mother is too wrapped up in her committees and her decorating schemes to see how horrid everything really is. I'm sure my father has been having an affair for years. That's why he must never find out about Max. He'll know I'm just like him and he'll hate me for it." She grabs her handbag. "I can't get into trouble with my father. I *have* to be allowed out."

"Because of Mr. Wheaton," I say.

"Yes." She looks at me, her eyes wide in the dim light. "I don't know what I'd do if I couldn't see Max. I hate having to share him, knowing he's married. It's a horrible kind of pain, Edie. You simply can't imagine."

"Maybe things will change," I say, following her into the hallway. I don't like to see Lucy agitated, but I know my words sound hollow, and I don't believe Mr. Wheaton will leave his wife, no matter what he tells Lucy.

"Thank you, Edie. I don't know what I would do without you."

I open the kitchen door, searching for my shoes, insisting I walk with her to The Gables.

"Don't worry," she says, placing her hand on my arm. "You stay here. This is Ludthorpe. It's perfectly safe."

12

1951

I'm standing in the church in the first pew. Above me, Jesus is levitating in a sunbeam. He's got his feet off the floor and is surrounded by brilliant yellow light, his arms raised, as if he's going to make an announcement, only he stays like that, watching me, watching all of us. Not that the church is particularly full. In fact, there is hardly anyone here at all. To the left of me is our next-door neighbor, Mrs. Cartwright, a widow who wears trousers and is therefore considered radical. She's the only person on our street who owns a telephone and a television, the aerial proudly sprouting from her roof. Behind me stands a friend of my mother's, a horsey-looking woman called Janet who is taller than her husband, a silent, suited man who looks as though he'd rather be anywhere but here. There is Mrs. Staines, who lives at the top of our road on her own because Mr. Staines couldn't get the day off work. Two men are lurking at the back of the church, their suits rumpled, an indication they are either bachelors or their marriages are in trouble. These men are regulars at The Bird in Hand and are friends of Reg's.

Then there is my mother. She stands at the front of the church, clutching Reg's arm, wearing a pink dress with a raspberry-colored trim, a matching hat, and gloves. She decided white wasn't appropriate for a second wedding. I think the pink was a mistake, but I haven't said anything. Reg is wearing a cream suit, which makes him look even more ridiculous than my mother. I'm wearing my best blue voile dress, even if it is a little small for me now, and holding the bunch of forget-me-nots she sent me out to pick yesterday. I stare at the tiny yellow centers. I'd rather look at the flowers than at my mother and Reg and Reverend Thurby, who is talking about the blessed union of marriage.

Reverend Thurby has been our vicar for as long as I can remember. He came to our house once, not long after my father's death, where he sat in the front room, sipping tea and scoffing cake. He gave my mother a pamphlet tilted "Beyond Life's Sunset" and talked about my father being in the arms of Jesus, something I could never quite picture. My father, although a gentle and quiet man, was tall and stocky, and all the pictures I've ever seen of Jesus show him as being rather skinny–in need of a good Sunday roast, Mrs. Cartwright might say. Definitely not strong enough to hold my father in his arms, even if my father was sent to heaven wearing only his bathing shorts, the shorts he died in, therefore being at his lightest possible weight.

I am sure Reverend Thurby has mixed feelings about my mother's evening occupation. Perhaps he would prefer his congregation visit him when in need of consolation or hope, as opposed to my mother, who may be guilty of stealing his customers. Perhaps he has a whole stack of "Beyond Life's Sunset" pamphlets in his office that he needs to get rid of in order to fit in more tins of pease pudding for the Salvation Army. I once heard my mother, when he asked her about her "endeavors to contact those passed," remind Reverend Thurby of that bit in the Bible where St. Paul states that some will be given gifts of the Holy Spirit embodying hearing, seeing and prophecy, and so on. He went quiet after that.

I look up. Reverend Thurby is still talking and Reg is grinning like a Cheshire cat. I blink and look away, shift my weight from one foot to the other, waiting for it to be over. How did it come to this?

Reg popped up everywhere after that first day, almost three months ago now, when I met him in our front room. He appeared behind us in the queue at the fishmonger's the following Saturday, offering advice on the haddock, the price of which my mother finds to be outrageous, especially as it's only from Grimsby. A few days later, Reg just happened to be driving his van down the High Street in the afternoon when we were walking home with bags of groceries. He offered us a lift, of course. Then he began to take my mother out dancing on Friday nights. He'd stand in our hallway, pacing up and down, holding a wilting flower or a bar of chocolate. He gave me a tin of Parkinson's boiled sweets, probably bought before the war and left forgotten in some cupboard or other. I couldn't bring myself to eat them.

"Oh, zip me up, will you, Edie," my mother whispered to me across the landing that first evening. "It isn't right to keep a man waiting *too* long, you know. Just long enough to make them understand you're worth waiting for." She giggled like a schoolgirl, as if we were in some kind of conspiracy together.

I tiptoed across the landing to her room, zipped up her dress, watched as she blotted her lipstick onto a tissue and studied her reflection in the mirror. When she was ready, she left the bedroom in a mist of Yardley's English Lavender.

I guess my mother must still be attractive for her age. She's slim with high cheekbones and bouncy curls due to the rollers she sleeps in each night. I don't look much like her. My face is fuller than hers, my hair thinner. I look more like my father: plain, round-faced, and with skin that burns easily in the sun.

Reg then began to appear on weekday evenings. He comes over after work, slinging the heavy set of keys for the garages down on the kitchen table, then sits there drinking beer. He apparently had lodgings he shared with a friend over the fish and chip shop. He couldn't have liked it very much, seeing as he spent most of his time at our house. Anyway, he's given notice to his landlady now.

My mother told me casually over dinner one evening a few weeks ago that she was going to marry Reg. I almost choked on my meat loaf.

"Marry him?" I asked, staring at her.

"Oh, come on, Edie. It can't be that much of a shock to you. It's a natural progression."

"From what?"

My mother sighed. "We've been courting, Edie. In case you hadn't noticed."

"But that doesn't mean you have to *marry* him."

My mother's face darkened. "Don't I deserve a little happiness? Can't something be about *me* for once?"

"But you've only known him five minutes."

"It's a whirlwind romance, Edie," she said, dreamily. "The best kind. Besides, I've known Reg longer than you think. I just waited until the right time to introduce you."

I didn't know how to tell her she was making a terrible mistake, that I knew Reg wouldn't make her happy, just like my father didn't. My mother is always searching for a man to solve her problems. I know she loves it when Reg flatters her over her talent and abilities, but there is something about Reg I don't like. It isn't just that he laughs too loudly, chews his food with his mouth open, slurps his tea. He is what my father would have called "a slippery old fish." He makes me feel uneasy. We hardly know anything about him. Apparently, he didn't fight in the war due to bad eyesight. When I asked Reg what he did to help the war effort, he mentioned something about "runway clearance" at the local Royal Air Force base during the winter of '41, which I took to mean he shoveled a bit of snow around.

"But where will we live?" I had visions of us squeezed into Reg's lodgings above the fish and chip shop.

My mother moved her half-empty plate away and patted her apron for her Player's cigarette. "Here, of course. He'll move in with us. It makes far more sense. It'll be a huge help financially. I can't be on my own for much longer, Edie. I really can't. It's impossible. Especially with you not working yet, although hopefully that will change soon. We need the extra income."

I'd pushed my food around on my plate. Even to me, this didn't sound like a good enough reason for marrying a person. I was also surprised my mother didn't think Reg beneath her. "But isn't he a bit..." I waved my hand, not wanting to finish my sentence in case I offended her.

"He's a self-made man," my mother said firmly. "Reg respects me. He appreciates my talents. He has a steady job."

I'd blinked at her and she'd turned her face away from me.

"You can't ask for too much after thirty," she added, bitterly.

Reg was in the hallway the following Friday evening, waiting for her to come down so they could go out, and I came through from the kitchen with a cup of Horlicks.

"You've heard our news, I suppose, Edie?"

I said I had.

He studied me for a reaction, and I must not have given him one for he looked at me warily.

"Your mother needs a man, Edie."

He leaned in and I could smell the alcohol on his breath. I've often caught him swigging at his hip flask when he thinks no one is watching.

"Someone to take care of things," he'd continued. "All women need that. You'll realize it when you get older. But your mother especially needs it. What with her nerves."

I eyed him with cool contempt, wondering what he knows or what she's told him.

There was a time, when my father was alive, when my mother went a bit funny. That's how my father and I used to refer to it: "when Mother went a bit funny." At first she became tearful and subdued. Then we found her loitering fearfully in strange places in the house; sitting on the kitchen stool by the back door, standing in the bedroom with one ear pressed against the wardrobe, or hovering at the bottom of the stairs, broom in hand, as if poised to strike. There were days when she put on her best clothes and our hopes were raised, but then we'd find her, in her heels, turban, and furs, madly scrubbing the kitchen floor. She said she was being haunted by a pesky Tudor court jester in red tights. "Shh," she'd say. "Hear those bells? He's dancing on the bed again." We were at a loss (this could, after all, have been the truth), but the doctor wasn't, and after a few months of this, it was decided she would be voluntarily admitted to the mental hospital at Sandy Bay. She was there for six weeks and we went to visit her twice weekly. I can still see her face, waving cheerfully to us when we left, her hair mad and disorganized. When Mother finally came home she went about the house, peering into cupboards, inspecting the curtains, studying the framed photographs on the sideboard, as if she had been expecting some great change that wasn't there. After that, she was better and we were pleased, although I couldn't help feeling some small yet vital part of her was missing. Whatever it was that had gone, I knew it would not return.

"You've got to look after your mother, Edie," my father said to me, not long before his death. I promised I would, thinking it silly because he would always be there.

Ever since Mother returned from the hospital, she's suffered on and off with "her nerves." When an attack comes on she alternates between being restless–agitated and unable to settle, complaining her skin feels like it's crawling with ants–to mournful and sad, staring into space and moving listlessly about the house. *My nerves are giving me trouble again*, she'll say, and after that she'll disappear into her bedroom for days on end where she does very little except lie in the dark.

I don't comment on this to Reg. It's true my mother hasn't had a bad attack of the nerves since she's been seeing him, that she appears to be happier, but I don't believe Reg is the answer to my mother's nerve trouble.

"What I'm saying, young lady," Reg said to me that evening in the hallway, "is that I'm going to be a permanent fixture around here. It suits the both of us, and it would be a good idea if it suited you too. Until you move out, of course. Which hopefully won't be too long."

He held my gaze. Before I could say anything, my mother appeared at the top of the stairs, and Reg's expression quickly changed. "Here she is! What a beauty, eh, Edie? Why, I could have sworn that was Lana Turner coming down the stairs."

"Oh, Reg. *Really*. Lana Turner is *blond*."

And now here I am, standing in the cool church on a Saturday morning early in June. After we've finished here, the wedding breakfast will take place in the function room above The Bird in Hand, the same room we used for my father's wake. Ham will be served with lettuce from Mr. Staines's allotment, followed by tinned fruit and Bird's custard for dessert.

"...I now pronounce you man and wife."

Reg is grabbing my mother around the waist and kissing her. She is no longer Mrs. Donald Green. Now she is Mrs. Reginald Drakes. She slips on a new name like she is slipping on a new dress.

The men at the back applaud and then I am ushered outside by tall, horsey Janet. We stand: me, Janet, Mrs. Cartwright, and Mrs. Staines, clutching small paper bags of confetti. My mother and Reg appear smiling in the doorway and we throw the confetti in the air. It's windy and I'm on the wrong side, so most of mine gets caught in the breeze. Pieces of pink and white paper are falling over me, clinging to my hair and my bouquet. A little piece lands in my mouth and I spit it out.

There are cheers and waves as they climb into Reg's van and he starts the ignition. I can hear my mother's laughter through the open window. 'We'll see you at the pub!' she calls out to me. Someone has already tied tin cans to the exhaust pipe and they clatter down the road. One night in Skegness. That's all they can manage for a honeymoon as Reg has a delivery to collect on Monday. They'll be setting off straight after lunch. Then once they return home tomorrow evening, Reg will be living with us. I shudder at the thought of finding him in the kitchen in the morning in his threadbare dressing gown, or having to wait for him to finish on the privy when I'm desperate.

I'm leaving the church–crossing the green, still holding my forget-me-nots–when I see Lucy cycling toward me. I wave vigorously, making sure she's seen me, and she stops and dismounts.

"You just missed the wedding," I tell her.

"Oh, what a shame. I completely forgot about it. I love a wedding. I *was* coming to find you, though–I was hoping you'd be in, but here you are. I need your help. It's rather urgent." Her forehead is creased with worry.

"What is it? Is it Mr. Wheaton?"

She smiles, glancing fearfully around. "No. Shh. It's not that." She lowers her voice. "I saw him yesterday. We went for a drink in a little pub miles from anywhere. Then we lay in the back of the car and kissed and looked at the moon shining down on us. Max says it won't be long before we'll be able to visit the moon. I told him not to be so ridiculous." She smiles again at the memory.

"What is it then?" I ask, a trifle impatiently.

"It's Hitler," she says with a sigh.

"Hitler?" I can clearly remember when the wireless

announced Hitler's death. Everyone on our street cheered and Mr. Pearson let off a firework. It was like VE Day all over again, except that on VE Day someone had too much gin and was sick over Mrs. Cartwright's buddleia tree.

"He's our cat," Lucy explains. "It's not his real name–that's Smudge–only George calls him Hitler as he's got this little patch under his nose. Anyway, he's missing. We haven't seen him since yesterday."

"Cats often go wandering off for a few days," I say, trying to comfort her.

She bites her lip and draws her eyebrows together. "But it's so unlike him not to come in for his dinner, and his breakfast. George is awfully upset about it. He made Daddy go out looking for him last night. And of course Mummy is upset too. She's so fond of that silly old cat."

"I'm sure he'll turn up."

Lucy sighs. "I do hope so, but I was thinking, perhaps you could ask your mother."

"My mother?"

"She could use her–abilities. To see if she can find him?"

"Oh." A weight forms in my chest. "I suppose I can ask..." I say, unsure as to whether channeling the locations of missing cats is a part of my mother's repertoire. I don't want to get Lucy's hopes up.

"Please, Edie. We're all dreadfully worried."

"She's just gone away–her honeymoon..."

Lucy looks defeated.

"But I can ask her tomorrow when she's back?"

Lucy brightens. "Thank you, Edie. You're such a good friend."

13

2018

Winterford Green Retirement Village is a new development a few miles outside of Ludthorpe. I've heard of it but never visited myself.

We step off the transporting thing—I can't think of its name just now—and onto the pavement. A large billboard shows a photograph of four silver-haired people sitting around a table drinking wine and smiling.

"Luxury living for the over fifty-fives," I read aloud. "To inquire or book your guided tour, please call—"

"This way, Nan," Amy says, linking her arm through mine.

We're in some sort of village. The buildings are new, the front gardens tidy and full of flowers. The streets are clean. There's even a fountain—a modern sculpture like a giant disco ball. It's all so neat and shiny, I feel like I've shrunk and am in a tiny toy town. I had a dollhouse once—my father made it for me—and a family of dolls that lived inside it: a mummy, a daddy, and two little girl dolls because I always wanted a sister. I can remember my mother getting cross because I dried the little doll girls' dresses over the fireguard and scorched them. *I shall have to make them new dresses now. And your father will have to sacrifice more handkerchiefs.*

"What are we doing here, Amy?"

She squeezes my arm. "We're here to see Constable Diprose. Although I think he was a chief inspector by the time he retired."

"We're here to ask about Lucy," I say, pleased, recalling how I'd seen it written on my calendar this morning.

"That's right," Amy says, leading me across the street.

I remember the telephone call I made. Was it yesterday? The day before? No, it was Wednesday. I wrote that on my calendar too. Then, in Saturday's square, I wrote: *Going to see C Diprose with Amy* and a little sun because I was feeling hopeful. I didn't write the "Constable" part out in full in case Josie or Daniel asked me about it. Not that they look at my calendar much. They've got calendars on their telephones, they tell me.

Amy thought it was best I make the call even though I hate using the telephone nowadays. I rang the local youth center.

"Is Peter Diprose there?" I'd asked.

The woman at the other end of the phone had sounded surprised. "Well, no. I'm afraid he hasn't volunteered with us for years. He helped buy some new kitchen appliances, but that was a while ago now."

"The charity fun run."

"Yes... Sorry, who's calling?"

"It's Edie Havercroft. I'm a friend of Peter's. A good friend." I'd glanced over at Amy and she'd nodded encouragingly. "I need to get in touch with him," I'd said, gaining confidence. "To send him a card, actually. But I've misplaced my address book." I'd felt both thrilled and appalled at the way the words tumbled so fluently off my tongue. It was quite fun to lie in the name of a good cause.

"Oh dear," the woman on the other end of the line had replied. "I'd be lost without my address book. I do think it's important to still send cards. Facebook isn't quite the same, is it?"

"No," I said, having no idea what she was talking about. "So you see, I was wondering if you could help me, if you had Peter's address to hand."

The woman cleared her throat. "I'm ever so sorry. We're unable to give out addresses over the telephone. It's data protection."

"Data what?"

"Protection. It's the new–"

"Oh, what a mess this is," I'd interrupted, mournfully. I'd paused but she'd said nothing so I carried on. "It's just, I've got no idea how to send this card to him without an address. In fact, I don't know how I would *ever* reach him again." I sniffed a little for effect. "Friends are just so important as you get older," I'd croaked, "and I'd hate him to think I didn't care."

There was a long pause. I could tell the woman was conflicted. "Well...I'm sure it wouldn't hurt on this occasion... If you could hang on a moment, dear, I need to go into the office. We keep all of our paperwork in there."

And now here we are. Going to visit Constable Diprose to see if he remembers Lucy. It's cold out and I'm wearing a thick duffel coat. I find a pair of brown leather gloves in my pocket and put them on.

Amy had said it might be best to go early in case Constable Diprose was going out for the day. She grumbled about getting up at "the crack of dawn" on a Saturday, but nevertheless she'd arrived on my doorstep with her rucksack at exactly eight o'clock. It felt like we were Girl Guides going on an adventure together. Not that I was ever a Girl Guide. All the nature put me off. It was bad enough at home having to go out in the garden to the loo, sitting there shivering among the spiders and Reg's pile of old newspapers, my breath coming out in front of me. Bathing was even worse, and I used to dread Friday nights. Our tin bath hung on a hook behind the kitchen door. It took ages to fill, and the water cooled down quicker than green grass through a goose. I was always terrified someone would walk in on me so I'd sit there tipping jugs of water over my head and scrubbing my armpits while singing "Mister Meadowlark."

Amy stops outside a small, newly built ground floor apartment. The front garden is very tidy, and there's a gnome with a fishing rod, although I can't see a pond. "This must be it," she says. "Number twenty-five." She rings the doorbell but there is no answer. She tries again. Still nothing. A woman with dark curly hair threaded with silver comes out of the neighboring apartment holding a shopping bag.

"Can I help you?" she calls to us.

"We're looking for Peter," Amy tells her.

The woman smiles. "At this time in the morning, he'll probably be at the pool."

"Oh, right, yes," Amy says, nodding.

"Turn left at the top there." The woman is pointing to the end of the street. "You won't miss it."

"Thank you," Amy calls to her.

The woman waves her hand at us then strides away in the opposite direction, her reusable shopping bag hooked over her arm.

We walk to the end of the street and turn left. In front of us is a building with a domed roof. The sign outside says JUBILEE SWIMMING POOL AND CAFÉ. I stop next to a board by the entrance and peer at all the notices: *Hatha Yoga with Selina Tuesdays 6pm. Chair Aerobics with Mandy Monday mornings at 10am. Pool closed on Sundays.*

We enter to find a young woman behind a reception desk. Through the glass to the right of the desk, I can see a swimming pool. I walk over and press my nose against the glass; a few gray heads are bobbing up and down in the water. My breath steams and I have to step back.

"Have you got your pass?"

The young blond woman behind the desk appears to be talking to me.

"Oh, no. We're just waiting for someone," Amy says quickly.

A door next to us swings open and an elderly man with a good posture enters the reception area. He's wearing shorts, socks, and sandals, despite it being November. His faded sweatshirt says LUDTHORPE RUNNERS 1986. A small blue towel is slung over his shoulders and I watch him taking a swig from his water bottle. He waves to the young woman behind the desk. "Have a good day, Scarlet. Oh, by the way, they're running out of shampoo in the gents' showers. Not that I've much use for shampoo." He grins and rubs his head. "But, well, you know."

The girl laughs. "I'll get right on it, Pete," she tells him, before disappearing into a large cupboard behind the desk.

"Constable Diprose?" I ask.

The man turns. He blinks, trying to work out if he knows us. "Sorry..."

I move toward him. "My name is Edie and this is my granddaughter, Amy. We'd like to ask you about Lucy Theddle."

Constable Diprose flinches. His eyebrows have disappeared into his forehead. He takes a step back. "That's a name I haven't heard in a very long time."

"But you know who she is?"

He nods uncertainly, gripping his water bottle. "Yes, I do."

Amy steps forward. "We won't take up much of your time. We'd just like to ask you a few questions."

"I was at school with Lucy," I explain. "My mother gave you the best china. You sat in our front room while you interviewed me."

Constable Diprose stares at us. The towel slips off his shoulders. He catches it and slowly wipes his forehead. I try not to look at his knobbly knees.

"You'll have to excuse me. This is unexpected." He looks from me to Amy. "You're here to ask me about Lucy Theddle?"

Amy nods. "About the investigation–after she disappeared. You were involved."

Constable Diprose blinks. "And who are you again?"

Amy opens her mouth to speak but I butt in. "She was my friend," I tell him. "I'm trying to find out what happened to her. I saw her outside the post office."

Constable Diprose studies me for a moment.

"The friend," he says slowly. "I *do* remember. I came to interview you. You and Lucy had grown close before her disappearance. You were at school together."

I nod vigorously as Constable Diprose studies me for a moment. He seems to make his mind up about something.

"Perhaps you'd like to join me in the café? I was just on my way there."

"Thank you," Amy says. "That would be brilliant."

14

2018

In the café, I ask for a pot of tea and Amy has a can of lemonade. Constable Diprose orders a "rejuvenate smoothie" that comes with a striped paper straw. We sit by a window that looks out on to the main street of the retirement village. I can see a tall building, apartments with balconies. At the table next to us, a woman is knitting something pink: a scarf, or a small jumper? I can hear the *click click* of her needles. She pauses every now and then to take a sip from a large mug.

"It's lovely here," Amy is saying. "This whole place."

"Isn't it?" Constable Diprose replies. He seems to have recovered from the shock of seeing us, from whatever memories Lucy's name invoked. "Best decision I ever made," he continues. "Of course, it costs a small fortune, all the fees and that, but it's well worth it. You can't take it with you, can you?"

"No," Amy says, agreeing with him. "I suppose you can't."

"A real little community we've got here," Peter continues enthusiastically. "Have you ever tried water polo, Edie?"

"I haven't," I say, dryly.

"It gets the heart rate up, I'm telling you." Peter takes a sip of his smoothie, sucking up the purple-colored liquid through his straw.

"I'm not sure I want my heart rate up," I mumble. "I'd worry I wouldn't get it down again."

But Peter doesn't seem to have heard me. "I'm a member of the chess club, the camera club, the current affairs discussion group, and I'm the only man who does legs, bums, and tums on Tuesdays," he says proudly.

Amy pops the ring on her lemonade. "Wow, that's great."

"But you didn't come here for a guided tour, did you?" he asks, glancing at us. "You're not looking to move in, I take it?"

"I'm supposed to be moving somewhere else," I say, the name of the place escaping me. "But I don't need to. I'm perfectly fine on my own."

"Devon," Amy says gently. "Nan's moving to Devon with us. We're looking for a granny annex."

"Lovely," Peter says, slurping heartily.

I frown and pour a little milk into my teacup. It's been a long morning and I need a proper brew. It's important to keep my strength up in order to find... I look up, remembering what I'm here for, that I won't have to move anywhere if I can find Lucy, prove I'm not only capable of deciding on my own dinner but of solving the mystery of my best friend's disappearance. "We came to ask you about Lucy Theddle. I want to know what happened to her."

"Well, wouldn't we all," Peter says, sighing.

"So you remember the case then?" Amy asks, leaning forward.

He scratches his forehead. "I remember the case well. I was young back then. Hadn't been on the job long." He stares into his smoothie.

Amy takes a sip of her lemonade. "We're trying to find out what happened with the initial investigation."

"Yes," I chip in. "I didn't think of Lucy for years, but now I'm remembering it all. I'm sure something must have been missed."

"Oh, I don't doubt that," Peter tells us. "But I'm guessing you don't have any new evidence? You should be down at the police station instead of sitting here talking to me if you do."

"We don't have any new evidence," I say. "Just a feeling."

"Well, a feeling won't get the case reopened if that's what you're after. You'd need evidence, or a body, of course." He looks at us suspiciously. "You don't have a body, do you?"

"Good God, no," I say quickly.

"It's like an episode of *Unforgotten* in here this morning," the woman at the table next to us announces loudly, putting down her knitting. "Who needs the television?"

Peter leans over. "Turn your hearing aid down, Dorothy. Or go and knit somewhere else. This is a private conversation."

The woman stuffs her ball of wool into her handbag. "Suit yourself, Pete. I was just leaving anyway."

After she shuffles off, Peter turns to us. "I'll be honest with you, Edie. I feel we let Lucy down, and her family."

I nod. I know how he feels. It's a feeling that wriggles in my gut; I should have done something more, something else. I knew something, and yet I locked it away inside myself and purposely lost the key.

"How?" Amy asks, gently. "How did you let her down?"

Peter sucks on his straw, then pushes his smoothie away. "She was an attractive girl. Bright, too. Most of the force back then, and indeed the town, thought she'd mostly likely run off with a chap. Or else she'd had an argument with her mother, gone to stay with a friend. Not a great deal was done in those first few days. Of course we found her bicycle, the suitcase, but even then..." He trails off, shakes his head. "I don't think anyone really thought she'd been taken."

"Do you think she was planning to go somewhere?" Amy asks. "The suitcase, I mean?"

"It's certainly indicated that she was. Of course, we asked at the train station but no one had seen her. It was quiet there that day. There had been a fete on in town. Maybe you remember it, Edie?"

"Perhaps I wasn't there," I mumble, feeling confused again; I don't remember any fete. I sip my tea, hiding my frown. "And after that," I ask, "when more time passed and you realized she wasn't coming back, you must have had suspects?"

Peter nods. "There was some focus on a local boy. His father owned the undergarment factory."

"Rupert Mayhew," I say, the name flashing in my mind like lights at the end of a pier.

"That's it," Peter says, "Rupert Mayhew. According to most people we spoke to, he was besotted with Lucy."

Pretty dresses. Paper streamers. Music. The sweet, syrupy taste of fruit punch. We're dancing together. He leans forward, close to my ear. *I'm going to marry Lucy.* I lean away from him, a slight chill running down the length of my spine.

"No one seemed quite sure if she was as keen on him as he was on her," Constable Diprose continues. "We wondered if they'd had an argument, if she'd rejected his advances, perhaps. But we didn't have anything on him, and the senior officers weren't too happy about us digging around into the Mayhews. They were influential people, like the Theddles. Many of the officers had family who worked in the undergarment factory; it was a huge employer back then. No one wanted to accuse Rupert Mayhew's son of having anything to do with the Theddle girl's disappearance. In the end, though, everyone in the town knew he'd been a suspect and I don't think the stigma ever really went away, not until he did, and especially as she was never found."

"So you don't think Rupert had anything to do with Lucy's disappearance?" Amy asks.

Peter rubs at the side of his face. "I just don't know." He sighs. "We lost valuable time—putting all the focus on the Mayhew lad. But it wasn't just that. There were other factors too. We were due a visit, you see. The week after Lucy's disappearance. From the chief constable. The boys—they were all male officers back then—were concentrating more on tidying their filing cabinets and polishing their boots than they were on looking for Lucy Theddle."

I trace my finger around the smooth rim of my teacup. "But did you have any other suspicions?" I ask. "About anyone else?"

Peter removes the towel from his neck and slings it over the back of his chair. "Well, there was one other suspect, of course. The one you told us about."

Amy stares at me, open-mouthed.

"Mr. Wheaton," I say.

Peter nods. "A teacher at your school. You mentioned him when we interviewed you, although you were very reluctant to tell us why you felt he might have been involved."

"It was Lucy's secret."

"Of course. You were trying to protect your friend. We realized that. We suspected they'd been having a relationship but we had no proof."

"That's *awful*," Amy says, stricken. "He was her teacher."

"And he had a watertight alibi," Peter continues. "He was at the fete with his wife and child. His in-laws were there too. His wife said he was with her the entire time and plenty of people saw him there. We were pretty sure he hadn't had anything directly to do with her disappearance, and like I said, with no evidence or anyone willing to testify over the affair... Not that we could have done very much at that time. She was sixteen, above the age of consent, so it wouldn't have been illegal, and there was no law against student-teacher relationships."

Amy sighs. "So the investigation just fizzled out?"

Peter leans forward and slurps the last of his smoothie. He gives Amy a sad smile. "I think that's probably fair to say." He leans slowly back in his chair. "The search became uncoordinated. The whole thing was a bit of an embarrassment. A few months later, our own chief retired. The new boss was given this huge hot potato—well, a cold potato—that he wasn't experienced enough to deal with. Everyone wanted to forget about it, move forward. The months dragged on. The efforts dwindled. We'd lost so much time in those first few weeks. I couldn't believe it, really, the way the whole thing was handled. But it wasn't my place to say anything. Not then."

Peter removes his towel from the back of the chair and folds it into a neat square, leaving it on the table. "I let Lucy down," he says finally. "I should have done more. Someone must have known *something*."

His words feel like a sharp object jabbing into my chest. My eyes are watery, so I dab at them with a paper napkin. I can hear the whir of the coffee machine, a clattering of trays. The waitress walks past carrying something green on toast. Mushy peas?

Peter breaks the silence. "Can I ask how you found me?"

Amy nods. "There was an article about you online. A fun run. You raised some money for the local youth center. We guessed you must have stayed local."

"Ah, yes," Peter says, smiling. "I don't think I could do that now. Running. I find swimming much easier on my joints these days. Running was a big part of my life though, at one point. But what about you, Edie?"

"Oh, I don't swim," I say, thinking of the cold swimming lessons we had to endure at school. The concrete hole–Ludthorpe's outdoor swimming pool–long since demolished. Shivering girls queuing up at the edge in green bathing hats. And I never felt like swimming much after my father drowned.

Peter grins. "I didn't mean that. I meant, what have you done with your life?"

"Oh, that," I say, waving my hand. "Well, I married, had a son. Now I have my granddaughter." I smile at Amy. "And I had a career too. I taught English at Ludthorpe Grammar for years."

Peter looks thoughtful. "You know, I did a lot of work for youth charities. And I used to go into schools. Talk to wayward kids. Try and get them back on track, you see." He holds my gaze. "It's funny, we both went on to work with young people. We tried to help them. Perhaps to make up for the fact that we couldn't help Lucy."

I push my napkin slowly under my saucer, thinking of the girls I taught. They'd come to me with their fears, their troubles.

They always knew my door was open. I'd give up my lunch breaks for those who were struggling with the texts. I wanted to help as many as I could. Did I do all that because of Lucy, because I couldn't help Lucy? "I hadn't thought of it like that before," I say quietly.

Peter glances at his watch. "Well, ladies, I'm afraid I must be going. I want to catch the minibus to Sainsbury's. It leaves at 10:15 and Marco won't wait for anyone."

Bus. I clap my hands. "We came on a bus," I say.

Amy smiles at me.

"Well, good luck." Peter is standing. "I hope you uncover something, I really do. I've never forgotten her disappearance, and I've often wondered what really happened to that girl."

Peter's words echo in my mind: Someone must know *something.* There is a horrible churning in the pit of my stomach. What if there was a time when I did know something, something more, something else? But what? What did I know?

15

1951

Saturday evening. My mother is sitting at her dressing table wearing her navy floral dress, putting the finishing touches on her hair and makeup. Reg is taking her to the pictures tonight to see *The Lavender Hill Mob*, which I can't help thinking is more his choice than Mother's. Not that she'll mind; she loves the pictures, whatever's on. I linger in the doorway, watching her apply her lipstick. The shade is called Leading Lady. I know because I tried it on once when she was out. It looked awful on me and I rubbed it off immediately. Standing on my mother's dressing table is a lamp with a violet pleated shade. I don't know how she can see to do her makeup in such dimness, but she despises bright lights. I, on the other hand, like to be able to see what I'm doing and was relieved when the war ended and we put the blackout curtains in the loft, when we no longer had to seal ourselves into the living room in the evenings like rabbits in a burrow. We were all just as frightened of breaking regulations as we were of

German bombers. Mr. Pearson from Cucumber Lane was fined five shillings in '42 for striking a match while looking for his false teeth; the local bobby was passing and saw the light. My father was terrified of a fine, of not doing his duty, of helping the Luftwaffe, and so my parents spent most winter evenings bumping into each other and cursing under their breath, or else going to bed early.

I've been putting it off all day, but I can't any longer. I'm going to have to ask my mother about Smudge. I made a promise to Lucy; I can't let her down. It just so happens my mother is holding a séance tomorrow evening so I must ask tonight–it's perfect timing if Lucy really wants to come along, if she can bear to spend a single evening away from Mr. Wheaton. This time tomorrow my mother will be sitting at her dressing table in her black taffeta dress, adjusting the feathers in her hair, clipping on her hooped earrings, draping a stole over her shoulders. She loves to get dressed up in her performance clothes, as she calls them. Most of the clothes are old; she's got a whole chest of furs and silks, relics from the twenties, from the time before my mother's family lost their house, their money, their status.

When I was young my mother would tell me stories of the big house. It was a modest house by country house standards but still, there was Nannie, a cook, a housemaid, and a manservant. The house was a large manor house with a farm and two cottages let to tenants. My mother was fourteen when they lost it. My grandfather was the nephew of my great-uncle Walter and, from what I can make out, the house was begrudgingly left to my grandfather due to lacking a suitable heir. After my great-uncle's death, the family had to pay a substantial amount in death taxes.

My grandfather had a lavish lifestyle he was fond of but could no longer support; he continued to spend money on antiques and art, dressing gowns, smoking jackets, kid gloves, and silk cravats. In an effort to reclaim some of what had been lost through tax and overindulgence, he made a number of bad investments. Finally forced to sell the farm and the cottages, he let the servants go, followed by the furniture, the paintings, the piano, the cravats. Eventually the house was sold at auction and my grandfather went abroad in shame, leaving my grandmother and my mother to fend for themselves, desolate and with few sympathetic relatives. My grandmother died not long after. *The shock of it all killed her, of course*, my mother liked to say. *She couldn't possibly be poor.*

My mother needed a wealthy man to save her, but wealthy men were in increasingly short supply. She met my father one wet November morning when, alighting from a train with several shopping bags, she got her dress caught in the door. My father helped untangle her (although she still lost a portion of the dress) and bought her a cup of tea at the station café. My mother thought it was all very *Brief Encounter*, and even though they were both unattached, and my father was only a train guard as opposed to a dashing doctor, she got caught up in the romance of his gallant actions, her torn dress, the rain lashing at the café window, that cup of tea he insisted was on him. He told her, not long after, rather bashfully, that she was the most beautiful woman he had ever met, which of course cemented things for my mother. She must have known my father was kind, adored her, and could provide her with a stable home. Glaring incompatibilities were overlooked, as these things sometimes are. To my father, I am sure my mother was beautiful and classy, from another world, a different time. He tried to make her happy, pandered to her every whim, accepted her changeable moods, but my mother always wanted my father to be more, to *do* more, whereas my father had no ambition beyond a comfortable life—a great disappointment to my mother, who longed for the luxuries of her childhood.

My mother has a photograph of herself on her dressing table. She's riding a white horse, sitting astride it, her back perfectly straight, her eyes full of fire. Behind her is the manor house, one of the last photographs before it was lost. The date: 1929.

"Is that you, Edie?" My mother's eyes don't leave her reflection in the glass.

"Yes."

"Well, what is it? Don't loiter like that."

"I wanted to ask you something."

My mother spritzes scent onto her wrists and rubs them together. "Well, go on then."

"Lucy Theddle's cat is missing and she thought you might be able to help. If perhaps she and her mother could attend a séance."

My mother turns to look at me. "You've been going about with Lucy Theddle?"

I shrink a little; this is the inquisition I had been dreading. "We just walk to school together," I say casually.

"And whose idea was it? To walk to school together."

"Lucy's," I say, my voice coming out small.

My mother considers this and smiles. "Perhaps she's realized who your family was. Who you *are*. Of course, it makes perfect sense that people like us would be friends with the Theddles." She dabs her cheeks with rouge. "You should have told me."

There's a plummeting sensation in my stomach, but my mother's gaze returns to her reflection where she smiles to herself. "Of course they can come. I've only got Mr. and Mrs. Staines down for tomorrow. You'll tell Lucy at school, will you? Eight o'clock?"

A heavy weight has formed in my chest. I can't help thinking this is a dreadful idea. "Yes, I'll tell her."

"How wonderful," she muses, "you being friends with Lucy Theddle... Perhaps you'll get an invite to one of their parties. Make sure you say you'd be delighted to attend, with your mother of course. You can tell Barbara I'm happy to make a trifle."

I wince, thinking of my mother appearing at The Gables in too much lipstick, carrying one of her wonky trifles.

"There are always parties at The Gables," she continues, "and I've never *once* been invited. You see what you can do, Edie. There's no point having friends in high places if you can't attend their parties. Lucy will be having a coming-out dance, I expect?" she says, a hint of jealousy in her tone.

"I'm not sure," I say quietly. "I don't think people go in for that much anymore."

My mother frowns. She doesn't like to think she's behind the times. "I've always thought Barbara and I would get on terrifically well if only we were introduced. They've got a beach hut, haven't they? Perhaps they'd let us borrow it. Or better still, invite us to go with them for the day."

I look at her in horror, picturing Reg squashed into a sagging deck chair, tucking into a chicken leg, attempting to make conversation with Richard Theddle.

"And why don't you sit at the table, Edie?"

"Sit at the table?" There is a thudding in my chest. I've never sat in on a séance before. "But what about the..." I gesture toward my bedroom where the broom is already in its place.

My mother waves her hand dismissively. "Oh, Reg can do that. And anyway, it's about time you got more involved. You're growing up now. You should take on more responsibilities."

I stare at my slippers. "Fine," I whisper. How can I refuse her? I have never been able to refuse my mother. And I rarely get the opportunity to please her. I can't tell her I'm frightened of her séances. She'll think me babyish. At least I'll get to sit with Lucy. I just hope my mother can come up with something, that Lucy won't be disappointed.

"Good, that's settled then." She rises from the dressing table, picks up the corner of her dress, and turns her back on me. "Are my seams straight?"

16

1951

Lucy was so pleased when I'd mentioned Mother's invitation: "Oh, yes, Edie. We'll be there. My mother is desperate. Poor old Hitler. It's been three days now. How much does she charge? I don't expect discounted rates or anything, just because I'm your friend."

At the time, I thought I'd done the right thing, but as the day drew on I'd felt more and more anxious, plagued by the harrowing thought of Lucy and her mother coming over to our house for a séance, and of my mother being unable to offer them anything that might solve the mystery of the cat's disappearance. What if Lucy is so disappointed, she no longer wants to be friends with me? What if my mother says or does something completely ridiculous or embarrassing or insulting? (Always a possibility.) I wish I hadn't been so keen to please Lucy, that I'd tried to put her off. Perhaps I could have offered to help her make posters, appeals for information: *Missing Cat. Answers to the name of Smudge or Hitler. £5 reward. No questions asked.* Instead I feel racked with nerves.

When the evening finally arrives, Barbara Theddle and Lucy are the first to ring the bell, and I show them, rather formally, into the dining room where the table has been cleared, the candles lit. Barbara is wearing a silk blouse with a cashmere cardigan draped around her shoulders, and her pearl and sapphire earrings, the earrings Lucy borrowed for the dance. Her soft clothes are expertly pressed and I can smell her perfume; expensive, pungent, and floral. Her hair is dark, unlike Lucy and George; they take after their father, who still has unruly blond hair. She glances around the room, clutching her handbag. "It is kind of your mother to let us attend at such short notice. We're all very concerned. Smudge is a part of the family. Anything your mother might be able to tell us—we'd be so grateful."

I mumble something about it being perfectly fine. Outside it begins to rain, and I can hear it thrumming on the glass. It's been threatening all day, the air thick, heavy, and slightly damp, the clouds low and ominously gray.

"Goodness," Lucy says. "We arrived just in time." She looks at the table, the lit candles, the burning incense. "It's terribly exciting, isn't it? But I suppose you must be used to all this."

I open my mouth to reply but my mother bustles into the room, the train of her black taffeta dress rustling along behind her.

"Barbara! Lucy. We're so glad you could come."

"Hello, Nancy," Barbara says, casting an eye over my mother's elaborate outfit. "It's very kind of you to see us. I was telling Edie, we're all dreadfully worried about Smudge."

"Yes, yes...Smudge... And isn't it lovely, our daughters being such good friends!"

I stare at her, mortified, but Barbara only nods, giving me a quick sideways glance. *I can't imagine why my daughter is friends with your daughter*, I imagine her thinking.

"You must excuse me if I don't *chat*. I've got to prepare my mind, you understand. Empty it of the everyday. It's important to allow space for the spirits." My mother rubs at her temples and we all jump at a loud knock at the door.

Mr. and Mrs. Staines from number eight stand dripping in our hallway. Mrs. Staines wipes her feet on the doormat, then peers curiously at the stuffed mallard. My mother saw a flamingo under domed glass in one of her *Homes and Gardens* magazines and tried to replicate it. I don't think the mallard quite creates the effect she was hoping for. Mr. Staines is shaking out his umbrella and hooking it over our banister. "I've always followed psychological research," I hear him telling my mother as she takes his jacket. "I believe in keeping an open mind about these things." He reaches into his pocket for a handkerchief to wipe his face with, then turns to see me, Lucy, and Barbara standing in the dining room. He looks impressed at the presence of the Theddles, and offers Barbara a strange little bow before inquiring after her husband and gushing about what a lovely ceremony it was when the new outdoor pool was opened last week. Richard Theddle, I now remember, had cut the ribbon.

Mrs. Staines is wringing out her hair.

"Would you like a towel?" my mother asks. "Edie, don't just stand there, for goodness' sake, run along and fetch a towel."

"Oh, it's quite all right," Mrs. Staines says cheerfully,

squeezing herself around the back of the dining room table. "We shall soon dry off. It's positively *autumnal* out there. In *June*. Such a lovely clock."

"It is very nice," Barbara says, glancing at our clock.

"Thank you," my mother says graciously.

The clock is a relic from the old house, something my grandfather never got round to selling or perhaps managed to keep from the bailiffs. I picture him clinging onto the clock, hugging it close to his chest while men carrying sofas and lamps and portraits of long-forgotten ancestors stride past him.

"Please, take a seat. Edie will be joining us tonight." My mother smiles at me but her eyes are full of warning. *Don't mess this up.*

"Feel free to inspect the room," she tells her guests. "Or the house." She gives a little laugh. "But I can assure you there are no gimmicks here, no trickery of any kind."

"We wouldn't dream of it," Mr. Staines says, firmly.

"Is Reginald out?" Mrs. Staines asks, looking toward the kitchen.

"Oh, yes. The Bird in Hand."

This is a lie. Reg is upstairs, waiting to play his part, usually *my* part. As much as I don't want to be sitting at the table tonight, at least I haven't been made redundant now Reg is here; at least my mother has decided she still needs me for something. I don't know why Reg has to stick his oar in with talk about flyers and advertising. What I do know is that Reg doesn't like me, that he wishes I wasn't here. I can tell by the way he looks at me, as if I'm a stranger in *his* house, not the other way around.

"Have you always had the gift, Nancy?" Barbara asks.

"Since I was a little girl." My mother turns the gas off, leaving us with only the flickering candles. "I saw people in the house I grew up in. A large house, you see. Full of dark passages and unlit rooms. I couldn't understand why no one else could see the people I saw." She smiles, recalling a fond memory. "I referred to them as the shadow people. They were my friends."

Mr. Staines's face in the dim light is pale and thin. "And has Edie inherited the ability to communicate with the spirits?"

Lucy glances at me with interest and I dig my nails into my hand and stare at the table.

"Not yet," my mother says, glancing in my direction. "I'm sure it will come. Although it can occasionally skip a generation," she explains.

Like twins or hereditary diseases, I think.

"How interesting," Barbara says politely.

"I imagine it's both a blessing and a curse," Mr. Staines replies sagely, reminding me of Lucy's words: *I suppose it would be a burden.*

"I wouldn't be without my gift," my mother says firmly, sitting and placing her hands on the table. We all do the same, taking our cue, linking our hands. I can hear the rain, the ticking of the clock. Despite the fact that my mother performs séances all the time, I still feel sick with worry. What if Lucy and Barbara Theddle realize it's all a performance? The Theddles are influential in Ludthorpe. What if they expose my mother as a fraud? Mother could be sent to prison for witchcraft, like that Scottish medium during the war. Hellish Nell, they called her. Have I really done the right thing, bringing Lucy here?

"It helps if we all concentrate," my mother tells us. "Close your eyes. Clear your minds. Let them be like a blank page, an empty vessel." She takes a long, shuddery breath, then sits, motionless, for a moment or two, before speaking again, more softly this time.

"If there are any spirits who wish to make themselves known to us in this room tonight, this is your opportunity. Please, come forward. Give us a sign."

The rain patters at the window. I can tell my mother has left it open a crack. She likes a chill in the air. I sneak a glance around the table. Mrs. Staines has a small black smudge under her eye where her makeup has run in the rain. Mr. Staines is frowning slightly. Barbara Theddle sits perfectly still, her eyes tightly closed. Next to me, I can hear Lucy breathing. Shadows flicker on the wall.

"We wish to communicate with those no longer on the earthly plane. Please give us a sign," my mother repeats, louder this time.

A banging noise from above us. Barbara jumps as I lift my eyes to the ceiling, imagining Reg with the broom. Lucy glances at me and I try to keep my face as neutral as possible.

My mother shivers violently. "There *is* someone here. Someone has made themselves known and wishes to communicate with us."

Lucy is squeezing my hand; Mr. and Mrs. Staines are sitting as still as statues. Barbara Theddle looks mildly astonished.

"I can hear the voice of a child," my mother whispers, in the dark.

All I can hear is the rain, the clock, Mrs. Staines sniffing. My fingers feel cold. *It's not real*, I remind myself. *I don't need to be frightened because it's not real.*

My mother moans loudly, then throws her head back. "Mummy, I'm hot. It's awfully hot in here," she says, in a strange childish voice that makes my cheeks flush. My hands are clammy and I long to release them; I can feel the hair lifting on the nape of my neck as I look fearfully into the dark corners of the room, worried I'll see a pale, malevolent ghost child with lifeless eyes. I can hear the wind in the chimney. The candle flames dance, creating larger shadows on the walls and I can't look in the mirror above the mantelpiece for fear of what I might see there. I watch as my mother opens an eye to take a quick peek at her guests. Satisfied they are all concentrating, all following her, she closes her eye again.

"Mm, yes... It's hard to tell if the child is male or female," she says, using her own voice again. "Does anyone here know of a child who may be trying to communicate?"

"No," Barbara says, breathless.

Lucy is shaking her head, so I look to Mr. and Mrs. Staines. I know they don't have children. It's something my mother remarked upon when they first moved in.

"I don't know who it could be," Lucy whispers.

"No," Mrs. Staines says, biting her lip. "I can't think either."

Mr. Staines is frowning. "I've no idea."

"A child who has been ill?" my mother suggests. "Or a child who never got a chance to grow up in this world? Perhaps a child who never got a chance to be here at all?"

I keep hold of Lucy and Mrs. Staines's hands, saying nothing, watching my mother looking at the pale, luminous faces around the table.

"I really don't know," Mrs. Staines says anxiously.

"The spirit is before me now," my mother tells us. "Not so much a child as a young woman."

"Is she right here in the room?" Lucy asks.

"She is with us." My mother confirms.

Barbara Theddle shivers.

"A young woman?" Mr. Staines confirms, still frowning.

"Oh, yes." My mother sighs, rolls her shoulders. "She has come to us from the spirit world."

There is a pause. The rain continues to patter.

They don't know what she's talking about, I think, my heart pounding. *They're going to realize she's a fake, that they're being swindled.*

"My mother had a sister who died when she was a child," Mrs. Staines says finally, her voice trembling. "Bright's disease. Her name was Pearl."

Barbara's eyes widen; she appears to have forgotten, for the time being, about Smudge. "Is it her, do you think? Pearl?"

Mr. Staines glances at my mother. "But you see a young woman now, Nancy, not a child?"

"It is Pearl," my mother confirms. "For all children get the chance to grow up in the spirit world but do not have to grow old. This is why I see a young woman."

"Goodness," breathes Mrs. Staines. "If only my mother were still alive to hear this. She was so fond of Pearl, and often spoke of her and how painful the loss had been to the family. She was my mother's younger sister, you see."

"Pearl has met with your mother, her sister, in the spirit world," my mother says firmly. "They have been reunited."

"Incredible," Lucy says.

Mrs. Staines blinks and smiles. "How wonderful."

"She wants you to know she has been happy in the spirit world, that your mother is happy too."

"Oh, how I miss my mother," Mrs. Staines murmurs.

"Pearl says your mother is telling you to go to church more often."

"Yes, that *is* the sort of thing she would say."

Mr. Staines turns in the direction of his wife. "Would you like a handkerchief, dear?"

"I might have one." Lucy fumbles in her pocket.

"Don't break the circle," my mother says, sharply. "Ah, but it is too late. Pearl has no further messages. She is going, drifting away. Drifting, drifting... She's fading now. There is nothing but light, such a bright light..." My mother moans again. Her breath catches in her throat and her moan turns into a wail, causing us all to look at her in alarm.

"It is a strange sensation when they depart," she explains, her voice shaky. "Like a strong wind blowing through... It leaves one feeling cold, an empty shell. For the spirits take so much from a medium..." She touches her hand to her head as if feigning a migraine.

"Are you all right, Nancy?" Mr. Staines asks.

"Just a little faint," my mother murmurs.

Barbara clears her throat. "We were wondering, Nancy, about Smudge?"

"Oh, yes," my mother says, making a quick recovery.

"Our cat," Lucy explains to Mr. and Mrs. Staines. "He's been missing for four days and we're dreadfully worried about him."

My mother takes a deep breath and closes her eyes, murmuring: "Smudge, *Smudge*," in a disconcertingly dreamy sort of way.

"Do you see anything?" Barbara asks fretfully.

"I'm getting... Yes, yes, a sense of something. It's dark. Yes, now I see it. A dark place."

"He's alive?" Barbara asks.

"Yes, yes," my mother says quickly.

"Can you see anything else?" Lucy asks.

My mother frowns and presses her thumbs into her temples. "I see dust, cobwebs..."

"It can't be our house then," Lucy says with a sigh.

"But now I see something else," my mother continues, and we all wait, holding our breath. I sneak a glance at Lucy; her eyes are tightly shut. Barbara Theddle is leaning forward, concentrating. Outside, the rain has eased.

"A single garment hanging on a hook," my mother says at last. "And, wait, yes, I see it: an old wooden chest with many drawers, a shaft of sunlight. Apples. I see apples."

Suddenly Barbara Theddle gasps. She rises to her feet, still clutching her handbag. "I know exactly where he is."

17

2018

I wake and it's dark, so I immediately switch the bedside light on. There's a tightening in my chest. I have recently been experiencing that horrible fear of the dark I had when I was a child. I don't know why, it's silly really.

The radio says it's five o'clock. I might as well get up and make a cup of tea. I used to get up at five thirty every morning during term time when I was a teacher. I'd be out there on the drive in the dark, scraping the ice off the car in the winter, knocking on Daniel's bedroom door, making sure he was getting up for school. It had surprised me, Daniel wanting to go into teaching. I'm not sure he knew what else to do. Daniel would never have wanted to teach English though. He hates Chaucer—all those bickering pilgrims—and he isn't too keen on Shakespeare either, especially Hamlet (*Why can't he just jolly well get on with it, Mum?*). No, Daniel teaches geography and sociology to sixth formers. Now he's an assistant head, involved in pastoral care and safeguarding procedures. Daniel has always been far more ambitious than me. I was happy to stay where I was, in the same classroom I had for twenty years, whereas Daniel has always been looking for his next opportunity, his next promotion.

Well, I don't need to go and scrape ice off the car today—the car is in my garage. Daniel is going to sell it, only he hasn't had the time. It wasn't that I didn't want to drive, but there was that day last year when I'd sat in the Co-op car park looking at the gearshift and the wheel, the engine running. I couldn't think how to get out of there. My feet were supposed to do something with the pedals only I couldn't remember what.

I didn't drive much after that. I was worried it would happen again—the fogginess, my brain unable to connect to my feet. It's a faulty signal, like an old black-and-white television I once had that used to constantly lose its picture, becoming nothing but gray crackling fuzz. Arthur would stand on a chair holding up the aerial, balancing it on the curtain rail. *Here, Edie?* he'd ask. *Is it better here?* I wish I had an aerial I could move around until my own pictures and connections sharpened.

I can hear the wind outside. As I swing my legs slowly out of bed, there's a creaking noise; I'm not sure if it's the bed or me. When my feet reach the floor, they land on something soft. They sink in a little. That's funny. I look down to find my feet have landed in golden sand. I can feel the hair lifting on the nape of my neck. Ever since I was a child, I've hated the sensation of sand between my toes. It was the only drawback of going to the beach. But I haven't been to the beach, have I? So why the sand? I hastily brush it off my feet. It's no use lying in bed worrying. I reach for my fluffy slippers. Daniel bought them for me from

M&S for Christmas last year; my feet go right inside them. Daniel says they're safer. *I can't stand the thought of you tripping up in those tatty things with no backs you wear.* I quickly put them on before any more sand gets on my feet, but I can still feel it there, a grittiness between my toes that sets my teeth on edge. I'll have to shake the slippers out later, the way we used to shake our shoes out when we reached the beach steps at Sandy Bay. I had to make sure every grain was gone. I was there with Lucy. I can see her now, the breeze lifting her hair as she stretches her legs on the blanket, the uncomfortable feeling of the sand underfoot as we made our way across the dunes. So that's where the sand has come from: my day at the beach with Lucy. My mother will be cross with me, bringing all this sand into the house. Reg too. He thinks I'm a layabout, that I should be working, not lounging about on the beach all day with the Theddle girl.

I open my bedroom door and there is more sand in the hallway, a thin trail of it. I switch the hallway light on. Shuffling along in my slippers, I follow the sand to the top of the stairs and then down, passing all my familiar photographs. I've got a whole wall of memories. Josie dusts them for me once a week as she knows what they mean to me. I look at Arthur on our wedding day; Arthur with Daniel on his shoulders, the three of us standing outside a castle. Then there are the more recent ones: Daniel and Suzanne's wedding, baby Amy. Amy in her primary school uniform, and my newest, taken a few years ago: Amy sitting on the swing seat in my garden reading *Wuthering Heights*, one of her favorites. I reach out to touch the photograph, tracing my fingers over the glass, over Amy's face. I study my photographs every day to make sure I remember. Will there come a day when the photographs no longer trigger the memories? A day when I look at my granddaughter and I can't remember her name? I take a deep breath; the thought is unbearable.

Something jolts me, causing me to drop my hand from the photograph: a banging noise, coming from the back of the house.

I follow the sand trail along the hallway. I'm like Gretel. But are the grains leading me home, or to the wicked witch in her house made of sweets?

Through my kitchen window, I can see half a moon. It shines its light into the room, breathing life into the shadows so I don't feel afraid. I don't bother to switch the light on. Instead I creep across the dark, silent kitchen, feeling my way along the worktop and the table.

My back door is ajar, letting in a draft. The wind bangs it shut again. Strange. I must have not closed it properly before I went to bed, although I don't remember opening it in the first place. A small pile of sand lies on the kitchen floor by the mat. Ignoring it, I open the door and step outside. The mossy patio stones are cold even under my slippered feet. Mint grows between the slabs. I used to try to get rid of it but I've given up in recent years. Amy goes out and collects the mint. She makes tea from it—a mug full of mint leaves. My mother used to read tea leaves for people. She didn't use mint though. She said China tea was the best. She read my leaves once; I remember her disappointed frown. *I can see a raven, Edie. An indication of an unsettled purpose in life.* People prefer to use bags now, and there isn't much to read about the future in a tea bag.

I'm standing on the patio in my nightdress, the hem catching in the wind. The sky is the color of a bruised fig, and the garden smells of damp leaves and something else. Roses. I can smell roses. Odd, to smell roses at night, and at this time of year.

The wind is picking up but I can't feel any rain, only the cool air on my cheeks. I can hear the rustling of the leaves on the tree at the back of the garden; it's as if they're whispering, trying to tell me something. I hope the birds are all in their nests, the rabbits and foxes in their burrows. It isn't the sort of night to be out. The wind wraps my nightdress around my legs.

It's dark, and I can't see much except for shapes and shadows: the trees, the shed, the outline of the fence against the sky. I look up at the clouds crossing the moon and feel my heart beating steadily. My breath catches as something moves in the garden. It's a figure, a shadowy figure. The scent of roses grows stronger. I blink and then I see her standing by the rose bushes. She's wearing the white dress with the lace collar she had on in the photograph of her and her brother George, which must have been taken in the Theddles' garden, the one they used for the papers and the posters that appeared on Ludthorpe's noticeboards and lampposts offering a reward for information. I stare at Lucy. She's got green ribbons in her hair. One plait has almost come completely undone. She'll lose a ribbon if she's not careful.

She smiles, her gaze holding mine. She doesn't want me to be frightened. She wants me to help her. Ribbons. Roses. The photograph in the paper. She's offering me clues, but I don't understand them. I want to tell her I can't help, that it was all so long ago, that I am old now, but my words are caught in my throat and she wouldn't hear them anyway. *Look at me*, I want to say. *My hair is as white as a gull's feather, and my skin is as wrinkled as an old apple. Look at me, Lucy, I got old and you didn't. I can't help you. How could I possibly help you? I tried, but I can't remember.*

Edie, she whispers.

It's as if she's saying, *Try. Try harder.*

A strong gust of wind and she vanishes, and I am standing alone in the garden, shivering, with nothing but the moon and the falling leaves. The wind howls and the trees wave their branches at me. I jump as a plant pot is knocked over on the patio. After I've righted the pot, I turn and head inside the house. All the sand has gone.

18

1951

Barbara Theddle turned up at our house again the following evening, this time with a bottle of sherry and a Madeira cake.

"I always tell Alan" (apparently the gardener) "to keep the shed door closed," she'd told us. "But Smudge must have got in somehow on Sunday when Alan was doing the lawn. I just couldn't believe it. There he was behind the wheelbarrow, a cobweb on his nose. You saw it so clearly, Nancy, in your vision: our seed chest, Alan's old gardening coat. Of course there are no apples left at this time of year, but still..."

"I'm glad I was able to help," my mother said modestly.

"We're all so incredibly grateful, Nancy. You'll have to come over for our garden party at the weekend. It will be a quiet affair. Nothing fancy. A few of us from the tennis club, the WI, and the Housewives' League."

My mother had smiled. "I'll bring a trifle."

And so my mother found herself somewhere on her way to social acceptance, back where she considered herself to belong.

The news of my mother's triumph spread quickly. It wasn't only Barbara Theddle who was impressed; a local reporter came over and took my mother's picture, and there she was the following week on page seven of the *Ludthorpe Leader* next to an advert for a vacuum cleaner: "Local Medium Finds Mayor's Cat."

"You're a star," Reg tells her. "Beauty and brains. We've got to up our game, not leave so much to chance. We're moving up in the world, Nance."

My mother has lots of visitors in the evenings now. Not only those who want to contact the dead but those who have misplaced something: wedding rings, wallets, glasses, husbands. "Yes, Mr. Pearson, your slippers are definitely under the sofa," I hear her say when I pass the dining room one evening.

Reg is chuffed to bits about my mother's newfound success, the business picking up, her becoming chummy with the Theddles and "their set" and "the dough rolling in." Not that Reg manages to hang onto money for very long; he's always out playing poker in the back room of the pub, going down to the dogs, or popping into Reynold's (the corner shop used as a front for the local bookie) to place a bet on a horse that's "a sure thing." He sits with his ear close to the wireless, wearing a tense, nervous expression, then storms out of the house, banging doors and cursing loudly. When I asked him why he bothers with it all, he gave me a cold stare and said: *A man's got to have a way of enjoying himself.* He never looks like he's enjoying himself to me.

Reg also has unpredictable moods, meaning my mother is often on edge. She gets upset if she thinks she's spoiled the dinner.

Goodness, are the potatoes overdone? she asks, prodding them with her knife while Reg is busy helping himself to seconds. I don't know why she worries. I'm sure Reg doesn't even taste what he eats. He wolfs his food down like a starved dog, then goes off to The Bird in Hand, not returning until late. My mother doesn't sleep until he comes home. I'm surprised she sleeps at all: I can hear Reg snoring from my room. I keep my door closed in an attempt to block it out. One evening last week he came home drunk and angry after an unsuccessful poker game and shouted at my mother. I could hear him banging about in the kitchen, calling her a floozy. She had been seen speaking to Mr. Goy, the fishmonger, outside the town hall. About what? Reg wanted to know. About a séance, my mother told him. The following morning she had a bruised cheek. When I asked her about it she said a tin of Spam fell on her at work. I arrived home from school to see a bunch of flowers sitting in a vase on the kitchen windowsill. Reg gives my mother other gifts, too, packages of meat that he brings home after we've used our ration, trinkets and odd bits of junk he gets from goodness knows where. Yesterday evening he came home with a large cast-iron doorstop in the shape of a rabbit. The rabbit has a chipped ear, but nevertheless it now props the kitchen door open and I have to remember to step around it so as not to stub a toe.

It seems cruel that just as my mother's social life has perked up, things have become difficult for her at home. Reg is always more interested in his van than he is in us. He goes off to the works garages in order to tinker about with it, even at the weekends. "Got to keep her in tip-top condition," he says. "You care more about that van than you do me," Mother replies, but really,

I believe Mother is still so flattered by Reg's praise, so excited about her newfound fame and friends, she forgives Reg for his rages and absences, makes excuses for him, or else she buries her head in the sand about his moods and demands. She doesn't seem to notice the money disappears as fast as she makes it. "Maybe one day we'll be able to afford a cottage by the sea," she said dreamily the other evening when we were eating our ham and chips. (My mother has always wanted to live by the sea.) "Don't be daft," Reg said, shoving a chip into his mouth. "I hate bleedin' seagulls. Noisy buggers."

As for Lucy, it's been three weeks since the dance and she hasn't mentioned Rupert, what happened between them. Whenever I broach the subject, she tells me not to worry, that it was just a misunderstanding. I expect she's keeping away from him.

All Lucy has wanted to talk about is Mr. Wheaton: how wonderful it is when they're together, how much he understands her, how clever he is. She tells me about being squashed into the back of his car, of having to wear sunglasses and a headscarf when she goes out to meet him, of snatched half hours and broken promises when he can't get away, which is often, by the sounds of it. It doesn't sound much fun to me: waiting around for a man, being a part of his lies and deceit, being let down when he doesn't show. I picture Mr. Wheaton taking Lucy's hands in his. *But you must understand, darling, it's all terribly tricky...* She writes him long letters that Mr. Wheaton apparently adores but has to burn immediately. He never seems to write to Lucy, nothing more than a quickly dashed-off note that he leaves tucked under the wheel of his bicycle—some kind of code telling her whether he can meet her that evening.

I worry about Lucy; I can't help feeling she's in over her head. She says she's happy but she's often anxious, concerned about upsetting Mr. Wheaton in some way or other. Her nails are bitten, and I catch her staring out of classroom windows, something I am usually guilty of. *Edie Green, the sky will offer no solution to Pythagoras*, Miss Munby said to me last week. Still, it's all terrifically exciting: to hear about Lucy's affair, to be friends with someone who is having a real grown-up relationship, to know that I am the only person who knows.

Yesterday, after school, we stopped off at the library as Lucy wanted to take a book out: *Married Love* by Marie Stopes. Mrs. Murdle, the librarian, asked Lucy how old she was before she gave her the book and Lucy had to lie. I am sure Mrs. Murdle knew Lucy was lying but she let her borrow the book anyway, slipping it to her in a brown paper bag. *I need to learn more about relations between men and women*, Lucy had told me. *I really don't know anything at all, and I don't want to look silly in front of Max.* I have to admit, I don't know much either. I remember when I began to bleed and my mother told me that I was to stay away from boys and never to sit on cold doorsteps. Then, there was that rather embarrassing biology lesson with Mrs. Lark, who announced it was time we learned how babies were made. She hastily explained that a male rabbit "deposits his fluid" into the female and that it works the same way for all mammals. This had left us feeling more perplexed than ever. Cordelia Keal, who has four younger brothers, all born at home, and who knows something of the male and female anatomy, was just as confused as the rest of us. *But how on earth do you squish it in and manage to keep it in for long enough?* she'd mused. *It must be like trying to get toothpaste back in the tube.*

I've had a lot to write in my diary; it's been hard to keep up and I've taken to carrying it around with me, making little notes about things I might want to write more about later. I write everything down if I can, trying to make sense of it all.

It's three thirty on Monday afternoon, the bell has just gone, and I'm hurrying along the upper corridor, on my way to meet Lucy at our usual place outside the gates. We've brought our bicycles to school and are planning to cycle to the beach. I haven't spoken to Lucy since Friday and I'm desperate to hear how it went with Mr. Wheaton on the weekend. His wife was planning to visit her sister in Harrogate, and Lucy was supposed to be spending the night with Mr. Wheaton in a hotel along the coast. *Of course, we'll have to pretend we're married*, she'd told me, chewing her thumbnail.

"Step into my office a minute, will you, Edie?" Miss Munby appears in the corridor in front of me, holding the door open, and I feel I have no choice but to reluctantly enter, wondering what she could possibly want. The sun streams through the windows. A picture of the King in his robes hangs on the wall, and another of a group of Victorian schoolchildren posing for a photograph. A brown teacup and saucer sit on Miss Munby's desk among piles of papers. The room smells of old school dinners, her small office being above the dining hall. She gestures for me to have a seat as she moves behind her desk.

"So, it's nearly the end of the term, Edie."

I nod agreeably, then look down at my hands. My pen leaked during maths and my fingers are stained; I rub at a mark on my thumb.

"We were wondering if you'd made any plans. If you know

what you might do when you finish here?" She fans herself with a sheet of paper.

There's a scuffle of footsteps and giggles outside the door as a group of girls rush by. It's the hottest day of the year so far and everyone is keen to be outside.

I haven't made plans, but I'm not sure I want Miss Munby to know this. I stare at a small trophy on her desk and dig my knuckles into the padded fabric seat of the chair.

"There are some girls, Edie," she continues, "who we know won't be returning to Ludthorpe Grammar in September."

I nod. Linda and Cordelia have already enrolled on a typing course, but neither of them intends to work for long. Ann's going into nursing but she sees it as short-term, something to be dropped as soon as there's a ring on her finger, I've heard her say. Judy is going to work as a secretary in her uncle's office. She doesn't even need to do a course. She's excited, as the office is "full to the brim with potential husbands." Her mother has already bought her a twinset and pearls.

"But there are plenty of other girls who *are* returning to us in the autumn, Edie," Miss Munby is saying. "Girls who wish to gain further qualifications, who want to give themselves more possibilities."

I glance up at the clock on the wall; I don't want to be late to meet Lucy, she might leave without me.

Miss Munby taps her fingers on the desk, then tries again. "You must understand, by getting a place here, you were offered a chance so many others don't get, a chance of a better education. If you stay and complete the new A-level qualifications, you'll leave here with something that many others don't have. A key to a better future, to a career. You're a bright girl, Edie." Miss Munby studies me for a moment, as if to make sure she trusts in her own judgment. "Well, bright enough." She rests her thin wrists on the desk in front of me. I can see a silver watch strap. The sleeve of her blouse is fraying and I avert my eyes to the floor.

She clears her throat. "I would highly recommend you return in September. The additional qualifications will stand you in good stead."

I look up at Miss Munby, cautiously. She smiles at me, trying to tell me that we are the same, me and her. I have nothing against Miss Munby, but I do not believe I am in any way like her. She is a different species, after all, an older person whose life is settled and dull. She may not be as old as some of our other teachers, like the Miss Drays of the world—women who never married after a whole generation of young men died, leaving a short supply. Miss Munby is probably only thirty-five, but to me she is old and washed up. She also hasn't secured a husband. For that, my mother would consider her a failure. When I look at her I see a cold cup of tea, a frayed sleeve, slim fingers with no rings, tiny wrinkles at the corners of her eyes, a weary smile.

"What I'm saying, Edie, is that you will have more options if you return next year. We're all very fond of you here, and of course we'd be delighted if you stayed."

I mumble that I will have to think about it. Although I don't know what I am going to do, I hadn't been planning on returning to school next year. I assumed I'd look for a job. I've no idea what job, only a sense that one will be there for me when I want it, and that it will be my first step out into the real world, a world away from cold classrooms, graying teachers, and cruel, giggling girls.

Oh, I am sure there will be cruel girls wherever I go, but I sense they will be less interested in me once they have their husbands and babies to deal with, once they are busy doing their duty, busy repopulating. Or perhaps I will be less interested in their interest in me. I will grow a thicker skin and at the same time grow into the one I have.

Then I think of Lucy. She is planning to come back next year. She wants to take the new A levels so she can move away to study to be a teacher in London. It never seemed possible that *I* could do something like that. Miss Munby appears to think it might be.

"Give it some thought, Edie. But don't think too long. You'd be very welcome back here next year."

I promise her I will consider my options, and then I stand, assuming I am dismissed, leaving her to her papers and her cold cup of tea.

19

1951

As I hurry down the stairs, I think more about Miss Munby's proposition. I enjoy studying, and it seems a shame I won't be able to do it anymore. Things will be different next year—those girls that are here will have *chosen* to be here. I'll be able to see more of Lucy. But could I really stand another two years of chalk screeching on blackboards, uniforms, and living at home with my mother and Reg? I've been feeling, more and more recently, that I need to get away from home.

I collect my bicycle and wheel it over to the front entrance.

"There you are, Edie. I was about to go." Lucy is leaning against the gate.

"Miss Munby kept me back," I explain. "She thinks I should stay on at school. Take the Higher. I mean, the new A levels."

"Well, it's something to think about," Lucy replies.

"My mother and Reg won't like it."

"It isn't their life, is it?" Lucy flicks her hair over her

shoulder. "You should stand up to them. Are we still going to the beach?"

"Yes, definitely."

It's then I notice Judy. She's standing close to the wall, in the shade of one of the trees, her arms crossed over her chest, staring at us. I pretend I haven't noticed her, but I can feel her eyes on me as I mount my bicycle. When I sneak another look, Judy turns and kicks the stump of the tree before walking off. Well, I'm not going to worry about Judy Simpson. She's just jealous. She's had Lucy to herself for long enough.

"Come on then." Lucy hops onto her bicycle and is already cycling out of the gates. I have to pedal fast to keep up with her; she's got a fancy new bicycle, whereas mine is a cranky old thing my father bought secondhand for me, an old butcher boy's bicycle with crossbars instead of a basket. When I first started riding the bicycle, it was far too big for me and, if I rode it to school, my father would lift me onto it outside the house, where I set off, wobbling along the road, praying I wouldn't have to stop at the level crossing. If I did, I'd have to ask the signalman to put me back on.

As we're cycling along the High Street, I think more about staying on at school, getting my qualifications–I could go to college with Lucy. I picture us arriving together in London, sharing a dorm room, climbing through windows after the curfew, drinking cocoa by the gas fire in the evenings, laughing late into the night. I see my life, full of possibilities and previously unimagined experiences, opening up before me and, just for a moment, it's a wonderful feeling. But then I remember my mother and Reg; I am sure they won't let me stay on at school, or go away to college. My mother thinks I should be courting, and Reg has already stated his opinion: he doesn't see why I'm still at school when I could be "out in the world," bringing in a wage to "help out the family." Going to college, getting out of Ludthorpe—it just won't be possible, and I wish Miss Munby hadn't put the idea in my head. "Get ideas above your station and you'll only be disappointed," Reg said to me the other evening when I was doing my maths homework. "I don't know why you bother with all that. You'll only need to know how to add up the groceries, won't you?"

We cycle through Ludthorpe, passing the green and the church, the malting factory—a mass of cranes and trucks, finally being rebuilt after it was hit in '42—then along the flat road to the sea, fields and hedgerows on either side of us. There is a haziness to the air and the breeze agitates the tall stalks of blond wheat, causing husks to float across our path. Lucy cycles ahead of me, her back straight, her pale hair streaming out behind her. We cycle by the abattoir with its horrible smell. It's a huge site consisting of several buildings and outhouses and tall, locked gates. I am glad when we pass it and the smell is lost on the breeze. The road widens and we ride side by side. Further along the coast, at Sandy Bay, are the amusements, the Beach View Café and, during the holidays, donkey rides and ice creams, but we are too old for such things; the novelty has worn off. When I was a child, the beach sounded almost mythical, something from a fairy tale. It was mostly prohibited, covered in barbed wire and landing traps. It wasn't as bad as it was further south—there were no mines—but still, we never went to the coast. Perhaps that's why my father was so keen to get in the water in '46. He'd missed swimming.

I always feel a sense of unease at the beach. It doesn't feel right that the place my father died is the place people come to enjoy themselves. I didn't want to tell Lucy this when she suggested it; I was happy she wanted me to go with her, and so I keep my feelings to myself.

The sea comes into view and I can now smell salt on the breeze. We glide past the long row of brightly colored beach huts. Lucy points out her parents' hut, striped red and white like a Christmas candy cane. We dismount and walk our bicycles down through the dunes. It's much cooler here on account of the strong sea breeze. Lucy takes her sandals off and hooks them over her handlebars.

"Aren't you going to take your shoes off, Edie? The sand is lovely."

"Oh, no," I say. "I don't like the feel of it."

Lucy laughs. "You are funny."

We find a spot in the dunes and sit on the blanket Lucy has brought with her. I finally remove my shoes and socks, taking care to keep my feet on the blanket. The beach is busy; clearly everyone else in Ludthorpe had the same idea as us. There are schoolgirls, groups of boys, mothers with toddlers. A few brave children run in and out of the gray surf, shrieking. A man and a small girl, father and daughter, are flying a red kite; it dips and dives in the wind. I try to avoid staring out at the sea as when I do, I can see my father's head, bobbing among the waves. There and then not there, and all because of me. I shake my head. Things are changing for me, and I no longer need to dwell on the past. I've finally found a true friend.

"Did you go away with Mr. Wheaton then, to spend the night?"

Lucy closes her eyes and turns her face to the sun. "Max

booked us in as Mr. and Mrs. Wheaton, and we had supper brought to our room on a trolley. I drank wine. He held me all night..." She opens her eyes and wraps her arms around her chest. "And we talked and talked. Max says he can talk to me in a way he can't with anyone else. He witnessed dreadful things in the war, you know. He was one of the first on the scene—after the Americans, of course—at a concentration camp in Northern Germany. He has dreams: piles of decomposing bodies, human beings like living skeletons, their faces nothing but bone and eyes. Hands pawing at him, begging him for food, for medicine, when he doesn't have enough. There is a woman who thrusts a baby into his arms. Take her, she tells him. Make her better. When Max looks down at the baby, it's dead."

For a moment, I feel sorry for Mr. Wheaton, but then I remember that he's our teacher, that he should know better than to have an affair with Lucy. There are no excuses, war or no war.

"So it all went smoothly then?" I press, wanting to know more, wondering about what it must have been like to spend the night with a man, with *Mr. Wheaton.* I want to know everything, but Lucy hesitates and I can tell she's holding back.

"Oh, yes," she says, evasively. "The only tricky moment was when the ring I borrowed from my mother's jewelry collection slipped off my finger as I was eating breakfast in the dining room and fell into my tinned tomato. An elderly woman saw and tutted."

"Where did you tell your parents you were?"

Lucy turns to me and smiles mischievously. "At your house."

I take a deep breath. "You could have told me. What if someone had wanted you?"

She leans over and squeezes my arm. "I knew you'd cover for me."

"I've hardly seen you in school," I say, a little cross with her.

"Well, you know..." She stretches her legs out on the blanket. "I've been in the music room most lunchtimes. Max can see me from his classroom window then. He likes to know where I am."

"Likes to know where you are?"

Lucy smiles to herself as the wind wraps her hair around her face. "Max says he can't help it that his feelings are so strong." She twists her necklace at her throat. "He also says it's better for me to stay away from the girls. You know, from Judy and Ann and the others."

From down on the beach, a dog barks and I can hear children playing a game, shouting instructions to each other. I frown. I can't see why Lucy should have to stay away from people for Mr. Wheaton's sake.

"But why?"

Lucy digs her toes into the sand. "Well, he wants me to himself, that's all. And he thinks the other girls are a bad influence." She shrugs. "He doesn't want me to tell anyone about our relationship even if I trust them. He says they'd only try and split us up. I daren't speak to any of the girls in school in case he's watching. Although of course I'd never tell anyone. Well, apart from you, but Max doesn't know I'm friends with you." She gives me a weak smile.

I return her smile, but I can't shake the anxious feeling that has settled in my stomach. No doubt Mr. Wheaton wouldn't want Lucy spending time with me either. What right has he to make decisions like that about Lucy? Telling her who she can and can't speak to and wanting to know where she is all the time? I feel like echoing her own words back to her: *It's your life.*

"Max gave me this." She hands me a small bottle and I run my finger over the grooves of the stopper. EVENING IN PARIS is printed on the gold label.

"Did he buy it in Paris?"

Lucy giggles. "No. He bought it in London. He went to see the Festival of Britain. So lucky. Try some," she says, gesturing to the perfume bottle.

"Oh, no." I attempt to give the bottle back to Lucy, but she insists.

"Go on."

I spray a little onto my wrists.

"Rub it behind your ears. Isn't it dreamy?"

I inhale deeply. I smell like Lucy—bergamot, lilac, rose, and jasmine. I smell of lust and passion and dark secrets. A shiver runs through me and I give her the bottle back, watching as she sprays some on herself. From her bag, she takes a Coty box with an orange and gold pattern. My mother would be envious; she'd love a Coty powder. Lucy lightly dabs the cream powder puff into the box. Using a small compact mirror, she expertly brushes the puff over her nose, cheekbones, and forehead. "I look a perfect sight. It's the wind."

I bite my lip—Lucy always looks beautiful.

"Let me do you, Edie."

I stay perfectly still as she scoots across the blanket, kneeling next to me. I push my face forward, holding my breath as she sweeps the powder puff lightly over my nose and cheekbones. She's so close to me, I can see her flawless skin dusted in powder, her eyelashes, her small earlobes.

"There you are, Edie. Beautiful, just beautiful."

"Did Mr. Wheaton buy you the necklace too?" I ask, gesturing to the tiny rose pendant at her throat.

"Oh, no," she says, touching the necklace. "I've had this for forever. I always wear it." She retreats across the blanket and tucks the Coty box and powder puff into her bag.

"Are you still seeing him in the evenings then?"

Lucy nods and adjusts her tunic so the sun can reach her knees. "If Max can get away, we drive out, try and find a little pub where we can have supper. Sometimes we drive for miles. Max is always so edgy about bumping into someone he knows." She sighs. "If he doesn't have time for supper, we meet for an hour or so over by Alderbury woods, in Max's car. I tell my parents I have extra orchestra practice, or a debate club meeting. In fact, I haven't been to debate club for weeks." She plucks a blade of grass and twirls it between her thumb and forefinger.

I picture them together. The windows of the car steamed. Mr. Wheaton's beard tickling Lucy's cheek as he murmurs sweet nothings in her ear, his hands creeping up under her blouse. My neck feels hot despite the breeze.

"I don't suppose you've seen Rupert. Since...you know."

Lucy looks sheepish. "Well, actually, yes. I went to the pictures with Rupert on Saturday."

I look at her in surprise. "After you got back from the hotel with Mr. Wheaton?"

A pink flush sweeps over Lucy's cheeks. "Rupert came round to ask me to the pictures, desperate to apologize, and wanting to know if I could ever forgive him for behaving in such a beastly way. He seemed so sorry and, I don't know, I suppose I felt sort of unhappy," she explains. "Max had gone home to his wife... Before he left, I'd asked him when I could see him again, and he got awfully touchy. He said it had been hard enough organizing the night we'd just had and that I mustn't put so much pressure on him. He said he gets enough of that from his wife. He was cross with me and it spoiled everything. I was upset. And then Rupert turned up, asking me if I wanted to go to the pictures. I didn't want to hurt Rupert's feelings."

I rub at my eyebrow. "But how could you go out with Rupert after spending the night with Mr. Wheaton?"

For a moment, Lucy looks stricken. "I don't know," she says. "To be honest, Edie, I feel awfully confused. When I'm with Max, it's so thrilling. But Rupert really is very sweet on me. We'd make such a wonderful couple. Everyone says so."

"Mr. Wheaton doesn't know anything about Rupert then," I say sourly.

"Of course not," Lucy replies. "And anyway, there's nothing to know, is there?"

"No," I say, although I can't help feeling Mr. Wheaton would see things differently.

"I saw *her* the other day," Lucy says, bitterly.

"Who?"

"Max's wife. Her name is *June*. Of course it's my least favorite name now. She was coming out of the grocer's with the baby in the pram, and I held the door open for her. She barely looked at me. I mean, she said thank you, but that was it."

"Well, she doesn't know who you are," I venture.

"But it was just *awful*. I kept thinking about her going home, unpacking her shopping, putting the dinner on, serving it onto the tableware they chose together, getting into bed with Max like she does every evening. I felt quite sick at the thought of it."

"You're bound to feel strange about her," is all I can think to say.

"She's quite pretty, really, for an older person," Lucy muses. "She was wearing pearl earrings and a blue dress. I liked the lipstick she had on..." Lucy frowns. For just a moment she looks sullen, but then she shrugs it off. Above us a gull cries out and the wind rustles the grass in the dunes. She reaches into her pocket and takes out a paper twist of Parma Violets, pops one into her mouth. I've noticed she uses them as breath fresheners.

"Max met June before the war," Lucy continues. "He promised her he'd marry her when he returned, only when he came back he wasn't the same. But she was, and he didn't want to let her down. She'd waited for him all that time, you see." She swallows her sweet and takes another. "Max said June went loopy after the baby was born."

I stare at her. "How do you mean?"

"Apparently she thought men were coming to take the baby away. Men in suits. Then she thought Max was one of them. She threatened him with a steak knife."

"Goodness."

"Anyway, she's all right now," Lucy says, matter-of-factly. "Although Max says she's always cold with him. He talks of leaving her, of us running away together."

I look at her, askance. "Run away? But where would you go?"

"Max says he's always wanted to go to Paris." She grins. "I don't know, Edie. Anywhere, really. I'd go *anywhere*, as long as I could be with Max, as long as it could be just us."

"But I thought you wanted to go to London to train to be a teacher?"

"Well, I do..."

I realize my right foot is lying on the sand. It must have slipped off the edge of the blanket. I attempt to brush the sand off; its gritty sharpness is irritating and agitating. But it isn't just the sand—whenever Lucy speaks of Mr. Wheaton, I experience a tight fist of anxiety in my chest. As exciting as her affair is, something about it just doesn't feel right.

"I think you should finish it with Mr. Wheaton," I say. "He shouldn't be telling you to stay away from people, or upsetting you."

Lucy drops the blade of grass. "Oh, he didn't really upset me. It was my own silly fault. I get too emotional about things, I know I do. And Max can't help his feelings. He's an emotional person too."

I press my fingernails into my palms. "But don't you see? He's making it that way. He wants you for himself when he is already married, and he doesn't even want you to have friends."

Lucy's face darkens. "You're not *jealous*, are you, Edie?"

My face burns. "Of course not."

We sit there for a moment or two in stony silence. I want to apologize but I also know I'm right. And would Lucy really run away with Mr. Wheaton? I suspect it's all just talk, but I still worry; I couldn't stand it if she got hurt, if she threw all her plans away.

"Maybe your mother could help me," Lucy says finally, breaking the silence.

"My mother?"

"She might be able to tell me my future, or which path to take. Does she do that too? Fortune-telling?"

"I'm not sure," I say cagily, feeling hurt. Why is my opinion never enough for Lucy? She always wants to involve my mother.

"It's just the séance, and finding Smudge like that–it was so amazing. Perhaps you could ask her?"

I give a reluctant nod. "I can ask her, but–"

"Great," Lucy says, stretching her legs out and wriggling her toes. "I'll come over tomorrow then, shall I?"

When I arrive home, entering by the kitchen door, Reg's large bunch of garage keys is hanging on the hook by the stove, always an indication he is in. He sits at the table, cleaning his boots. My face is flushed from the sun; my hair still smells of the sea. He eyes me suspiciously.

"Where have you been?"

"Sandy Bay."

He puts one boot down on a sheet of newspaper and I creep across the kitchen, hoping he'll forget about me.

"Been hanging about with the Theddle girl again, have you?"

I stop, halfway across the kitchen, pressing my elbows into my sides.

"Yes," I mumble.

"Isn't she a bit posh for the likes of you?" Reg grins at me.

I can feel my shoulders stiffening. I want to tell him to get lost, that it's none of his business but, like my mother has recently learned, I am aware it is best not to anger him.

"I don't know," I say, stupidly.

"Been in the house, have you?"

I shake my head.

Reg laughs. "'Course you haven't. She's not likely to invite *you* in, now, is she? Little Edie Green. There isn't anything fancy about you, my girl. She wants to see how the other half lives? Feel sorry for you, does she?" He sets the boots down on the floor, then turns to me, his gaze hard and cool. "You might be interesting to her right now, because of your mother's talents, but mark my words, she'll drop you quick enough when all the fuss dies down. I've told your mother the same—they won't mix with us for long, not with all their airs and graces. People like that will only be a friend when they want something from you."

I can feel tears pricking the backs of my eyelids even though I know he's wrong. Lucy isn't friends with me out of charity or because she wants something from me. I *know* that's not true. That just isn't Lucy. She wouldn't have asked me to go to the dance with her, and to the beach this afternoon. If Lucy did invite me to The Gables, Reg is the last person I'd tell. I don't trust him. Not one bit. In fact, I hate him.

I mumble something about not knowing Lucy very long and Reg grins. "Well, let me know if you do get a butcher's at the house, Edie. I bet they've got all sorts of things that are worth a bob or two." He laughs darkly. "And it's about time you helped out around here more. You need to get yourself a job."

"I'm still at school," I say, defensively.

He snorts. "Not for much longer. You can look for something part-time until you finish. This isn't a bleedin' hotel. And you can help out more with the family business." He bangs a boot down on the table and I flinch. "You know Mrs. Goy, the fishmonger's wife?"

I nod, confused.

"She lost a son in France. Find out what his name was."

I blink. "Why? And how am I supposed to do that, anyway?"

Reg gives me a sharp look. "Just find out. Use your initiative."

I don't wait to hear anymore. My legs are tired and my feet feel heavy.

"And go and wash yourself," Reg calls after me. "You stink of perfume. It's giving me a headache."

20

2018

It's Sunday and Daniel, Suzanne, and Amy are coming over for lunch. It's there on my calendar but I remembered anyway. They want to celebrate something and I told them I'll cook a chicken. I've written it down: *Cook chicken.*

I take my pen and write underneath *Saw Lucy last night*, not unaware of how barmy that sounds but not wanting to forget. Am I really seeing the dead? Just like my mother? But wasn't my mother a fraud? Or did she just embellish her gifts? And is Lucy really dead? No one knows what happened to her, whether she's alive or not. I haven't thought about it all for so long. I suppose I haven't wanted to.

I shake my head. For now, I need to concentrate on today. Everyone likes my chicken, especially Arthur. He's probably tinkering away in the shed as usual. He's got into wood turning, bought himself a lathe. He makes wooden bowls and gives them away as gifts. Never anything else, just the bowls.

"Don't be silly, Mum," Daniel had said on his Friday-evening visit. "We'll bring something with us to heat in the oven. Suzanne can make a vegetable lasagna."

"Nonsense," I said. "I'll do a proper Sunday dinner. Chicken with potatoes and vegetables."

Daniel was reluctant. "That's a lot of work, Mum. Why don't you let us take care of it?"

"No," I told him firmly. "I've cooked more chickens in my life than you've had hot baths. I'm doing a chicken and that's the end of it."

Daniel had smiled, held up his hands, and I'd sat back on the sofa, satisfied.

I don't like the thought of Suzanne having to make something in her house to bring over to mine. And my chicken is always much better than Suzanne's. She doesn't let it rest for long enough. I've never said anything, but to be honest, her meat is always a little on the dry side.

"Amy's been making noises again about becoming a vegetarian," Daniel warned me on Friday evening.

"Oh, don't be silly," I said. "She'll soon forget about that after tasting my chicken."

"I don't think that's the point," Daniel had said, but he let it go.

I step outside with my scissors to gather some chives from the garden. I can't hear Arthur. Perhaps he's gone out. Back in the kitchen, I put my apron on, the one Josie wears now more than I do.

I can't remember the last time I cooked properly. Josie buys me these ready meals; cottage pie, fish pie, hotpots, macaroni cheese, that sort of thing. She sticks Post-it notes on the meals before she puts them in the fridge: *Tuesday, Wednesday, Saturday.* I always put the Post-it notes in the bin. I'm perfectly capable of deciding which day of the week I'll have a cottage pie over a macaroni cheese. And I'm still capable of cooking as long as I keep an eye on things and remember to set my timer. I only forgot about the egg that one time. Daniel found it shaking in the pan. I'd left the gas on and all the water had boiled away. "You were lucky it didn't explode," Daniel had said, tipping the egg into the bin.

"I only forgot about it for a minute," I told him, but they were worried after that. There may have been other times, too. I seem to remember a black apple crumble, charred sausages. And there was that time I dropped a whole casserole on the kitchen floor. It slipped straight out of my hands. I told Daniel I needed new oven gloves, that's all.

I peel the plastic wrapping from the chicken. I've been using this chicken recipe since 1975 when Arthur bought me a copy of *The Times Cookery Book* by Katie Stewart.

Arthur. I swallow hard. I suppose we were together for so many years that I occasionally forget he's gone. I wish I didn't. It makes it all come back to me when I realize.

I take a deep breath, trying to focus on the task at hand, spooning in the buttery, herby mixture. After my potatoes are peeled and cut, I scatter them around the chicken on the roasting tray and pop it all in the oven. From the drawer, I take the M&S napkins I've been saving and lay the table: mats, cutlery, my best crystal glasses. I set the kitchen timer and, just to be on the safe side, take it with me when I leave the room. If I carry it around, I'll be able to hear it wherever I am.

Daniel, Suzanne, and Amy arrive just after twelve, letting themselves in and stomping around noisily in the hallway, traipsing in wet leaves. They pile into the living room. It's always strange to see the room so full of people when it's usually just me. They smell like the outdoors and Suzanne's musky perfume. She's brought a cheesecake: shop-bought, I notice.

"How are you doing, Mum?" Daniel makes himself at home on the sofa. He's wearing a checked shirt, and trousers with large pockets.

"Fine," I say, winking at Amy.

Amy returns my wink with a smile, and I can see she's told Daniel and Suzanne nothing of our adventure to Winterford Green Retirement Village last weekend to speak to Constable Diprose.

"How's the chicken? Can we do anything to help?" Daniel asks.

I shake my head. "The chicken is fine. It's in the..." I can't think of the word. "Cooking machine," I say, quickly.

Suzanne looks at Daniel, one eyebrow raised.

"We've got good news," Daniel tells me, changing the subject. "Our offer has been accepted on the old dairy. We're moving to Devon." He smiles and his eyes sparkle with excitement. "We've already got a buyer for our house, and yours is going on the market next week."

I can see how pleased Daniel is but my stomach churns. "I don't think so," I mutter. "There are things I still need to do..."

"Don't worry. We'll get everything done before you go. Perhaps we'll get someone in to help with the packing."

I twist the rose pendant at my neck. I wasn't thinking about packing, I was thinking about Lucy. Once I find her, I'm sure Daniel will drop all this moving nonsense. I am about to tell him this but Suzanne appears, hovering in the doorway. "I'll put this cheesecake in the fridge and make us some drinks, shall I?"

I've noticed Suzanne can't sit still in my house for more than five minutes. Last time she was here I went upstairs to the bathroom and found her vacuuming my landing. I should be making the drinks, really, playing hostess, but I know she has to keep busy. Besides, I've been on my feet all morning and I seem to remember I was up in the night.

Daniel offers to help Suzanne, and then it's just me and Amy in the living room. She's wearing jeans with a hole in the knee. I am guessing the hole is meant to be there, and not just for ventilation. Some of the girls nowadays wear them so tight, their legs look like sausages in skins. They don't look any more comfortable than our itchy school stockings. Lucy used to hate them.

"I've seen Lucy again," I tell Amy.

She looks surprised. "Where? When?"

"Last night. She was in my garden over by the rose bushes." I pause, take in a sharp breath. *Roses.*

"What is it, Nan?" Amy comes over and sits next to me on the sofa.

I think of the photograph of Lucy on the front of the *Ludthorpe Leader*, the photograph I remembered when I told Josie I'd seen Lucy outside the post office, when I thought of my mother in the kitchen, the sound of Eddie Fisher on the wireless. In the photograph, Lucy was standing in front of the rose bushes in her garden, wearing her best Sunday dress. She'd been holding her brother's hand, his small fingers curled around hers.

"Lucy had a brother," I say. "About five years younger than her. George. He used to own the dentist's practice in town. Perhaps he's still alive. He might be able to tell us something. He might know more about Rupert."

"I'm surprised George stayed in Ludthorpe," Amy says thoughtfully. "You'd think they might have all moved away. After Lucy disappeared, I mean. It must have been horrible. Being stuck in the same town with everyone who knew her."

"That's exactly *why* they stayed, in case Lucy came back. Or in case the police discovered something. They never stopped looking for her. They moved out of The Gables, though. I'm sure they did." I knit my eyebrows, trying to remember. Didn't I go to The Gables recently? I went to speak to Lucy but she wasn't there.

"Do you have any idea where George is now, Nan?"

I seem to think I *have* seen George Theddle recently. Well, maybe ten years ago or so. When you've so many years behind you, ten years can feel like last week. *Seventy* years ago can feel like last week. Although ask me what I had for tea last night and I'll probably be unable to tell you.

I close my eyes, trying to think, trying to remember. "I did see him," I tell Amy. "It was something to do with Arthur. There was tea and mince pies, and a Christmas tree in the living room." My eyes are screwed tightly shut. I can see George's wife pouring tea, handing out napkins. There are lots of people there, people Arthur knows from... I open my eyes.

"Choir," I say. "Sarah Theddle was a member of Arthur's choir. She invited us over for a Christmas tea once. It was mostly the choir. I wasn't a member, but husbands and wives were invited. I went along with Arthur."

"Great," Amy says, excitedly. "Where did they live? Can you remember?"

"They lived on the road that goes out to Melfork. I can see it now–a bungalow with a cherry tree outside. That's where George and Sarah lived. That's where we had the mince pies. I have to go and see George," I tell Amy. "I am sure he'll help me remember. Maybe he'll be able to tell us something. I have to go now before it's too late."

"Okay, Nan," Amy says, reaching across and squeezing my hand. "We'll go. Although I've got no idea how we'll get to Melfork." She takes her telephone out of her pocket as if it might offer her a solution. "I'm not even sure the bus stops on that road and, even if it does, it will take forever–" Amy stops talking as Daniel and Suzanne appear in the doorway. They look distressed.

"Mum? What is it?" Amy asks.

"There's a funny smell in the kitchen," Daniel tells us.

"What smell?"

"It smells like gas." Suzanne looks worried. "You can smell it in here too."

Amy sniffs the air. "I *can* smell it." She gives me an apologetic look.

I wrinkle my nose. They're right. There is *something.*

"It's not carbon monoxide, is it? We should get out of the house. Call someone." Daniel looks panicked.

"I'll google it." Amy reaches for her phone as Suzanne marches off back to the kitchen.

I follow and so does Daniel. In the kitchen Suzanne pauses, her nose in the air. She looks at the oven, grabs my gloves, and opens the door. *Oven*, that's the word I was looking for. Black smoke pours out. Daniel coughs and Suzanne bats away the smoke before reaching in and pulling out my oven tray. The chicken looks lovely. Golden. Perfectly cooked. It's almost ready. But there is something black and gooey in with the potatoes.

Amy comes into the kitchen, waving her hand in front of her face.

"A knife," Suzanne says. "You left a knife in the tray. It wasn't gas we could smell. It was burning plastic."

I look at my knife. It's the one with a black plastic handle. Or it was. The handle has mostly melted. "We can still eat it, can't we?" I say hopefully, looking at my chicken.

Suzanne pinches her lips. "Don't be silly, Edie. The chicken will have soaked up all the plastic fumes."

"It'll be toxic," Amy adds. "Sorry, Nan."

Daniel is busy opening my back door to let the smoke out. He comes over and pats my shoulder. "Sorry, Mum."

"We need to open *all* the windows." Suzanne is still batting the air with the oven gloves.

"We don't want this smoke in our lungs," Amy adds.

I can feel my heart pounding. I have ruined lunch. I have polluted my family. The frustration is swelling inside me, the exasperation I've been trying to push down for months. It was a simple mistake, and yet they'll use it against me. I know I forget things, make mistakes, but I'm not mad, I'm not ready for the scrap heap just yet. I've still got all my marbles, even if they're sometimes in the wrong order. I'm fed up with people patting my shoulder, all the sighs and sympathetic smiles. Before I can stop myself, I pick up a glass, hurl it across the kitchen and against the wall where it smashes, making a satisfying sound, leaving a mark on the paintwork. There are shards of glass all over the floor. Everyone stops what they're doing. "It could have happened to anyone!" I shout. "It wasn't my fault!"

Daniel looks at the glass and then at me. I can't believe it either; my anger just fizzled over. One second I was staring at the glass, the next it was on the floor.

"Are you okay, Mum? Did you hurt yourself?"

"No, I didn't bloody hurt myself," I mutter.

Daniel tries to touch my shoulder but I shrug him away. He looks to Suzanne for support but she says nothing.

"No one is suggesting it's your fault, Mum," Daniel says gently. "There's no need to get so worked up."

Amy is reaching into my cupboard. "I'll fetch the dustpan."

"No, I'll do it." Daniel takes the dustpan from Amy, shooting me a sideways glance as he does so, perhaps checking I'm not going to do anything else crazy. "You help your mum," he tells Amy, glancing over to where Suzanne is scraping my lovely roast potatoes into the bin.

I sit slowly down at the kitchen table while they busy themselves with clearing the toxic air, soaking my pan, and sweeping up the broken glass. I begin to tear one of the paper napkins. It calms me and I start on the next, creating a pile of shredded tissue.

"I can't do anything anymore," I mutter. But it's useless. Lunch is ruined and no one wants to hear an old lady whinging. I take a steadying breath, trying to calm myself. Suzanne is wrapping the chicken in a plastic bag. I can't believe she's going to throw it away. What will the neighbors think, wasting food at a time like this? "Better pot-luck with Churchill today than humble pie with Hitler tomorrow," I mumble.

Suzanne stares at me, then shakes her head and ties the bin bag.

"Why don't we get a takeaway?" Amy suggests.

Daniel and Suzanne think this is a good idea. They all perk up.

"Turkish?" Suzanne adds. "There's that new place. We can go and collect it."

"*Turkish?*" My hand has bunched itself into a fist.

"It's just chicken and rice, Mum," Daniel says, impatiently. "You'll like it."

Amy is tapping away on her phone. "They do a vegetable wrap." She looks pleased. "We can get hummus to share."

"Do they have a lamb shish?" Daniel is trying to look at Amy's phone over her shoulder.

I stare at the shredded napkins, the ones I'd been saving for a special occasion. They all crowd around Amy's telephone, talking about stuffed mushrooms and flatbread.

21

1951

A week later and I've got myself a job in the hope Reg will leave me alone. I take Mrs. Underwood's baby out for an hour each afternoon when I get home from school. His name is Paul. He's got pink cheeks and he smiles if you play peekaboo with him. I like lifting him out of the pram and bouncing him on my knee when we get to the park. Mostly though, I just wheel him around Ludthorpe while he gurgles and kicks his chubby little legs in the air, or peers out at me from beneath the thick blankets Mrs. Underwood swaddles him in. Mrs. Underwood is chuffed to bits about our arrangement. "A whole hour to myself! Whatever shall I do with it, Edie? You're a godsend, you really are."

One afternoon when I dropped Paul off, she didn't answer and I stood there for ages, banging her door knocker as loudly as I could. She'd fallen asleep on the sofa; I could see her stockinged feet up on the sofa arm when I peeked through the letterbox, and when she finally answered the door, she had the imprint of the embroidered sofa cushion on her cheek.

She pays me ten shillings a week, which I'm supposed to hand over to Reg (although I always keep a little back). My mother gives me apologetic looks but says nothing. "She's got to earn her keep, Nancy," Reg says. "I was out at work at her age. What does she think this is, a free boardinghouse? All meals provided?"

It's where I am today, walking Paul through the park, earning my keep. It's early evening. The air is dry and still and the neatly mowed grass is striped with long shadows from the trees.

I push the pram up onto the bandstand and rock Paul gently. I wonder where Lucy is now. Is she at home, having dinner with her parents, waiting for it to grow dark so she can sneak out of the house and meet Mr. Wheaton at the woods? They've got a new signal. On Tuesdays and Thursdays, during our history lessons, Lucy knows that if Mr. Wheaton places his hand on her desk at some point during the hour, it means he will be waiting in his car by the woods for her at nine o'clock that night. If he doesn't, it means he can't meet her. Once she went and waited a whole hour for him, but he didn't show. Apparently his wife made a fuss about him going to the pub, and he couldn't get away. *I was freezing*, Lucy had said to him the following night. *You could have given me three rings on the telephone or something.* Mr. Wheaton had apparently got cross, told her not to be so ridiculous, that he was risking enough as it was. He'd asked Lucy why she was always ruining the short amount of time they had together and so Lucy had walked home, cold and tearful. I hate Mr. Wheaton for making her feel that way. *It was my fault*, Lucy had said. I didn't agree, but it's useless telling Lucy. Nothing is ever Mr. Wheaton's fault.

Lucy is coming over this evening to have her fortune told. She needs direction, she tells me. She wants to know if Mr. Wheaton will play a part in her future. I feel guilty she's pinning so much hope on my mother's ability to offer her a solution.

Thanks to her new friendship with Barbara Theddle, my mother has managed to get herself on the summer fete committee. In a few weeks' time, she'll be there on the green in a booth behind a curtain, telling fortunes and reading palms. The summer fete is always a big day in Ludthorpe. Everyone goes. There'll be a coconut shy, a tombola, and guess the weight of the cake. The church committee ladies sell their knitted bonnets and homemade jams, and Reverend Thurby puts himself cheerfully in the stocks, where delighted children get to throw wet sponges at him. "He's a good sport," my father used to say.

I decide it's probably time to push Paul home. I'm crossing the park, wheeling him along the path, when I see Judy coming toward me. I smile but she glares at me.

"I suppose you think you're clever, do you? Stealing people's friends."

"Sorry?"

She narrows her eyes. "Lucy. She was my friend first."

Even though I think Judy is being awfully silly, she speaks with such venom that I find I am clutching the pram handle. "Lucy is my friend too," I say weakly.

Judy scoffs. "No, she isn't. Not really. Can't you see? Everyone thinks it's strange. Everyone can see you must have some sort of a hold over Lucy. You've probably put a spell on her or something."

My throat feels tight. "I haven't put a spell on her."

"Well, you've done *something*. Lucy would never want to be friends with you. Not through *choice*."

She spits the word at me and I flinch. I want to get away, but the pram is heavy and Judy is standing right in front of me.

"Everyone knows your mother is a trickster and a fraud," she continues.

I shrug, trying to keep my cool, trying not to let Judy rattle me, but my pulse races. "Well, everyone knows why Lucy is friends with you," I say. "She has to be, because of your mother, because your mother cleans her house. I bet Lucy gives you all her old clothes and was told to be nice to you."

I don't like to be so mean but I enjoy the way Judy's face flames.

"That's not true," she hisses.

"Well, it's what Lucy told me," I lie.

"She didn't. She wouldn't. You're a liar. Your whole family are liars. You don't know what you're talking about."

"Maybe she isn't the friend you think she is," I suggest, enjoying myself now.

Judy begins to say something but only manages to make a spluttering noise. Her fists tightly clenched, she turns on her heel and walks away, not wanting to let me see her cry. I release the breath I hadn't realized I'd been holding and look down at Paul, who seems to be frowning at me.

"Thank you, Edie," Mrs. Underwood says, pressing coins into my hand. "And were you a good boy?" she asks Paul in a silly voice.

"He was very good," I say, as Paul can't yet answer for himself.

Mrs. Underwood smiles. "I'll see you same time tomorrow, Edie."

I nod, then remember something. "Do you know Mrs. Goy?" I ask.

"From the fishmonger?" Mrs. Underwood confirms, although we both know there is no other Mrs. Goy.

"Didn't she lose a son in the war?"

Mrs. Underwood stops jiggling Paul and gives me a sad smile. "She lost her eldest, Billy. Shot down over the Dutch coast, I think. Why do you ask?"

"I couldn't remember, that's all. I wanted to remember."

"Well, of course, we *all* want to remember their sacrifice, dear. Although best not to mention it to Mrs. Goy. A day won't ever go by when she won't think of him, but we mustn't go around talking of the war, reminding people and upsetting them." She lowers her voice. "My Cliff nearly fainted when I served him rice last year. I thought it would make a change. Something exotic. You should have seen his face. He was in Burma, you see. But it doesn't do to keep on about any of it."

I nod, and Mrs. Underwood shifts Paul to her left hip.

"You run along now, Edie. I expect you don't want to be late for your tea. And don't worry yourself about things. We've all got to move on. It's the only way, even with the times as they are." She sighs. "It's over, that's what we've got to remember."

"Thank you."

Mrs. Underwood gives my shoulder a friendly pat and after I've promised to be here the same time tomorrow, I let myself out of the front door and walk quickly along the street, feeling nicely unburdened but also slightly empty without the pram to push.

As I turn into Sycamore Street, I hear hurried footsteps behind me. Someone catches my arm.

"Edie."

It's Rupert. I shake him off. "What are you doing?" I ask, crossly. "Were you waiting for me?" *What is it with people accosting me?* I wonder.

"I need to speak to you, Edie."

I shake my head. "I'm afraid I'm in a rush. If you'll excuse me—"

"Edie, please. It's Lucy."

I hesitate. "What about Lucy?"

Rupert shoves his hands into the pockets of his cuffed trousers and stares at his shoes. "She won't see me. She keeps—putting me off."

"It's no business of mine," I say, impatiently. What right does Rupert have to be loitering on street corners, grabbing people's arms?

"But you're her friend," Rupert says. "She trusts you, I know she does."

This pleases me but I don't let on. I fold my arms across my chest.

"I wondered if you might know why she's avoiding me. If you might be able to speak to her." He looks hopefully at me. "I know you know why she won't see me."

I say nothing. What can I say? I obviously can't tell him about Mr. Wheaton.

"If it's because of what happened at the pictures last week..."

"What happened at the pictures?" I ask, confused.

Rupert's cheeks color. "I put my arm around her. I thought it was what she wanted. Please tell her I'm sorry, Edie. I should have thought about how it would look. It's just, well, everyone knows we'll be going steady soon, so I thought it would be all right."

I blink at him as he runs a hand through his hair. I can see he's sweating.

"I'll do anything, Edie," he says, desperately. "If only she'd see me again." He moves toward me, his eyes bright, his hand twitching nervously. I can see the protruding veins in his neck.

"I'll talk to her," I say, taking a step back, wanting to be rid of him. "Now I really must go."

As I hurry up the street toward home, I can feel his eyes following me. I open the gate with a shaky hand and go around to the kitchen door without looking back.

Lucy is in the kitchen with my mother, sipping tea.

"Oh, hello, Edie," she says, as if I'm a visitor who has just popped round. "I've come for my fortune-telling. We were just about to get started."

My mother smiles at me, then crushes the stub of her Player's into the ashtray. "There's tea in the pot."

"Thanks," I say, bewildered. I take a few steadying breaths. Rupert must not know Lucy is here. I can still see the desperate look on his face and I realize, now, that he will not take Lucy's rejection well. But he'll get over it, I remind myself; he'll find someone else.

"Nancy is going to be telling fortunes at the fete," Lucy says, excited.

"Yes." I wonder when my mother became "Nancy." I wouldn't dream of calling Barbara Theddle by her first name.

"Do you want some privacy?" I ask.

"Oh, no," Lucy says quickly. "You can stay."

I take a seat awkwardly at the table and pour myself a small cup of tea with what's left in the pot; it's dark and stewed, and I have it without milk as there's none left in the jug.

My mother draws the curtains, then returns to the table.

"I need to know about the future," Lucy says, reminding us why she's here.

"The future is always uncertain," my mother sagely replies. "But my visions will offer guidance." She takes hold of Lucy's hand, then closes her eyes and draws in a breath, preparing herself. She's quiet for several moments, and I try to put the teacup down in the saucer without making a clattering noise. Outside, over the low garden wall, I can see Mr. Staines walking up the path to the privy, a newspaper tucked under his arm.

My mother knits her eyebrows together and rolls her head on her shoulders. She begins to hum, a strange, low-pitched noise, while Lucy gazes hopefully at her.

"Ah, yes, the mists are clearing... I see...I see–eggs."

"Eggs?" Lucy looks blank.

My mother is still concentrating. "Mm. Yes, eggs."

"In my future?" Lucy confirms.

"Eggs, and...something else..."

Lucy leans forward in anticipation and I take another sip of stewed, bitter tea.

"It's difficult to get a clear picture. Wait. Yes, there it is... Rabbits," my mother pronounces.

Lucy wrinkles her nose. "Rabbits?"

My mother takes a deep breath, opens her eyes, and smiles. "Eggs and rabbits. That's what I see."

Lucy frowns and chews on her lip. She looks to me but I shrug helplessly, unable to offer her an explanation.

"And that's all you see, Nancy? You don't see anything else? Anything perhaps a little more..."

My mother shakes her head. "That's what I saw," she says, releasing Lucy's hand. "I can't help with interpretations, I'm afraid, but things usually become clear."

"At least you got something," I say helpfully.

Lucy looks glum and begins to open her purse, but my mother waves her hand in the air. "Oh, no, consider this one my treat, Lucy."

"Well, thank you..."

I see Lucy out and, when we are on the doorstep, she turns to me, her forehead creased. "I don't know what to make of it, Edie."

"I shouldn't worry. Her visions are just a guide, after all."

"I was hoping she might see something else. You know, Max, or Rupert, or something to help me decide about the future."

"She doesn't really deal in specifics."

I decide not to tell her about speaking to Rupert. It might only confuse her more. My feeling is she should get away from the both of them. A dilemma, my father used to say, is nothing but two bad options.

Lucy sighs. "Maybe I should come along to another séance. The last one was so successful. Maybe the spirits will be able to guide her."

"Well, maybe," I say, doubtfully.

She checks her watch. "I'd better go. My father saw me sneaking out the other night. I had to make up a story about leaving something over at your house. I'm sure he's getting suspicious.

Last week I found him in my room, going through my things. Goodness knows what he was looking for."

"What do you think he'd do if he found out about you and Mr. Wheaton?"

Lucy shakes her head. "I daren't even think about it. My parents must never know. They're terribly conservative. I'm surprised they let me out without a chaperone. Do you know they voted *against* when we had the Sunday cinema vote? My mother thinks the pictures are corrupting us."

"My mother was all for the Sunday opening. She loves the pictures."

"It would destroy my father," Lucy continues. "Can you imagine it? His only daughter having an affair with a married man. He'll *hate* me for it. He already thinks something is up. Last week he threatened to burn my records. If he found out about Max, he'd take me out of school and I'd be trapped in that house forever." She shudders. "That would be it, my life would be over. They must never know," she says firmly.

I lower my voice. "I really think you ought to break it off with Mr. Wheaton."

Her face darkens. "Edie, I couldn't do that. Max understands me, and the way he kisses me...I just couldn't give it up. And of course he's clever too, even if he does go on all the time." She sighs.

"Go on about what?"

"Oh, I don't know. He just *talks*. It's all, Attlee this and Attlee that, and those two chaps who ran off to Russia. Can't we talk about *us*, I say. He tells me it's important I know what's going on in the world, and I suppose he's right, but it's all terribly boring."

"Still, I think you should finish it. He's unkind to you, and anyway, he'll never leave his wife and child," I add, wincing at the harshness of my words. She has to hear this, I think. Someone has to tell her.

Lucy's eyes flash with anger. "I told you, Max is in love with me. His emotions run high, that's all. You wouldn't understand. Really, Edie, I don't even know why I'm talking to you about this. You don't know anything about Max, about *us*."

"I know that he's old, and married," I say defensively.

"We're in *love*, Edie."

I can feel my cheeks reddening. Lucy thinks I'm stupid, that I don't understand anything. She's the one being stupid, not me.

"But how can he love you? It's all just silly. You shouldn't carry on with it, not if you don't want to get found out. I think you should forget all about it now before something awful happens. You just said yourself it would be terrible if your father discovered what's going on. Why risk your whole future?"

Lucy glares at me. "I thought you were on my side, Edie. I thought you were the one person who understood."

"I'm trying to look out for you."

"Well, don't," she snaps, collecting her bicycle from behind the front wall. "I don't need you. I don't even know why I'm here. I only started walking to school with you because after you saw me that time with Max I was terrified you'd tell someone, but I needn't have worried. Who would believe *you* anyway?"

Her words feel like a sharp slap. I try to speak but a horrible pressure is building in my chest, and I place a hand on the door frame to steady myself. Lucy only wanted to walk with me, to be friends with me, because she thought I might tell someone? She only wanted to make sure I kept her secret safe? That can't be true, it just can't be. My face burns and I can feel the tears forming behind my eyes. I open my mouth to call after her but she's already cycling furiously away. She doesn't look back.

22

2018

"Is this even legal?" Amy asks.

"Of course it is. I've held a driving license since 1959. You just need a driver in the car with you. And I *am* a driver."

"But you haven't driven a car for over a year, Nan." Amy tightens her grip on the wheel, checks her mirrors again.

"Never mind about that."

It had taken us several attempts to start the car, and I'm not entirely sure I've still got insurance, although I don't remember canceling it. Anyway, now here we are, out on the country road to Melfork, looking for George and Sarah Theddle's bungalow. I used to go blackberrying along here when I was a girl.

"You haven't told Dad about this, have you?" Amy asks.

"Of course not. I'm not daft."

She nods, satisfied, keeping her hands firmly on the wheel at ten to two as we drive slowly down the long road.

"We'll need to tread carefully, Nan. With George. I know it's been a long time but she's still his sister. I'll tell him I'm doing a school history project."

History is nothing but death and mess and wasted lives. Who said that?

"And I don't think we should mention our visit to Peter, um, Constable Diprose."

"Whatever you think best," I say, cheerfully. "We'll have to find Rupert next. He might remember something too."

"I can have a look into Rupert, Nan, but let's focus on George for now."

I nod and look up at the sky. There always seems so much more of it once you get out of Ludthorpe and into the flat open countryside. China blue, with a few fluffy white clouds. I can see an airplane; it cuts through the sky like a pair of scissors tearing through blue cloth, like my mother when she cut my favorite blue dress to make napkins from it. *It's too small for you now, Edie. I'll make us a set of napkins.*

I wonder if I'll ever fly on an airplane again. I expect not. You always think there's so much time to do things, to see places, then you realize there's hardly any time at all.

"Can you see the house yet?" Amy asks.

I press my face close to the window and look out at the fields and the odd house whizzing by. We pass a few brown cows grazing in a field, then cross a small stone bridge. I remember the bridge. I used to cycle over it on my way to Sandy Bay. Lucy would have cycled over this bridge many times. She must have cycled over it the afternoon she went missing. The bridge hasn't changed at all, apart from a sign advising that it is weak and not suitable for large lorries. I squeeze my eyes shut. I'm standing on the bridge, staring numbly down into the brown water. It's hot and I'm sweating terribly, yet shivering too, but barely aware of myself, or of anything around me. I'm holding something. What is it? Now I'm letting it go and it's falling, falling...

I open my eyes and the image disappears. Glancing over at Amy, I can see she is busy concentrating on the road. I take a deep breath, calming myself; we're going to see George, who will be able to help us.

"Nan, are you concentrating?"

"Of course I am." I wipe the window where my breath has steamed the glass. Then I see it just ahead of us. The bungalow with the cherry tree in the garden. "There," I tell her. "That's it."

The car slows as we carefully pull to a stop outside. The cherry tree is almost bare.

We make our way up the overgrown path. The paint on the front door is peeling. On the porch sits a plant pot with something brown and dead in it next to a pile of old catalogs that never made it to the recycling bin. The bungalow looks different from the day Arthur and I arrived for minced pies, tea, and mulled wine. It had been December, cold and wintry, and yet the outside had been more cheerful somehow. The paint wasn't peeling. There had been a wreath on the door; holly and red berries. I brush away a few dry branches to reveal a plaque on the wall that reads WYM COTTAGE. I can see nets, just like mine, giving away the age of the occupants.

"I wonder if anyone's in?"

"There's only one way to find out." I press the doorbell.

For a while, we hear nothing, then Amy leans forward. She can hear something, footsteps perhaps?

The door opens just a crack, the latch is still on, and I can see a pair of eyes looking out at us from the gloom. They belong to a man with a wrinkled face and a wisp of white hair clinging to the top of his otherwise bald head.

"George Theddle?"

"Who is it?"

He peers down at us suspiciously and I notice he's got a graze on his forehead.

"We've come about Lucy–"

"You people!"

Before I can say anything else his expression changes to a fierce glare.

"Why can't you just leave it alone? I don't want anything to do with you and your cold case podcasts. I've told you already. Get off my property!"

He slams the door in our faces.

We stand blinking in the autumn sunlight next to the dead plant and the pile of moldy catalogs.

"Well, that went well," I say.

23

2018

Amy knocks loudly on the door. "Mr. Theddle," she shouts. She turns to me. "We've come all this way. He has to see us."

"What's a codpast?" I ask.

But Amy is banging on the door again. "Mr. Theddle," she calls out.

The front door opens, still on the latch. The eyes appear.

"I thought I told you—"

"Mr. Theddle, we're not making a podcast. You've got us confused with someone else." Amy stands firmly, gripping the shoulder straps of her rucksack. I can see George's eyes taking us in. He grumbles something indecipherable then reluctantly removes the latch.

"I'm Amy, and this is my nan."

George eyes us doubtfully. "My sister disappeared seventy years ago, and people from all sorts of places still come around poking their noses in. Last month someone wanted to record me."

"Mr. Theddle, we're local. We both live in Ludthorpe. Nan's lived here most of her life. She knew you, and your sister."

George stares at me and I see a flicker of recognition. He can't quite place me. That's fine—I expect I've changed a bit in the ten years or so since I was last here. George looks different too. He's got the same broad forehead, the same blue eyes as Lucy, but he's smaller than I remember. His hair is thinner and whiter and he doesn't stand as straight; he looks like a plant in need of watering. He no longer resembles the proud, ambitious man who owned the small dental practice in the town center for thirty years. Neither does he resemble much of the man I met here ten years ago, the man who handed out his wife's homemade mince pies and who was keen to show off the photographs of his two grandchildren. Boys, I seem to remember. Two blond-haired boys. I hadn't thought of Lucy at all that day. Well, I'm trying to find her now. Better late than never.

"It's Edie," I say. "My husband, Arthur, was in the Ludthorpe Singers with Sarah. I went to Ludthorpe Grammar."

George studies me more closely. The lines around his eyes deepen. "Edie Green."

I can't tell if he's pleased to see me or not.

"Well, yes. Only I've been Edie Havercroft for quite some time now."

"Can we come inside?" Amy asks. "We won't keep you long."

George sighs. He steps back. "Yes, I suppose so."

He leads us into a dusty living room. It's dark, due to the heavy curtains not being properly drawn. Dust motes float in the air. There's a greasy, lingering smell—his oven probably needs a clean. A pile of papers litters the coffee table. The cushions haven't been plumped in a while, and the two sofas sag in the middle, a little like George.

I realize that George is terribly lonely. The thought hits me in the chest and I have to stop myself from saying out loud: *You're lonely, George. How did that happen?*

George sits down, so Amy and I do the same. I can see the photographs of the two small blond-haired boys on the mantelpiece. There are others now, too; the boys in graduation robes. They must have grown up. There is a photograph of Sarah standing in front of a waterfall. Sarah Theddle is dead, I'm sure of it. The dust in the bungalow, George's sagging shoulders, his smart but poorly ironed shirt, are all giveaways.

"How did you get that graze on your head?" I ask.

"Oh." George touches the graze as if he'd forgotten about it. "I was in a car accident."

"Good grief," I say.

"Was everyone okay?" Amy asks anxiously.

George coughs. "Well, it was only me. I drove into some bins. They were gray, you see, the same color as the road. Only they had yellow lids, that's what the policeman said. *Yellow lids.* I dented my car, knocked the bins over. They wanted me to go for a new eye test. They asked me if I was sure I should still be driving. Should I still be driving!" George coughs again.

"I don't drive anymore," I say, trying to be helpful. "I've given it up."

George closes his eyes briefly and I can see I've said the wrong thing.

"Tea?" he asks.

"That would be lovely," Amy says for both of us.

The sun has come out, and it filters through the net curtains, creating a dappled light on George's faded orange rug.

"Nan," Amy whispers. "Is there anything here? Anything to help you remember?"

I look around, noticing a collection of china thimbles on the mantelpiece, a large picture on the wall, a shepherd herding sheep up a country lane on a frosty winter's morning, and another—a Constable, or something in that style—cows grazing by water. There is nothing here that might have been important to Lucy. She liked Picasso, even though her mother said his paintings made her feel ill. And the photographs are too recent. It's all George and Sarah's life. Unsurprising. Why should George keep anything belonging to Lucy? It was so long ago, and so upsetting of course. Why would anyone want to remember their sister disappearing, their parents' suffering? George would only have been around ten or eleven, probably still in short trousers. I doubt much was said to him, they would have tried to protect him. Not only that, people bottled things up in those days. No one talked much about Lucy as the months dragged on, and it became clear she wasn't coming back.

George returns with a tray and three, thankfully, small cups of tea; my bladder these days is somewhat unpredictable. I note the absence of biscuits. Lifting my mug, I resist the urge to sniff my tea to check if the milk is off, not that he's put much in. He places the tray on the side table, and a faded Charles and Diana on their wedding day stare up at me.

"The truth is," Amy says, "I *am* interested in Lucy, George. Not just Lucy, but Nan's other friends too."

I am about to tell Amy that I didn't really have a lot of friends at school, but she carries on before I get a chance.

"I'm gathering research, you see. For my Extended Project Qualification. It's all about Ludthorpe Grammar School for Girls through the ages, with a focus on how education for women has changed. I asked Nan if she had any photographs from when she was at school, but she doesn't keep much."

Well, this is true. I have the photographs in my hallway, of course. But I haven't got many photographs from the past, certainly not from my school days. My mother didn't hang onto anything for more than a few years. *Cluttered house, cluttered mind*, she used to say. I got used to throwing things away.

"What I'm looking for," Amy continues, "are any old photographs, or anything from that time, really. Anything belonging to a 1950s schoolgirl. I appreciate this might be difficult for you, but Nan, I mean Edie, thought you might have something."

George sighs heavily, then lifts himself out of his chair. Despite the sigh, I can tell Amy has won him round. She has that effect on people.

"There might be a box in the spare bedroom somewhere. I don't know what's in it. It's been a long time since I've looked, but I suppose if you really wanted–"

"Oh, that would be fantastic! Thank you so much, Mr. Theddle. Really, anything at all would be incredibly helpful for my project. It's so difficult to bring the past to life when you've only got facts and dates. I've always thought there's so much more to history."

History is nothing but death and mess and wasted lives.

"It's in the spare bedroom," George is saying. "On top of the wardrobe. You've got to stand on a chair–"

Amy is already on her feet. "Let me help."

She follows George out of the room, and I take the opportunity to pour a little of my tea into the plant pot behind me. The plants in this house could do with watering. I notice a thin layer of dust on the TV cabinet. He wants to get Josie round. Perhaps I'll pass her number on. Outside, a supermarket delivery van is passing. I take a quick sip of what's left of my tea; it's got a tangy, muddy taste to it. I can hear banging, the sound of Amy's voice, then George appears carrying a large cardboard box.

Amy carefully clears a space on the coffee table, pushing the old newspapers and piles of unopened letters aside. George puts the box down, then returns to his armchair.

Sitting next to me, Amy leans forward and pries the lid off. There are several loose black-and-white photographs.

"It all came from my parents' house," George mumbles. "We cleared the house out after my mother died. I was going to get rid of it but Sarah thought it should be kept."

Amy lifts a photograph out of the box: a small boy wearing a knitted jumper and holding a cricket bat that's almost bigger than him.

"Aw," she says. "So cute."

There is the tiniest flicker of a smile on George's lips. "That's me."

Amy takes out another photograph. A group of girls; I recognize the uniform. We're in our skirts, blouses, and cardigans, our hair above our shoulders, our neat side partings. Eight of us with Miss Munby, who is holding her hat in her hands. Her brown hair is tightly curled and she wears a dress with a turndown collar. How young we seem. How little we knew of life. Miss Munby is so proud of us. I have always thought of Miss Munby as old and yet here, she looks youthful.

"Nan, are you in this?"

"That's me." I point to myself. I'm on the far left. One of my socks is slightly higher than the other. "And that's Lucy." Lucy stands center right. Her hair, the longest, is in two plaits tied at the ends with ribbons. She smiles, her hands neatly tucked behind her back.

Amy glances at George for his reaction but he stares at the fireplace.

"That's Ann, Linda, Judy, Millie, Cordelia..." I point out those faces I recognize.

"You can keep that if you like," George is saying. "I shouldn't think I'll have much use for it."

Amy slips the photograph into her rucksack, thanking George, then reaches for something else: a small handheld mirror with a pink flower design at the edges. She gives it to me and I look into it as Lucy must have done many times, expecting to see Lucy there, or perhaps a younger me, the me from the photograph, but the woman who looks back at me is old and wrinkled. I hardly recognize her. I blink and the eyes in the mirror blink back. Reaching a hand to my face, I touch my cheek; my skin feels smooth and soft despite the wrinkles.

Amy is holding a Coty powder box. The box is a faded orange, decorated with powder puffs of cream and gold. I can see Lucy on the beach, dipping her powder puff into the Coty box; she sweeps the powder expertly over my nose and cheekbones. *There you are, Edie. Beautiful, just beautiful.* It's a warm and sunny afternoon, and yet I am worried for Lucy. My mouth is dry, my throat tight. I brush the sand from my feet. *Max likes to know where I am.*

"Wow. They don't make them like this anymore," Amy exclaims.

George shrugs. "They're all my sister's things. My mother kept her room the same for years. She was reluctant to throw anything away." He's staring at the fireplace again. "I think my mother always expected her to walk through the door. For a while, after she first disappeared, we'd find portions of dinner saved in the oven, just in case. My father had to throw the food away when my mother wasn't looking. My mother bought her a birthday card for years."

Amy has put the Coty powder back and is looking at something else. I lean over. She's holding two train tickets in a faded pink: *British Railways, Single 2nd, Ludthorpe to London.*

"Ah, yes, the tickets," George says sadly.

"Did she take a trip to London?" Amy asks. "Keep them as a memento, perhaps?"

I study the two tickets. "They're not punched."

George nods. "That's what my father said, and the police. It looks like they were bought but never used. They gave my mother great hope though, as you can imagine." I take the tickets from Amy, rubbing the smooth card between my fingers. "She thought Lucy might have gone to London..."

"But why would Lucy leave these tickets behind if she was planning to use them?" Amy asks.

George rubs his eyes. "Of course, we came up with all sorts of theories. She might have left in a rush, had to buy more. She changed her mind and went somewhere else..."

"And why two tickets?" Amy muses, peering inside the box again.

George wipes his glasses. "My mother had the idea Lucy had gone to London in her head for years. It was as if she knew something, something more than the tickets, something we didn't. Once a month or so she'd book herself into a hotel in London for a couple of nights and go about walking and inquiring, searching for Lucy."

Amy places a piece of folded paper in my hand. The paper is old and foxed and deeply creased. It's a note written in a black fountain pen; there is a splash of ink in the top right corner. It isn't dated.

Dear Lucy,

I've hardly seen you since we went to the pictures, and that was last month now. I know you are busy with your studies, my darling, but that will all be over soon. I can't help thinking you've been avoiding me. Was it what I said? I know it must seem like it's all happening so fast but you see, I simply can't wait to make you mine and I want the world to know how I feel about you. We'd have a splendid wedding, and while I'm away I'll be able to think of it and of coming home to you to begin our life together. Don't avoid me, darling. The sun doesn't shine when I don't have you, and I'll do whatever it takes to make you forever my girl.

Love always
Rupert

"Hm." Amy is peering over my shoulder. "Sounds a bit sinister, doesn't it? I'll do whatever it takes..."

George shrugs. "Or perhaps just the outpourings of a heartsick teenage boy."

I put the letter back in the box. "Is that what you think, George?"

"I don't know," he says, wearily. "All I know is that Rupert Mayhew was questioned. The police had the letter for a while until my mother insisted they return Lucy's possessions to us." He coughs again and his eyes water. "Such a dreadful business," he murmurs, spluttering into his handkerchief.

"This has been really helpful," Amy says, looking from George to me. I know what she's thinking: it's all getting a bit much for George.

Amy begins to put Lucy's things slowly back in the box. I lean over to see what else is in there: a white comb, a few hairpins, a tiny cushion embroidered with Lucy's initials and, at the bottom of the box, a green ribbon. I reach for it, threading it through my fingers. The color has faded but it is still silky.

"Thank you for showing us this, Mr. Theddle. It's been so useful. To see these objects–it really brings the past to life."

Outside, a bird is scuffling around in the bushes below George's window, and I think of the crows laughing at him. Amy drains the last of her tea and I push myself up using the sofa arm, a little unsteady on my feet, and yet, seeing Lucy's things, holding the photograph of us, I feel a new, fierce determination. I must find out what happened to Lucy. I *will*.

"Yes, thank you," I say to George. "This has been most helpful for my granddaughter. You know how curious young people are about the past."

"It's never interested me much," George says, leading us along the hallway. He coughs again, a deep hacking sound. "I learned not to look back. It worked best for me." He shrugs. "But I know you were a good friend to my sister."

I look at George. Was I a good friend to Lucy? Either way, I know what I have to do now: I have to find her.

He undoes the latch and we step outside.

"George," I ask. "Do you think Lucy is still alive?"

Next to me, I feel Amy tense.

But George only shakes his head sadly. "No," he says. "I don't believe she is. She never came to my mother's funeral. I looked for her, but she wasn't there. If she was still alive, she'd have come."

24

1951

It's six o'clock in the evening, and I'm sitting at the kitchen table with my mother and Reg, trying to eat the tea my mother has cooked—pork chops and peas—even though I don't feel hungry. My mother and Reg have their dinner in the middle of the day, so we always have a light tea. Reg, like many men, expects his dinner on the table at a certain time, unless he's on the road; then my mother makes him a sandwich or gives him a slice of leftover pie to take with him.

It's a warm evening, and Reg has the sleeves of his shirt rolled up above his elbows. The kitchen door is open, and a fly buzzes lazily around the stove as I pick at my dinner. The pork chops are rather small, and I expect they came from Reg. I don't know how he gets away with it; I've seen him setting off for the pub, carrying small packages I know to contain various pieces of mystery meat. He's stealing them, I'm sure he is. I've even seen him doing it, bringing meat into the kitchen, slicing off thin strips or small cubes, then rewrapping his packages as if they've never been opened.

I'm feeling thoroughly miserable; Lucy hasn't spoken to me for almost a week, not since she came over for her fortune and we had the argument about Mr. Wheaton on the doorstep. She wasn't at the postbox the following morning. I saw her but she cycled by without saying a word. She's ignored me at school too, spending lunch break in the music room practicing her violin, or revising in the library. When I think of the coldness in her eyes: *I only started walking to school with you because you saw me that time with Max*, I just want to curl up into a ball and disappear. I shouldn't have been so foolish—of course Lucy wouldn't have wanted to be friends with me, and yet I still can't believe Lucy really meant what she said. There must be a way to put things right.

I think of Miss Munby: *You're a bright girl, Edie.* Could I really stay on at school, train to become a teacher? It's what I'm clinging onto. I'd see Lucy then. Perhaps, after a time, we could begin to rebuild our friendship. Surely she'd have to speak to me if we were both in the sixth form together.

I decide to broach the subject. My mother might not object to me staying on at school if she knows Lucy will be there, and if she realizes what the extra qualifications could give me.

"Miss Munby thinks I should stay on at school," I say. "She says I should come back in September."

Reg is taking a slurp of tea. He puts the mug down on the table. "What, stay at school for another two years?"

"Yes."

"Waste of time. What do you want to stay at school for when you can go to work? You expect us to feed and clothe you for another two years, do you? Can't you see we're struggling, girl? Can't you see your mother could do with the extra wage coming in?"

I look to my mother, who studies the tablecloth, avoiding my eye.

"But Lucy will be there. And I might be able to earn more. Eventually. If I pass the new exams, get my certificates–"

"Certificates!" Reg leans forward on his elbows. "Worthless. All of it." He waves his fork at me. "When you grow up you'll learn that fancy qualifications and fancy friends don't count for much in the real world. Hard work and common sense. That's what gets the likes of us a job. Not bleedin' certificates. Not that you'll be in a job long. Hopefully some gullible chap will come and take you off our hands soon." He chuckles. "Anyway, I've been giving it some thought. We both have, haven't we, Nancy?"

My mother swallows, puts her knife and fork down. She won't defend me. She is on Reg's side. Of course she is.

"We have been giving it some thought," she says nervously, pulling a cigarette out of the packet on the table. She glances at the kitchen clock. She's missing *Mrs. Dale's Diary*.

Reg makes a stab at a pea. "I've heard there are jobs going at the undergarment factory."

"The undergarment factory?"

"It's plenty good enough for most of the young girls around here. I don't know why it shouldn't be good enough for you."

There's a lump in my throat and I don't know how to reply. I turn to my mother, but she looks pained. She watches Reg give up with his fork and scoop the rest of his peas up with a spoon. She's waiting for him to finish so she can light her cigarette. Not that

Reg would mind, but my mother wouldn't think it proper. I can tell she doesn't like Reg scooping his peas in that way. I believe she thought, when she first married Reg, that she could train him, improve him. It is not turning out to be the case.

Reg fixes me with his gaze. "Listen here. We're giving you a chance, don't you see? Working in the factory, helping us out with the family business in the evenings—it's an opportunity for you to make something of yourself in the world, the *real* world, not a world that doesn't belong to you. Because let me tell you now, you won't last five minutes in those fancy colleges with those Lucy Theddle types. You'd never fit in."

My mother swats half-heartedly at the fly as it circles the kitchen table. "But you mustn't forget *who we are*, Reg. Perhaps Edie could—"

Reg bangs his fist on the table, causing us to jump.

"It's about time you *both* got over your airs and graces. We've all got to make money, one way or another. We can't be gallivanting about at garden parties and beaches and avoiding a hard day's work."

After a moment, my mother speaks. "Reg is right, Edie," she says quietly. "The factory will suit you very well. You might at least like to inquire."

I stare at my cold, inedible pork chop, my neck bent forward. I told my mother the pork chops were too green but she insisted they'd be fine if she gave them extra time. I think of myself, clocking in each morning at the factory, spending all day loading bobbins onto a buttonhole machine; the whir of a hundred other machines, girls with their hair in scarves shouting to each other across the noise, traipsing home with sore feet and sore fingers, handing my meager wage packet over to Reg.

I want to tell them both they're wrong, that Miss Munby thinks I have a different kind of chance. That I can make something else of my life. But deep down I also know they're right. I am not like Lucy, despite what my mother tells me about our family history. That's all in the past, even if my mother can't accept it. And perhaps, if my ancestors couldn't hold onto what they had, then they deserved to lose it.

Reg wipes his mouth on a tea towel and pushes his knife and fork together on his plate, and my mother reaches for her matches, finally able to light her cigarette.

My life has been decided, mapped out. How stupid I was, thinking there could be something else.

Reg is rolling a newspaper. He slams it against the wall, squashing the fly, and my mother looks at the mark on the wall with distaste. The doorbell rings and she pushes her chair back with a sigh. "I hope it isn't that ex-serviceman with the dishcloths again. I thought they said this sort of thing wouldn't happen this time round."

"Oh, they don't give a jot, do they, that lot up there." Reg slides a packet of Woodbines from his shirt pocket. "Churchill would have looked after them, that's for sure."

"I'll answer the door," I say, desperate to get away.

I quickly leave the table and dash across the kitchen, being careful to step around the cast-iron rabbit. In the hallway I open the door to find Mrs. Cartwright on the doorstep wearing corduroy trousers.

"Hello, Mrs. Cartwright," I say, glumly. "They're in the kitchen."

She smiles. "Cheer up, Edie. It's you I came for. There's a telephone call for you."

I blink, wondering why anyone would call me on the telephone.

"It's Lucy Theddle."

There's a sinking feeling in my stomach. The telephone, in my limited experience, is usually used to convey bad news.

"I'll come right away," I say, stepping out and closing the door quietly behind me. I can just imagine Reg's reaction. *Taking telephone calls now, are you? Fancy as that, eh?*

Mrs. Cartwright's telephone sits on a table in the hallway. She bustles off to the kitchen and I lift the heavy receiver to my ear. I'm not quite sure what to say when the call has already been picked up by Mrs. Cartwright, who no doubt answered in the proper way.

"Hello?" I say, tentatively.

"Edie, it's Lucy. I'm sorry to call here. I know you don't have a telephone, but then I remembered Mrs. Cartwright does and thought she wouldn't mind."

I fumble with the telephone cord. "Oh, no, it's fine to call here," I say, not really sure if it is or not but expecting Lucy to know about such things. From the kitchen, I can hear the wireless, a clattering of saucepans. Mrs. Cartwright is humming along to "Pennies From Heaven." Bing Crosby's voice, as smooth as honey, floats into the hallway and I press the receiver closer to my ear.

"I wanted to say, I'm sorry for walking off like that last week, for not speaking to you in school, but especially for what I said."

I say nothing. I still feel hurt and betrayed, and I don't know what to make of her apology, if I will be able to accept it, not when she never even wanted to be my friend.

"I know you were only trying to look out for me, and I want to apologize for the things I said. They weren't true, and I didn't mean them. I've been feeling out of sorts recently, and I think I was a little disappointed about what your mother told me about my fortune. I shouldn't have taken it out on you. It wasn't fair."

"What you said–about only wanting to be my friend because I saw you–"

"There may have been some truth in that, Edie. But only at first. Then I realized how interesting you are, how thoughtful and kind. I felt I could trust you. I *wanted* to be your friend."

"Really?" I can feel my resolve softening. "I shouldn't have said what I did either," I say, humbly. "I shouldn't have got involved."

"Yes, you should," she answers quickly. "And you're right." She sighs heavily. "I know you're right." She lowers her voice and I can just imagine her in the hallway of The Gables: fresh flowers next to the telephone. An umbrella stand, a Persian rug with gray tassels, a stained glass window. "I am going to *have* to break it off with you-know-who."

I think she should, but I don't say anything. I tried to get involved and I almost lost Lucy. I won't make the same mistake again.

"But that isn't the only reason I'm calling," she says. "I need to tell you about what happened yesterday. It's Max's wife. She found one of my ribbons in Max's car. On the back seat. Apparently, she went berserk."

I let out a small gasp. "What did Mr. Wheaton say?"

"He said he'd given a girl a lift to school. That's all."

"Did he say which girl?"

"Well, yes. You."

I almost drop the phone.

"He had to think of something, Edie. I suppose when he said your name he knew that if June were ever to see you, she would think..."

She would think *there is no way my husband would be having an affair with that girl. That girl is awkward and shy and not a bit pretty.*

My lip trembles.

"I knew you'd be a good sport about it, Edie. I told Max as much. That we could trust you."

"You told him I know?"

Lucy hesitates. "Well, not exactly. He wouldn't be happy about *that.* I just said you were a good friend to me and wouldn't ask questions when I told you he'd said it was your ribbon and not mine."

I wrap my free hand around my stomach, trying to take all of this in. "But did she believe him? That the ribbon belonged to a girl at school, to me?"

"I don't think she had any choice." There is a pause and then: "Edie, I'm sorry, I'd better go."

I picture her, glancing toward the stairs, the sound of footsteps.

"Will we be able to walk to school together this week?"

Lucy hesitates. "I don't think it's a good idea. In case Max sees me."

My chest feels heavy. I need to get her away from Mr. Wheaton.

"Are you still coming over for the séance tomorrow?" I ask. "You wanted to come..."

"Of course," she replies cheerfully. "I'm looking forward to it."

After I've hung up the receiver, I find Mrs. Cartwright in the kitchen drying her toast rack. I wonder why she bothers with a rack when it's just her. For some reason I think of how she took in a small boy during the war and was sad to see him go home. I didn't like the boy much, no one could understand his accent and he used to dig up worms and dangle them in front of people's faces, but I wonder, now, if Mrs. Cartwright still misses him. I also wonder if she knows the children always run past her house, never lingering, because of her privy being haunted.

"Is everything all right, dear?"

"Oh, yes. Lucy just wanted to make an arrangement with me."

"The telephone is very useful for making arrangements," she says thoughtfully. "I'm not sure what I ever did without it."

25

2018

Saturday. Twenty past four, my kitchen clock tells me. I don't know where the time goes. I sleep in late these days, have a little nap in the afternoon. Sometimes I wake in the evening to find I'm in my chair in the living room. A whole hour gone. I never used to sleep so much. I didn't have the time. Even after I retired, I was always busy driving off somewhere: the shops, the garden center, my keep-fit class, the cinema. And of course, I was looking after Amy then. I'd pick her up from school and she'd spend a few hours with me, have her tea. It meant Suzanne could go to work. I think that's partly why they moved back to Ludthorpe when Amy was three; they knew I'd love to see more of my only granddaughter, that I'd be happy to help.

It's the third Saturday in November according to my calendar—I've got a picture of Peru. It's almost a whole week since we went to see George. I've written in today's square: *Ask Amy about Rupert*. I want to know where Rupert is now. I want to look him in the eye and decide for myself if I think he had anything to do with Lucy's disappearance. I think of his note: *I'll do whatever it takes.*

I'll go into town to see Amy. She'll be finishing her shift soon. I can't sit around here all day turning it over in my mind.

I slip on my coat and shoes and then I'm out in the late-autumn afternoon. The pavements glisten from an earlier rain. I turn down Willow Avenue, avoiding Sycamore Street as I always do. I use the new zebra crossing and walk along the path by the green, passing the war memorial. The plane tree leaves have fallen now, creating a carpet of brown and yellow.

Then it happens; the fogginess descends.

One minute I know where I am and where I'm going. Now, I don't know anything. I stop and take a few deep breaths. I need to keep breathing, keep moving. It always returns to me—where I am, what I'm doing, I just need to be patient, wait for the fog to clear. The panic rises in my throat and my neck feels hot and prickly. The more I fight it, the more the panic takes over.

Lucy.

The name pops into my mind.

I mustn't let Lucy down. But where is she?

And where am I?

Nothing looks familiar. A busy street. Cars passing. People with shopping bags. A woman talking into a mobile telephone. A poodle on a pink lead. No one is looking at me. No one seems to know me. I look for some sign, something to let me know where I am. My pulse is racing; the blankness is terrifying.

I find myself outside a coffee shop. It looks warm, inviting. There are cakes in the window on an old-fashioned tiered stand, fairy lights, some kind of fake snow that looks like confetti. I can feel it in my mouth, the papery taste, before I spit it out. Only when I look down I'm no longer wearing my blue voile dress, and I can't hear wedding bells, only music coming from inside the shop. The sign in the window says THE TEA TREE.

I flop into an available chair at a table for two, glad to be away from the busy street. I can hear the clinking of teacups, the whirring of a coffee machine, chatter. The café is playing a song by The Beach Boys. I can't remember the name of the song, but the melody and some of the words are familiar. It is something comforting to hang onto.

A young girl behind the counter spots me. She's wearing an apron and a pair of those black basketball shoes young people like to wear. Her dark hair is up in a bun; a tiny silver stud in her nose catches the light as she moves. She's heading over, pulling a notepad out of her apron. She pauses when she realizes how heavily I'm breathing.

"Um, excuse me, are you okay? Do you need some help?"

I glance around. No one is looking at me. There doesn't appear to be anyone here I know, anyone I'm supposed to be meeting. "I've lost my way," I tell her. My voice sounds small and shaky and I cringe at the sound of it, sliding down into my chair, my neck and ears hot. I don't want to be a burden to anyone, and I don't know how to explain about the fog, that if I just sit here for a minute it's bound to lift.

The girl tilts her head, still holding onto her notepad and pen. "Where were you trying to get to?" she asks kindly.

I feel so stupid. *Come on*, I tell my brain. *Give me something. Something other than The Beach Boys.* "I'm looking for Lucy."

The girl glances around. "There's no one here called Lucy. No one who works here, anyway..." She stops and stares at me. "Wait. You're Amy's nan, aren't you? I came over once after school. You made us toast."

"Did I?"

The girl nods.

"I'm afraid I'm in a bit of a muddle. I'm not quite sure how to get home."

She tucks her notepad back into her apron. "Perhaps I should go and fetch Amy for you? She's only down the road. We got the jobs at the same time. I'm glad I'm here and not at Exquisite. I'm not one for fashion, really. I prefer coffee. Anyway..." The girl waves her hand in the direction of the street. "Maybe I should tell her you're here? If you're not feeling well?"

The sound of the coffee machine, the chatter, and the clinking teacups, The Beach Boys, are all too loud. Colors swirl in front of my eyes, making me feel unsteady.

"I think I should get her," the girl says, peering down at me. "Just wait here for a sec. I'll ask Seb to make you a cuppa. I'm Ella, by the way."

She rushes over to the counter where a tall boy with dark floppy hair is busy arranging a mug and a slice of cake on a tray. She whispers something in his ear. He glances at me, then nods and I look away, embarrassed.

The girl leaves the tea shop without even putting a coat on. I stare out of the window. I don't remember it ever happening as bad as this before. I just need a moment, I tell myself. Everything will be fine in just a moment. I have to wait it out, like a visit to the dentist.

A cup of tea arrives in front of me. The boy has placed one of those little wrapped biscuits on the side of the saucer.

"On the house," he says, smiling.

I put as much milk in as I can without it spilling over, my hand shaking. Out of the tea room window, I watch a young woman in a brown jacket pushing a buggy. Then the door opens and a girl with wavy hair steps in. She's wearing a flowery dress with a long cardigan and chunky boots; she's got lots of rings on her fingers.

She rushes toward me.

"Lucy?"

The girl stops, blinking rapidly. I can see I've surprised her. "No," she says softly, pulling up a chair. She sits down and takes hold of both my hands. "Nan, it's Amy."

For a moment, I don't know her. Then I do. Of course I do.

My eyes fill with tears, my chin trembles. "Oh, Amy," I say. "I didn't know you."

"It's okay, Nan," Amy says, smiling at me, trying not to show her disappointment, her sadness. "It was just for a moment. You know now, don't you?" She bites her lip.

I nod, rummaging in my bag for a tissue. I find one and dab at my eyes.

"I got in a muddle and I ended up here."

"How about we get you home?" Amy puts a hand on my arm.

"Isn't there somewhere you should be? I don't want to be a burden..."

Amy shakes her head. "Don't be silly. It's fine. My shift's nearly over. And Sheila–she's very understanding. She's got a dad with–Well, she's got a dad who gets in a muddle sometimes."

I stand, gathering up my bag, and Amy helps me with my coat.

"Can we walk through the park?" I ask as she holds the door for me. Amy will leave when we get home. I don't want her to go. I want her to stay with me a little while longer.

"Sure. I wouldn't mind the fresh air. I've been running backward and forward from the fitting room to the shop floor all day. Or else I've been stuck in the cupboard–Sheila calls it *the stockroom*–hanging the new knitwear." Amy chuckles, then gives me her arm. I take it gratefully: it feels steady, reassuring. We walk slowly along the road and enter the park.

"Can we cross the bridge?" I ask.

"Of course."

We stand on the bridge and I peer over the edge. The water is clear but I can't see any fish.

"We used to play Poohsticks on this bridge, Nan. Do you remember?"

I do. I can see Amy running from one side to the other in her little pink coat. We used to give her the best sticks.

"I went for tests, didn't I?" I ask. "Tests about my brain."

Amy grips the side of the bridge. "Yes," she says quietly. "Did you forget?"

I look down again at the trickling water. The air is filled with the scent of wet leaves and woodsmoke. "How long has it been?" I ask her. "Since I went for the tests?"

She glances uncertainly at me. "About six months. But you'll have to ask Dad if you want the exact date."

I shake my head. "I just wondered how long it had been. When did they say I should come back?"

"I think they said a year," Amy says softly, pulling her cardigan more tightly around her.

"I failed, didn't I? I failed the tests."

I recall a room with white walls, a woman in a gray blazer who looked at me with sympathy. It was a look I didn't like, a look I wasn't used to. She asked me questions and I didn't get many of them correct. She sprang them on me, I didn't have time to prepare, I hadn't checked my calendar. Then there was a maths question. I've never been very good at maths, just like my mother. I tried to tell her about my mother messing up people's change at the grocer's, but she wasn't listening to me. She just nodded politely and said, "Let's move on then, shall we, Edie?" She reeled off a list of objects and I was supposed to repeat the list back to her. It was just like when Arthur and I used to watch *The Generation Game* on Saturday evenings. We'd try and remember more objects than the contestants did. Only at least on *The Generation Game*, you could see them all whizzing by: the toasters, the footballs, and the teddy bears. How is anyone supposed to remember a list of objects if you can't even see them? The woman had a piece of fruit on her desk, perhaps for her lunch, and she asked me what it was. Such a silly question! Only when she asked, I couldn't think. The word had wandered off. They do that sometimes. It's as if there's a door in my brain marked EXIT and they've all jumped through it, laughing at me over their shoulders as they go. "Orange?" I tried.

"It's a peach," the woman said, giving me that awful sympathetic look again.

How ridiculous to have a peach for lunch—the juice will go everywhere. No wonder I couldn't think what it was.

We leave the bridge and walk toward a bench. I tell Amy I want to sit for a minute; I'm not quite ready to go home. I look at her, wanting to know the answer to my question, wanting to know if I failed, but I can see she's struggling. She twists one of the rings on her fingers.

"They said you're in the early stages of dementia, Nan. That's all I know. They explained to Dad about the different stages, and how we need to keep an eye on you."

Dementia. That was what the woman had said that day. Dementia is what's stealing my time, my memories. It's responsible for the fog, the static, the lost words. I've tried to fight it but I'm losing.

I touch the pendant at my neck, the tiny rose, pressing it between my fingertips. I don't ask Amy anymore. I don't want to upset her. It's enough that she's here with me, that I *know* she's here with me. The fog has lifted, as I knew it would. I'm just having a bad day, that's all. There will be more bad days, but there will be good ones, too. I am fortunate to still have those. I will hold tightly onto each good day.

"Is that why I'm seeing Lucy?" I ask.

"I think so," Amy says slowly. "Changes in perception. Hallucinations. It's your brain misunderstanding the information being received from your senses."

"I thought I was seeing ghosts."

Amy reaches into her bag. "Here, I've got something for you."

She gives me the photograph George said we could have, the photograph of all of us with Miss Munby.

"Thank you," I say, slipping it into my pocket. "I forgot all about it." Then I remember something else. "I was going to ask you about Rupert. It's on my calendar. Are we going to visit him, like we did Constable Diprose, and George? Maybe he'll be able to tell us something."

Amy hesitates. "I did manage to find out about Rupert. It wasn't too difficult because of his father owning the factory, although I had to do a bit of digging." She swallows. "I'm sorry, Nan. Rupert was called up for national service in October 1951. He completed a few months of training, then he was sent straight to Suez. He was killed by a sniper in January 1952."

I stare down at my hands. "If he had anything to do with Lucy's disappearance, we'll never know, will we?"

"I don't think so, no."

I feel a sudden sense of despair. It was all such a long time ago. Everyone has gone. Time is running out. I can no longer pretend this isn't happening to me, that the fog isn't spreading, curling itself into every corner of my mind. Right now, I can find clear patches, and sometimes, if I'm lucky, whole rooms of lucidity. But it won't always be the case. Before long I'll be fumbling about in the dark, unable to see my hand in front of my face. By then it will be too late to find Lucy.

26

1951

Lucy is on the doorstep; I've been expecting her. She's here for the séance tonight, although she's a little early.

"Edie, can I speak to you for a moment?" she says quietly, glancing anxiously behind me to see if anyone else is there. "Outside?"

"Of course," I say, putting the door on the latch and closing it behind me. We cross to the other side of the road and sit on the wall. Along the road, three children are playing hopscotch. It's teatime, and the air is infused with cooking smells.

Lucy glances around the street, then whispers: "Edie, I'm pregnant."

It takes me a moment to register what she is saying. She must have got it wrong, or I must have misheard her, but when I look at her face I know I heard correctly. I feel slightly dizzy: the houses, the front gardens, the children playing, all swell and recede in front of me. It can't be true, I can't be hearing this. As girls, it is our worst fear, the thing we dread happening before it is supposed to, the reason we know we must wait until our wedding nights.

"Are you sure?" I murmur. "You might be mistaken—"

"I'm not mistaken."

The children down the road begin to sing: *Bluebells, cockleshells...* "Have you been to the doctor?"

"Of course I haven't been to the doctor."

"Then how can you be sure? And how can you be pregnant? I mean, is it even possible?"

She looks up at me and I suddenly realize how frightened she is.

"I'm sure, Edie. I feel exactly like my cousin Lilian did when she was first pregnant—sick and dizzy, and tired all the time. And I missed my monthly. That's never happened."

I want to comfort her but don't know what to say. It is a truly dreadful thing to have happened and I still can't believe it has and that, specifically, it has happened to Lucy.

"Couldn't it be something else? You missing your monthly. Couldn't it be—"

"I know, Edie. I just *know*."

I try to gather my thoughts. The children playing in the street are being called in. I can hear a woman's voice: *Gregory. Hilary. I said now!* "How long have you known?" I ask.

"I've only been sure of it this last week. It's been so awful. I've felt sick with worry. I've hardly been able to eat. Mummy served us chicken and tinned asparagus last night, which was meant to be a treat, but I took one look at the chicken and turned green. I don't want to eat anything but blackberry jam. And I think I've gone into some kind of shock. I simply can't believe this is happening to me, I keep praying for it not to be true, and I've avoided Max completely, I can't even think about him right now. I just don't know what to do. You know it's possible, from just a few times, but you don't really think it's possible."

I scuff my shoe against the brick wall, not knowing what to say, feeling as desperate as Lucy looks. I should have done something sooner, made Lucy see sense, then this would never have happened. "Will you tell Mr. Wheaton?"

She gazes at a point ahead of us and I wonder if she's heard me. The hem of her dress flutters in the breeze and I can see her calves have caught the sun.

"At first I had all these ideas," she says, twisting a button on her cardigan. "Max would leave June, we'd go away together, begin again, start a new life in a new town. We'd live there with the baby in a little house, just the three of us, but then last night when I saw Max... I was going to tell him, but sitting there in the car, listening to him going on about the Americans testing bombs in the ocean and the effect it must be having on marine life, all those dead fish floating about, I realized how stupid I've been, that he'll never leave June."

"You know this because of dead fish?"

"We're too different," Lucy says glumly. "Max is always thinking about what's going on in the world, whereas I'm always thinking about what's going on in *my* world. I know he won't be happy, that he won't throw his arms around me and tell me how pleased he is. He'll be angry. He'll never want to see me again. He won't want anything to do with it."

I can't help thinking she's probably right. "I'm sorry," I say.

"A few weeks ago, he drove past my house and saw me outside by the gate talking to Judy. The next day he kept asking me what I was doing with her and what we were talking about. I told him: her mother works for us. She waits for her mother at ours sometimes. I've known Judy since I was tiny. But he wouldn't have any of it. He told me I should keep away from her, and when I protested, said that would be impossible, he accused *me* of not trusting *him*. I told him I just couldn't take it anymore and he said I didn't appreciate his sacrifices, only I realize now, everything he does has nothing to do with us, it's all about him. We had a terrible row that day, but of course I went back to him. Now, I'm not even sure I want to see him again. It's like waking from a dream, realizing it's actually been a nightmare."

"What are you going to do?"

"I can't have a baby, Edie. I just *can't*," she says desperately. "I'll have to, you know..."

We both consider this.

"But how?"

"I don't know," she says miserably. "But I know there are places you can go, people who can help."

"Do you know where you can go?"

"Of course not. That's the problem. I can hardly start asking around, can I? It's not like I'm looking for a new hairdresser. Imagine if word got back to my father. And I can't risk going to the doctor. They're all in the Rotary club with him."

I don't know what to say to Lucy: it's too much to take in and I need some time to think.

"I was wondering if you might be able to ask your mother," she says, hopefully. "She was so helpful with Hitler, and of course she was right about the eggs."

I give her a blank look.

"The symbol of fertility," she says with a sigh.

"Oh, right..." I rub my eyebrows. "I don't think my mother will be able to help with this," I say diplomatically.

Lucy stares at the pavement. "I know she can't make it magically go away—I'm not stupid—but I thought perhaps she might have an idea. She seems to know about things..." I frown and, seeing my expression, Lucy gives me another desperate look. "Please, Edie. Just ask."

I shake my head. It doesn't sound a good idea to me.

"I did think of Rupert, of course," she says.

I look up. "Rupert? What's he got to do with it?"

"Well, he'd probably marry me."

"Lucy! What, tell him it's his? You couldn't do that! And could it even be possible?"

"Well, no," she says miserably. "But of course, I could make it possible. He's very keen on me... And then if I told him in a few months' time, perhaps the dates wouldn't matter so much. Not if I act quickly."

"I can't believe you're seriously considering this."

"It's not what I want," she says firmly. "I'd be stuck then, wouldn't I? Stuck with Rupert. Stuck in Ludthorpe. And of course I could *never* tell him. But it's an option. If there are no others. Please," she says. "Please ask your mother." She sighs. "We had better go in. She'll be waiting."

"Are you sure you want to attend tonight?" I ask, surprised that she still wants to come. Hearing of Lucy's dilemma, I'd forgotten all about the séance. "You don't have to, you know."

"No, I'd like to. All this worry is dreadful. It will help to take my mind off things, even if it's just for an hour."

We slide off the wall and head numbly inside the house. My thoughts are still racing: Lucy... A baby... There was a girl in school the year before last, two years older than us, who was pregnant. We weren't supposed to know, but of course everyone knew. One day she disappeared and didn't come back until four months later, no longer pregnant. Her mother told everyone she'd been in Switzerland getting fresh air for her asthma. She didn't even have asthma. And when we asked about Switzerland, she couldn't tell us a thing. No one knew what had happened to the baby. Is that what will happen to Lucy? Will her parents send her away? Will she ever come back?

In the hallway, Mother is coming down the stairs.

"Lucy, how lovely to see you. How is Barbara?"

"She's fine, thank you." Lucy attempts a smile.

"I *am* looking forward to our next Housewives' League meeting. I agree with Barbara entirely: the voice of the ordinary housewife *should* be heard. And your mother's mutton recipe was superb."

"I'll be sure to let her know."

My mother ushers Lucy into the dining room just as the doorbell rings; it's Mr. and Mrs. Goy from the fishmonger's.

While my mother is greeting them and showing them to their seats, and the Goys are busy inquiring about the health of Lucy's family, the doorbell rings a third time.

"Get that, will you, Edie?" my mother says.

I open the door and let out a yelp of surprise. "Mr. Wheaton." I take a step back, feeling disorientated, unable to think clearly.

He's standing on the doorstep in the same brown suit he has on in school, only with no tie. Next to him, his wife is wearing a felt hat and red lipstick, her short dark hair perfectly waved and tucked behind one ear. I blink several times as if what I'm seeing can't possibly be real. I know from listening to Lucy that Mr. Wheaton exists outside of the classroom, and yet it has somehow always been hard to fathom; he belongs to the world of chalk and rolling blackboards, of polished wood floors, inkwells, dates, and maps. For a moment, I can't think what they're doing here, then I realize: they must have seen my mother's adverts.

"Hello," Mr. Wheaton says, giving me a curious look.

"Is this number six?" his wife is saying.

I try, desperately, to think of a way to get rid of them, but only nod stupidly. Footsteps behind me. The scent of my mother's perfume. The door opening wider.

"Max. *June*," my mother gushes, stepping in front of me. "Do come in. So lovely you could join us tonight."

In the hallway, June is slipping her jacket off. Mr. Wheaton is so tall, the top of his head brushes against the fake chandelier. "Nice duck," he says, looking at the stuffed mallard. He lifts his gaze. "Edith, isn't it? I take you for history."

"Edie." My heart hammers in my chest. *Mr. Wheaton can't be here. June can't be here. They mustn't see Lucy.*

At the mention of my name, June's eyes flick to me briefly. She gives a small, tight smile, then looks away.

"Well," my mother says, "I don't think we've had a teacher before, a man of *education*. They're often the skeptical type."

Mr. Wheaton's eyes sparkle playfully as he glances at his wife. "June is the open-minded one. I'm just here to keep her company."

June turns to my mother. "My sister is staying with us.

Babysitting. I don't get out much since the baby. We thought we'd give it a try. A little entertainment if nothing else, although I *am* open minded. I'm always telling Max–there's got to be something in it, hasn't there?"

"Well, you'll soon see," my mother says with a small smile. "Make yourselves comfortable in the dining room. We've got a full table tonight!"

I follow them into the next room where Lucy is sitting with Mr. and Mrs. Goy, her expression frozen; she must have heard Mr. Wheaton's voice in the hallway. Mr. Wheaton looks as surprised to see Lucy as she does to see him.

He clears his throat. "And Lucy, too."

"Hello," Lucy says weakly, hardly able to look at him.

Mr. Wheaton has no choice but to sit down. However mortified I feel, I know it must be worse for Lucy. She holds my gaze for a moment and I try to communicate to her that I understand how awful this is, that I had no idea Mr. Wheaton would be here, that I am so sorry, that I don't know what to do.

"Would anyone like a small drop of sherry before we begin?" my mother is saying. "I find it helps to relax the mind and open the senses."

There are nods all around the table.

"Not that I often take a drink myself." She laughs. "Just a tiny drop every now and then." She turns to me. "Fetch the bottle and glasses, Edie. The best ones," she adds, leaning in close to my ear.

In the kitchen, I take a few deep breaths, then begin to arrange the glasses on a tray, my mind spinning. Lucy is here. Mr. Wheaton is here. June is here. Lucy is pregnant. This final thought sends a cold shiver through me and I turn from the drinks cupboard, the sherry bottle in my hand. There's someone there. A slap across my face. A ringing in my ears. I put my hand to my hot cheek, stumbling backward into the cupboard, almost dropping the bottle.

It's June, her eyes cold and hard. "My husband gets bored with silly little girls very quickly. Do you understand?"

I stare at her, my limbs frozen, my hand still at my burning cheek.

"And don't for a second imagine you're the first." She gives a shrill little laugh. "I wouldn't flatter yourself about *that*." Her face is close to mine, her eyes narrowed. "You are a surprise, though. Not his usual type. Gullible. I suppose that's it."

I can hear my heartbeat thrashing in my ears. She takes hold of my chin and lifts it, her fingers gripping me tightly. Her nostrils are flared and I can see the powder settled into the tiny creases in her skin. There is a smell of Pond's cold cream.

What is she talking about? What's happening? Then I remember. The ribbon. She found it in Mr. Wheaton's car. Lucy said it was mine.

"But it's all going to stop now, isn't it?"

Her flinty eyes bore into mine. My shoulders tremble and all I can do is nod.

"Good."

She releases my chin, forcing my head back, then calmly takes the sherry bottle from me and puts it on the tray.

"I'm glad we understand each other, Edie. Now, let's get this little charade over with, shall we?"

I watch her striding along the hallway. My legs are like jelly; I feel slightly faint.

I stumble into the dining room with the tray, where my mother pours the sherry out carefully. The candles flicker on the table and I slip into my seat, between Lucy and Mr. Goy, my eyes down. I can't look at June, or Mr. Wheaton, and I don't know how to help Lucy. For once, I am grateful for the dim light; my cheek burns from the slap, and I feel both horror and shame, although I'm not sure what I am ashamed of.

"Lovely candles," Mrs. Goy is saying.

"They're from Rome," My mother replies, proudly. "Blessed."

"Funny," Mr. Wheaton says, peering at them. "I've seen some just like them in Woolworths." He takes a sip of sherry, then looks at me over his glass and smiles but I look away, my heartbeat still racing. He doesn't know his wife just slapped me. He doesn't know Lucy is pregnant. I close my eyes, trying to steady my breathing. When I open them Mr. Wheaton is whispering something to his wife. On his other side, Lucy sits, trapped. Mr. Wheaton looks smug and satisfied, sitting there between his wife and Lucy, and despite feeling sick and wobbly, I have the urge to hit him.

At the top of the table, my mother takes her seat. She's wearing a long purple silk dress and her flapper-style headband adorned with new feathers. "Welcome," she says, "to all those here at the table this evening, and to all those who may wish to join us from the other side."

Mr. Wheaton looks amused.

"Now," my mother says, placing her hands elaborately on the table, "we will begin."

The rest of us mimic her, our hands flat on the table, palms down. June's wedding ring glints in the candlelight and Mr. Wheaton takes her hand in his as if it's the most natural thing in the world, then reaches for Lucy's. I think of that same hand creeping up Lucy's blouse, unfastening her underwear, signing them into a hotel register. *I know about you. I know what you've done to Lucy. Lucy is too good for you.*

My mother clears her throat. "There is often, when a soul departs this world, so much left unsaid, but tonight we will have the rare opportunity to make contact with those passed."

I can see Mrs. Goy is nodding. I feel an ache at the back of my throat and I swallow, trying to shift it. I long for time to speed up, for this to all be over. When I look at Mr. Wheaton sitting opposite me, at his serene face, my jaw clenches.

I join hands with my mother and Mr. Goy, whose hands are thick and meaty. I try not to think of all the fish guts he must have handled. My mother begins to breathe heavily, her eyes closed. My shoulders curl forward and I lower my chin as she rolls her head around, loosening her neck, searching for the spirits. She lets out a small moan as the breeze lifts the curtains at the window, causing them to billow into the room.

"Ah, my spirit guide has joined us."

June raises an eyebrow and I can see a small smile playing at the corners of Mr. Wheaton's lips. I glance at my mother. *They don't believe in you. They know you're a fake. You're embarrassing yourself and you don't even realize.*

"Who is the spirit guide?" Mrs. Goy whispers.

"A native," my mother replies.

"A native of where?" Mr. Wheaton asks, his voice full of skepticism.

"From the other side," my mother replies, impatiently. "A Native American man. Over six foot tall. Bare to the waist. He wears a loincloth, a black headband. A fine specimen of manhood," she adds.

Mrs. Goy looks hopefully around the room as June opens her eyes and stares at me. I can see the whites of her eyes glinting fiercely in the dark. I'm hot and my skin feels too tight. *Let her think it's me, I don't care.*

"He is trying to show me something, something about someone here tonight." She lifts her chin. "Ah, yes. A new moon, a white dove. Beginnings. Arrivals. Someone here will soon enter into a new phase of life."

Lucy grips my hand in surprise, and I know what she's thinking: Mother is hearing of her pregnancy. I open my eyes and Lucy glances at me, her face pale and fearful.

"Now he tells me there is someone who wishes to make contact with us tonight," Mother continues.

"Who's there?" Mr. Goy asks. "Who is it, Nancy?"

"A young man," she breathes.

Mrs. Goy looks up hopefully and I feel a pang in my chest, a dull ache that spreads outwards. *No*, I think. *Not this. You don't need to do this.*

"An airman in uniform," my mother continues. "I can see him clearly."

Mr. Goy's hand is growing warm in mine; with his other I can see he's tightly squeezing his wife's.

"He tells me his name is Billy."

I breathe in sharply.

I want to get up, to leave the table, to tell her I will have no part in this, announce that she's a fraud, that she embellishes her gifts, spare Mrs. Goy. And yet I can't. I don't want to give June and Mr. Wheaton the satisfaction. Perhaps I am no better than my mother. I am her flesh and blood, after all.

I look to Lucy and can see what torture this is for her, holding Mr. Wheaton's hand, being in the same room as his wife, knowing that he won't want anything to do with her when he finds out what his actions have led to.

Mrs. Goy lets out a small sob. "My Billy."

"He tells me he was shot down over the Dutch coast," my mother continues, gaining confidence. "It happened quickly. The fuel tank was hit. I can see flames." She fans her face with her hand dramatically. "It's terribly hot, oh, so terribly hot... He isn't in any pain."

Mr. Wheaton lets go of June's hand and tugs at his shirt collar, breaking the circle.

Mr. Goy is gripping my fingers so hard I wonder if he'll crush a bone. He has his head bowed and his shoulders are shaking. I look away, staring at the tablecloth, unused to such displays of emotion, especially from men. June is sitting perfectly still.

"He misses you both, and Flossie too," my mother tells Mr. and Mrs. Goy. "But he says he's happy. At peace."

Mrs. Goy's breath catches in her throat. I look up at her and, in the candlelight, I can see her face is wet with tears. "Tell him we love him," she whispers.

"He knows," my mother replies. "He doesn't want you to worry about him. He's smiling, telling you both to enjoy life, to take care of yourselves, to be at peace, as he is." My mother opens her eyes, her gaze sweeping around the table, satisfied with her performance. "He's going now," she says, closing her eyes. "We thank you, Billy, for your sacrifice."

Mrs. Goy is crying quietly but Mr. Goy's shoulders grow still and he slowly reaches into his pocket for a handkerchief. I try to keep my eyes on the table. I still feel I should not be here, should not be witnessing this private grief. Mr. Wheaton looks embarrassed and I hate him for it. Why should he be sympathetic to someone else's suffering when he won't feel any sympathy for Lucy? They all think he's the perfect husband, the perfect teacher, a steady pillar of our community, but I know the truth. I hate him for what he's done to Lucy and I make a silent vow to help her any way I can.

27

2018

"You've stolen my photograph."

Josie is in the kitchen using the dirt-sucking thing. She turns it off. "Sorry, Edie, what did you say?"

"You've stolen my photograph."

She sighs, unplugging and winding the cord in. "I haven't stolen anything, Edie."

"Yes, you have. You don't want me to have it. You don't want me to help her because you'll get into trouble. But I *have* to help her. It's the least I can do. Soon it'll be too late."

Josie puts the kettle down. "Edie, I don't know what you're talking about. What photograph?"

"The photograph of Lucy. Someone's stolen it."

Josie undoes her apron, then slides it off over her head. "I haven't taken anything. And I don't like being accused. But if you calm down, I'll help you look for what you've lost. How does that sound?"

I nod, keeping an eye on her as she hangs the apron on the back of the door.

"What does it look like, Edie?"

"It's the school photograph of Lucy, me, the girls, and Miss Munby."

"And where did you say you last had it?"

"I put it under the *Radio Times*."

In the living room, we search the coffee table, even though I've already been through everything. Josie gets down on her hands and knees and looks underneath. Then she checks down the back of the sofa. She finds half a packet of Polos (Daniel's), a Co-op receipt, and ten pence, but not the photograph.

"Perhaps you left it upstairs?"

"I don't think so."

But Josie insists we check, so we go upstairs and into my bedroom and there is the photograph on my bedside table next to my reading lamp and a pair of my glasses.

Josie reaches for the photograph and holds it up. "Is this it?"

I snatch it from her and hug it close to my chest, sitting down on the edge of my bed, touching the black-and-white faces with my fingertips.

"You must have taken it to bed with you. You forgot you'd moved it, that's all."

"I suppose so," I say, still clutching it tightly.

Josie sits next to me on the bed. "It must mean something to you, Edie. Can I see?" She peers at it. "Is that you?" she gestures to the me in the photograph, and I nod. "You haven't changed a bit. I'd recognize you anywhere."

I move my finger over the faces of the girls and Miss Munby. "And that's Lucy," I say, pointing her out.

"Your old school friend?"

"I'd forgotten about her. But now I'm going to find her."

Josie hesitates then smiles. "There's so much we forget, isn't there?"

"I forget a lot more now," I say, and then we both laugh.

Josie pats me on the shoulder. "I will miss you, Edie."

"Because I'm going to Devon?"

Josie smiles. "Yes, because you're going to Devon."

"Aren't you coming with me?"

She shakes her head sadly. "I'm afraid not. I've got Ocean, remember? I've got to stay here. My life is here, and my other jobs. There are people who need me."

I look down at the photograph in my hands. People are always going away. Now it's my turn. I'm moving far away where I won't know anyone and everything will be unfamiliar. I did it once before, I remember. I did it because Miss Munby and Lucy thought I could. Only this time I won't be coming back.

"It'll be fun, choosing things for your new place. Daniel says it's lovely. Your bedroom has a view of the fields. There are sheep. And the neighbors have horses, apparently."

"Maybe I could learn to ride a horse?" I ask hopefully. "My mother could ride, but I never learned."

Josie stares at me and then, after a moment, we both start laughing. I look down at my unsteady legs, my feet tucked into my slippers. I can hardly get into the bath nowadays, let alone onto a horse. Still, for just a moment, for some reason, it seems entirely possible.

"I can just see you," Josie says, grinning at me, "galloping across the meadows. The wind in your hair."

"Me too."

"Come on, Edie." She holds out her hand, helping me to my feet. "How about I make you a cup of tea before I go?"

After Josie has left, I sit in my chair, still feeling worried. Wasn't I supposed to be doing something? *Lucy.* That's what I have to do. Find Lucy. There's no time to waste. I'll tear this town apart if I have to. I'll speak to everyone. Lucy must have had other friends. What about the girls at school? I'll speak to them all. It doesn't matter that no one wants to help me anymore. I don't need help, I've always been independent. I'll show them all how sharp I am when I find Lucy.

I realize the doorbell is ringing. Who could it be? I grip the fabric of the chair. A woman will be at the door, a man too. The woman doesn't like me. She thinks I've done something wrong. *My husband gets bored of silly little girls very quickly.* I touch my cheek, recalling a burning sensation. Perhaps if I sit here quietly, she'll go away.

The doorbell rings again.

But what about Lucy? She's in trouble and I must do all I can to help her, even if it means dealing with angry wives with false accusations.

I push myself up, determined not to let Lucy down. In the hallway, I open the door to find a woman on my doorstep, dressed in a smart black suit jacket, matching skirt, and red blouse. She's wearing purple high-heeled shoes. A large camera hangs around her neck.

"Edie?"

"Yes?"

"Kate. Sorry, I'm a few minutes early. Can I come in?"

The woman isn't who I was expecting and I experience a moment of confusion. She smiles and I smile back, relaxing a little. She looks friendly enough. Perhaps she's here to help.

"Of course." I move back to let her pass. I'm supposed to check people's ID cards before I let them in. Daniel gave me a pamphlet about it. It's to make sure I'm not accidentally letting in a burglar or someone trying to sell me a time-share, but I don't believe this woman could be a burglar. She wouldn't be able to run very far in those heels.

The woman wobbles along the hallway so I follow, watching as she peers around the living room door, then steps inside.

"Very nice," she says, nodding.

"Would you like a cup of tea?" I ask.

"Oh, no thank you." She is busy squashing herself into the far-right corner of my living room. Now she's taking a photograph. "I do like these thirties semis. The living rooms are a good size. Three-bedroom, is it?"

I nod.

"It'll be quite nice, really, when it's modernized. But that's what people want, isn't it? To put their own stamp on a place. Of course it'll knock the price down a bit, but you need a quick sale, don't you?"

"A quick sale?"

But she's too busy fiddling with her camera to answer me. "God, I always forget how to work this thing. It's a bit dark in here, what with the nets. You don't know how to adjust the ISO, do you?"

"No," I say. "But you can lift the nets."

"Oh, super. Yes, that would work."

I can hear the sound of the key turning in the lock. Perhaps it's Josie. I don't remember her coming this morning. Maybe she'll be able to tell me why this stranger is taking photographs of my living room.

"Josie?" I call out, unable to remember if she's been today or not.

But it's Daniel. He appears, wearing his work suit and tie. He's still got that funny tag around his neck that lets everyone know he's the teacher. Silly, really. No one's going to mistake a man with a balding head and graying beard for a sixth former.

"Sorry, Mum. I got held up."

"Never mind," I say, cheerfully. "Would *you* like a cup of tea?"

"I'm on my lunch break. Haven't got time. How's it going?"

"Fine," I say. "Although I'm stuck on the crossword."

"Go on then," Daniel says.

"Grow rapidly. Eight letters."

"Hm. Mushroom?"

I look down at the paper in my lap. He's right. "I don't know why I didn't get that one." M-U-S-H-R-O-O-M. I carefully write the letters down.

The woman has finished with her camera. "I'll head upstairs, if that's all right?"

"Of course." Daniel tells the woman. He looks around the room as if he's lost something. "It was good of Josie to give it a bit of a spruce up, wasn't it?"

"Daniel, who is that woman?"

Daniel rubs his neck. "She's the estate agent, Mum. She's

here to take photographs. She's going to put the house on the market. Hopefully today. I told you on Friday she was coming this morning."

"Oh, yes," I say, as if I knew all along. "Am I moving house?"

Daniel draws his breath in, then releases it slowly. "Devon, Mum. We're moving to Devon, remember? Our offer was accepted."

I look at Daniel, bewildered. "Why on earth would I want to move to Devon? And why has no one told me about this?"

Daniel closes his eyes briefly. We can hear the woman moving about upstairs. *Stomp, stomp, stomp.* It's a good thing I remembered to make the bed. At least I think I did. I don't like the thought of her photographing my unmade bed, like that artist. She put her bed in a gallery for the whole world to see. I remember when people thought Picasso was bad enough. *My mother says his paintings make her feel sick*, Lucy told me once, gleefully. *I think he's wonderful. So does Max.*

"Mum, we've talked about–"

"Well, I can't," I snap. "I'm not going to Devon. I'm not going anywhere until I've found Lucy."

"Who's Lucy?"

"Lucy Theddle. She disappeared in 1951 and everyone's looking for her."

Daniel stares at me.

The woman in the heels is making her way down the stairs. "Nearly done. I'll just snap the kitchen and the garden." She clomps past us, camera in hand.

"Mum, I don't know what you're talking about," Daniel whispers. "Do you mean a cat? Did you have a cat?"

"Lucy wasn't a cat! That was Hitler." I can feel a sharpness in my chest, my pulse rate rising. My voice must have been louder than I intended it to be. My fist is clenched and Daniel has taken a step back.

The woman appears again, glancing from me to Daniel. "Um. Does anyone have the keys to the back door?"

"Of course," Daniel says, quickly. He gives me one final look, then follows the woman. I can hear him jangling the keys, opening the back door, the woman's heels tap-tapping across the kitchen linoleum. "Ooh, seventies retro," she exclaims loudly. "So fashionable right now."

I sit down in my chair. Devon! It's ridiculous to think I can go anywhere when Lucy is still missing.

Daniel returns with the dark-haired woman.

"I'll send you the details before it goes live," she's saying, and then something else I don't catch. They walk into the hallway and Daniel opens the front door.

"Do you think you'll get interest?" I hear him say.

"Oh, definitely. These kinds of small semis make excellent starter homes, family homes. A short walk into town, a garden—it'll be snapped up. In fact, I've already got someone in mind. I wouldn't be surprised if it's sold by the weekend."

They step outside and their voices fade. Then Daniel is here again. "I've got to get going, Mum. You haven't had your lunch, you know."

"Haven't I?"

"It's in the kitchen. Josie's left it for you on a plate. A cheese roll. Don't forget."

I tut. Daniel is talking to me like I'm a child. He's the one who forgets his lunch. I'm often running down the road after him with his lunch bag. There is always something more important he's thinking of: the conkers in his pockets, football with his friends.

"You don't forget *your* lunch," I say.

Daniel smiles. "I've already eaten. Pasta from the school canteen. I've got to get off. I'll see you Friday for fish and chips." He leans forward and gives me a peck on the cheek then dashes out of the room.

"See you Friday," I echo as the front door shuts behind him.

I watch from the window as he gets into his car. I've never liked his visits. He brings me sweets and cheese and knockoff meat as if that makes everything okay. He's after my mother. I'm sure he is.

I let the net curtain drop, then wander into the kitchen. Someone has left their lunch on the counter. There's a note next to it that says, *Edie's lunch.* Well, that's nice. I can't remember the last time anyone made anything for me. I can't think who it might have been.

28

1951

I've had a lot to write in my diary recently: Lucy's terrible situation, her idea about marrying Rupert, that awful evening of the séance. Each day has required a storm cloud. I've also been writing down all that's happening here. A strained and frosty atmosphere has lingered in the house the last few days after Reg asked my mother to lend him three pounds. My mother refused and I could hear Reg shouting at her, telling her, *I'm your husband, for Pete's sake, if that still counts for anything*, and that what's hers is his, and doesn't she want him to be happy? Doesn't she trust him when he hears about an opportunity? *We'll lose the house if you carry on like this*, my mother had said. *I don't know why you have to make such a big deal out of it, Nancy. Show me a man who doesn't have a bit of a flutter every now and then.*

Tonight, we've had fish and chips straight from the paper. Once we've finished and Mother is tipping the scraps into the bin, Reg goes out to the privy and I decide now has to be the time to ask. If I'm going to do it, I need to get it over with. I remind myself I'm doing this for Lucy. She believes my mother might be able to help, that Mother might have some idea of what she should do.

I take a deep breath, praying I'm doing the right thing.

"Lucy is pregnant."

My mother turns and stares at me.

"Are you sure? Did she tell you?"

I nod miserably. "She's sure."

My mother considers this. She sits at the table, fumbles for her cigarettes. The first match goes out and she tries again. "Well," she says finally. "Who'd have thought."

"She didn't mean it to happen," I say, feeling I ought to defend Lucy.

"No, I should think not," my mother replies thoughtfully.

The kitchen door bangs. Reg is back sooner than I thought he would be. He looks from me to my mother. "What's this then? Who's died?"

"It's nothing," I say quickly.

Reg glares at me. "I don't like secrets in this house."

"Lucy Theddle is pregnant," my mother says.

I shake my head; my fingers twitching. How could she have told Reg? I glance at her crossly but she won't meet my eye.

There is a moment's silence, then Reg begins to laugh. "Well, that's a turn-up for the books. Lucy Theddle. Pregnant. I'd have thought it far more likely you'd be the one to get yourself in that sort of mess."

My mother flinches but doesn't say anything.

"She's very worried," I say through gritted teeth. "She's...

desperate." I turn to my mother. "She wanted me to ask you if there is anything you might be able to do to help her."

Reg grins at me. "Your mother's a very talented woman, Edie, but there are some things–"

"Yes, I know," I interrupt him. "I told her the same, but she insisted I ask."

"Poor Barbara," my mother mutters.

"Her parents don't know," I say quickly. "And she needs to keep it that way."

Reg reaches for his pipe. "And who's the father then?" he says, a glint in his eye. I can see he's enjoying this, reveling in Lucy's misfortune, in something like this happening to the Theddles.

"I don't know," I lie. "She didn't tell me. And you're not to tell anyone," I say sternly. "She trusts me."

Reg chuckles and sits at the table. "Is she going to marry the father?" He packs tobacco into his pipe.

"She doesn't want to keep it, not if she can...find another solution."

"Oh." My mother considers this. Outside in the garden, a bird trills noisily.

Reg lights his pipe and puts the match out with a flick of his wrist. "If that's what she's after, perhaps we might be able to help after all."

"What do you mean, Reg? I really don't think there's anything *we* can do," my mother says, anxiously.

"I mean that I've heard rumors."

"What, about Lucy?" I ask, panicked.

"Not Lucy. Other girls. There's a medical chap who drinks

in The Bird in Hand. I've heard it said he assists girls in that way. For a fee, of course."

I feel a swell of hope in my chest. I hate having to ask Reg for anything but I haven't got much choice, not if I want to help Lucy. I remember her words: *I wouldn't know where to go.*

"Do you think you could ask him then?"

"I reckon I might just be able to do that," Reg says with a sly smile. "There'd need to be something in it for us, though. Twenty percent ought to do it. On top of his fee."

"You can't do that," I say, horrified.

"I most certainly can. We've got to think of the risk. Getting involved in something like this. It's bleedin' illegal, isn't it?"

I look to my mother, but she shakes her head as if to warn me not to argue.

I sigh and rub my temples with my fingertips. I can't believe I am having to rely on Reg.

"Leave it with me," he says. "I'm sure we can fix her up. And people like the Theddles, people with money, well, their problems have a way of disappearing, don't they? Funny, that. I'll find out what he asks for. I'm sure she'll be able to stump up."

"What about Lucy? The procedure, can it be risky?"

"Don't be daft," Reg says. "He's a professional. Does it all the time from what I've heard."

29

1951

The house is ordinary. Quite nice, really. A large semidetached with a bay window and a porch. I notice a nameplate fixed to the wall: Dr. Pentland, Chiropodist. I feel reassured by the Dr. part.

"Is this it?" Lucy asks.

"Yes, I think so."

Lucy bites her lip but doesn't move and I feel it is down to me to ring the bell. All we know is that Lucy is to see a Dr. Pentland and that no one must know we are here. I've come with Lucy because she couldn't bear to go on her own.

It hadn't taken long for Reg to make the arrangements. He'd come home from The Bird in Hand on Tuesday night to find me in the kitchen, waiting up. "He'll see her," he said. "Thursday. Six o'clock." He thrust a piece of paper at me. "This is the address. You're not to tell anyone a thing about it before or after."

"Thank you," I'd said, hating to be in his debt.

The front door is answered by a tall, slim man with glasses. He glances up and down the street, then ushers us quickly inside. I find myself next to the hallstand, full of coats, hats, and umbrellas. The hallway is papered and family photographs line the walls: two men in uniform, a stern-looking woman in a large Victorian dress. There is a smell of boiled vegetables. From somewhere at the back of the house, I hear a child's cry.

"Does anyone know you're here?" the man asks.

"No," I say for the both of us. "It's only my mother and Reg who know. Reg, who you spoke to–"

"Yes, yes." He looks from me to Lucy. "And which one of you needs assistance?"

He speaks as if we require help lifting heavy shopping or opening a stuck door.

"Me," Lucy says in a small voice.

He nods, then raises an eyebrow in my direction. "It's usually husbands who come along for support." The way he says "husbands" with a slight pause before it makes me wonder if the men who come along are really husbands after all. I imagine frightened women wearing oversized wedding rings like the one Lucy wore when she went away with Mr. Wheaton.

"I'd like Edie to stay," Lucy says softly.

"Very well. If you can follow me, please."

He's a professional, I remind myself. *He knows what he's doing.*

He leads us upstairs and into a small room at the end of the landing and I worry, for just a moment, that he's going to show us into an ordinary bedroom, a child's room perhaps, but the room is clearly a room for patients, which causes me some relief. A doctor's examination couch on wooden legs sits in the middle of the room, covered in a waxy sheet. The shelves are full of glass jars, and the room smells of rubber and polish and leather. The pictures on the walls all show feet, and I suddenly realize, with a sinking heart, that a chiropodist must be a foot doctor. I feel I ought to say something, inquire into this man's qualifications and expertise when it comes to what he is about to do for Lucy. But we are already here; it seems all too late, and besides, Lucy has no other options.

He tells her to lie on the couch, and I find myself staring at a labeled picture of a pair of fleshless feet, the skeleton toes long and gnarled.

"The date of your last period?" he asks Lucy.

"I-I'm not sure," Lucy stutters.

Dr. Pentland sighs and then he is pressing and prodding at Lucy's stomach. "About seven or eight weeks, I should think. You've been a silly girl, haven't you?"

Lucy flinches. "I didn't know," she says, a tremble in her voice.

"And is this the first time you've found yourself in this—situation?"

"Yes, of course," Lucy says, her eyes wide.

"Well, I expect you won't be so careless in the future. Have you told the father?"

"No," Lucy whispers.

"And you're sure he won't do the right thing?"

"I can't have a baby," Lucy says, her eyes filling with tears.

I press my knees together, wishing Lucy didn't have to go through with this, wishing I could make it all go away for her.

"All right, all right." The doctor says hastily. "Well, let's see what we can do then. Do you have the money?"

Lucy reaches for her bag and hands him a stuffed envelope. I wonder how she managed to find so much cash.

The doctor quickly counts what's in the envelope, then tucks it into his pocket. He leaves the room and I am left alone with Lucy. I reach for her hand and give it a squeeze; it feels small and sweaty. "It will all be over in a moment," I say, not knowing if it will be but desperate to offer her some comfort. "He's done this many times before."

Lucy nods but doesn't speak; her gaze is fixed on a spot ahead of her.

The doctor returns with a bowl of water. He is wearing an apron and gloves and has his shirtsleeves rolled up to the elbows. He looks like a butcher.

From his bottom desk drawer, he takes out a pale orange syringe and a small bottle of something, from which he measures several drops into the water. His desk is littered with shoe lasts and foot supports, and I wonder what his foot patients would think if they knew of his other occupation, of what else goes on in this room.

"Do you have a handkerchief?" the doctor is asking Lucy. He is still at his desk and isn't looking at us.

"Yes." Lucy quickly fumbles in her pocket and produces a handkerchief. "Do you need it?"

"It's not for me. It's for you. You'll need to bite down on it."

"Oh."

He turns then, holding the bowl, and seems surprised to see me there. "You'd better wait outside," he tells me.

I try to give Lucy one last encouraging look, a look that is meant to tell her everything will be just fine, then slip out through the door.

"You'll need to take off your underthings," I can hear him telling Lucy as I close the door behind me.

I wait on the landing, unsure of what to do, staring at the carpet—plum-colored squares with orange and blue flowers—and at the chipped yellow varnish on the banisters. A small oval mirror hangs from the picture rail and as I peer at myself in the smudged glass, I realize a small spot has formed on my chin. I look away in disgust. My stomach churns, and when I think of Lucy lying on the couch, of the orange syringe and the doctor's rolled-up shirtsleeves, I think I might be sick. *Please let Lucy be okay.*

It's taking an awfully long time. Why is it taking so long? Downstairs, someone has switched the wireless on: *don't sit under the apple tree with anyone else but me.* The song is too jolly and I want to run downstairs and make it stop, throw the wireless out of the window, beat it with a hammer. *Stop, stop!* Instead I stand on the landing, pressing my fingernails into my palm, waiting, listening.

A little way along the landing, there is a wooden dresser. On top of the dresser are a number of china figures: a woman in a large dress demurely holding onto her bonnet, another woman with a dog on a lead, and a small boy in red trousers, with garish red cheeks and lips, holding a basket of cherries. I shudder and look away.

From behind the closed door comes the sound of a sharp but stifled cry and I resist the urge to push open the door and run to Lucy, to comfort her. The sound causes an ache in my chest and I find my knees are shaking.

Whatever the doctor is doing seems to take forever, and I will him to hurry and finish it.

Finally, after an unendurable length of time, the door opens and Lucy is there, fully dressed, her face pale and bewildered. The doctor motions for us to descend the stairs ahead of him, and Lucy leans heavily on the banisters for support.

We stand by the front door, Lucy blinking back the tears. All I want is to get us out of this house. "It'll come out," the doctor says. "Later. Maybe tomorrow. There'll be bleeding." He pauses. "Remember, you're not to mention me under *any* circumstances. If you experience complications, you're to get help, but *not* to mention where you received the treatment, or who you received the treatment from. Understood?"

"Yes," I say, fearing Lucy won't be able to reply.

Outside the evening is still warm, and the sunlight plays through the vivid green leaves of the trees; spring is turning into summer, an unstoppable bursting and blooming. A blackbird darts into a hedge. I give Lucy my arm and she takes it, leaning into me, putting one foot carefully in front of the other.

30

2018

It's Saturday and I'm in the car. Daniel is taking me to the garden center for tea and cake. I saw it on my calendar this morning in Daniel's writing, then I noticed something else—written on a Saturday two weeks from now—*Moving Day.*

I stare out of the window at the bare, wet fields, pressing the tiny rose charm at my throat between my thumb and forefinger, feeling its familiar shape. It's raining, and the drops slide down the glass, obscuring my vision. Not that I'd know where we are anyway. Everything changes too fast these days. It's hard to keep a handle on things. According to my calendar I'm moving away from Ludthorpe in two weeks' time. I sit up a little straighter. *Lucy*. There will be nothing in Devon to trigger any memories of Lucy. I must find her before I move, otherwise she'll be lost forever. What am I even doing here when there is still so much to find out?

"Are we going to look for Lucy?" I ask.

Next to me, Daniel sighs.

"Not today, Nan," the girl in the back seat says. Her voice sounds sad and I'm not sure she understands the gravity of the situation.

We're pulling into the car park, finding a space, and I realize Amy is here too. Outside, it's cold and drizzly, and I pull the scarf I'm wearing tightly around my neck even though it isn't mine—far too mauve. There's an umbrella being held over my head. Daniel is locking the car and I turn to Amy and whisper, "I remembered something else about Lucy. Green ribbons. That's what I remembered. Is it a clue, do you think?"

Amy coughs. "I don't think so, Nan. Come on. Let's get you inside, shall we?"

I frown. Amy is acting as though I'm confused when, in fact, things have never been clearer. Fine, I think. I don't need any of you.

"Where are we anyway?" I ask, grumpily.

"We're at the garden center," Daniel replies. "You always used to like it here."

"Ah, yes," I say. *The Garden Center.* And perhaps I did. It seems like a place I might like. Not that any of us can be buying pretty plants at a time like this. We need to be growing vegetables. Last week we swapped several carrots for a tub of Mrs. Cartwright's broad beans.

"Are we here for vegetable seeds?" I ask.

Amy smiles. "No, Nan. Just cake. Why vegetables, anyway? You've never grown vegetables, have you?"

"Well, we had to give it up, see. For the shelter. There wasn't any space left for beans."

Amy nods and we approach the entrance: STEEPLETREE GARDEN CENTER. NOW OPEN SEVEN DAYS A WEEK.

"I don't do much gardening anymore," I say. "Why not?"

"It was getting hard on your joints," Daniel explains. "All that kneeling and digging. But you'll love the garden in Devon. It's huge. You can sit out on the terrace under the umbrella all day, like the Queen."

"I don't think the Queen has time to sit around," I mumble. "Not with her growing family, and her Canadian tour."

Amy pulls her bobble hat off. "I used to help you do the watering, Nan. Do you remember? I had that little green watering can."

I think of a small girl running around barefoot, following me about. "I do," I say. "I think you watered your feet more than anything else."

Amy grins and we enter through a sliding door. It doesn't look much like a garden center. There aren't many plants, just shelves of pricey-looking food: jars of chutney, tins of strange beans, and bottles of cloudy apple juice. I can see Christmas decorations everywhere, on the tables and on the walls: wreaths, baubles, snow globes, bags of glittery pine cones, and statues of twiggy reindeer. It all reminds me of when I used to help my mother with the church jumble sale. She got involved because the other wives did, and because Reg said someone might have thrown out something valuable by mistake. We had to sort through all the chipped china, baby clothes, and moth-eaten suits that had been left in the backs of wardrobes by neglectful wives while their husbands were away during the war. *They should have used mothballs*, my mother would mutter. Then there were the dull silver photograph frames containing Edwardian relatives. I didn't like having to take the photographs out of the frames and throw them away. It felt like the families of the relatives had discarded their memories, decided they were nothing but old rubbish. That'll be me soon—put out with the jumble.

Daniel and Amy are looking at some of the pricey food, and I walk over to a display of Christmassy ornaments: mini flashing trees and candles in the shape of snowmen. I pick up a small figurine, a boy in a red duffle coat holding a lantern. It's cheerful and bright but I almost drop it, remembering another ornament: a boy with a basket of cherries, garish red lips, and cheeks. A song on the wireless. Chipped yellow paint on the banister. A closed door. My churning stomach. I replace the ornament with a shaky hand. *Lucy*. I must find Lucy.

There's a board on the wall: COMMUNITY NOTICEBOARD. A photograph of a cat stares down at me but it's the wrong sort, too ginger, it doesn't look like Smudge at all. MISSING. FIFTY POUND REWARD. I reach into my cardigan pocket, take out my crumpled piece of paper, the one Halim printed for me in the library, then pin it next to the photograph of the missing cat.

"Do you have a pen?" I ask a woman with a basket full of glittery pine cones.

"Oh, hello. Um, yes. Hang on a sec." She digs into her handbag and hands me a pen, one of those felt-tip types. I write on the top of the pinned piece of paper. *Still missing. Appeal for...* I can't think how to spell the last word. How ridiculous. I've gone blank. Fancy an English teacher forgetting how to spell a simple word. I almost giggle but then I write carefully and slowly, sounding the word out phonetically in my head like I used to do when I was teaching a small boy the alphabet. IN-FOR-MA-TION. Who was that small boy? And where is he now? I hope I haven't lost him. You hear about these things, don't you–children wandering off in supermarkets.

I give the woman her pen back. "Have you seen a boy?" I ask.

She gives me a worried look. "I don't think so..."

"Excuse me." There's a loud voice in my ear and I am forced to step aside. A tall man wearing glasses is wheeling a Christmas tree in a trolley up to the till point. He looks stern and businesslike. *And which one of you needs assistance? You've been a silly girl then, haven't you.*

Amy appears. "Nan, what are you up to? We couldn't find you."

"Nothing," I say defensively, turning away from the noticeboard. "What's all this paraphernalia, anyway?" I ask, waving my hand in the air. "Where are the vegetable seeds?"

Amy takes my arm. "It's Christmas, Nan."

"It's only just December. I checked this morning. I've got penguins in Antarctica."

Daniel comes over, a small smile on his face. "People start early, Mum."

"That tree will be dead as a doornail by Christmas Day," I say loudly, pointing at the tree in the man's trolley, causing him to glare at me.

"She thinks she's lost someone," the woman with the large handbag tells Daniel.

I nod, earnestly. That's right. "Lucy," I tell them. "Have you seen her?"

The woman glances at Daniel, then back at me. "I thought she said a boy..."

"It's okay," Daniel says. "She hasn't lost anyone. Come on, Mum. Let's get a cup of tea, shall we? The café's through here."

Daniel is hastily leading me away. I suppose I wouldn't mind a cup of tea. We walk past all the glittery things and up two large steps. The café smells like tea and toast and something sweet—strawberry jam.

Once we're seated at a table, I pick up the menu. "Vegan Breakfast," I read. "Soup of the Day."

"We're just here for tea and cake," Daniel tells the waitress when she comes over.

"Coffee and walnut," I say, reading from the menu.

"Mum, you don't like coffee." Daniel is peering at me over his glasses. "Or walnuts. She'll have the Victoria sponge, please," he tells the waitress, who nods but doesn't write anything down. Perhaps she's like me. She doesn't need to. She remembers what's important.

Daniel wants a cappuccino and a chocolate brownie. If you ask me, he's getting slightly rounded at the middle and shouldn't bother with the brownie, but I don't say anything. Amy offers to share a pot of tea with me, only she wants a different kind of milk. She orders a slice of cake made from something with a funny name, Polenta. It sounds like a foreign language or a small, sunny county. There are lots of things people don't eat nowadays. Imagine if we'd been so fussy during the war. We'd have wasted away.

The waitress brings the cakes over first, which seems the wrong way around to me. I pick at a few crumbs, nibbling at them like a bird.

"Here." Daniel passes me a fork but I frown because it's the wrong sort. Too large. It isn't the proper one for eating cake with. My mother won't like it.

I check the color of the tea by lifting the lid off the teapot—just about strong enough. Weak as gnat's piss, Reg always says when Mother doesn't use enough leaves.

I reach for the teapot and try to pour a little into my cup but the teapot is too heavy and my hand is shaking. Whoever replaced our teapot with this monstrosity anyway?

"Here, let me help you."

A young girl is leaning across the table, reaching for the teapot, trying to help me pour like I'm old and senile.

"I'm fine," I tell her loudly. And it's true, the tea is finding its way into my cup, despite a little of it splashing onto the table.

"But look, it's going everywhere. Just let me help you—"

"I don't need help!" My hand is flying across the table, knocking over the mug half-full of hot, steaming liquid. It falls onto the girl's arm and she yelps.

"Bloody hell," the man says, getting up out of his chair.

"I told you I didn't need help," I shout. "I told all of you but you won't listen. You'll see. You'll all see when I find Lucy."

The girl is clutching her arm and the waitress is rushing over. "Come and run it under cold water, love. There's a sink behind the counter."

The girl is staring at me, her expression stung. I can see tears forming. "Tears won't help anything, will they?" I say crossly. "And who are you? Is it your first day? Shouldn't they be training you?"

The café has gone very quiet. I can no longer hear the chatter, the chinking teacups. The girl's eyes have clouded over. Her shoulders shake and she makes a small choking noise. “I’m sorry, Dad. Sometimes it’s just too much.” She turns away and follows the other waitress, still clutching at her burned arm.

The man is putting his coat on. He tries to help me to my feet but I shake him off. “I haven’t finished my cake.”

“I don’t care about your bloody cake, Mum. Look what you’ve done. You’ve hurt Amy.”

I look to where the man is pointing. Behind the cake counter by the coffee machine, the girl is running her arm under the tap. Everyone in the café is staring at me.

“I don’t know what you’re talking about,” I tell the man, but my voice is beginning to wobble. I’ve got a feeling I’ve done something terrible. “I’m sorry,” I say, but no one is listening. “I’m very sorry,” I say again, louder this time. “I’m sorry, I’m sorry, I’m sorry.”

“It’s all right, Mum. It was an accident. Let’s just get home.” The man is slipping someone’s coat over my shoulders. He steers me in the direction of the door. It seems the girl with the burned arm is coming with us. I stare at her but she won’t look at me.

As we leave the café, I realize I’m not even sure what I’m sorry for.

31

1951

Monday morning. Lucy still isn't in school and I'm beginning to feel concerned. Last Thursday evening, I'd walked with her all the way to The Gables and had been reluctant to leave when we reached the gates. "I'll be fine, Edie," she'd said, although she didn't look fine. "I just need to lie down."

And she hasn't been in school since. I was sure she'd be back today. My stomach is tight and I am unable to concentrate on anything. The splayed-out frog I am supposed to dissect with Linda in biology causes me to run to the bathroom heaving. I can't help thinking of that orange syringe in Dr. Pentland's room, of Lucy lying, trembling, on the couch. If Lucy is unwell it will be all my fault. I could have said no to her request to ask my mother for help. I could have persuaded her not to go to Dr. Pentland.

Even though I am preoccupied with thoughts of Lucy, I hear of the rumor going around school. The rumor is that Barbara Theddle has sacked Martha Simpson, Judy's mother. At first I don't listen properly, irritated that this is the important gossip of the week, that no one knows what Lucy is going through, but it's difficult not to overhear. *I've heard she was caught stealing. Judy must be mortified, her mother–a thief.* And Judy isn't in school either, which only arouses further speculation: *She couldn't face everyone*, I overheard Ann say. But I am not worried about Judy, I only want to know that Lucy is well.

After my last lesson of the morning, I slip away, collecting my bicycle and cycling, rather brazenly, straight out of the front gates. I don't care if I get into trouble. I have to see Lucy.

It's a hot day and I can feel beads of perspiration forming on my forehead as I cycle. There is a single, lonely cloud in the sky, shaped like Australia. On the High Street, a woman in a pale pink dress is pushing a covered pram and I can hear the mewing cries of a small baby.

When I reach The Gables, I turn into the driveway and come to a halt outside Lucy's front door, jumping off my bicycle, removing my hat, and ringing the bell.

At first there is no answer and so I take a step back, staring up at the house, wondering if anyone is in, anxious about where Lucy might be if she isn't at home. At one of the top windows, the curtains flutter and there she is, looking down at me, her face pale and moonlike. I give her a small wave and then she is gone. A few seconds later I can hear light footsteps in the hallway.

"Edie." Her hair hangs limply around her face. Her skin lacks any color at all; she's wearing a faded floral blouse and a long skirt, both of which look slightly too big for her. She keeps one arm protectively across her stomach, and I feel sad to see her not looking at all like her usual bright and polished self.

"I came to see how you are."

She blinks at me. "To be honest, Edie, I don't feel very well at all. I haven't since... I had to tell my mother it was my monthly. She wasn't very keen on me having time off."

"I'm sorry."

"Let's not talk on the doorstep. Why don't you come into the garden? My mother has gone shopping and won't be back for an hour or so."

Leaving my bicycle by the fuchsia bushes and slipping my satchel onto my shoulder, I follow Lucy into the house, passing the elegant staircase with its sparkling banisters. The floor is a checkered black-and-white stone and when I look up, a huge chandelier hangs above me, tiny glass droplets catching the light. Several paintings are displayed on the walls: portraits of girls in white dresses, and one of The Gables with a horse and carriage outside. Lucy takes me straight through the kitchen with its shiny linoleum floor, clean turquoise cupboards, and modern appliances. There are cut flowers on the large table, which is covered in a fresh white cloth; the curtains are a cheerful yellow.

Trying not to linger, I follow Lucy out to the garden, where we sit on the swing seat, Lucy wincing a little as she lowers herself carefully onto the padded cushion. The garden is full of color, blue hydrangeas, pink rhododendrons, purple perennials; I can smell the roses and the fruit trees ripe with black currants and gooseberries.

"What a beautiful garden."

"Oh, thank you," she says, vaguely. "I'd forgotten you haven't been over before."

"Lucy, if you still aren't feeling well, I really think you should see a doctor."

She looks alarmed. "Oh, no. I couldn't."

"But Dr. Pentland said if there are any complications–"

"I think it's all over now," she says quietly.

I pause, unsure of what to say. "I'm sorry. Was it dreadful?"

Lucy nods, her lip trembling. "A sort of slipping and bursting all at once. It was incredibly painful, Edie. I was clutching at the bathroom sink, trying to breathe... Trying not to cry out in case someone heard me. It seemed to go on and on. I had to throw away several towels. I could hardly look, but of course it was right there in front of me: life and death." She pauses. "To be honest, I don't think I'll ever be quite the same as I was before. The things that happen to us, they change us, don't they?"

I nod, and neither of us says anything for a moment.

"But if you're still not feeling well, perhaps you should see someone," I say finally.

Lucy puts a hand on her stomach. "I just couldn't face going back to school."

"I still think we should call for the doctor. You don't look very well."

She shakes her head. "Please, Edie, I don't think I can go through all that. Explaining everything..."

I sigh. "But if you feel any worse, you really must," I say, defeated.

She closes her eyes and we sit together, the swing seat gently rocking. The sun is warm on my arms and face. A butterfly lands on the lawn.

"I suppose they'll always be there now, won't they?" she says quietly.

I frown. "Who?"

"The child. Or the ghost of the child, the not-child. They'll always be there, the absence of them, I mean. And I'll wonder, I'll always wonder."

I don't know what to say to her. It was the sensible thing to do, of course, the only thing, but I also know she's right. "Do you think you'll ever tell Mr. Wheaton about what happened?"

Lucy slowly opens her eyes. "No, I don't suppose I ever will. We aren't seeing each other anymore. I think June finding the ribbon really rattled him." She pauses. "And I don't know if things can ever be what they were, not after..." She shakes her head. "He's a coward, really. I should have seen that. I'm angry with Max, and angry with myself too. I have this overwhelming desire to smash everything in my room. I want to break a gramophone record over Max's head like Amanda in *Private Lives*."

I frown. "What?"

"It's a play. But things like that don't happen in real life, do they? People don't go around breaking gramophone records over other people's heads."

"I wouldn't be so sure."

She turns her face away from the sun, dropping her chin. "What a dreadful mess."

"It's over now," I say, trying to console her.

"I suppose you heard at school... About my mother letting Martha Simpson go."

I glance at her. "Yes. The other girls were talking about it this morning, and Judy wasn't in."

"Well, it's true," Lucy says, with a pained expression. "As if I haven't got enough to think of right now."

I picture Barbara Theddle telling Martha Simpson she's

letting her go, giving her a final envelope, Martha in tears as she leaves The Gables for the last time.

"Whatever was she let go for?" I ask. "I thought Martha had been working for you forever."

"She has," Lucy says miserably. "She's like part of the family, really. That's why Judy and I have always been close. Well, until recently. All this..." She waves a hand to indicate the events of the past few months. "I suppose it's created a distance between us, but I couldn't tell Judy about Max, she's a terrible gossip." Lucy swallows and gently rubs her temples. "The fact is, my mother dismissed Martha for stealing from us."

Although I've never particularly liked Judy, I do feel a stab of sympathy for her. If the girls are already talking about it at school, it won't be long before everyone in Ludthorpe will know.

"What did she steal?"

"Oh, bits and pieces," Lucy says vaguely. "Trinkets, jewelry."

"And you're sure it was her?"

"Yes," Lucy says flatly. "Oh, let's not talk about it anymore. It's the last thing I want to think about."

"Of course."

"Do you think you could get us some lemonade? It's in the jug on the kitchen table. My mother left it for me. There are glasses in the cupboard."

"I'll get it now." I stand, feeling glad to be useful at last.

In the kitchen, I quickly find the jug full of iced lemon and take two glasses from the cupboard. I glance around for a tray but, not wanting to snoop, settle on carrying the jug and glasses as best I can.

When I return Lucy is leaning forward on the swing seat,

reading, her brows furrowed. My satchel is lying on the grass, and it's only as I draw closer that I realize she's holding my diary. She looks up and her expression frightens me. Her eyes are wide and accusing, her mouth slightly open.

"How *could* you?" Her chest hitches.

"Did you go through my bag?" is all I can think to say.

"No, I *didn't.* Your satchel slipped off the seat and it fell out." She waves the diary at me. "You've written about everything. All of it." She stares at the pages again. "About me and Max. *Everything.* H-how could you do that?"

She looks hurt and bewildered and I feel immediate remorse.

"Lucy, I'm sorry, I–"

"How you must have enjoyed yourself!" Now her eyes are dark and fiery. "Listening to me day after day, then running home and writing it all down!"

"It wasn't like that," I say, indignantly. "I've always kept a diary. I like to write–"

"Well, you certainly had something interesting to write about, didn't you? Do you have any idea what this would do to me if someone found it? And there you are, just carrying it around with you in your bag. Scribbling away, writing whatever you like about the intimate details of *other people's lives.* I guess friendship doesn't mean very much to you, does it?"

Her words sting and I bite down on my bottom lip.

"How I wish you weren't so stupid and forgetful. If you hadn't forgotten your scone tin that day, you'd never have seen me."

"And then I wouldn't have been able to help you," I say coolly.

Lucy narrows her eyes. "You'd better destroy this," she says, waving my diary at me. "Burn it. In fact, no, I should do it myself."

"You can't do that," I say, horrified at the thought of my writing disappearing to ash. Before I know what I'm doing, I'm reaching forward and snatching the diary from her, taking her by surprise. She cries out and almost falls from the seat, clutching at her stomach.

"Lucy, I'm sorry..." I stand back in horror. "Did I hurt you?"

She blinks and stares at a spot beyond the trees. "Just go," she says, not looking at me, her eyes brimming with tears. "I don't want you here anymore."

"Please, let me help you. You're not well. I really think you should see—"

"Didn't you hear me? I said *go*."

32

2018

I wake early in the morning from a dream. I was holding a huge ball of green ribbon. It was unraveling so fast I couldn't stop it. It had a mind of its own, this ribbon, as though it were possessed, wanting to take me somewhere. In my dream, I was a girl again. I wore my best blue voile dress as I chased the ribbon through Alderbury woods, falling over tree roots, twigs cracking under my bare feet. The ribbon, I'm sure, was taking me to Lucy. I could hear her whispering in my ear, the scent of Evening in Paris on the breeze. *Edie. I'm here, Edie*, she said, her whispers growing more urgent. I felt something land on my arm. Rain? I looked up at the sky and it was raining Parma Violets; they showered down on me, hundreds and thousands of them.

And then I woke, and now it's too late to find her, to follow the ribbon. Only perhaps it isn't.

I get out of bed. Lucy is in trouble and I must reach her. She didn't look well. This time I'll insist she calls the doctor. This time I can make everything all right.

I open my wardrobe doors and slip a gray wool cardigan off the hanger. It smells musty but I don't care. I wrap myself in the cardigan, pull on a pair of thick socks, find my slippers, then make my way downstairs. I take the key from its bowl, put it in my pocket.

It's still dark out. It rained in the night and under the streetlamp I can see jewellike dew drops hanging from the bare branches of the trees. I walk quickly and purposefully, pulling my long cardigan tightly around me. As I reach the High Street, the sky has cleared and the sun begins to rise, the darkness lifting slowly as though someone is peeling it back; the sky is as pink as a peony.

I walk past shuttered shops and rubbish bins, reaching the post office on the corner, but there is no sign of Lucy. A car passes and I shrink into the shadows, not wanting to be seen.

There is the library and the Co-op, not yet open. The pavement narrows to nothing and then I am heading out of town, on Alderbury Road at last. I keep to the edge, my slippers getting muddy, but I don't care. The woods are silent and watchful with that early-morning stillness. A pale orange mist is beginning to appear through the trees as the sun rises. I hear a rustling from somewhere within the undergrowth, a muntjac perhaps. A few birds call to one another, those that haven't already flown south, hardy little birds that will stay to tough it out. Another car passes, ignoring me. It's probably someone on their way to work; they don't have time to stop and talk to me. I am grateful—I must find Lucy.

It's almost fully light now. The sky is a pale pinkish gray, the color of new plaster. And there is the driveway to The Gables, the open gates. I make my way up the path toward the house. The driveway is covered in yellow and brown leaves; they squelch under my slippers and the air smells damp and woody.

Two cars are parked out the front. I've seen them before, I'm sure I have, even though they don't belong here. I stand, looking up at the house, thinking of a black-and-white floor, portraits on the walls, a fresh white cloth on the kitchen table. I notice someone—probably the gardener—has taken an ax to the wisteria, cut it right back. It used to creep up the side of the house, wrapping itself around the windows. The circular grass plot in the middle of the driveway has gone, the fuchsia bushes too, but then, it isn't the time of year for fuchsias. I take the steps up to the porch and knock using the large brass knocker.

No answer.

I step back onto the driveway and look up at her window. The curtains are drawn but, as I watch, they flutter at the edges. Her face is pale and her hair hangs limply over her shoulders. She stares at me; she wasn't expecting me. Still, she's pleased. I know because she gives me a weak smile.

I climb the steps to the porch again, waiting for her to come down and answer the door. This time I can make it all right.

I stand, waiting, but she doesn't come.

I knock again.

Unfamiliar voices in the hallway. My shoulders stiffen. Isn't Lucy the only one home?

A man answers the door. He's dressed in a shirt and tie, ready for work. My stomach flips.

"Oh, it's you," he says, taking me in—the cardigan I've pulled on over my nightdress, my socks and slippers, my bare legs and wild hair. He looks alarmed. "You must be freezing." He glances around anxiously, as if there might be more of me, a whole army of elderly, slippered women come to beat down his door.

"I'm on my own," I say. As I speak the words I get a strange sense of déjà vu. Have I said this before? I ignore the feeling, it's a common one these days. I mustn't get confused, lose focus, not when Lucy needs me. "I'm here for Lucy," I tell him.

He shakes his head. "Where have you come from?"

I look at him, blankly. What's he talking about? "I'm Lucy's friend," I tell him.

He sighs. "I mean, where do you live?"

I shiver. I am about to tell him I live on Sycamore Street, but then I'm not sure. Perhaps I moved. I knit my eyebrows together, trying to remember.

"Look, you'd better come in for a moment. You'll freeze..." He steps back, uncertain, but gesturing for me to step inside.

I hesitate. "Are you the doctor?"

The man looks surprised. "No, but my wife is."

Satisfied, I step up onto the doormat in the hallway. The house smells of soap and washing powder, something uplifting and lemony. It's all making sense at last. Lucy must have called for the doctor herself and now she is being taken care of. As I follow the man down the hallway, the warmth of the house hits me. I hadn't realized how cold I was. Good. Lucy needs to be kept warm. Now I can smell something else—coffee and toast; homely, comforting smells.

I enter a large kitchen with a range and cream cupboards.

Nothing is like it should be. A woman in smart gray trousers and a pretty red blouse is packing a lunch bag over by the fridge. A girl wearing a school uniform is sitting at the kitchen table, messily buttering a piece of toast. Opposite her, an older boy is reading a textbook, engrossed. I'm sure I've seen him before, but I can't think where.

"Oh," the woman says, her posture stiffening. She looks from me to the suited man, who shrugs apologetically.

"She was on the doorstep," he says. "She's the one who came once before. I told you about her... I think she's a little confused."

"I'm not confused," I say, irritated. "I'm just here for Lucy."

The boy has looked up. "It's you," he says, grinning. "I didn't realize it was you..." He glances at his mother. "I met Edie in the library."

Of course. It's Halim. "Hello, Halim," I say, "fancy seeing you here."

I'm not sure what I've said that's funny, but the small girl giggles.

"Well, I'm glad you two have met." The woman gives her son a questioning glance. "Where have you come from, Edie?"

I hesitate. Where have I come from?

"She didn't seem sure," the man says.

"Well, we'll have to find out, won't we?" The woman smiles. "My name is Ridi. And this is Alisha." She gestures to the girl, who is eating toast and glancing shyly at me. It all feels unreal. Who are these people in Lucy's house?

"Perhaps you'd like a cup of coffee to warm you up," Ridi says gently. "And we'll see if we can get you home, shall we?" She glances at the kitchen clock and I realize the man has disappeared. Perhaps he's gone to check on Lucy. But shouldn't the doctor be doing that?

"I only drink tea," I tell her.

She nods. "Tea then."

I suppose I wouldn't mind a cup of tea now I come to think of it. Perhaps they've got biscuits. Still, it doesn't feel right to be drinking tea with strangers when Lucy is ill in bed. "But have you seen Lucy?"

She begins to shake her head but then seems to remember something. "Yes," she says, softly. "Yes, I've seen Lucy."

"Will she be okay?"

"She'll be fine," she says firmly.

The boy is sliding the textbook into his bag. "Have you made any progress, with Lucy, I mean?"

For some reason the woman, Ridi, shoots him a warning look but he ignores it.

"I've made progress. Plenty," I say, thinking of the memories that have been returned to me: Lucy and Mr. Wheaton, Rupert, the dreadful séance, Lucy's pregnancy, and the foot doctor. I'm not sure yet what it all amounts to but it must be progress, mustn't it?

Ridi places a steaming mug in front of me. "Edie, is there anyone we can call? Anyone who might come and get you?"

"In the library, you mentioned your granddaughter," Halim says, helpfully.

"She's at school," I tell them. "Daniel, too. He works there. He's a deputy headmaster." I feel disorientated at the mention of Daniel, and cling onto the back of the kitchen chair for support. The past is colliding with the present like tectonic plates, sending up eruptions I am unsure how to navigate. Here is Halim from the library talking about Amy, yet Lucy is upstairs and has been seen by the doctor.

"Sit down for a minute, Edie." Ridi puts a hand on my shoulder, then pulls out a chair for me.

"Thank you," I murmur. *Never forget your manners, Edie*, my mother used to say. *Whatever the circumstances. There is always room for manners.*

"Is Daniel your son?"

I nod.

"Which school does Daniel work at?" She reels off a list and I stop her when I recognize the name.

"Hillcliff," I say. "That's it."

She glances at the clock again. "It's a bit early, but we could try..."

"Oh, he'll be there," I say, cheerfully. "He's a workaholic. That's what Suzanne says."

The man returns wearing shoes and a coat. "I'm sorry, love. Are you sure you don't want me to..." He glances in my direction, but Ridi shakes her head.

"No. I'm not due in until a bit later. I'll get her sorted."

The man gives Ridi a kiss and murmurs something in her ear that I only catch fragments of. *So sorry. Got to go. If no luck. Call police. Not your responsibility.* Ridi is nodding, reaching for her mobile telephone, stepping into the hallway.

A chill runs through me. Why is the man talking about the police? I realize my hands are shaking. I didn't realize how cold I was. The tea will help. I look down at myself. "I'm in my nightdress!" I say, horrified.

The girl sitting opposite me at the table giggles again, then puts her hand over her mouth.

I smile at her, letting her know it's okay. We've got to laugh, haven't we?

"Come on, Alisha." The man says. "Fetch your bag. You'll be late for school, and I'll be late for work."

The girl slides off her chair. "I have to go to school now. Daddy's taking me. I'm in Year Five."

"Well," I say. "That's marvelous."

My eyes follow her out the door. She's carrying a red reading folder. Amy used to have one just like it.

"I'd better go too," Halim says. "I've got a mock exam this morning. I hope the search is going well, Edie. And hope to see you again soon."

Search for what? I wonder, as he slings a rucksack over his shoulder. I can hear him whispering in the hallway. *I met her in the library. I didn't realize she was the woman who knocked on the door.* But then the door slams and I don't hear anything else. Everyone in this family has somewhere to be. Not me. I need to be here. With Lucy.

Ridi reappears holding her phone. "You were right, Edie. He's just got in and they were able to put me straight through. He won't be long. He's coming right away."

"Okay," I say, as if I know what she's talking about.

She pulls up a chair and sits down next to me with a cup of coffee. We seem to be waiting for something, but I suppose it doesn't matter that I can't remember what. Lucy is safe upstairs and Ridi, the doctor, is here. That's all that matters. I feel a huge wave of relief.

"I'm so glad you've seen Lucy," I say. "I messed everything up and now I'm trying to put it right."

Ridi reaches across the table and squeezes my hand. "I'm sure, whatever happened, you did all you could. Sometimes we have to forgive ourselves, Edie."

I look down into my tea.

I wish I could stay forever in this kitchen with Ridi the doctor, the remnants of her busy family's breakfast strewn all around us, the smell of toast, the warming mug of tea in my cold hands. But I know I can't stay here forever. Someone is on their way and I suppose I'll have to go soon. I want to ask Ridi who is coming and where I'll be going, but perhaps it doesn't matter. Perhaps it's enough to be in this moment, in this warm, familiar yet unfamiliar kitchen, with this kind stranger.

33

1951

I keep thinking it must be awful for Lucy, seeing Mr. Wheaton at school all the time, knowing what he put her through, knowing that he can just carry on with his life as if nothing happened while she must carry her secret and her pain.

Not that I can say any of this to Lucy, seeing as she still isn't speaking to me. She's back in school at last, which means she must be better, but she hasn't so much as looked in my direction.

I'd like a chance to explain myself, to tell Lucy that my diary is just for me, that she doesn't need to worry, her secrets are safe, but I am worried about approaching Lucy and being rejected. I don't think I could stand it if she rejected me again. At least I'm not the only one she has fallen out with; I've noticed Lucy and Judy aren't speaking, which isn't surprising after what happened with Judy's mother.

I've heard a rumor that Mr. Wheaton is leaving at the end of term. I hope he does leave. Looking at him makes me angry, and it's hard to concentrate when you are angry. I got a low mark for my last history essay. He gave me a D, writing in the margin: *This reads like fiction!* which I suppose it was. I've always thought history is about making up the bits we don't know about in order to join things together in a more satisfying way.

At home, Reg has been in an unusually good mood after a recent windfall. He's going about the place whistling "The Lambeth Walk," and has bought my mother a sewing machine and a new pair of dancing shoes. He thinks we don't know where he keeps his money, but I've seen him stuffing cash into the empty Rinso box at the back of the kitchen cupboard. *I told you our luck was in*, he said to my mother. He is also in a good mood about the upcoming fete. He thinks my mother should raise her prices. "You've got to remember you're a star," he tells her. "They'll be queuing all the way to the fishmonger's." His cheerfulness makes me suspicious; I don't trust it. I also don't want to be at home anymore, but I know the only way to move out would be to get a job and try to find lodgings, which would mean I won't be able to return to school in the autumn. It's a dilemma that runs continually through my mind. I haven't been over to the undergarment factory like I promised; I just can't bring myself to.

At Friday lunchtime I'm walking along the side of the gymnasium with my English exercise book and a copy of Thomas Hardy's selected poems (Miss Munby loves all the Emma ones—*we've got to realize what we've got when we have it, girls!*) when I spot Judy Simpson coming the other way. As soon as she sees me, her expression clouds and her eyes narrow. I try to give her a wide berth but she stops right in front of me, trapping me by the side of the gymnasium wall.

"I know this all has something to do with you," she hisses.

"What are you talking about?" I ask, genuinely bewildered.

"All of it. Lucy not wanting to see me, her acting so strange all the time. What happened with my mother."

I almost laugh. "What happened to your mother had nothing to do with me. I didn't steal anything, did I?"

Judy looks as though she might strike me; her anger palpable, her fists tightly clenched. "My mother didn't steal anything. She was framed."

"Framed?" It sounds like Judy has been spending too many Saturday afternoons at the pictures, and I try to swallow my amusement, reminding myself that I should feel sympathy for Judy and her mother. Martha Simpson must have been desperate if she needed to steal from the Theddles, and I know what it's like to live without much, to have a mother who must scrimp and save and who always yearns for more.

"You have no idea what this has done to my family, do you?"

"I'm sorry, but I really don't know a thing about it," I say, edging carefully away then breaking into a brisk walk. How can Judy possibly believe her mother's dismissal is my fault, that it could have anything to do with me? I know she's always disliked me, but I'm beginning to think she might be slightly barmy.

"I know it all comes back to you. And I'm going to find out how. You won't get away with this," Judy calls after me.

I'm cycling along the High Street on Saturday morning, running errands for my mother (*Can you get me some peppermint oil from the*

chemist's, Edie? Oh, and see if Mr. Goy has any kippers in). I haven't gotten far and am passing The Bird in Hand and the pawnshop when I see Lucy. I do a double take, drifting unintentionally into the middle of the road, not quite believing it's her, that Lucy would be at this end of town. The only reason I can think of her being this way would be to see me, and she certainly isn't doing that. She's coming out of the pawnshop, wearing a headscarf and sunglasses and, as I watch, she glances up and down the street as if someone might be watching her. I am about to wave but something stops me: she clearly doesn't want to be seen. Her manner is guarded, hesitant, secretive; it's the way she looks left and right, the slight hunch of her shoulders, how she pulls at her cardigan as if trying to cover up as much of herself as possible.

I drag my bicycle up the curb, watch her walking hastily away, then approach the shop, peering into the window, as if it might give me a clue as to what she was doing.

JEWELRY BOUGHT AND SOLD reads the handwritten sign.

There in the window display are the earrings Lucy wore to the dance a few months ago, the ones she borrowed from her mother, the tiny pearls and sapphires. Next to them is Lucy's rose pendant, the necklace she always wears. I stare at them, a fuzzy feeling in my head. It doesn't make any sense. Lucy said her mother was given the earrings by a sweetheart. Why would she part with them now? And why would Lucy give up her favorite necklace? Was that what she was doing in the shop? Selling her mother's earrings and the necklace, or more of her mother's possessions? Why?

An uneasy feeling claws at my stomach. Nothing about this is right. I remember Lucy's words when I asked about Martha Simpson, what it was she had been stealing.

Trinkets. Jewelry.

I look again at the earrings and necklace so brazenly on display. What else has Lucy brought to the pawnshop? Is she in on something with Martha Simpson? Another thought slowly dawns on me. What if Martha didn't steal from the Theddles? What if it was Lucy? But why would she steal from her own family? From her mother?

I hop back onto my bike and take off, skidding around the corner by the hairdresser's, flying up the High Street in the same direction as Lucy, my feet driving at the pedals, going as fast as I can on my rickety old bicycle.

I finally catch up with Lucy by the cinema, slowing my pace to cycle alongside her. She stops when she realizes it's me.

"What do you want?" she asks crossly.

At least she's acknowledged me. I hop off my bicycle, wheeling it alongside her.

"I saw you just now."

"I can see that." She carries on walking.

"No, I mean I saw you coming out of the pawnshop. What were you doing?"

"Sorry, I didn't know I was required to tell you my business these days." Her manner is cool yet I can tell I've startled her; she wasn't expecting to be seen.

We're reaching the end of the High Street and she cuts up Cucumber Lane, meaning I have to walk behind her with the bike.

"What's going on?" I say, when we emerge by the church. "I saw your mother's jewelry in the window."

Lucy says nothing and so I take a deep breath. "Judy's mother didn't steal anything, did she? It was you."

Lucy stops walking and stares at me. Her steely expression wavers.

"I know it must have been you," I press, praying I am right, not wanting to create a deeper rift between us.

"In here," she says, opening the gate to the churchyard.

I leave my bicycle tucked behind the gate and follow Lucy along the path between the gravestones, a smell of flowers and newly turned earth in the air. Someone has left a bunch of sunflowers on a grave and they're beginning to wilt.

She stops by the old yew and turns to me. To my surprise she buries her head in her hands. "I didn't want to do it, Edie. You can't imagine how I've been feeling. I'm so fond of Martha. After all she's done for us..."

She looks at me, her eyes bright and feverish. A small bird scuffles around in the tree.

"So why are you stealing things?"

She hugs her shoulders and glances around desperately, "It was so difficult to get the money together. For the, you know..."

I nod.

She lowers her gaze. "And then when he asked for more."

"Who asked for more?"

"Reg," she says, biting down on her lower lip. "He said I'd been given the wrong price, that the doctor needed more money. I got what I could but then, afterward, late that evening, he just turned up at my house, saying that it had been such a risk for the doctor, and for your mother and him, given whose daughter I was and my age and everything, and that he needed more money. I had to get rid of him, I couldn't have him coming to the door, standing on my doorstep. I told him I didn't have any more money, but he said if I wanted it all to be kept quiet then I was going to have to find what he'd asked for. I did, but then he came to me when I was on my way home from school the other day and told me I still hadn't given him enough, that he was going to need even more. I sold some jewelry to the pawnbroker."

My body tenses. Reg. I can't believe it. I picture him coming through the door with the sewing machine under his arm, splashing out on cigarettes, whistling cheerfully to himself. All the time I thought he'd had a win at the races.

"And then my mother noticed a few things were missing." Lucy draws a hand down her face. "I didn't realize she would catch on so quickly. Oh, Edie. It was just *awful*. Martha in tears and my mother so upset about having to let her go, my father going on about getting the police involved and my mother begging him not to. Of course I couldn't tell them it was me. They would have wanted to know why I needed the money."

"I'm so sorry," I say, suddenly realizing Judy was right in her accusation: it *is* all my fault. If I hadn't asked Reg to help, he'd never have taken a cut from the doctor, never asked Lucy for more money, and she wouldn't have stolen from her mother. Martha Simpson would not have lost her job.

My breathing sounds loud in my ears and I sit down on the space between the graves, my shoulders slumped. I've been so stupid. I should have guessed.

"You don't need to be sorry," Lucy replies, sitting next to me and hugging her knees to her chest. "I got myself into this mess, didn't I?"

"Don't give Reg any more money."

"But he said he'd tell my father."

"He won't."

"How do you know that?"

I stare at a sun-bleached cherub. She's right. I don't know for sure.

"I feel so trapped," Lucy says.

I nod. I do too. Trapped with my mother and Reg. Trapped in this town. Soon I'll be trapped in a job I'll hate.

An idea begins to form. I can't believe I haven't thought of it before.

"Let's go away," I tell Lucy, my thoughts all crowding in on me at once. "We could go somewhere. Anywhere. I need to get away, and so do you. We'll leave this. All of it." I wave my hand in the air, gesturing toward the town, to Reg, Mr. Wheaton, his wife, Rupert, Lucy's parents. *Everything.*

Lucy stares at me. "Where will we go?"

"London," I say, the idea of it just coming to me. "You want to go to London. Well, we'll go now. Why should we wait?"

Lucy blinks. "But where will we live?"

"We'll find somewhere. There must be hundreds of rooms to rent in London. We'll get jobs for the summer. In a hotel or a shop or something. When the autumn comes, we can study in the evenings. Then once we've got our qualifications, we can go to college together."

Lucy glances around. "I don't know if I can just leave, Edie. My parents..."

"You can contact them when you're settled. We both can. I can't stay here," I tell her. "I just can't stay any longer."

"Neither can I. But what would we do for money?"

"I can get some," I tell her, thinking of the stuffed Rinso box and not feeling any guilt about stealing from Reg. Anyway, it's Lucy's money. I'd just be taking it back. "It will keep us going for a while," I tell her. "Then we'll get jobs as quickly as we can."

I picture us riding cramped red buses, walking down famous streets under black umbrellas, sitting in sophisticated cafés wearing berets and putting cubed sugar into our tea. We'll find lodgings and make a little home for ourselves. The landlady will be a kind old widow with a gray cat. She'll invite us down for tea and treat us as if we are daughters of her own. We'll come home each evening tired but happy, cook our supper on the gas ring, go out to the pictures at Piccadilly Circus or to dance halls where we'll dance with Irish boys until our feet hurt and our dresses stick to us.

"When would we go?" Lucy says, getting excited.

"Saturday," I tell her. "It's perfect. Everyone will be at the fete. No one will miss us. By the time they're all wondering where we are, we'll be far away."

"Will we leave a note?"

I shrug. "If you like. But we should avoid telling anyone where we're going."

Her expression clouds.

"What is it?"

"Rupert. I'll have to tell him."

"Why?" I ask, crossly. "What's *he* got to do with anything?"

"We've been friends for such a long time, and he thinks he's going to marry me. I can't just leave without giving him some kind of explanation."

I shake my head. "You mustn't tell him you're leaving, or where we're going. You don't owe him anything. Not after what he did to you. You don't owe Rupert Mayhew or Mr. Wheaton a thing."

Lucy looks conflicted. "I think I at least ought to tell him that it's never going to happen. Me and him. Then he can move on and find someone else."

"Fine," I say impatiently, determined not to let anything spoil our new plan and my good mood.

"I said I'd go to the fete with Rupert on Saturday." Lucy looks at me apologetically. "Well, you and I weren't speaking, and I did really want to go to the fete." She stands, brushing down her dress. "I'll meet Rupert and tell him he should forget about me, that we can never be together, and then I'll come straight to the station." She grins at me. "I can't believe we're really doing this."

"I'll get the tickets," I tell her.

34

2018

Daniel is cross with me. I can tell because he isn't speaking, and he's got that moody look about him, the look he used to get when he was a teenager and I told him he had to finish his homework before he could go out with his friends. He drums his fingertips impatiently on the steering wheel as we sit at the traffic lights. He's late, I expect, although I can't think what he would be late for.

It's early in the day. A pale, sobering morning light glints through the bare branches of the trees in the park; the grass is covered in a dusting of dewy frost. The traffic and the schoolchildren are also a giveaway. We're waiting at the lights. *Beep, beep, beep.* Ahead of us, children are crossing the road; small ones holding the hands of parents, older ones carrying bags and folders. I can't think of where we've been, but I know it was somewhere nice. There was a cup of tea, a kind smile, a smell of toast.

Tap, tap, tap go Daniel's fingers.

The lights change and the car moves forward.

Daniel glances at the clock. "I'm going to be late for registration."

"Are we going somewhere?" I ask.

"Home," Daniel says. "I'm dropping you home. To your house."

I fumble with my seat belt. "Aren't we going in the wrong direction?"

"No, Mum."

We pass the library, the library they reopened to search for Lucy, to check she hadn't been locked in. And they searched elsewhere for her, too; the whole town got involved. There were people crawling over the fields and lanes; a large sum of reward money was raised by local residents. My mother insisted we help with the search party. We took a thermos and a torch and went out with Mrs. Cartwright and Mrs. Staines, who brought homemade gingerbread wrapped in cheesecloth (*to sustain the troops*). I didn't want to go. *We've got to do our bit*, my mother had said. *Besides, I thought she was your friend.*

"They said you'd been there once before," Daniel says, his eyes fixed on the road.

"The library?"

Daniel shakes his head in exasperation. "No, not the library, Mum, The Gables. Apparently you knocked on the door a few weeks ago asking about Lucy. You mustn't go over there again, do you understand?"

I shrink down in my seat. Daniel is telling me off like *I'm* the child. I don't know what I've done wrong. I should be able to go where I like. I always used to go all over the place on my bicycle.

Besides, I *had* to go, Lucy needed me. I wasn't about to let her down. It's Daniel who doesn't understand.

"I had to see Lucy," I mutter.

Daniel breaks sharply at the mini-roundabout. "You've got to stop this Lucy business. I'm very sorry about what happened to her–"

"No one knows what happened to her, that's the point."

"Okay, then," Daniel blows air into his cheeks. "I'm sorry she vanished. It must have been really hard on you, if the two of you were friends."

"We were." I look out of the window as Daniel turns a corner, his face a mask of grim determination.

"I realize that, for some reason, it's all coming back to you now, that you've been thinking about her, that you need to...process the emotion." Daniel glances at me, his face softens. "But the thing is, Mum, it was over *fifty* years ago. No one remembers her. No one's *ever* going to find out what happened to her. You need to forget about it all."

I realize I've scrunched up some of the fabric of my nightdress in my hand. Why am I wearing my nightdress? And how can Daniel say that? *No one's ever going to find out what happened to her.* It's not true. It can't be. Lucy knows I can help her now, that I'm ready to help her. It's why she came back. She's counting on me.

"I really don't want to, Mum, but we're going to have to think about making sure you stay in during the day."

"Don't be ridiculous. I won't be a prisoner in my own home."

"I've been looking into getting you a GPS tracker, too. You can put it on a key ring. That way, I'll always know where you are."

"I'll do no such thing."

"Maybe a microchip then. I've read about them–"

"I'm not a dog!"

Daniel sighs. "Well, we've got to do something. It was lucky they found me. You had nothing on you... And they were very nice about it, but it can't happen again."

We come to a standstill in the traffic. A long line of people are waiting for a bus, and there is a girl about Lucy's age. Her hair is loose though–she isn't wearing a ribbon.

"I had to go to The Gables. She needed the doctor."

Daniel grips the wheel. "This is the end of it, Mum. You can't be going over to that house again. And I don't want to hear another word about Lucy. It's all over, okay?"

My neck and ears feel hot but I say nothing. What's the point? Daniel doesn't want me to look for Lucy. Amy has given up, too. I'm all on my own, and I'm about to be tracked or chipped or whatever it is. This was my chance to put things right, to show them all I'm perfectly independent and not in a muddle. My search for Lucy has led nowhere. I haven't been able to find her, and now my family thinks I need locking up. I glance out of the window as Daniel slows for a speed bump. There is a dead pigeon at the side of the road, a mess of feathers and guts and wings. Grimacing, I look away.

35

1951

I've been awake since 5 a.m. watching a faint glow creeping around the curtains. Never have I longed for time to go more quickly. When I rise, I move quietly around my bedroom, tiptoeing across the creaky floorboard, packing my clothes into my small brown suitcase, running through my mind what I need to take: *toothbrush, soap, hairbrush, underthings, two pairs of stockings, two blouses, cardigan.* I'm going to wear my best wool skirt and my favorite pale blue blouse. I know it's too hot for the wool skirt but it will take up half the space in my case, and it's my best skirt, so it should come with me. Once I've packed, I lie on my bed, looking at the ceiling, thinking that this is the last time I'll do so, that tonight I'll be sleeping under a different roof. The fact that I don't know where it will be excites me.

Around nine, I finally go down for breakfast. Reg is sitting at the table, drinking tea and reading the paper. My mother is dressed in her performing clothes: her black silky dress, gold hoop earrings, feather boa. Of course–her booth at the fete.

"I had better get going," my mother says.

"I'll get my own breakfast then, shall I?" Reg says, grumpily.

My mother glances at Reg but says nothing. She turns to me. "I need to be there early to set up. Edie, do you want to walk over with me?"

I feel a pang of guilt that I won't be at the fete to help my mother, and that I am leaving her here with Reg for good. I make a promise to myself to write to her as soon as I can.

"I'm going to pop along a bit later," I say, avoiding her eye.

My mother turns hopefully to Reg.

"Reg?"

He takes a slurp of tea, then sets the mug down. "I think I'll do the same, Nancy. Go along a bit later. Once I've had a bit of breakfast. There is no point me hanging around all day, is there?"

I feel a flutter of anxiety. I had hoped my mother and Reg would go to the fete together, that there would be no one to witness me leaving the house with my suitcase.

"Fine then." My mother sighs and I have a sudden urge to embrace her, but that would look strange and there can't be anything strange about this morning. I mustn't do anything to arouse suspicion.

Once my mother has left and Reg has gone off down to the privy, I know I only have a small window of time to get what I need and leave without him seeing me.

The Rinso box is stuffed full of notes. I've never seen so much money. I quickly shove a ball of cash into my skirt pocket and replace the box. I don't feel at all guilty. We'll need it to get ourselves settled, and it belongs to Lucy. Once again, I only feel bad for my mother, that I am leaving her behind. I shake my head. I can't let any doubts creep in. Not now.

I strap my suitcase to the back of my bike and then I am off, cycling out of the front gate and away from Sycamore Street forever. I've got plenty of time, and so I stop at the pawnshop on the way to the station. Barbara Theddle's earrings have been sold, but Lucy's necklace is still there. I point it out to the man behind the counter and make my purchase. Lucy will be so pleased when she finds out I've bought it back for her. Terrified it will fall out of my pocket, I put it on, fastening the chain at the back of my neck, dropping it under my blouse.

The streets are quiet, just a few people on the High Street with their shopping bags. I reach the church and Alderbury Road, and then I am passing fields of tall golden wheat. It's already hot, and I think what a good day it is for the fete, for ice cream and cold lemonade and throwing sponges at the vicar. But all that is in the past and I can't wait to get started in my new life.

I picture Lucy already at the station, waiting. Then I wonder if she went to speak to Rupert before she left. Well, none of that matters now. The world is bigger than Ludthorpe, and I am about to take a first step toward finding out what it has to offer. I can't help but feel I've been waiting for this day all my life. I can't wait to lose myself in the city, to live somewhere where no one knows your name or your business or who your parents are.

Perhaps one day I'll come back, but if I do it will be because I want to, and in different circumstances, ones which will mean I won't have to live with my mother and Reg.

The suitcase makes cycling harder work than usual, but I am

filled with adrenaline and smile to myself as I fly along the lanes, the hedgerows full of honeysuckle and wild raspberries, yellow and blue butterflies flitting between them.

From nowhere a small black cat darts across the road, and the next thing I know the front wheel is slipping from under me and I am flying sideways, unable to keep hold of the handlebars. A quick flash of blurred hedges and sky, a thud and a jolt, and I find myself on the ground.

After a second or two, I pick myself up, stumbling to my feet, dizzy with the shock of the fall. A pain, sharp and stinging, spreading into a warmth. It's my knee, I realize. Then I notice my hands: grazed and dirty, my palms littered with tiny pieces of gravel. I brush them on my skirt, desperate to get rid of the grit, then chance a look at my knee. It's grazed and bloody, and embedded in my gravelly flesh is a piece of flint from the road. I shut my eyes and pull it out, drawing in a sharp breath, trying to be brave. A trickle of blood runs down my leg toward my ankle sock and I take a handkerchief from my pocket and catch the drip. After tying the handkerchief tightly around my knee, I glance about; the cat has disappeared.

I'm all right.

Nothing is broken.

I can still make it. It's not too late.

I hobble over to my fallen bicycle and manage to get it upright, which isn't easy with the suitcase still strapped to the back and my newly acquired limp. I'll have to push the bicycle the rest of the way. Luckily I haven't far to go; the station is almost in sight.

Finally I make it, parking my bicycle and hobbling into the

station. Of course my bicycle will be found and then, if they haven't worked it out already, everyone will know we left on the train, but I am not worried about that. London is a big place, even if they do know where we've gone. I'll write when we have an address, but I can't for a minute imagine my mother coming after me, turning up in London, persuading me to come home. Reg would never let her do that; he'll be too glad to see the back of me, to have my mother to himself.

My knees almost buckle with relief when I see Lucy sitting on the bench, her suitcase at her feet.

As soon as she sees me she scrambles to get up.

"Goodness, whatever happened to you? Are you all right?"

"Fine. Just a grazed knee. I came off my bicycle."

Lucy tuts. "I can't say I'm surprised. You will go about riding that rickety old thing. We'll have to get new bicycles in London. Or will we even need bicycles? Perhaps we'll just use the buses."

"I expect so," I say cheerfully.

I notice Lucy looks better than she has done in weeks; her cheeks full of color, her hair soft and shiny. "Have you done something to your hair?" I ask.

"I shampooed it, that's all. Listen, Edie, our train is running late. About half an hour. Some signaling problem at York or something. It should be in at eleven now."

"Oh," I say, feeling disappointed, hoping there won't be any further delays. "Did you speak with Rupert?"

"Yes. I was very clear about things. I'm sure he didn't believe me, but that doesn't matter. I've told him there won't ever be anything between us."

"Good. I think it's right."

"I brought us sandwiches for the journey." She glances at my suitcase. "I hope you've brought everything." She smiles, but then for some reason she shudders.

"What is it?"

"Your diary. You did destroy it, didn't you?"

I dip my chin, unable to reply, feeling caught out. I thought, with the excitement of us going away, that she'd forgotten about it.

"We'll burn it together when we get to London," she says firmly. "It will be symbolic. We don't need any memories of the last few months, do we? Nothing that will remind us."

She registers the change in my face, my slow intake of breath. "Edie?"

"I forgot it," I whisper.

She stares at me.

"I'm sorry. I just... I was in a hurry to pack."

"Goodness, Edie. That diary has got *everything* in it. How could you *forget* it?"

"But it doesn't matter," I say desperately. "We're going away now. Who cares?"

"Of course it matters," she says through gritted teeth. "My family is still here. They must never learn about any of it. Where do you even keep the stupid thing, for goodness' sake?"

"Under the floorboard next to my bed. It's completely safe." I try to reassure her. "I expect it will be there forever."

She shakes her head. "I can't risk it, Edie. We have to get it."

I glance at the station clock. "What do you mean? There isn't time. There isn't anything we can do. We'll just have to—"

"I can't leave knowing it's in your house," she interrupts me crossly. "You'd better stay here. You can't go anywhere in that state." She gestures to my knee.

"No, Lucy. Please. We'll miss our train."

"No, we won't. Not if I go now. There's still plenty of time. Quick, give me your house key."

I reluctantly give her the key. "The back door is usually unlocked anyway," I mumble.

"No one will be in, will they?"

"I shouldn't think so. My mother has gone to the fete, and Reg has probably gone too now. But Lucy, do you really have to—"

"Which floorboard is it?"

"On the left as you look at the bed, under the corner of the rug," I tell her, my voice urgent but miserable, a dropping sensation in my gut. She's really going. She had better be quick.

"All right. I'll obviously be as fast as I can." She smiles then gives me a hasty embrace. "Don't look so worried. In half an hour we'll be gone."

I watch her tie her scarf around her hair, and then she is rushing over the bridge and out of the station gate. I can see her cycling quickly along the lane, her back straight, her skirt tucked under her knees. *Please hurry.*

36

1951

The large hand of the station clock creeps across to five to eleven. Where is she? Using my hand as a visor, I scan the station road. Nothing. She should be here by now. She should be back. It's getting hot and I fan myself with my hat. *Come on, Lucy*, I will her, desperately, as if the force of my thoughts will be enough to cause her to appear. It shouldn't have taken this long. All sorts of scenarios run through my mind: she was stopped by someone she knows on the High Street; she took a tumble off her bicycle like I did; she forgot which house is mine.

A black speck appears on the horizon, white smoke puffing. It can't be.

Stop, I want to yell. *She isn't here yet.* But the train continues its approach, the gentle *chug chug.* I can smell the thick oily smoke.

Feeling numb, I watch the train pull into the station, catching a glimpse of the driver in his cap, and the stoker, his face streaked with coal. A carriage door opens and a mother and daughter, both carrying luggage, step onto the platform. They rush along, not noticing me.

This is my chance to get away. But instead I stand, rooted to the spot. How can I leave without Lucy?

Gripping my suitcase, I brush a hot wet tear from my cheek and make my way to my bicycle. How stupid I must look, watching the train arrive and depart, standing on the empty platform clutching my father's battered old suitcase, wearing a bloody handkerchief around my knee. I'll have to ride my bicycle back into town, even with my scraped knee. It will take me forever to walk. I feel angry with Lucy; she should never have tried to go back, I told her there wasn't time. If she wasn't so worried about what other people might think, we'd never have missed our train, and I know no one would have found the stupid diary anyway. It was stupid, stupid, stupid.

Each push of the pedals hurts my knee. My hands are sore and I have to keep brushing away the tears. I'm hot and sticky and it's hard to cycle when I feel so utterly wretched and crushed with disappointment. Perhaps we'll get another chance, but what if we don't? Today was perfect. *Today* was our chance.

I expect to bump into Lucy cycling the other way, going as quickly as she can, her face creased with worry that she's late, her cheeks red with exertion, her hair flying out behind her, but she doesn't appear. Where is she? Surely I should have seen her by now. I can't believe the High Street is still going about its business when all our hopes have been dashed, when our train has left without us. There is still no sign of Lucy. When I reach Sycamore Street, her bicycle is leaning against the lamppost at the end of the road. She's still here?

I leave mine outside the front, then go round to the back of the house, unable to believe I'm back here so soon, that our plan has gone so horribly wrong. We should be on the train by now, watching the fields and hedgerows whizzing by, the sunlight streaming onto our laps, tucking into the sandwiches Lucy brought. From the garden I can see Reg sitting in the kitchen. My heart thuds. What is he still doing home? Did he see Lucy? I consider going around to the front and creeping straight up the stairs to see if Lucy is still in my bedroom. Perhaps she didn't hear my instructions about the diary being on the left side of the bed; maybe she's still up there, searching. But something about Reg's posture makes me feel curious. Why is he just sitting there? I can see his untouched breakfast in front of him: two fried eggs and a slice of bread. I approach cautiously; he hasn't seen me yet. I'm almost at the door and realize that he is rocking a little, backward and forward. How can he be drunk already? It's not even twelve o'clock. I frown and push open the kitchen door.

Lucy is lying on the floor. My first thought is that she looks uncomfortable with her head turned toward the hallway at an odd angle, one arm crashed beneath her body, her ankle twisted. Then I see the blood. It's pooled around the back of her head, dark and sticky; some of it matted into her hair. She'll be upset at having to shampoo it again.

Then, somehow, I understand that she isn't going to be able to shampoo her hair again, that something about the way she's lying there is wrong, very wrong. I continue to stare at what I see in front of me as if it can't possibly be real. And then I am rushing toward her, no longer in control of what I am doing, letting out a moan that seems to come from some deep, animal place inside me. I touch her arm, her cheek. Her skin feels cool. Her eyes are open and glassy and she's staring, unblinking at a point beyond me. I can't seem to get enough air into my lungs and my cries are strange and strangled. Lucy is heavy, rigid, and unmoving like an abandoned doll, limbs left at strange angles, hair matted, unloved. I want to shake her and watch her eyelids open and close. I want to breathe life back into her. I don't understand. *Lucy...Reg...*

My arrival, the startling sound of my moan seems to have brought Reg round from his stupor.

"I-I didn't do anything," he stammers. "It was her fault. She gave me a fright."

I turn to him, trying to form words but unable at first to do so. "What...what have you done?" I say, finally, my voice coming out a hoarse whisper.

"Oh, God. Oh, God." Reg rushes over to the sink where he begins to heave.

"Tell me." I'm shouting now. "Tell me what you did!" The tears are spilling over my cheeks, hot and fierce. "Tell me!" *This can't be real. This isn't happening.* "She needs help," I say, looking wildly around the kitchen. "Look, she needs help. Do something. We need to do something."

Reg shakes his head then takes a step away from the sink, his face gray, his hands trembling. "I checked on the money and it was gone. There was a noise upstairs and then she was here in the kitchen. She was stealing from us." He staggers back to the chair and pushes the palm of his hand into his forehead. "She should have let go," he murmurs.

I can see it: how surprised both Lucy and Reg must have

been to find each other; Reg demanding to know what Lucy was doing, where his money was. Perhaps Lucy said something to make him angry. Or perhaps she denied taking the money and Reg didn't believe her.

"But what did you *do*?"

Reg leans forward, clutching at his stomach. I can see the sweat on the back of his neck. He lifts his head. "She was holding something. I couldn't see what it was. I told her to give it back, but she wouldn't, then she laughed at me." Reg shakes his head. "She shouldn't have laughed at me."

I try to make sense of what he is saying, but it doesn't make any sense at all.

"I tried to get it off her, didn't I? But she wouldn't let go."

I can see it: Lucy laughing, Reg launching himself at her.

He glances at Lucy then looks away. "She didn't let go," he says again. "She should have let go."

I turn my head, tightly closing my eyes. "I took the money," I say, my voice a hoarse whisper.

I open my eyes to find Reg staring at me. Then I notice my diary. It's lying on the floor, close to the table leg. And the blood. More of it on the linoleum, on the doorstop, seeping into the hallway.

Reg follows my gaze. "She fell back, hit her head on the rabbit. I tried to stop it but..." He makes a gesture with his hands. "She just fell."

I look in horror at the cast-iron rabbit propping the door open.

"You pushed her."

Reg's right leg is jittering uncontrollably. "I only tried to see what she had," he moans. "How was I meant to know it was just a book? I thought she had my money."

I dig my nails into my hand but I don't wake up. I am still standing in the kitchen with the lingering smell of recently fried eggs. Outside it's a beautiful sunny day: most of Ludthorpe are throwing balls at coconuts, playing tin can alley, guessing the weight of the church ladies' cake, while Lucy is still lying unmoving on our kitchen floor, that awful dark stain around her head. We should be on a train. We should be far away from here. I press my hands over my ears and squeeze my eyes shut, but when I open them she's still there. A sob escapes my throat, the sound of it strange and unfamiliar. *This isn't happening. This isn't happening.*

"We have to call someone," I manage to say. "An ambulance. I'll use Mrs. Cartwright's telephone." My voice trembles.

"There's no need for an ambulance. You can see that," Reg says numbly.

"The police then."

Reg blinks several times. "No," he says firmly, my mention of the police apparently snapping him out of his shock. "You'll not call the police."

"You can tell them what happened, what you did." My fists have curled themselves into tight balls. I'm talking, moving, but it isn't really me, and Lucy isn't really lying on the floor. In just a minute things will be put right. Lucy will wake. Reg will be gone. There must be a way I can make this go away. It all needs to go away... There's a horrible twisting in my gut. My fingers feel numb.

"Don't be stupid," Reg says. "I'll go to prison if they don't believe what happened, that it was an accident. I could hang."

He looks up at me. "And what about your mother? What do you think she'll do without me?"

Lucy looks cold and uncomfortable and I want to put a blanket over her, tell her everything will be fine, that someone is coming to help her, but it's too late. *I was too late.* I think of her family: her mother and father and George. They are probably eating ice cream, checking their raffle tickets, queuing for lemonade or ginger beer. Then I think of my mother, reading palms, telling fortunes, doing what she loves to do, not knowing her life has also changed forever.

"My mother will be better off without you," I choke.

Reg slowly shakes his head. "But think what it will do to her, Edie. She'll never recover from this." He waves a hand in the direction of Lucy, as if she is no longer Lucy but a thing to be dealt with, a situation that must be rectified, a problem for everyone. "Your mother isn't strong, you know that." His voice is calmer now. "Everyone will know," he continues. "Think of it: your mother's husband. Mixed up in something like this. Accused of *murder*. Because I could be, you know." Reg's voice is steady but his eyes are wide and frightening.

I realize with a jolt that he's right. There'll have to be an investigation, surely. It will all come out: Lucy, *in our house*. My mother will be shunned, gossiped about, ostracized. I picture her going about Ludthorpe, getting her groceries, the whispers that will follow her, the averted eyes of the shopkeepers. As people pass the house they'll stop and point it out: *that's where it happened*. Even if we were somehow able to move away, it would follow us. We'd always be waiting for the day someone said: Nancy *Drake*. My mother wouldn't cope; she'd sink into the depths of despair again, take to her bed, only this time she might not get up. And I'd never be able to leave her. Or what if she was taken away, back to the asylum? Only this time she wouldn't get out. I can't let that happen to her. I won't. And of course it will all come out about Lucy, it's bound to. The police will examine her, will know she had an abortion. Or else they'll take my diary away as part of their investigation. My mother could be sent to prison for her involvement in the abortion. She will end up either in a prison cell, or locked in a bare room, strapped to her bed. If the shock doesn't kill her first.

I made a promise to my father to look after my mother, and I can't let him down. I may have been responsible for my father's death, but I won't be responsible for my mother's.

I realize Reg is speaking to me. His voice sounds echoey and far away "Edie." He reaches for my shoulders, trying to shake me. "Did she come on a bicycle, Edie?"

I take a step back, flinging his hands away; I don't want him to touch me. "What are you talking about!" I say, faintly hysterical. *This just isn't real. It's not, it's not...* I can feel my mind shutting down, closing in, all the doors slamming shut at once. *Bang. Bang. Bang.*

"Lucy's bicycle. Where is it?" Reg is saying.

His voice sounds slow and thick and I shake my head, trying to get rid of the thrumming in my ears.

"Where is it?" he repeats.

"It's at the end of the road," I manage to say. My voice doesn't sound like it belongs to me.

"Take it away," Reg tells me. "Leave it somewhere else. Can you do that?"

I gape at him, trying to comprehend what he is asking me to do.

"I'm going to sort this out," Reg says, his eyes fixed on mine. "And we're going to forget it ever happened. Lucy was never here. We were never here. You never saw her this morning."

He's crazy. What's he talking about?

I only know I can't be here in the kitchen with the blood, and the doorstop, and with Lucy unmoving.

I stagger outside and take several deep breaths. Mother can never know.

The bloody handkerchief still tied around my knee, I leave the house and stumble down the road, where I mount Lucy's bicycle.

37

2018

Edie Green, the sky will offer no solution to Pythagoras. I look from the window to the blackboard. The sums are all still there, white unfathomable markings. Dust motes float in the air. I can smell wood polish and boiled cabbage. My hands are stained with black ink. I return my gaze to the window and there I am, walking with Lucy up the High Street, the sun behind us. *It's my secret, Edie.* We pass the church, our satchels on our shoulders. In the churchyard they are lowering my father into the ground. Reverend Thurby says a prayer as my mother dabs at her eyes with her best handkerchief. I spit a piece of confetti into my hand, then turn and run through the church gate, all the way home. *There goes ghosty girl*, Judy says. *They found her bicycle in a field.* At home my mother is in the garden with Smudge in her arms. *He was in the shed. Who'd have thought? We've been courting, Edie, in case you hadn't noticed.* I lower my eyes, and when I lift them, my father is there digging up the lawn. *We'll be safe in here, Edie. They've saved lives, these shelters. Will you fetch me a glass of water, love? There's a good girl.* My mother stands in the kitchen, her hands on her hips. *Have you ripped your dress again, Edie? Whatever will people think?* I take him his glass of water, hardly spilling any, then pick up my spade, the spade I bring to the beach where I build castles and squat down by the surf, looking for pink shells. Lucy stubs her cigarette out with the heel of her shoe. *I get this delicious pain just thinking about him.*

"Mum, are you even listening to me?"

I stare out of the window as Daniel turns the engine off. Words, images, fragments—they drift through my mind like scattered dandelion seeds, blowing hither and thither on the breeze. They seem useless, nothing more than thistledown, pieces of a puzzle that won't fit together. Only I know they *do* fit together, somehow. There are important bits, gaps I need to fill in.

We've pulled up outside a house with a SOLD board outside. Someone has staked it into the front lawn. "Where are we now?" I ask.

Daniel ignores me. He opens the car door and gets out. Then he is round at my side, undoing my seat belt, offering me his arm.

"I can manage," I say, crossly. But I take his arm anyway.

He pulls a key from his pocket and then we're inside a familiar hallway. "Look, you'll be all right, won't you, Mum? Get yourself a cup of tea. Put some warmer clothes on. Or go for a nap. I'm sorry, I've got to get to work, I'm late enough as it is." He glances at his watch. "I'll give you a call later, okay?"

"Don't go. Please don't go."

But the door is closing. I see him outside, through the colored glass, fiddling with the lock, a blur of features, suit and tie.

His footsteps on the path, crunching on the gravel. He's right. I should put some warmer clothes on; I'm in my nightdress but I can't think why. How embarrassing. I hope no one saw; I'd be mortified.

Once changed, I make a cup of tea in the kitchen and sit at the table. I wonder where Arthur is. I suppose he's at work. Didn't he just say he was going to be late? He seemed to be in a rush. I sip my tea and reach for the crossword, remembering I was stuck on something. I drum my pencil against the folded paper. Ah, yes, there it is: *leporid mammal.* Six down. What is a leporid mammal? I know this, I'm sure I do.

Leporid mammal.

Rabbit. Of course.

I begin to fill in my squares. It's the last clue, and I feel a sense of satisfaction at completing the crossword. R-A-B-B-I-T.

Rabbit.

Eggs and rabbits. Rabbit and eggs. Weren't they what my mother saw?

I grip the arm of my chair; the room is swaying, objects sharpening then blurring. A cast-iron rabbit with a chipped ear. Two untouched fried eggs. Blood pooling on the floor. Reg's trembling hands, my mother's voice: *people will interpret my visions in all sorts of ways when they're looking for answers.*

It can't be right. It can't be true.

Feeling wildly disorientated, I take Arthur's magnifying glass from its leather case and place it over the photograph we took from George, pressing the glass over our young, hopeful faces, lingering on Lucy. It seems like only yesterday we were there together with Miss Munby. Lucy is smiling; the collar of her blouse is neatly pressed, and she wears a thin chain around her neck, a tiny charm resting at her throat.

The chain I found at the bottom of my jewelry box, the one I've been wearing all along—it had slipped under the lining and I couldn't think where it had come from. Now, I see it in the pawnshop window. A hot July day. I'm on my way to meet Lucy, but I never got a chance to return the necklace to her.

I see myself, an awkward girl of fifteen with sore hands and a bloody handkerchief. There I am in a too-hot tweed skirt, resting my bicycle against the wall, entering the house by the kitchen door. And then it returns: the memory, a splintered-off part of the jumbled narrative of my life, forgotten and dusty, but also as fresh as if it happened yesterday. Lucy, lying on the kitchen floor; Reg, noticing me come in, the panic in his eyes, his insistence that we could never tell anyone, that we had to forget we had anything to do with it. What I did in order to protect my mother.

Lucy Theddle is missing, they said.

I ease myself up from my chair, my legs heavy. In the hallway, I slowly climb the stairs, standing, looking at my picture gallery, at all the photographs of my family. All the photographs of the life I've led, the life I never deserved to lead. I take one from the wall and throw it down the stairs onto the hallway tiles. I do the same with the next, and the next. One by one I pull the pictures down off their hooks and throw them. I enjoy the sound of the photographs bouncing down the stairs, the musical note of the smashing glass. My hallway is littered with parts of frames, broken glass, and discarded pictures. Once I have a bare wall, I carefully step over the broken frames and shards of glass and go into the kitchen.

Then I begin to panic. I can't forget. Not again. I reach for a pad of paper, the pad Josie writes my shopping lists on. I grab a pen and write in large shaky handwriting: *Lucy was on the floor. She fell on the rabbit. Reg said we couldn't tell anyone. Reg made it go away.*

I look down at what I have written. I am ready to face the consequences, to sacrifice the rest of my life so that Lucy and her family can finally have their peace, the closure they deserve. I've got to work out a way of getting out of the house when I'm locked in; I must confess to what I've done. I'll call them now. I'll call the police and tell them what I did.

Putting the note in my pocket, I leave the kitchen and wander along the hallway. I feel ever so unsettled, although I can't think why. What was it I was about to do? I'm sure there was something. It was just there and now it's gone. Perhaps there is an untouched cup of tea in the living room. That could be it. I'm always making cups of tea and forgetting to drink them. It wouldn't be the first time. Then I notice someone has made a mess in the hallway. There are shards of glass on the floor. I'll have to get the dustpan and brush.

38

2018

I've been locked in all day," I tell Amy when she arrives at three thirty. "Your father locked me in."

"Oh, God, Nan," Amy says, shrugging off her coat. "Why? What's happened? Where have all your photographs gone?"

"They fell down," I explain. "I've put them on the coffee table. There was all this broken glass—I swept it up. I'll have to get Daniel to put them back, won't I?" I give Amy a watery smile, then follow her gaze to the bare wall—nothing but hooks. I feel a burning sensation in my throat. I turn toward the kitchen, not wanting to look at the empty wall.

"I don't know why Daniel locked me in," I tell Amy. "I'm sure there is somewhere I need to be, something I need to do. I thought Josie would come and I'd be able to go while she did the vacuuming, but she didn't come. No one came."

"It's Thursday. Not her day," Amy tells me.

"Are you sure?"

"Yes. I've got double physics on Thursdays." Amy shudders.

"Well, that explains why I haven't got any biscuits in."

Amy hesitates, then follows me through to the kitchen. I sit down at the table while she flicks the kettle on. She goes to my cupboard, puts several bourbons on a saucer and places them in front of me. I nibble anxiously at one, unsure as to whether I've had lunch. A few crumbs fall into my lap and I brush them away. I can see a small black mark on the table, probably from where Reg has been polishing his boots. I trace it carefully with my finger.

"I'm sorry about the other day," I tell Amy. "In the café. I hurt you, didn't I?"

Amy turns, a teaspoon in her hand. "It's okay, Nan. It doesn't matter. It was nothing. I assumed you'd forgotten."

I shake my head. "I know I hurt you. I didn't forget."

"Well, you should. I have." She smiles and I feel comforted. She's forgiven me, even though I probably don't deserve it. Her forgiveness doesn't untangle the tight ball of worry in my stomach.

She brings the two mugs of tea over and I peer inside mine; she's left a vicar's collar, but I'm not bothered. I wonder if I've got any Parma Violets. They're Amy's favorites. She's always buying them, offering them to me. She uses them as breath fresheners. I put my hand in my pocket but I can't feel any sweets, only a crumpled piece of paper, probably an old receipt. I take it out and realize it isn't a receipt but a note in my handwriting, a note that explains everything. "I have to call someone," I say. "I need to tell them what happened to Lucy."

Amy gives me a questioning look, so I put the piece of paper into her hand and watch as she reads. She swallows hard, then lifts her eyes to meet mine.

"It's difficult to make sense of this, Nan."

"But I remembered. She was on the kitchen floor. Reg pushed her and she fell and hit her head. My mother never liked that rabbit, she said it was an eyesore and a liability but she had to pretend to like it because Reg gave it to her."

Amy is staring at me. She looks down at the piece of paper in her hand. "I think we'd better call Dad."

Daniel and Amy are talking loudly in the kitchen. Are they arguing? Is Daniel cross again? He seems to be cross a lot recently. I'm putting my coat on, fastening my buttons, ready to go out. I slide my hand into the pocket of my mackintosh and pull out a packet of Parma Violets. How did they get there?

Voices carry from the kitchen, although I can't make much sense of what they're saying.

I've had just about enough of all this, I really have.

She wrote it down, Dad. Look. What if she's right?

She gets confused. She doesn't know what she's saying, or doing, half the time.

And the other half of the time? What if it's true, Dad? We need to take this seriously. She's convinced she needs to tell the police something.

I can hear a stomping noise, the scraping of a chair. I shove the Parma Violets back into my pocket.

She was at that house at seven o'clock this morning. Seven o'clock! She just turned up at the door. In her nightdress!

A silence.

Fine. Let's listen to her story. She can tell it to the police if that's what she wants.

I'm waiting patiently by the front door in my coat when they appear. Daniel waves a small piece of paper at me. "Is this true, Mum? Do you know what happened to Lucy? Did it have something to do with your stepfather?"

"True?" I echo. I don't want it to be true. I never wanted it to be. But I can't hide in the dark anymore. I can't keep parts of myself hidden, not when there's so little time left.

Daniel is asking too many questions at once. I can't get it all straight in my mind.

Amy is here too. She isn't wearing her hat, though. She'll get a detention if Miss Munby catches her without her beret. "You'd best get changed," I tell her. "You don't want to spoil your uniform." The words taste like ash in my mouth. They don't belong to me but to someone else.

"Do you know where Lucy is, Nan?" Amy asks.

I shake my head slowly. *Lucy, Lucy.* "She disappeared and everyone's looking for her. But I know what happened. I'm not in a muddle anymore."

Daniel and Amy exchange glances.

I go to the telephone, lift the receiver, and begin to dial.

"Who are you calling, Mum?"

"The police. I should have called them sixty-seven years ago."

39

1951

Reg decides we should go to church. He mumbles something about *keeping up appearances* and it being *good for business*. It's another sunny July day, but I barely notice. I feel a sense of separateness from everything around me, as if I'm not really part of the world, because how can it be going on as normal? Did yesterday really happen? There is no evidence that it did; there is no confirmation from Reg and, if I can avoid his eye, perhaps I won't see what's there.

We put on our hats and our Sunday bests and traipse down to the church. Judy is walking with her parents and younger brother, but she ignores me. As we near the church, Linda breaks free from her family and sidles up to me. "Edie, have you heard about Lucy?"

I manage to shake my head.

"She's gone," Linda announces. "Disappeared."

"Disappeared?" My throat feels dry.

Linda skips along beside me. "No one's seen her since yesterday."

Blood on the floor, her glassy, unblinking eyes. The strange angle of her limbs. I realize Reg is looking over in my direction. *Think what it would do to your mother.* "Where is she now?" I ask numbly.

Linda giggles. "That's just it. No one knows. Apparently she was with Rupert first thing yesterday morning, but no one has seen her since then. She didn't go to the fete, and she was supposed to be home for tea, but she didn't turn up. At ten o'clock her parents called the police."

"Oh." The world is closing in on me, narrowing to a point, hazy and gray. All I can see is Linda's face, her eager eyes, the neat freckles on her nose.

"They drove around looking for Lucy. They looked *everywhere.* They even called on Mrs. Murdle at home and made her go and open the library in case Lucy got locked in. They did the same with the pictures. They couldn't find her *anywhere.* She didn't come home *all night.* The police wondered if she might be staying with a friend, but Mrs. Theddle said she would *never* stay away from home and not tell them."

I swallow hard, trying to dispel the solid lump in my throat.

"And then this morning..." Linda leans in close to my ear. She lowers her voice. "They found her bicycle. In a *field.*"

I squeeze my eyes tightly shut.

We're nearing the church, and my mother glances over her shoulder to see where I've got to. "Sorry," I tell Linda, moving quickly away. My mind is spinning, and I wonder if I might be sick. Linda's words are stuck on repeat like a broken gramophone record. *Disappeared, disappeared... Her bicycle in a field.*

I picture myself, but it's as if I'm watching someone I don't know very well. There I am, riding Lucy's bike, stopping and wheeling it off the road, into a field, behind a tree. A nice shady spot, I think. I'm taking the train tickets from my pocket, opening her suitcase, and slipping them alongside her neatly packed things; she should have them, I decide. And then I am walking along the lanes, among fields of golden wheat and green summer cabbages, a skylark circling above me. It seems to take hours, this long walk home. And nothing is quite real anymore, as if I've stumbled into some alternate world where things like this can happen, and all I have to do is walk and walk and eventually I'll return and everything will be all right again. I stop on the small stone bridge and stare down at the brown water, feeling numb and cold even though the sun is shining. I still have my diary with me. And then I am throwing it into the river. A plopping sound. A single ripple. I imagine it sinking down among the weeds, down into the depths of the riverbed. Lucy's story, gone forever. When I do finally arrive home, Reg is gone, and so is his van. The keys to the garages are missing from the hook. The kitchen smells of Vim, lemony and too clean. Later, much later, Reg comes back looking dirty and haggard, his boots covered in a thick gray silt. He returns the keys to the hook, puts his clothes straight in the dolly tub, and lights the copper for a hot wash. I watch him scrubbing his hands in the sink, getting the gray dirt out from under his nails. I don't speak to him and he doesn't speak to me, because if we speak it becomes real and it can't be real. My mother brings scones home for tea and wants to talk about the fete: whose fortune she read, and *wasn't it a lovely day*, and *where were you two anyway?*

"Come along, Edie," my mother says. I realize I am standing at the edge of the road, that she is beckoning me to join her and Reg as they near the church.

"It's Lucy," I tell them, my voice coming out strange, unable to look at Reg. "She's missing."

"Shh," my mother replies as we enter. "Yes, we've just heard. I'm sure it's nothing to worry about." She touches my shoulder, steering me toward an empty pew. Although it's cool, I can feel a trickle of sweat at the back of my neck. It's clear everyone knows Lucy is missing; there are murmurs and glances, an air of anticipation and anxiety. News travels fast in a small town. The Theddles, who usually sit in the front pew, are not there. No one has taken their place. But of course, they are thinking, it is too early, really, to be very concerned. Lucy has not even been gone twenty-four hours. The congregation are still shuffling in and I catch fragments of conversation. *Gone off with a chap, I expect. Having a great time of it. She'll be home this evening.*

I notice Rupert sitting with his parents and brother, his head bowed. The church is unusually full, but of course Reverend Thurby says nothing about Lucy or the absence of the Theddles. He ignores the four empty spaces in his front pew. The door behind us closes and we rise as, seated at the cranky old organ, Mrs. Murdle begins to play the opening bars of "When I Survey the Wondrous Cross."

40

2018

I'm sitting in a small room with cream walls and uncomfortable chairs. I seem to have been here a long time. I've gone to the bathroom along the hall twice. A woman in uniform has to stand outside the door of the ladies', perhaps to make sure I don't run away. "I'm not a fast runner," I tried to explain. "I was always better at cross country."

The woman had smiled a little. "I'll be right outside, Edie."

And now I'm back in this room. I've already spoken to someone, a woman who arrived with a tag around her neck. She came to assess me, they said. She asked me all sorts of questions, just like the ones before at the hospital, as though I was a contestant on a quiz show. What day of the week is it? Where do you live? Who is the prime minister? I'm pretty sure I got that one wrong. It all changes so quickly, it's hard to keep up. Once they decided I'd done well enough at the quiz, they brought me back here and explained lots of things to me. I've tried to remember them all.

I keep repeating the words they used, wanting to make sense of them. *Under caution*, they said. *Due to your admission. Anything you say can be used as evidence. Video- and audio-recorded. Entitled to a legal adviser.*

Two police officers enter the room. They're sitting in front of me, a man and a woman. The man is slim, clean-shaven, not much more than a boy. But then I remember: it isn't him who's young but me who's old. There is a woman officer too; she's got reddish-brown hair that's been neatly tied back, green eyes, pale skin.

"Did I pass the quiz?" I ask them.

"Yes," the female police officer says. "We're going to begin the interview now, Edie. Are you sure you don't want a legal adviser at this stage?"

"Oh, no," I say. "I know I'm going to prison."

The two officers exchange glances. "This is an interview, Edie," the female officer says. "We'd like you to tell us what you told the officer on the telephone, what you said about Lucy Theddle, her disappearance."

"She disappeared in 1951." I know I have got this question right. I'm sure it's been on my mind. The answer, Lucy's name, rises easily to the surface. The typewriter key has finally come unstuck.

"Yes," the female police officer says. "And you say you have some new information, about what happened to Lucy?" She glances at the male officer.

I fumble for the piece of paper in my pocket, the one that answers all the questions, but it doesn't seem to be there. "I had it just a moment ago," I murmur.

The female officer is looking at me but her face doesn't give much away.

"She was on the kitchen floor," I say, my voice wobbling a little.

The female officer keeps her eyes on me. "Where was this, Edie?"

"At home. Reg was there. He said it was an accident. He said we mustn't say anything, because of my mother, how awful it would be for her. He said we were to pretend we didn't know anything."

The female officer glances down at her notes. "This was your home. Six Sycamore Street?"

I nod.

"And you're referring to Reginald Drakes, your stepfather?"

"Yes," I say, remembering the half-empty church, the paper taste of the confetti on my tongue. "My mother wanted to go dancing, you see. They'd been courting." Before I can stop it, a small sob escapes my throat. "She's dead," I say.

"Lucy?"

"My mother."

"Yes." The female police officer exchanges another glance with the male officer, who is leaning forward in his chair.

I can see my mother smoking in the kitchen, Lucy's picture in the paper. Eddie Fisher is singing on the radio. *I hope they're doing all they can to find her*, she had said, and I'd wanted to tell her then, but of course I couldn't.

The male officer coughs and I'm back in this small, bare room with the recording device on the desk and the two officers waiting patiently for me to remember, for me to get it right.

"Can you tell us how Lucy died, Edie?" the male officer asks.

I frown and look down at my hands in my lap. I shift my

sitting bones on the uncomfortable chair. It is *very* uncomfortable. They don't need to torture me, I've already confessed. They should have cushions. Perhaps being this uncomfortable helps people to remember. I think of Lucy crying on the bin bench, dancing in Rupert's arms. *I've got a secret, Edie.* We're on the beach, our legs stretched out in front of us. Mr. Wheaton is at the board, a piece of chalk tucked behind his ear. The ordinary house with the neat driveway and the pictures of feet on the walls, Lucy's cry of pain.

"Death and mess and wasted lives," I mutter.

"Sorry, Edie. Can you speak up?"

"It was all because of my diary. We were ready to leave, but she didn't want anyone to find it."

The police officer tilts her head, just a fraction, perplexed. I know how she feels: it's taken me so long to make sense of it all.

"Reg was blackmailing her about the abortion. It was the final straw. We decided to go. But then she went back."

The officer nods encouragingly.

"Reg found Lucy in the house. He thought she had stolen the money, but she hadn't, I took it. We were going to use it to run away with. Reg must have pushed her. She hit her head on the doorstop. That's what Reg said. My mother predicted it. Eggs and rabbits, you see."

No one says anything for a moment, and I wonder if I'll be allowed a cup of tea. I wouldn't mind a biscuit, but then the female officer is speaking again.

"Do you know what happened to Lucy? After the accident?"

I shake my head. "Reg was gone all afternoon. He took the van. He took the keys to the garages too."

"Which garages would this be, Edie?"

"The garages at the abattoir. Reg used to drive a van for them. He was a mechanic, too. He was always up there, fiddling about with that van. My mother said he loved the van more than he loved her. When I got back, the kitchen had been cleaned, and when Reg came in, his boots were covered with a thick gray dirt."

The male officer frowns. "Are you saying, Edie, that you believe Reginald Drakes disposed of Lucy's body, after she died in an accident in your house?"

I nod. I can see Lucy lying on the floor. Blood, dark and sticky, pooling around her hair. Her hand limp underneath her body. I close my eyes, not wanting to think of it, not wanting to remember anymore.

"Take all the time you need." The female officer is speaking to me, but her words sound far away, distant and echoey.

"We couldn't tell my mother. She wouldn't have coped. That's what Reg said. He didn't want to go to prison. He didn't think he'd be believed when he told them it was an accident. He said they could both go to prison because of the abortion. I thought my mother might have another breakdown, that they might send her away. I only remembered because of the rabbit. It was on my crossword. And I was wearing Lucy's necklace all along. I bought it back for her, from the pawnshop, but I never had a chance to give it to her. I've had it with me all these years. It slipped under the lining of my jewelry box."

"I see." The female officer glances at her notes. "You had time off school, Edie. A month or so in September 1951, due to a fever that began in August, a few weeks after Lucy Theddle disappeared. It's here in your medical records. Do you remember?"

I screw my eyes tightly shut—flannels, damp sheets, anxious bumps on my skin, ginger tea, small spoonfuls of chicken soup, drawn curtains. And then, one afternoon, when I was feeling a little better, I walked to the park and saw Miss Munby. I finally broke down then. I sobbed and sobbed and I remember how she put her arm around my shoulders and said: *Oh, Edie.* Of course I couldn't tell her why I was really crying, what I knew about Lucy's disappearance. But I told Miss Munby about living with Reg, how I couldn't be there any longer, how I had to get away, how I'd had a plan but it had all gone horribly wrong. By October, I had moved in with Miss Munby. She had two rooms she let to lodgers, and I took the smallest. I realized, after a while, that the lady who had the other room wasn't really a lodger at all but was a particular sort of friend of Miss Munby's, only things like that weren't acceptable in those days. They took care of me and didn't charge me very much, which meant I could stay on at school and only work at the weekends. I saw my mother regularly but I never went home, I never saw Reg. Then I went away to a teaching college in London. I went even though Lucy couldn't, perhaps *because* Lucy couldn't. And then there was that afternoon when I'd stood in the hallway of the college holding the telephone. Girls coming in and out, bringing in gray sludge on their winter boots. A cold, icy day in February. Reg had been caught stealing from his employer, my mother told me on the telephone. He was going to prison. Two years, she said. My mother only went to visit him once, after which she declared he'd turned religious. Apparently he thought my mother finally coming to visit him meant he was on the path to forgiveness. My mother said that kind of pressure was a bit too much and never went back. *The Lord's forgiveness! He only stole a few sausages*, she said to me once. By the time Reg came out, my mother had sold the house and moved to the coast. She got a job as a doctor's receptionist and bought a little flat with a balcony and a sea view. Reg found her of course, but by then she wanted nothing more to do with him.

I heard that not long after Lucy's disappearance, Mr. Wheaton left Ludthorpe, that he moved away. Several years later, my mother mentioned to me in passing that she'd heard from someone who knew June, that Mr. Wheaton had lost his job at a school somewhere in Surrey after allegedly having a relationship with a fifteen-year-old girl. I never found out if he was prosecuted, but this acquaintance of June's, so my mother told me, said he was unlikely to ever be able to teach again, and that June had taken her child and moved in with her parents.

"Edie?" Someone is saying. "Do you need to take a break?"

"I forgot what I did," I tell the two police officers, dropping my chin to my chest, a thickness in my throat. "I never told them what I knew." My shoulders begin to shake and my face is wet. Why is my face wet? I reach up to touch my cheek and realize my hand is shaking. I can't seem to breathe properly. The room is too bright and I hide my face in my hands. A large, fat teardrop falls onto my lap. A machine is being switched off. The door is opening. The young male officer is helping me to my feet. *Is this it?* I wonder. Is it all over now? Am I being led to my cell? I don't know what happens next, but I know I'm ready.

41

1951

The doorbell rings late in the evening. It's been three weeks now since Lucy disappeared. Her picture was in the *Ludthorpe Leader* again on Saturday, and other papers too. The headlines have got more sensational. *Appeal for Information: Mayor's Daughter Missing. Disappearance of Local Schoolgirl Rocks Small Town. Desperate Hunt for Missing Girl Continues. Factory Owner's Son Questioned over Disappearance of Ludthorpe Schoolgirl. Come Home Lucy, says Distraught Father.*

School has finished, and I've been spending most days out on my bicycle, cycling like my life depends on it. Everywhere I go, I see Lucy. She waits for me on the corner by the postbox, irritated as I cycle on without her. She sits on the bench by the church and stands, smoking a cigarette, outside the town hall, or on the edge of a field, her hair the same color as the wheat, wearing a blue dress, although I don't remember her in blue. She always looks serious and watchful, but never as cross as I imagine her to be. Each day I cycle so far and for so long, my legs constantly ache, my muscles throb, and I fall into bed at night exhausted and tearful. During the day, there is a constant queasiness in my stomach, a dizziness behind my eyes. Reg barely speaks to me. It's as if what happened never occurred, as if we didn't have anything to do with it. I've even begun to convince myself that perhaps we didn't. My mother is picking up more shifts at the grocer's. Reg has given up on his plans to make my mother a star.

I answer the door to find Barbara Theddle standing on our doorstep. It's August, a balmy summer evening. She's wearing a silk blouse, a cardigan over her shoulders, and a scarf around her hair. She looks neat, moneyed: flawless makeup, expensive white-rimmed sunglasses. She gives me a small smile. "Hello, Edie."

I freeze, my heart skipping a beat.

"Is your mother in?"

I nod slowly, unable to speak. *Act normal, act normal.*

She smiles again and I back away from the door, moving clumsily along the hallway where my mother and Reg sit in the kitchen, Reg picking at a back molar with a cocktail stick, my mother reading a magazine, circling dress patterns.

"Who is it, Edie?" my mother asks as I stand there, digging my nails into my arm.

"It's Barbara Theddle at the door," I whisper.

Reg coughs, almost choking. "What does she want, Edie?" he hisses.

"I don't know. She wants to see Mother."

My mother rises slowly from her chair as Reg grabs hold of her arm. "Don't let her in, Nancy. It's got nothing to do with us."

"Good heavens, what are you on about?" my mother says,

shaking Reg off. "She's my friend and she's going through a terribly difficult time, of course I'm going to *let her in.*" She leaves the room while Reg and I stand by the kitchen door, listening. "Oh, Barbara. I'm really not sure..." I can hear my mother saying. And then: "Of course, if you really think..."

After a moment, the front door closes. My mother is ushering Barbara Theddle into the dining room. I dig my nails into my palm again, and Reg and I both move away from the kitchen door as my mother enters.

"She wants a séance," my mother announces, her voice an urgent hush.

Reg's eyes bulge. "Surely you said no."

My mother gives him a sharp look. "Of course I didn't say no. I could never turn away a friend, not at a time like this. You can both sit at the table," she tells us, "offer me a little support."

I shake my head. "I don't think I can..." Just as Reg is making his own excuses.

My mother looks from me to Reg. "What's the matter with you two? Poor Barbara is asking for our help."

Reg clears his throat. "Of course," he says grimly, recovering himself, and I feel I have no choice. We follow her into the dining room, my footsteps dragging. My legs are stiff and I'm having difficulty swallowing.

Barbara Theddle is sitting at the table. She has taken the scarf from her head and is threading it anxiously through her fingers. Her makeup doesn't disguise how tired she looks; there are dark circles under her eyes.

"I should have booked," she says, nervously. "I hope I haven't disturbed your evening." She looks from my mother to Reg.

"It's perfectly fine," my mother replies, giving her a reassuring smile. She turns the light off, then takes a box of matches from her pocket.

"We completely understand," Reg adds, trying to behave normally. "Given the–circumstances." He coughs into the dark but Barbara doesn't seem to notice. My mother briskly lights a candle, her face appearing in front of me, full of concentration.

"I thought you might be able to help," Barbara says quietly. "Richard–he doesn't believe. He doesn't know I'm here. He thought you finding Smudge was a coincidence, even though we know it wasn't." She looks down at the tablecloth. "I have to try everything, you see. I have to believe."

"Of course you do," my mother says firmly. "You haven't had any news, I suppose?"

Barbara Theddle shakes her head.

My mother nods and hesitates, and I wonder if she's having second thoughts, if perhaps she realizes it will be too much, even for her, but then she takes her seat at the table and mutters a prayer. We all bow our heads. The atmosphere in the room is stifling, and I feel as though I might stop breathing altogether.

"Let us make a circle," my mother says.

Barbara Theddle's hand is cool and smooth. It is not a hand that does the weekly laundry or daily dishes. Reg's hand is large and sweaty, and I feel a wave of disgust that I have to touch him.

"Let us clear our minds and concentrate," my mother says into the darkness. Next to me, Barbara lets out a shuddery breath she must have been holding.

My mother sits in silence for several seconds, then begins to twitch and moan.

"I believe I'm getting something. Oh, yes. I think I am... There is an image, something trying to come through. Lucy? Is it you?"

My body is thick and heavy and I am surprised I don't sink into the floor. That's all I want to do, sink into a giant Edie-shaped hole in the ground, escape this horror.

"I see her as she was," my mother says. "She's in the garden at The Gables. At least, that's where I think she must be. There are rose bushes behind her. She's happy, so very happy..."

I think of Lucy's picture in the paper last weekend, the photograph taken in front of the rose bushes, and then I think of the day I cycled to The Gables to see how Lucy was feeling and we sat in the garden, the day we fell out over my diary. If only I'd destroyed it like she'd wanted. The guilt burns in my stomach. Lucy is gone and it's all my fault.

I open my eyes. Reg's features in the glow of the candle appear contorted with severe discomfort, his expression a mix of fear and dread.

Barbara Theddle smiles. "She loved the garden," she whispers.

"Yes, yes..." My mother murmurs, her eyelids fluttering. "She was happy. So happy..."

"But now?" Barbara asks. "Can you see her now, Nancy?"

Reg's hand is growing damp in mine, and I fight the urge to pull away and wipe my hand on my skirt. I hardly dare breathe in case I cry out in shame, giving us up.

My mother sighs. "Now...now..." She moans again, as if what she is doing is terribly strenuous. Watching her, I feel a sense of revulsion.

My mother frowns. "I'm afraid I'm not getting anything. I can't see her."

Barbara sniffs. "Please, Nancy. Please do try. Anything you see could be helpful. Anything at all."

I lower my head and stare at the tablecloth. The ticking of the clock is slow and torturous. Barbara's desperation cuts through me and I feel I don't deserve to live.

"I see only darkness," my mother says.

Barbara begins to cry softly. "Oh, Nancy. What does that mean? Does it mean...? Oh, no..." I fight the urge to comfort Barbara Theddle, to put my arm around her, tell her I'm sorry, so dreadfully sorry. But how can I? All I could do is tell her the truth, and then all of our lives will be over. My mother would never cope, and before long she'd be back in that hospital and I'd have failed my father and lost both of them. I keep my lips tightly pressed together, afraid of what will happen, of what I might say if I open my mouth.

"It may not mean anything," my mother says, her voice faltering.

Reg is struggling, too: I can see more sweat on his brow. Luckily, Barbara doesn't notice, she breaks the circle without thinking, dabbing at her eyes with a handkerchief. "Oh, I couldn't bear it, if that meant—"

"Perhaps I see something," my mother says quickly.

Barbara swallows. "What do you see, Nancy?"

My mother rolls her neck. "Ooh, yes... There she is. Feeling happy. So happy..."

"Where?" Barbara whispers, her voice almost inaudible.

"Somewhere. Somewhere... A city. Yes, that's it. I see tall

buildings. Traffic. A large city. I can't quite tell where it is. She's there though. Feeling happy, and free, but guilty of course. Oh, terribly guilty for leaving as she did. But it's all going to be fine, just fine. She plans to be in touch soon. She's enjoying herself so much. So very much."

Barbara sobs quietly into her handkerchief. Bile rises in my throat.

"Oh, dear... She's fading, fading... But still happy, so happy..." My mother exhales and drops her chin. After a moment, she opens her eyes and looks up. We release our hands. Reg has gone green.

"Oh, Nancy. Did you really see her?"

"Of course," my mother says, standing and blowing out the candle. "My visions have always been correct." She turns the gas on, bringing a dim light back into the room.

How could you?

Barbara is fiddling with her purse. "This has given me such hope, Nancy. Really, I can't thank you enough." She looks from my mother to Reg. "How much do I owe you, please?"

"Sixteen shillings," Reg says quickly.

Barbara opens her purse as I stare at Reg open-mouthed.

"Well, thank you. Thank you all." Barbara smiles at Reg, then turns to me. "I know you were a friend of my daughter's, Edie, and I know you've spoken to the police already. They've been so thorough. But..." She pauses, gives me a kind smile. "You don't have any idea where she went, do you, Edie? There were train tickets, and a suitcase... She didn't say anything to you, did she?"

The shame burns in the back of my throat. A sudden chill sweeps through me and yet I'm sweating terribly. The floor seems to be giving way and I'm having trouble standing upright. I can feel Reg's eyes on me, his hand on my shoulder, a tight squeeze.

"No," I manage to say, almost choking. "I'm sorry," I add. My eyes are filling with tears as my mother ushers Barbara Theddle into the hallway.

"What a warm night," I can hear my mother saying, as she opens the front door.

"I appreciate your time, Nancy. I'm so incredibly grateful."

Everything is spinning, shapes and colors distorted; my head throbs. I turn and run upstairs to my room.

42

2018

I'm sitting on the end of the sleeping thing, but it hasn't got any clothes on. It's bare, undressed. I can't think of its name.

It doesn't help that nothing is in its proper place. My bedroom curtains have vanished, for one thing. Who would steal a pair of curtains? The wardrobe is empty—even the hangers are gone. There are several boxes in the corner where my dressing table used to be, a suitcase at my feet, one of those modern ones with wheels. I don't know how I'll get it down the stairs. Perhaps there is a hotel porter I can ask.

A man enters the room holding a box. I am about to ask him about the suitcase; he might want a tip but I'm not sure where my purse is. As soon as the man sees me, he smiles. "All right, Mum?"

Of course. It's Daniel. Just Daniel.

"Where are my curtains?"

"Packed, Mum. Along with everything else. Are you ready?

The guys need to get in here to get the bed and wardrobe down. The rest of the furniture is in the vans now."

"Am I going somewhere?"

"Yes, Mum." Daniel smiles again. "It's moving day."

He offers me his hand but I don't take it.

"Am I going to prison now?"

Daniel's smile freezes. "No, you're not going to prison." He sits down slowly next to me on the sleeping thing, creating a dip.

I look at my new shiny suitcase. "Why not?"

Daniel runs a hand across his head. He hasn't got much hair left on top now. I suppose he takes after Arthur. I liked kissing the top of Arthur's bald head.

"There are lots of reasons, Mum," Daniel says, slowly, patiently, as if he's told me this before. Perhaps he has. My memory isn't quite what it used to be. It's to be expected, I'm sure, at my age.

"What reasons?"

Daniel looks toward the window. The sky is white and the tree branches are bare. I've got a feeling it will be Christmas soon. They've been playing carols on the wireless.

"Lack of supporting evidence," he says. "You being the only witness. It all happening so long ago. Your mother and Reg gone. Your–current mental capacities." He glances at me then looks away again. "Lack of public interest," he adds.

"But...I knew what happened. I'm an accessory, aren't I?"

He shakes his head. "You had nothing to do with her death."

"I don't know." My voice sounds small and I fumble with the sleeve of my cardigan.

"I'm sorry, Mum."

"What are *you* sorry for?"

"For never asking. I don't know...I suppose, because you were such a good mum to me, I just assumed your own childhood had been...normal. I didn't realize that Reg was such an unpleasant character."

I stare at the tiny flowers on my carpet, thinking that I played a part. I accept that now. I could have acted differently that day. I have to live with that.

"Did they find her?" I ask.

"They've found a body," Daniel says slowly. "They're working to ascertain if it's Lucy."

"Where? Where did they find her? How did they know where to look?"

Daniel is uncomfortable. He shifts his weight and I give him an encouraging smile. He's trying to protect me but I have to know.

"What you said about the garage keys, the state of his boots. They went out to the abattoir. That land is full of old outhouses. Well, they found the site of the garages. They've found a body in an old inspection pit. Someone had filled the pit with cement. They don't believe the pit was in use at the time when Reg was there so it's unlikely anyone would have noticed it had been filled. I'm so sorry, Mum."

I think of Lucy, alone out there for so many years. How could I have left her there?

"If it wasn't for you, she'd never have been found," Daniel tells me.

"But what about George?" I ask. "Have they told him? And have they told him what happened?"

"They'll tell him when it's confirmed." Daniel pauses, rubs

his chin. "George isn't too well, Mum. I don't think he has any interest in prosecuting. The police have explained everything to him, your story, the lack of evidence..."

I fumble for a tissue in my pocket, then wipe my wet eyes.

"I think she'd like her ashes to be scattered over the beach. She loved the beach. She should be thrown into the wind so she'll go up with the red kite."

Daniel reaches for my hand. "Perhaps that's what they'll do, Mum."

He squeezes my hand and I nod, satisfied. Then I think of something else. "Do you think she's forgiven me?"

Daniel hesitates. "I don't know," he says finally. "But..." He holds both my hands in my lap. "I think what's important is that you forgive yourself."

"Someone else said that. I can't think who."

We sit for a moment, listening to the sound of furniture moving below us, until Daniel says, "Oh, I nearly forgot. I bought you a present." He hands me the box he was carrying. "Go on, open it."

Inside the box is a camera. I turn it over in my hands. "Thank you," I murmur.

"Here," Daniel says, taking it from me. "It's a really easy one. You just press this button to turn it on and the same button to take a photograph. You can look through the viewfinder." He puts the camera to his eye, demonstrating. "Or you can look at the screen. Whatever you see on the screen is what you'll be taking a picture of."

He gives it to me, and I hold it up to my windows and press the button. There is a satisfying click.

"Not bad," Daniel says, taking the camera from me and studying the picture. "That's pretty good, Mum. You're a natural."

"Maybe it isn't too late to learn new things after all."

"It's never too late, Mum."

He shows me how I can look at the pictures I've taken by pressing another button.

"There's no film, just a memory card," he tells me. "You can take all the pictures you want and it won't run out. You can capture all our new memories. And we can print any photographs you want. Just ask."

"Thank you, Daniel. It's a lovely gift." And I mean it. I'm going to take lots of photographs in Devon. I'll add them to my others, those that have been reframed. I'm going to build a whole wall of new memories to help me remember where I am and who my family are.

"Shall we go down?" Daniel stands, offering me his hand, and I take it, sliding off the bed.

Bed.

The word came to me. I remembered. I usually do.

"Can I say goodbye to my room first?" I ask, glancing around my empty bedroom.

"Of course. We can say goodbye downstairs too. I'll tell you what, I'll take this first, then I'll come back for you." He reaches for the suitcase at my feet. "I'll just be a minute, Mum."

I listen to the sound of his footsteps descending the stairs. I can hear other noises now too: Suzanne's, and Amy's. At the front of the house, men are calling to one another. There is the sound of the radio, although it isn't Eddie Fisher. It's something more modern with a bouncy beat.

I walk over to the window and look out over my small garden. My father is there in his tweed cap and work shirt with his shovel. The Anderson shelter kit is laid out on the grass. He's giving up a part of his vegetable patch, building the shelter for us, to keep us safe if the bombs fall. The grass is damp and dewy, still slightly frosted. A single leaf clings to a tree branch, and a squirrel jumps from the fence to the tree. My father looks up, gives me a wave, and I wave back. I'll go out and help him in a minute.

The winter sun is breaking through the clouds and I close my eyes, breathing in deeply, letting its warmth wash over me. I'm going on a journey soon. I can't remember where but it doesn't matter. I can hear the murmur of the sea, the waves crashing against the beach. The wind rustles the long grass by the sand dunes. I see us: our legs stretched out on the blanket. Lucy tucks a strand of blond hair behind her ear, smiling at something. She reaches for her Coty powder and sweeps the soft powder puff across my nose, my cheekbones, her face close to mine. *There you are, Edie. Beautiful, just beautiful.* I can smell the salt on the wind, and something else: Evening in Paris. I breathe in the familiar scent, savoring it. High above us, the red kite dips and dives, dancing in the wind.

Epilogue

1954

A sunny October afternoon. I'm walking along Tottenham Court Road, passing the Lyons tea shop, thinking that I might stop somewhere for a brew and a slice of something sweet.

The London I have come to know and love is still scarred but healing slowly; the skyline is dotted with cranes; new blocks of flats springing up everywhere you look, the modern merging with the ancient. I have come to love the hustle and bustle, the way it is possible to lose yourself in a city, to walk anonymously through its crowded streets; the sense of freedom that accompanies the fact that no one knows your name, or who your mother is, or what you bought at the shop yesterday.

I am now enrolled at Lady Margaret's Teaching College For Young Ladies Under Thirty. I live in the college, a plainly furnished but spacious Victorian house, its bedrooms partitioned into dormitories. When I have any time off, I like to wander the streets of London, occasionally jumping on a bus and seeing where it might take me. I have to stop and pinch myself, remind myself that I really am here, that this is my life now, that a different future awaits me, a future full of possibility.

It's been one of those strange autumn days of sunshine and light showers. The trees are brightly illuminated, showing off their autumn colors; golds, russets, and ambers, but the sky is a deep, threatening mauve. The fallen leaves—yellow, red, and dark spotted—are like tiny promises stuck to the damp pavements.

I pass a confectionery shop and wonder if I have enough money to buy a bag of marshmallows to toast on the fire tonight. But then I remember it's Friday and that Friday is a dancing night. We have a strict nine o'clock curfew, but it's easy to be back for curfew, then sneak out again through the small laundry window on the ground floor (we all have to watch our figures in order to not get stuck). The laundry window can, of course, also be used to sneak in boyfriends. Not that I partake in boyfriends. I like to dance and I sometimes take up an offer of a walk home, but my studies are important to me and I need as few distractions as possible. I feel grateful to be here, for the opportunity to make something of myself. I won't let my mother or Miss Munby down.

I'm passing Heal's, glancing in at all the shiny new furniture, thinking how much my mother would love the new modern sideboard with its walnut doors. But then I stop.

There, a little way ahead of me, peering into a shop window, wearing a blue tweed coat and brown boots. Blue ribbons at the ends of her blond pigtails.

So clearly. So quietly.

Her movements precise and familiar.

Lucy.

It can't be. Can it?

She looks at her wristwatch, then hurries on. For a moment I find I can't move. I stand, rooted to the spot, feeling dizzy, watching her as she walks quickly, darting daintily around a lady with a large dog. The city moves on around me but time has slowed down, become shattered and distorted. I want to call out to her, but I know she is unlikely to hear me above the roar of the traffic and the slush of tires on the wet road.

I take after her, trying to keep her in sight.

She cuts in front of a group of schoolchildren on an outing, and for a moment I think I've lost her; all I can see are pairs of children in maroon berets, but then there she is: a flash of blue tweed coat and blond pigtail. Why is she moving so fast? I hurry ahead of the schoolchildren. It begins to rain and a man in front of me stops to open his umbrella.

"Sorry," I say, almost colliding with him.

Where is she? I clutch my bag, breathing rapidly, pressing forward.

There she is.

I try to keep her in sight, imagining reaching out, touching her shoulder, the way she'll turn, her face breaking into a smile. "Edie!" We'll go and sit down in a small cafe and eat freshly baked Battenberg while she explains the whole thing, how she couldn't get in touch, how it had to be this way.

"I'm so glad you found me, Edie," she'll say.

She's crossing the road. A bus passes and I strain to see beyond it, my movements jerky, my throat tight with frustration. I go to cross, barely looking, and am hooted at by a black cab.

On the pavement, a man steps out in front of me, thrusting

a leaflet into my hand. “Try the new Wimpy Bar, love. Straight from America. Food cooked with atomic-age efficiency.”

I shake my head but he won’t let me pass.

“Oh, go on, love. Take a leaflet now, will you?”

I push his arm aside, the panic rising in my chest. “No,” I say, trying desperately to see around him.

“No need for cutlery!” he calls after me.

But it’s too late. She’s turning the corner, disappearing into Oxford Street, absorbed by the crowd and a sea of black umbrellas.

I run this way and that, crossing the road, crossing back, hurrying forward, looking left and right, calling out her name, not caring what I must look like.

“Have you seen a girl?” I ask. “She was just here. Blond hair. Pigtails.”

People shake their heads, move out of the way, avert their eyes.

I continue to search for Lucy, even though I know she has gone, that I have lost her; checking in shops, walking up and down the length of Oxford Street until my feet hurt and the afternoon wanes, the light thinning, the sky darkening, the streets filling with office workers returning home from a long day.

Eventually, I buy a cup of tea from a street vendor and find a bench in Soho Square gardens, passing the chestnut roaster’s stand. Soon the lamps will come on. From my bench I can see a couple, arms linked, walking with heads down, laughing. A woman is rocking a pram. A man in a brown trilby hat, holding a small bunch of flowers and with a newspaper tucked under his arm, stops to ask the woman with the pram the time before hurrying on. I imagine his wife at home waiting for him, his tea already in the oven. He'll watch her face light up as he gives her the flowers; it's the moment he's been waiting for all day.

The rain has stopped and the air smells of wet leaves, roasted chestnuts, and cozy evenings in a far-off future I am unable yet to envisage. The paper cup of tea warms my hands. I watch a few pigeons scrabbling about on the damp grass and think of Lucy, peering into the shop window, dashing along the street, finally turning the corner and disappearing into the crowd. I take a sip of tea and am surprised to find I'm smiling.

Reading Group Guide

1. Edie is suffering from memory loss, which makes remembering even the smallest details of her life difficult. What does she see one day outside of the post office, and why would that be confusing for her? How would you feel if this happened to you?

2. Edie soon becomes plagued with flashes of her old friend Lucy. What is her goal in remembering Lucy Theddle?

3. Do you think Edie is an unreliable narrator? Why or why not?

4. The story is told in two separate timelines, one in 2018, the other in 1951. How did these pieces connect, and what did this add to the suspense of the story? What time period were you most drawn to in the story?

5. What did you make of Edie's mother's occupation? How did that affect the way the people of Ludthorpe saw their family? How would you have felt if you were Edie?

6. This is not your typical mystery. As Edie says to Halim, "I think the clues are buried in me." What did she mean by this? How did this type of mystery compare to others you've read?

7. Coming to terms with her dementia is hard for Edie. How did Edie grapple with some of the changes in her life? How does her memory loss evolve throughout the narrative?

8. How did you relate to Edie on her mission?

9. Why is Edie's independence so important to her, and why does she feel it's being taken away? If you were in Edie's position, would you also want to prove your abilities, or would you accept help more willingly?

10. What was Lucy and Max's relationship like, and how did Edie feel about it? If you were Edie, how would you have handled being put in the middle of their relationship? Would you have done anything different?

11. Compare Lucy and Edie. What were differences between them that might have acted as barriers to their friendship? Do you think their relationship was genuine? Why or why not?

12. Near the end of the novel, it is revealed that Lucy has another secret. How was this situation "dealt with"? Why would that have been dangerous in this time period?

13. Edie has the idea to leave Ludthorpe behind and to take Lucy with her. Why does she want to leave, and what do they plan to do? What happens to this plan?

14. The novel ends with a shocking twist. What do you believe happened to Lucy? Do you think there was any ambiguity to the conclusion of the story?

15. Discuss all the ways memory plays a vital role within the narrative. Then, think about what memory means to you. What memories do you hope to never forget?

A Conversation with the Author

This story is unique in the sense that the mystery takes place within Edie rather than events happening in the outside world. How was the process of writing a story like this? What inspired you to do so?

I am interested in memory and its distortions. I believe it is possible to forget memories that may be painful, but memories can also be found and returned to us, whether we are searching for them or not. As a writer, I am fascinated by what drives and motivates people, where our fears come from, and how our personalities have been shaped by our experiences. It felt right to me that Edie was not only searching for external clues but also the clues she'd buried inside herself.

Was it hard to write from the perspective of someone dealing with memory loss? What are some things you had to do to make Edie's condition feel realistic for readers?

After writing the first couple of chapters of *One Puzzling Afternoon*, it became clear to me that Edie was in the early stages of dementia. There are moments when Edie is lucid, and others when she's very confused. I wanted to show how this can be upsetting, both for the person themself and for family members. I wanted to be kind to Edie, but I also felt a responsibility to research as much as I could about the condition and make Edie's situation, her confusion and frustrations, feel truthful and realistic.

This novel takes place in two time periods, one set in post–World War II England. What was the research process like? Were you surprised by anything you learned about life in the 1950s?

I really enjoyed the research process and read a number of novels set in post–World War II Britain, as well as several works of nonfiction and diaries. Rationing was still in place in England in the early 1950s, and life was hard despite the war being over. Sugar, butter, milk, cheese, meat, and tea were all still on ration. During the war, people become very industrious, and there were some wonderful wartime recipes, but I think, by the early 1950s, the general public was feeling quite fed up. Most major cities were still bomb sites, and there was a shortage of housing. I was surprised to learn that in 1950, around half of UK homes still didn't have an inside bathroom.

Why do you think Edie's and Lucy's stories are important to tell? What do you hope readers get out of this novel?

I believe the experiences we have in our childhood or teenage years can leave lasting impressions. Lucy, whatever her faults, is only fifteen when she becomes involved with a much older man, and it is Lucy who ultimately suffers as a result of the relationship when she finds herself in a difficult situation. Nancy also suffers because of her relationship, and Edie in 1951 lives under the shadow of her bullying stepfather. I think it's important that women's stories, both past and present, are heard. *One Puzzling Afternoon* is a work of fiction, but nothing that happens to any of the characters is outside the realms of possibility. In 2018, I wanted to show Edie's struggle with an incredibly cruel condition yet also show how it is still possible to find moments of joy. I hope readers will take away the fact that it's never too late to try to solve a mystery or reconcile with the past and that even in the darkest of days, hope can be found.

What does your writing process look like? Are there any ways you like to find creative inspiration?

I take inspiration from life experiences and from the books I read. A writer has to always be curious and has to want to understand what life must be like living in another person's shoes. I am always looking for good stories and new voices.

What are you reading these days?

I recently read Kate Atkinson's marvelous *Life After Life*. Set partly in wartime Britain, it's a book that explores the different paths our lives can take and the consequences of events that are outside of our control. I've also been reading *The Maid* by Nita Prose—a mystery novel featuring a character you can't help rooting for who is also on the margins of society. Next on my TBR pile is *Women Talking* by Miriam Toews. I really enjoy discovering novels written by forgotten or neglected authors, particularly midcentury female writers. A few of my recent favorites include *Our Spoons Came from Woolworths* by Barbara Comyns, *Mrs. Palfrey at the Claremont* by Elizabeth Taylor, and *The Weather in the Streets* by Rosamond Lehmann.

Acknowledgments

Thanks to my amazing agent, Hayley Steed; to Elinor Davies; Georgia McVeigh; Valentina Paulmichl; Liane-Louise Smith; Amanda Carungi; Chloe Seager, and all the team at Madeleine Milburn Literary TV & Film Agency. Thanks to my editor, MJ Johnston; to Jessica Thelander; Anna Venckus; and the team at Sourcebooks in the U.S. Thanks to my UK editor, Sophie Orme; to Isabella Boyne; Clare Kelly; Elinor Fewster; Ellie Pilcher; and all the team at Zaffre and Bonnier Books UK. Thanks to Caroline Hogg and Jenny Page for your thoughtful comments and suggestions, and Teddy Turner for your eagle eye. Thanks to Amal Adam, Francesca Alberry, Sandra Brown, Sarah Dale, and Ronan Fitzgerald for reading those first early chapters and encouraging me to keep going. Thanks to Ena Hartland for answering my questions about growing up during, and just after, WWII and for giving me an insight into education for women in the early 1950s. I am grateful to the following works of nonfiction: *Somebody*

I Used to Know by Wendy Mitchell, *Perfect Wives in Ideal Homes: The Story of Women in the 1950s* by Virginia Nicholson, and *Our Hidden Lives: The Remarkable Diaries of Post-War Britain* by Simon Garfield. Thanks to booksellers who work so hard to get books into the hands of readers. Thank you to my parents for answering my questions about the lives of my grandparents, and thanks to all my family for your constant love and support.

About the Author

Emily Critchley grew up in Essex and has lived in Brighton and London, where she worked in one of London's biggest bookshops. She has an MA in creative writing from Birkbeck, University of London. She lives in Hertfordshire.